FLAMES
OVER
FROSTHELM

DAVE DOBSON

To my wife, Christina, and my children, Nick and Bri.

BOOKS IN THE INQUISITORS' GUILD SERIES

Flames Over Frosthelm (2019)
The Outcast Crown (2020)
Traitors Unseen (2020)

Chronological Notes and a Guide for Readers

Flames Over Frosthelm is the first book written about the Inquisitors' Guild in Frosthelm. *The Outcast Crown* is set a year after *Flames Over Frosthelm* ends, and it relates the further adventures of some of the main characters of the earlier book. Both books are novel length (about 120,000 words).

Traitors Unseen is set about ten years before the events of *Flames Over Frosthelm*. It shares a few characters with the later stories, but it is a separate story set in a different time. It is novella length (about 39,000 words).

All three books are complete adventures, fully resolved, and they can be enjoyed in any order. If you're new to the Inquisitors' Guild, I recommend starting with either *Flames Over Frosthelm* or *Traitors Unseen*. Starting with *The Outcast Crown* is fine too, but you might enjoy it a little more if you've read *Flames Over Frosthelm* first.

TABLE OF CONTENTS

1

THE SOTTED SWAN

The man in the corner leaned against the wall, his chair tipped back on two legs. His feet rested on the table in front of him, and a coarse brown hood framed his face. This restful pose was a sham. The man's eyes gleamed in the firelight as he scanned the room. A battered pewter mug sat on the table, but he hadn't touched it in a half hour or more. A huge staff, six feet of oak, stood against the wall nearby, in easy reach of his enormous right hand, and I could see a glint of steel at his belt under the folds of his cloak. The staff had some unsavory reddish-brown stains on it, soaked into the wood. All in all, he appeared ready to break heads at the slightest provocation, and the other patrons at the Sotted Swan kept their distance. No doubt about it — he looked like trouble, the kind of trouble that required mopping afterward.

He was my partner, Boog. He and I were part of the Inquisitor's Guild, tasked with investigating crimes and upholding the laws of Frosthelm. Today, our intrepid service to Frosthelm consisted of sitting near-motionless in a tavern for three hours. It had been a distinctly unremarkable experience. I sat at the other end of the room from Boog, near the fireplace, also with a clear view of the door. The chimney wasn't drawing, and soot coated the walls and ceiling all around me. My eyes were red from the smoke, my nose was running, and my throat felt like I'd swallowed a nail, or maybe a bucket of nails. I wiped my nose yet again on my once-gaudy kerchief. Next time, I vowed, I get to pick where we sit.

The door opened, letting in a blast of cold but thankfully smoke-free air. I caught a glimpse of the muscular tavern guard outside, and then a smaller man pushed past him. This new arrival paused in the doorway, hands on his hips, surveying the room as if he were its lord and master. He was dressed in a red jacket with a green silk sash, orange trousers, and embroidered floppy boots. His hair was long, brown, and shiny, and he'd pressed it into curly ringlets at the ends. After a quick glance, I was careful not to look his way or attract attention, but I saw that Boog had spotted our target as well. Stennis Shortsaber, probably guilty of theft, definitely guilty of dressing himself this way.

My partner lowered his feet from the table and picked up his mug. As he took a drink, he flexed the fingers of his free hand, still resting on the table. I squinted through my watery eyes. Boog was using our guild's hand speech, the Argot. Though his gaze was focused on his mug, his fingers were busy. *Wait*, he signed. Of course. We'd already agreed to see whom Stennis was meeting. *Armed. Sword. Dagger boot.*

Stennis' long fencing blade was obvious, but I hadn't noticed the small hilt poking up from the flowery cuff of his boot. I put my kerchief back in my pocket and replied. *Wait for other.*

A hint of a grin crossed Boog's face. *Chicken is love.*

I squinted again, then rolled my eyes. Boog's thick fingers weren't quite nimble enough for the Argot, and as a result, he didn't like the lessons much. He frequently got parts wrong. I signed back. *What?*

Boog looked faintly annoyed. *Chicken. Is. Love. You. Idiot.* His motions were still subtle, but his knuckles whitened a bit on "idiot."

I raised an eyebrow. Stennis slapped the bar loudly and called for the tavern keeper's finest ale. I had to give the guy some credit for flamboyance. Most thieves would rather not be noticed, but he was awfully sure of himself. Sable, the burly bartender, gave Stennis the eye. Then she picked a mug off a shelf — the shelf for already-used mugs, I noted with some pleasure – and poured a foamy draft from the large keg set in the wall behind the bar. She set the glass in front of Stennis.

Stennis quaffed his ale with audible swallowing sounds and slapped the glass down again with a thunderous belch. I guessed that he probably practiced this in front of a mirror at home. "Another, milady," he called, waving a finger in the air.

"I'll be seeing the color of your coin first," growled Sable.

Stennis smirked, reached into his crimson jacket, and dropped a fat pouch onto the counter with a resounding tinkly thud. A few gold coins spilled out, enough to buy a number of rounds for the whole establishment. Or maybe even the establishment itself. That wasn't good. Our prior investigation indicated that Stennis was quite the dandy, but that he was often near poverty from gambling, drinking, romancing, or general incompetence. If the rest of his pouch was filled with gold, it meant he'd probably sold the stolen jewelry already, and our chances of recovering it were remote.

Sable smoothly refilled the mug, and as Stennis turned to survey the tavern, she just as smoothly plucked a gold coin from the top of the pouch and dropped it into the pocket of her greasy apron. Stennis was none the wiser, though what he was now slurping had cost him what I was paid for three months' work. *Bottoms up*, I thought.

The door slammed open again, blown by the wind, and a hooded woman stalked in, pausing only to wipe her feet and brush some snow off her cloak. She pushed back her hood, revealing a thin, worn face with coal-black eyes. She wore a dull brown cap that extended from her close-cropped hairline in front down to the back of her neck, and there was a thick purple line, a scar, running from the left side of her chin down to where it disappeared under her cloak.

The woman saw Stennis at the bar. Not surprising, as Stennis shot his hand up in greeting and then beckoned with both arms, his face beaming. The woman pursed her lips and headed over. She spoke to the bartender, who pulled a small glass and a bottle of red liquid from behind the bar. The barkeep filled the glass, pushed it across, then retreated to the other end of the bar.

Interesting, I thought. The woman must be a regular patron, or maybe it was on Stennis' coin?

The woman spoke to Stennis, quiet and earnest. Stennis threw his head back, laughing, and then put his hand on the woman's shoulder. She looked at the hand as if it were a dead fish, and Stennis pulled it back, a bit chastened. Stennis listened, attentive, as the woman continued to speak. Stennis occasionally nodded or said a few words I couldn't overhear. The woman grew more agitated. Stennis' smile became strained, and he made placating gestures with his hands. Finally, the woman slammed her palms on the bar and shouted "Where is it?" The babble of conversation running through the tavern ceased for a moment as the patrons turned to look.

This was interesting. Who was this woman? A jewelry merchant? Stennis' partner? Or someone else? I cast a quick glance at Boog, and he gave the faintest of shrugs. If I was correct that Stennis had already turned over his haul and been paid, what was going on here? Had Stennis held back something important? Tried to keep something for himself?

Stennis was taken aback at the woman's display of temper. He tucked a stray ringlet of hair back behind his ear, straightened his shirt, and then reached into a pouch at his belt. He pulled out a necklace and held it up to show the woman. A shiny silver and gold talisman dangled at the end of a gold chain.

We had to do something. That amulet matched our reports. *Stolen*, I signed. Boog nodded. I hopped up from my seat and strode toward the bar where the two stood. Boog stirred as well. His fingers closed around his staff as he rose from his chair. He moved to cover the door.

"Inquisitors!" I shouted, trying for my deepest, loudest voice. It turned out a little croaky, but authoritatively so, I hoped. "Stennis Shortsaber! Halt!"

Stennis turned toward me, his face first showing alarm but quickly twisting into a sneer. His companion looked down at me and frowned. I'm not a big man. In fact, most would call me short, and scrawny to boot. But I was trying my hardest to be the intimidating presence of the law. It wasn't working – the cloaked woman with the vicious scar looked less like she feared arrest and more like she'd found a hair in her soup.

Ignoring me, the woman turned and lunged for the pendant in Stennis' hand, but Stennis was too quick. He danced back, his eyes bright, holding his prize above his head. "Twenty more in gold, or you'll never get it." Stennis took another step back and leapt across a table. A mug crashed to the floor.

The cloaked woman's eyes were cold, and her expression dour. "You'll get what you deserve," she said, her voice low. I was reasonably certain she didn't mean twenty sovereigns. She turned her attention to me.

I swallowed. "I'll need to bring you in for questioning, citizen," I said. "You are associating with a wanted criminal."

The woman gave me a grim smile. Her lips formed low syllables, but the words were in some foreign tongue. She raised her arms, her cloak billowing behind her. An icy cold bit my cheeks, and a tingling ran down my arms and legs. I grimaced. Just what I needed, a miscreant who used the arcane arts. I yanked my warding rod from my belt, hoping to absorb whatever she was going to throw at me. I held up the rod between us. There was a chorus of cries and frantic chatter as the tavern patrons backed away.

The woman wore a simple band of gray metal on her right wrist, and as her chanting intensified, blue sparks arced from this bracelet to her hand and fingers. She thrust out her right hand, palm first, and a bolt of sparking energy flew from it. Not at me, though – at Stennis. The bolt struck the amulet Stennis held. He yelped in pain, but he did not drop the amulet, even as sparks buzzed and crackled around it. All but the drunkest of customers now scrambled for cover. I heard a shout from somewhere behind me. "Bloodmother!"

The woman's chanting changed to short, guttural syllables. Some new spell. Had the last one not worked? I could feel my hair stand up, pulled toward the cloaked woman's magical aura. I raised up my warding rod and hoped that whatever was about to happen wouldn't hurt a great deal.

There was a resounding *POP!* It was accompanied by a flash of green light that left spots in my vision. The woman vanished. A moment later, I had a disturbing feeling of a wave of energy passing through me. It didn't hurt, exactly, but it was not altogether pleasant. My mouth went bitter, and I felt a pang of fear and discomfort, as if I were watching a small child stumble next to a cliff's edge.

Blinking, I looked around. I appeared to be unharmed, but the woman was nowhere to be seen. A silence had descended over the tavern, and all of the patrons were rubbing their eyes or staring slack-jawed at the space so recently vacated by the cloaked woman. All save one, that is – Stennis stared at the amulet in his hand. It jumped and twirled, dancing with sparks, glowing faintly in the orange-red color of ripe milkmelon. Whatever magic the scarred woman had worked, it had brought the amulet to life. As Stennis and I stared, the amulet's gyrations and light intensified, and it gave off a sound like a distant, unending scream.

Stennis looked back at me, and then he was a blur of motion, stuffing the amulet into his shirt, diving over the bar, scrabbling to make an escape out the back. I started after him, but I needn't have. In the confusion over the cloaked woman's disappearance, Boog had come up to us from his position at the door. Now, he reached over the bar, grabbed Stennis by the back of his jacket, hauled him back across the bar, and dumped him on the floor at our feet. But rather than sprawling amid the ale-soaked rushes, Stennis landed on his toes and leapt up again, drawing his saber in one fluid motion. "Heyya!" he yelled, waving the tip of his blade at Boog, who glared back with obvious disdain.

"Yes, heyya." I said, pushing my way over to them. "You really don't want to do that. It will go much better for you if you come peacefully to answer some questions."

"Stennis goes peacefully with no man!" he cried, slicing the blade dangerously about. That didn't make a lot of sense, but I think he was focusing more on style.

Boog grew irritable. "Put down the blade, Stennis." He hefted his staff with both hands and put on his I'll-eat-you-for-breakfast-with-kippers face. He was about a foot taller than Stennis, even if you gave Stennis his teased-up hair.

"I warn you, sir, I'd sooner unman you as look at you!" Stennis made a small feint at Boog, who didn't flinch.

"Unman me? Really." Boog frowned. "But you're the one they call Shortsaber."

Stennis gasped, and his eyes widened. "You'll pay for that!" He lunged.

Boog knocked the saber easily aside and swung for Stennis' head, but the fop was quick. He ducked and sliced again, his quick blade raking across the leather covering Boog's chest. Boog was more than competent with his staff, but the saber was a weapon of far greater finesse, and for all his dandified appearance, Stennis fought with a deadly grace.

I struck the end of my warding rod with my palm, and the rod hummed with magical energy. It would paralyze anything it touched now. I circled around behind Stennis as he traded blows and insults with Boog. I swung the rod at Stennis a few times, but the thin thief dodged and pranced so quickly it was difficult to land a blow. Boog was sweating, and his forehead bled from a deep cut. Stennis took a step back, toward me, and I lunged at his back with my small rod. Just as I did so, however, Stennis dropped to one knee and pulled his dagger out of his boot. My rod barely grazed his right cheek, not nearly enough to put him down, but I did hear a satisfying "Yeoww!"

He spun to me in a rage. "Youw doghh. Ah kih you wheh you stan!" Apparently, my rod had numbed his face somewhat. "Yuh bluh wih rung redh ovuh mah blayed." Boog's staff whistled at Stennis, but he dodged and kicked Boog hard in the chest, toppling him backward into a chair. Stennis then flung his dagger at me, but I ducked easily under the hurtling blade. From somewhere behind me I heard a surprised "Hey!"

"Dah, you pigh!" shouted Stennis. The front of Stennis' jacket writhed and bucked as the amulet moved underneath it, and I could hear the eerie screaming noise intensify. I held my rod in front of me, barely a foot long against Stennis' three feet of steel. Stennis swung madly at me, but I blocked his first four blows, the blade clanging against the stone of my rod. The fifth, though, sent my rod spinning to the floor. I saw Stennis attempt an evil grin with the left side of his mouth. He lunged at me with his blade, and I pondered which of my organs would soon be punctured.

With a rush of wind, Boog's staff swung down, crunching on Stennis' wrist, diverting his blade down between my knees, and leaving me happily free from unwanted holes. I looked down at the saber as Stennis cried out and dropped his sword, and Boog swung back with an expert counterstroke at Stennis' head.

One thing I'll give Stennis – he may have had horrible taste in clothes and a lousy head for money, but he was good in a fight. With a grunt, he launched himself backward onto the bar, slid across it, and dropped down. Boog swore as his staff met only air.

"Youw bastahs wih nevah take me awive!" cried Stennis, cradling his damaged sword hand. He spat at us awkwardly and dashed toward the kitchen and freedom. "Nevah!" His voice faded as he turned the corner. "No mah cah beeh me! No mah—"

There was a terrific blast from the kitchen. The bar patrons cringed, and I took a quick step backward. A mass of dark liquid flew out the kitchen doorway and across the bar, coating most of my upper body. I felt disgustingly warm and sticky.

I'll be the first to admit, I have a healthy aversion both to conflict and to injury, but I try very hard to suppress this when performing my duties, and I think I do a pretty damn good job most of the time. I say this because this particular instance was not my finest hour. I gurgled, I scraped at the liquid and the warm bits it contained, I hopped around in circles spitting and yelling. Finally, a huge hand on my shoulder stopped my gyrations.

"Stew," said Boog.

"Whuh?" I replied.

"Stew, Marty. It's stew." Boog pulled something off my cheek. A large slice of carrot. I stuck out my tongue and licked my face. Salty, but good. Needed something — maybe more tomatoes.

"Let's go," shouted Boog. He vaulted the bar, his staff in one hand. I clambered over it after him.

We needn't have hurried. As we entered the kitchen, I stumbled over an embroidered boot. We passed the upended stew pot among the other dishes, spoons, and cutlery scattered on the floor. As we neared the tavern's back door, the floor took on a reddish hue, and we began to see bits of charred flesh and bone mixed with expensive, gaudy shreds of orange and red fabric. The air was smoky and the odor oppressive. We found most of a leg. I felt a bit light-headed, but Boog pressed on undaunted.

On the floor of the kitchen, in the center of a torn and smoking red jacket, lay the pendant Stennis had kept from the mysterious scarred woman. It was clean, untouched, and it no longer danced or screamed. The talisman at the end of the chain was of a strange design – a metal ring containing two symbols. On the right was a moon of beaten silver, and on the left, a sunburst of gold, peeking out from behind the moon.

Boog went over to one side and picked up something. I glanced over and immediately wished I hadn't. Boog put it down and pulled a few long, brown, oily, curly hairs off his hand. "Looks like we caught him, Marty."

I nodded, not trusting my voice, and sighed. This was going to be hard to explain. It's not every day your prisoner explodes.

2

BAR EXAMINATION

It took us several hours to sort out the situation. First off, I ordered everyone to stay at the tavern. Given the recent display of sorcery, the fight, and the unfortunate thunderous demise of Stennis, this was not a popular idea. I wondered if I might suffer either disobedience or bodily harm, until I hit upon the grand scheme of using one of Stennis' coins to buy a few rounds of ale for the surly patrons. Their resulting inebriation sometimes helped and sometimes hindered our questioning, but the important thing was that the Swan's inhabitants no longer wanted to rip me limb from limb.

Boog ducked outside and gave a girl a copper to summon the city guard. I wiped off the stew as best I could. While we waited for our support, we questioned the bartender and the regular patrons. With my charming manner and incisive intellect, we made some real progress. It also helped that Boog stood next to me fiddling with his staff.

The bartender was a good source. Sable told us the mysterious sorceress first arrived a week and a half ago. She sought out Stennis right away, on the first night. They didn't know each other before that night, but they spoke a great deal then and for the next few nights. The bartender didn't know the woman's name. Early on, the woman put some silver on deposit to pay for food and drink, enough for a few weeks. She spoke with a northern accent when she spoke at all, and she seemed like a decent person. She worked no magic before tonight. Her drink of choice was Gortian bloodwine, and Sable had tracked some down a few days previously.

An old man with few teeth, a regular at the Swan, said that he'd once heard Stennis call the woman Novara. He also recalled that this Novara frequently wore a pendant like the one Stennis had, which now lay on the bar in front of me. I was a bit reluctant to touch it given its recent history. The old man didn't think this was the same one Novara had worn. I thought he was probably right, because this matched one of the pieces of jewelry Countess Moriff reported stolen a week earlier. We had more than enough evidence now to place Stennis as the thief, especially after his face had appeared in the Augur's Pool back at headquarters.

We asked several other patrons but learned little else of interest about Novara. No one recalled Stennis having much money recently, but one serving maid recalled seeing Novara and Stennis conferring the previous night at a table in the back, and she thought she saw Novara push a purse across the table to Stennis at one point. She remembered that Stennis had given her a silver coin as a gratuity at closing time, and she proudly produced the coin, probably more than she made in a week serving the wretched population of the Swan. The trident stamped on the side showed that it was of Gortian origin.

This prompted us to check the contents of Stennis' pouch, still sitting on the bar. Boog picked it up and rather indelicately dumped its contents on the stew-covered counter. The room quieted a bit, this silence followed by a great deal of whispering. There must have been nearly fifty gold coins there with a number of other lesser ones. Sable's eyes bulged, and the serving maid's pride at her silver coin seemed to evaporate somewhat. Almost all of the coins bore the Gortian trident, which was quite rare here in Frosthelm.

"Is that a fair price?" asked Boog. "For the jewels?" He glared at the other patrons, hopefully quashing any ideas they had of liberating the treasure.

"Hard to say," I replied. "From what her ladyship Moriff said, many of them are very rare – black pearls, fire emeralds from Zindis, and a number of other stones and pieces of more sentimental value. They're worth much more than that on the open market, but they'd be hard to sell. Maybe as stolen goods, this is fair. And who knows what Stennis would take for them?"

Boog grunted and began scooping the coins back into the pouch, apparently oblivious to the muttering and neck craning going on behind him. "I'm guessing this is Stennis' fee, and that Novara has the jewels. All except the one thing she wanted most." He gestured at the moon and sun pendant on the bar.

I nodded, chewing my lip. "But why's the pendant so important to her? What's it for?"

"Blowing up Stennis?" replied Boog.

"Could be," I said, remembering how the pendant had glowed and danced after Novara's departure. Could Novara's spell have triggered the explosion? "But that can't be what Novara wanted it for. Neither of them knew we were here, or that we were going to interfere with them. And Novara definitely didn't want Stennis to keep it." I rubbed my eyes, still stinging from the smoke and the stew. "Also, why does Novara have one like it? I doubt she wants to explode herself."

"Well, something had to blow up Stennis. I don't think it was the food here, though I'm not ruling that out." Sable glowered at Boog. "And the pendant has to be enchanted – it glowed, and it survived the explosion unharmed."

I stretched. "What was that business about the chicken?" I wiggled my fingers.

"Chicken?" asked Boog, incredulous.

I signed to him. *Chicken is love. You idiot.*

Boog slapped his forehead. "Agh. Trap. Set. The trap is set. I forgot the pinkie." He looked at his traitorous fingers with disgust. "I always get those mixed up."

There was a commotion at the door, and several armed guards pushed through. I knew the sergeant, Serena Wolfhorn. She wasn't a pleasant woman, but she'd handle the crowd here with her typical competence. She pushed through the patrons to us.

"Inspectors." She nodded at us.

"Sergeant Wolfhorn," I replied.

"What's going on?" she asked.

Boog spoke up. "We were observing two people, one a thief under warrant, male, the other an unknown foreigner, female. When we tried to arrest them, the foreigner used magic to escape, and the thief fought us."

The sergeant looked at Boog, and then appraised my physique. "You won?"

I felt heat come to my cheeks. "Boog disarmed him, and then he, er, tried to run away."

Boog pointed silently toward the kitchen. Wolfhorn walked around behind the bar and vanished into the kitchen, returning shortly thereafter, her nose wrinkled. "You two did that?"

"No," said Boog. "He did that all by himself."

After some discussion, Boog and I agreed that we were done at the Swan, but we needed Stennis' remains collected for the Augur back at headquarters. Wolfhorn gave a short whistle and summoned a spindly lad over. He looked a bit silly in his ill-fitting shiny chain mail and carrying his big sword, but he had an honest, open look about him. I did not envy him the remainder of his evening.

As he left for the kitchen, a linen sack in his hand and his face full of misgivings, we headed for the front door. I requested an escort, given the amount of gold we were carrying, and Wolfhorn provided us with two guards, a burly fellow who smelled a bit off and a fierce-looking woman with an intricately scarred cheek.

I suddenly remembered something. I walked over to the bar, reached behind, and grabbed the glass and the bottle of wine the wizard had used. "Ah, for an augury!" said Boog. "Good thinking."

On our way out, a thin-lipped old woman suddenly rose from her stool and grabbed my arm. I gave a little yell, but it soon became clear she was pretty deep into her cups. And she had a lot of cups. I recovered my composure, and Boog shook his head sadly, his eyes casting skyward. The woman leaned close to me.

"I've heard of that symbol – the moon and sun," she rasped. "My grandfather told me. His sister killed her family, her children. The blood…everywhere…" She paused, lost in memory or in the ale. "Beware, son. Beware of…" She sank back into her chair and closed her eyes. I waited a bit, but she remained silent. What further dire warnings would she offer? Boog tapped her on her shoulder, and the woman slumped over onto the table, snoring loudly. I stood there, lost in ominous thought.

"Boo," said Boog, poking me in the back. I flinched again.

3

HEAVY WAIT

Early the following morning, Boog and I sat in uncomfortable silence outside the door of our superior, the High Inquisitor, Sophie Borchard. I looked up at the large map of the city on the wall. It showed all the incidents investigated by the Inquisitor's Guild in the current month. There was a small flag (black, for theft) sticking out at the site of the jewel robbery. The case number there would allow an inspector to locate all the relevant information – Countess Moriff's initial report, the augury results, and our notes on Stennis.

I saw that our recent adventure at the Sotted Swan had been marked overnight. The new flag showed the same case number. A junior clerk had taken our testimony in excruciating detail upon our return. The Guild's clerks were extremely efficient, often annoyingly so. The flag was orange, for "miscellaneous incident." It was somehow comforting to me that the clerks didn't have a specific color for exploding swordsmen.

Boog blew air up his face, making his short brown hair lift in the breeze. The cut on his forehead was still crusty with dried blood, but he didn't seem bothered by it. He studied a grubby fingernail, then spoke. "Think she'll pull us off the case?"

I pondered this. I should confess – we were men of very little importance. We were provisional inspectors, in the second month of service following five years of training, both of us merely eighteen years old. It was hard to see how Sophie would consider this a successful investigation, and we didn't have a long history of clever sleuthing and glorious arrests to fall back on. I was surprised that we got the case at all, considering the rank of the noble involved.

The heavy door creaked open. I wasn't sure what or who had kept us waiting. It turned out to be one of our fellow provisionals, Gueran Declais, who strode out as if he were a hero in a play, off to storm a castle or climb a mountain or achieve some similar feat of dauntless prowess. I wondered if his eyebrows were naturally so high on his forehead, or if he had to remember to keep them raised all the time around his perceived inferiors.

"Ho, there, Marten," called Gueran, turning to me. My, someone who actually says 'Ho, there,' I thought. "I understand you had a bad night. Blew one up and lost the other. Nice work." His sneer was quite polished, no doubt from heavy use.

I struggled mightily to keep a straight face, because Boog, unseen behind Gueran, was noiselessly aping his words and accompanying them with elaborate hand gestures. "Well, Gueran, we can't all be as daring and talented as you," I replied, muffling a snort with my fist.

Gueran tipped back his head and gave a sardonic laugh, which Boog mimicked silently but with great flair. "Well, better luck next time. I'm off to wrap up the murder case I've been working on. A tricky one, too, but I've got my man. And he's alive in a cell, not in pieces in a seedy tavern somewhere." Gueran resumed his striding. I wished heartily that he would trip and fall as he made his exit, but my luck isn't that good.

Gueran came from a minor noble family, a third child, but that put him far above the rest of us in the social hierarchy of Frosthelm. He made sure none of us forgot this, talking frequently about his days at court functions, or his servants at home, or the soirées he attended, or his highly placed sources of gossip and information. I considered it one of the major disappointments in my life that he actually turned out to be a very good student — one of four (out of the initial group of thirty selected five and a half years before) to be named inspectors after the long training period. It was also disappointing that he was dashingly handsome – strong and graceful, with jet-black hair and pale blue eyes. A wart, an ugly birthmark, a hint of pox, or maybe even just bristly nose hair would have gone a long way toward consoling me, but alas – no luck at all.

Clarice Jerreau emerged from Sophie's office now. She smiled faintly at us and followed Gueran out the door. I didn't know how she could stand working with him without killing him or at least causing him severe bodily harm. Perhaps she was just immune to his abrasiveness. Despite five years of training, eating, and working with her, I knew nearly nothing about her background or family, other than that she had an uncle who was an Inquisitor – she'd mentioned that once, in passing. But her position came in no way from nepotism. She was very, very clever, and she missed no detail or clue in studying the scene of a crime, poring over information in the library, or questioning a witness or a suspected criminal.

She and I had been the quickest to learn the bits of magical lore we were taught, as well. It was just we two of all the students who had been able to get the warding rods to function. Only a small number of inspectors currently in the Guild, including even the most senior, had mastered the rods, maybe ten in all, including Clarice and me. These devices were centuries old, crafted for the Guild by a forgotten wizard in a time long past, the records of their origin lost or destroyed. The source of the rods' power was likewise mysterious. No modern scholar could produce such a device, though several had studied them closely. Nonetheless, the Guild had several written guidebooks (often conflicting) and knowledge passed from old inquisitors to new.

For me and Clarice, and the others who could use them, the rods were often very effective at turning violent situations calm and protecting us from harm without hurting those we sought to arrest. I had loved studying with Clarice. After the other students had tried and failed, we'd trained together for a couple of months under the less-than-watchful eye of Inspector Surrey, who would rather read books than speak with us. It was over that time that I'd gotten to know Clarice a little better, and when I think I could say we'd become friends. She loved reading and studying history and politics, and she often shared with me tidbits that she'd discovered while reading in the Guild library, which is where she spent most of her limited time off. She knew more about Frosthelm's past rulers than anyone in the Guild, I'd guess, even our instructors. She also had a love of spicy Turzek food, and we'd stolen out occasionally to the southern market where an immigrant family had a stall.

I would be remiss not to mention that Clarice was beautiful, too – deep red-brown hair over creamy skin, green eyes, with just enough freckles. I'd been smitten from the day I met her, although I suspected this was unrealistic on my part. Gueran made some gallant advances toward Clarice during training, but she rebuffed him, gently but firmly, just as she did the others who tried. I suspected she was either uninterested or that she might even have a paramour she met when off work, although she never spoke of this. I envied this imaginary person and wished upon him or her all manner of ills.

All in all, I considered myself very lucky to have been partnered with Boog. He and I had become fast friends during training, rather improbably, I thought, but we complemented each other very well. He was strong, menacing, and skilled with weapons, while I was none of those things, although I'd worked hard to better myself with the dagger and short blade. Boog was huge, too — easily the tallest and strongest at the Inquisitor's School, a good foot and a half taller than I was and almost twice as heavy. He wasn't exactly handsome, with short, ruffled brown hair and a number of scars from a rough childhood in the poor neighborhoods near Beggar's Row, but this weathered appearance often helped him avoid conflict and loosen tongues. Befriending him had greatly reduced the number of times I was beaten up during our training.

Boog was also quite clever. He was quick on the uptake, intuitive, and full of humor. The only subjects he'd had trouble with were those at which I excelled – languages, including the

Argot, research, infiltration, picking locks, and magic. During school, we'd train each other, with me helping him through long nights in the library, and him leaving me bruised and limping in the weapons hall. Mistress Fennick, our combat instructor, loved to pattern our exercises and maneuvers after the natural world. One day, after Boog and I had performed *Snake Takes Mouse* and *Crab's Choice* with uncharacteristic grace, Fennick had paid me her greatest compliment ever. "Mingenstern," she said. "It's possible you won't die as young as I thought."

Yes, I owed Boog a great deal. I don't think I'd have made it through the School, much less have been selected as a provisional inspector, without him at my side. But he had a sharpness about him, sometimes, too. He was at times quick with a cutting remark, though usually meant as a joke, and he was willing to use his strength and size to get what he needed or wanted. But he was a genuinely good person, with a well-developed sense of justice, and as loyal to his friends and to the Guild as I was. With his help, I had already grown in confidence, although I'd likely never have his presence or command of a room.

Despite our many differences, we did have one thing in common, and that was our commonness. We were both of quite humble birth. Boog did not know who his father was. He was probably some patron of the lowly tavern where his mother worked, most likely a very large patron. Boog's mother had died when he was only ten, but a well-to-do tradeswoman had taken pity on him and given him employment in her shop. There, he'd received some schooling as he performed his various duties. As for me, I had a more traditional childhood. My mother worked as a scrivener in our tiny cottage, and my father was an assistant in a locksmith's shop. We never had more than a few coins to spare. I'd helped both of my parents in their work as a child, which left me both literate and skilled with locks and tools.

The Inquisitor's Guild was unusual in that it took apprentices into training based on their talent rather than their birth, although in practice there were still some favored children of high-born or wealthy families who slipped in on their parents' name rather than their own merit. We were fortunate, Boog and I. There was much room for advancement in the Guild, and even as provisional inspectors, we had already achieved a status (if not wealth) far above our birth. The Guild had saved my life, too, in a way. In the second year of our apprenticeship, a plague swept through Frosthelm, and it had taken both my mother and father. Had I not been already apprenticed, I'd have died with them or been left a penniless orphan. Well, actually, I was pretty much a penniless orphan, but at least I had a job, a bed, and a home.

Sophie appeared at the office door. "Come, lads," she sighed, and disappeared back inside. I fretted as we entered and found seats in the cluttered office. I hated to have let Sophie down, but I didn't see where we could go from here unless we could somehow track down the mysterious Novara.

Sophie, the High Inquisitor, was stuffing some cheese in her mouth as we entered. It was rather pungent, but she was a great lover of cheeses, the more discolored and unpleasantly aromatic the better. She also led the Inquisition, a complex organization tasked primarily with the investigation of crimes and disturbances in the city of Frosthelm and the surrounding lands controlled by Jeroch, Prelate of the Northern Realm. In practice, our duties sometimes extended beyond crimes to counter-espionage, espionage, or other missions requiring a measure of subtlety, all at the whim of Jeroch, for the High Inquisitor answered directly to the Prelate. This made the Inquisitor's Guild equivalent in stature (if not in numbers or in funding) to the other three service branches of the Prelate's government — the Prelate's Brigade, the Frosthelm Guard, and the Justiciary.

"What's happened?" asked Sophie through her meal, spewing some yellow crumbs on her desk. "I've heard rumors."

I related the prior evening's events in detail, with Boog supplying occasional additional remarks. Our saga was rewarded with one raised eyebrow at the disappearance of the magician, and the other went up to match it at the demise of Stennis. I had the moon and sun amulet with me, on loan from the evidence chamber, and I unwrapped it and placed it gingerly on her desk. The money we had turned in to the clerks. It would probably be given to Lady Moriff, although it would hardly be full compensation for her loss.

Sophie was silent for a moment, absently brushing cheese crumbs off her chin and her red inquisitor's tunic. "Well, boys, you certainly dived in headfirst. I send you off after a simple theft, and you return with magic and murder."

"Murder?" asked Boog.

"Well yes, Beauregard." Sophie was the only one I knew who used Boog's given name. That is, more than once. Boog was a bit touchy about it, and those who didn't know that often ended up bruised or bleeding. "We can safely assume, I think, that Master Shortsaber didn't opt for his own detonation. The question now is what to do next."

I swallowed. "Inquisitor, we would like to continue the investigation. Inquisitor."

Sophie eyed me, her face inscrutable. She pushed an errant gray lock back up behind her ear. "I see. And how would you propose to do so, Marten?"

I had an answer for this. I'd spent a good deal of time in the library the previous night after we returned, researching and thinking. "Inquisitor, I've searched our references for symbols involving the moon and sun, and while I haven't found a perfect match, I did turn up records of a religious sect, active over a hundred years ago in and around Frosthelm, that used the moon and sun, in silver and gold, as symbols. They were reported to have mystical powers, perhaps related to what we observed. The cultists were rumored to be trying to bring about the end of the world. If they've returned..." I trailed off as I noticed Boog drop his head into his hands.

Sophie's smile was not unkind. "So, you start with a jewel thief, and in less than half a day's time, you're proposing the resurgence of a century-old cult of suicidal moon-worshipping mystics?"

My confidence fled me. I felt somehow naked. "Well, Inquisitor, when you put it that way, I...er..."

Boog stepped in before I could do more damage. "Chief, we'd like to take the amulet and what's left of Stennis to the Augur and see if we can learn anything to help us track down the jewels and this Novara, if that's her real name."

"Now that sounds like a reasonable course of action," replied Sophie. "But why should I trust it to you two and not assign a senior inspector? The matter has grown more serious, it seems." She grinned. "Especially if we're dealing with sorcerous cultists."

I shifted uncomfortably but found my voice. "Well, Inquisitor, we're short-handed, which is why I think we were assigned this case in the first place. With forty inspectors out east at the border, and all the incidents on the map out there, I'd think there might be more urgent business for the senior inspectors than wrapping up a case where the suspected thief is already dead and the stolen property likely lost."

Sophie placed her hands on the desk. "Ah, now you're talking sense, boy. Though I do appreciate your initiative in the library – there's always a chance that such unlikely inquiries could bear fruit. I've seen it happen, more than once." She rose, her red tunic rumpling as it settled over her broad hips. "All right. You two carry on, but I want a report daily, and sooner if you find something interesting." She pointed at Boog's injured forehead. "Stay out of trouble, too. Tell the Augur to give this case high priority on my order – I'm sure I'll be hearing from Countess Moriff about her precious jewels at least another three times today." She gestured at the door. "You're dismissed."

As we made our way through the door, past the incident map, Boog muttered, "Cults? Marty, really." A huge hand cuffed me sharply on the back of my head.

4

AUGURY

They had the roof window open, so the Augur's chamber was mighty cold. I think the idea was that the pool responded better in sunlight, but in the winter, that made mystical scrying a real test of endurance. Boog was stoic and indifferent, as always, but I stamped my feet, clapped my hands together, and tried to keep my teeth from chattering. Next time I was going to bring a sweater or an extra cloak. Maybe both.

The Augur stood up by the pool, gazing intently into its waters, walking slowly around the edge of the marble basin. I didn't know what she was working on currently, but I figured she'd better hurry, or the Augur's pool would become the Augur's block of mystical ice.

"Inspector Mingenstern. Your dance routine is somewhat distracting." The Augur's sonorous voice echoed through the chamber. Her eyes didn't leave the pool.

I hunched over, hugging myself, but ceased my fidgeting. "Sorry, Augur." She grunted, and then sprinkled powder into the pool from a brass tureen. This would calm the waters and end the scrying, I knew. I'd used the pool myself a number of times while training under the watchful eyes of the Augur.

Those watchful eyes turned to us, unnaturally pink and unblinking. "Back again so soon?" she asked, pulling her rough brown hood up over her short white hair. She stepped down from the dais towards us. "What do you seek?"

"A mysterious sorceress, who magically escaped from a tavern last night," I replied. "We think she was tied up in the robbery we are investigating. Also, her accomplice was killed last night, maybe through her magic."

"And what have you brought to guide the waters?"

Boog held up the linen bag of Stennis parts. "Her accomplice." Even in the cold weather, it was starting to emit a rather noisome odor.

I pulled out the wine bottle and the glass. "These, which she used at the tavern." I set them down and pulled out the pendant. I held it up. "And this, which she desired greatly. It may be enchanted, and it may have been the cause of the death of the man in the, uh, bag."

The Augur glided over to me, her brown robe dragging silently on the floor. She stretched out a bony hand to grasp the moon and sun. "A thing of power, this," she rasped. She closed her eyes.

I waited for her to continue. She stayed stock still, her hand covering the amulet resting in my palm. I waited some more, time enough for the silence to move past mysterious into awkward. I gave Boog what I hoped was a questioning look. He shrugged and put down Stennis. My arm started to cramp up.

"Aaaaah," gasped the Augur at last. "Very interesting. We shall see what the pool can reveal." She turned and moved toward the door. "Set up the objects around the pool, Marten. You know the methods – you were an apt pupil. I shall return shortly."

"Are you going to seek more information on the amulet?" I asked, hopeful.

"No," she said. "It's damned cold in here, and I need to visit the privy."

Boog grabbed the bloodstained bag, and he and I crossed the ornate black and white tiles to the raised platform in the center. We walked up the curved steps to the pool, illuminated in the cool blue-white light from the window above. The chamber was circles within circles, the pool basin set into the circular dais, the dais surrounded by a diamond pattern of runed black and white tiles, themselves interrupted by a circle of seven carved columns reaching up to the edge of the window in the ceiling thirty feet above.

The basin atop the dais was six feet wide, curving down to a depth of about three feet at its center. The enchanted waters of the pool rippled and gleamed, although there was little enough breeze in the room to stir them. Around the basin, carved into the marble platform and filled with gold, were seven large runes, where objects related to the subject of the scrying were placed. It was better to have a full set of seven objects, but it was even more important that the objects connected in different ways to the subject. A cherished belonging, a lock of hair, and some soil from a dwelling would provide much better results than, say, seven socks, unless you were particularly interested in the subject's bunions.

For our initial augury, we had used a number of articles from Countess Moriff's house – a splinter from the strongbox she'd used to store the jewels, the key to its lock, mud scraped from a footprint in the hall nearby, some of the other contents of the treasure room and strongbox, and a strand of the lady's hair. The shimmering waters quickly resolved to show a man examining the jewels. With his description, a sketch, and a few hours of questioning at various taverns, we were able to identify him as Stennis. Our efforts were aided, no doubt, by his none-too-subtle wardrobe, hairstyle, and personality.

This time, it would be a bit trickier. I placed the amulet carefully on the topmost rune, reserved for the most important object. Then I added the wine bottle and glass from the Swan on the second and third spots. I then looked at Boog and held up my hands. "What now?"

Boog heaved the bag over to me. I caught it, barely, and almost stumbled back into the pool. That wouldn't have been good. "Uh, sorry," said Boog in response to my swearing.

I swallowed, trying to fight the metallic tang building in my mouth. Finally, I opened the bag and then promptly closed it. "What the hell am I supposed to do with this?"

"Well, you've got four more runes."

"But...I don't...ugh." I set the bag down. I picked it up. I set it down again. It was heavy. "This is...repulsive."

Boog nodded in sympathy. "I'd, uh, be glad to help, but your skills at augury far outshine mine, O Apt Pupil." He wiggled his fingers at me sarcastically.

"Thanks. Thanks a lot." I opened the bag again. Stennis' head was thankfully face down. I'd rather have used some of the more unrecognizable bits, but I figured the head might be more important. Grimacing, I pulled it out by the hair and set it on the fourth rune. I added what was left of his jacket on the fifth, figuring it was most directly affected by the explosion and the amulet. What else to use? I put the dagger from his boot on the sixth, although that seemed only marginally connected. I was making a terrible mess on the dais. Hopefully one of the Augur's apprentices would be around to mop up.

What to do for the final rune? I could add more of Stennis, but he wasn't really the target here, and fishing through the bag was getting pretty unpleasant. I considered using one of the Gortian coins from the pouch, but money tended to be a poor choice, because it changed hands so frequently and contacted so many different people. We didn't have anything else belonging to Novara, or even anything that she'd touched. I pondered a moment more. Boog handed me a towel from a pile in the corner, and I wiped my hands.

"Wait here," I said, finally. "I'll be back in just a bit." I ran down the steps, out the door, and through a series of passages to the evidence storage chamber. There, I signed out the countess' strongbox key, thinking that this might connect our augury more directly to the robbery. On my way back to the pool chamber, I hesitated. A potentially foolish thought had occurred to me.

I turned and ran up the stairs to the library. There, on the table I'd used the night before, lay the book on cults I'd been reading, *Weirde Woorships of Froosthelme*, by Sir Neggin Boniface, a long-dead inspector who, despite his predilection for extraneous vowels, was an informed and valuable resource.

I picked up the book and headed back to the pool chamber, still unsure of whether I'd use it. The danger, and it was quite real, was that the book and its contents would have nothing to do with Novara or the amulet. In that case, the pool might well delve into some useless connection between them – a time that the book and the amulet were in close proximity, for example, or a glimpse of Novara's favorite book, and our efforts would be wasted. The pool could only be used a few times each day, at most, as it sapped a great deal of the Augur's strength. It was very unlikely we'd get another chance.

I reached the room and saw that the Augur had not yet returned. I held up the key, and Boog nodded. "Good idea."

"How about this?" I held up the book.

Boog took it and read the cover. "Are you insane?"

"Maybe. We could just play it safe, I suppose. But what if I'm right about the cult? I have a strong feeling about this."

"Just like the strong feeling you had that Melovian history would figure prominently on our exam?"

"Won't you ever forgive me for that? It was two years ago, and we passed it, after all."

"No, YOU passed it. I, on the other hand, had Remedial Antiquities for two months with Lady Entlemousse. I can still smell her oniony breath." He frowned at the memory.

I sighed. "It's all right. We can leave it out, and I'll be fine with that. It's up to you."

Boog chewed his lip. "A strong feeling?"

"Yes. Pretty…very strong."

Boog looked annoyed. "Pretty strong, or very strong?"

"Very strong."

Boog sat down hard on a bench. "All right, then."

"So…?"

He made a submissive gesture toward the pool and slumped down in his seat. I ran up eagerly and removed the dagger, dropping the key in its place. Then I placed Sir Neggin's manuscript carefully on the seventh rune.

As I dropped the dagger back into the bag of Stennis bits, the Augur returned. She glanced at Boog and climbed the steps to the pool, where she surveyed my choices carefully. She gazed at the book for a long time, her eerie pink eyes impossible to read. Finally, she picked it up. I feared she was removing it from the pattern, but instead she walked around the pool.

"An interesting choice, Marten. But if we're going to try that, let's move it up a bit in the ranking." She swapped the book for the wine bottle on the second rune and moved the wine down to the seventh position. I felt quite proud of myself and shot a triumphant look at Boog. He rolled his eyes.

The Augur began her preparatory ritual, sprinkling all seven objects with blue powder. I'd known its recipe for our augury examination, but I've forgotten the details. Saltpeter, ground eye socket bone, bat ears, something like that. Spiders, too, definitely spiders. Next, she pricked her finger with a slim silver dagger and dripped seven drops of blood carefully into the center of the pool. The water bubbled a bit. She pulled a small jar of salve out of her robe and rubbed some on her injured finger. This wasn't strictly part of the ritual, but without the healing balm her fingers would be covered with scars by now with the incessant bleeding.

She stood, clasped her hands before her, and then proceeded to pull on each finger, cracking each knuckle, then pushed each finger to her palm with the opposite hand, cracking them again. Then she flexed them repeatedly, giving rise to numerous additional pops and cracks. Then she grabbed her head and chin and rotated her neck to both sides, giving out a startlingly loud series of crackles and crunches.

"Why does she do that?" whispered Boog, who'd come up to observe the pool.

"*How* does she do that?" I replied. I wasn't sure, but I suspected it was mostly for show. The Augur was an odd individual.

Everything was ready. The Augur began to chant. It was ancient Arunian, the same language as the runes, often used in wizardry. I'd become crudely versed in it during our studies, and

I knew the routine here, having done it myself on several occasions. I knew better than to hum along with her, though.

The augur's pool was a mystery, its origins buried in a time long before Frosthelm rose around it, though some researchers had struggled mightily to track it back at least eight hundred years. Many attempts had demonstrated that the pool's design and use weren't reproducible elsewhere, though scholars had tried to construct duplicate pools to exacting measurements. But even with the same ingredients, dimensions, and runes, the copied pools never provided more than random colors and fuzzy shapes. There must have been something special about this location to have prompted the original augurs to build the pool here, or maybe we did not understand some key part of its design.

By contrast, the use of the pool was quite well understood. The objects selected determined the scope and subject of the augury, but it was the augur who steered it. It is hard to describe. Through force of thought and will, one can guide and select the images in the pool, focusing on one part or one aspect, or changing the perspective. The few times I had tried had left me dazed and exhausted, and even so my control of the pool had been limited.

Though many visions were of the present time, it was frequently possible to shift the pool into the past, especially if the strongest connections between the items were from previous times. Very, very rarely would the pool show images of the future. There was a great deal of scholarship on this in the library. Most thought the pool's glimpses of the future were absolute destiny, immutable. Others thought that they were merely likely and could be changed or avoided. It didn't happen often enough to say definitively, and the future images were usually vague, flighty, and hard to control.

The Inquisitor's Guild was very lucky to have such a tool, not only for our own investigations, but also for paying our bills. Many traveled to Frosthelm to seek answers from the pool, and for a respectable fee, we usually obliged them. Merchants, nobles, explorers, leaders, scholars, jealous lovers – all would pay for the information the pool provided. This income probably constituted half our budget.

The Augur ceased her chanting. Boog and I gathered at the edge of the water to see what might appear. The water roiled, shimmering blue and white and silver, and then an image started to coalesce as the water calmed. It was Novara! I recognized the scar on her chin and neck immediately. She was seated at a table in a chamber. The Augur skillfully willed our viewpoint around the room with small gestures. The image was by necessity always centered on Novara, but around her we saw a bed with embroidered pillows, a bright green tapestry showing three goats and a bear, and a chest-of-drawers with a water ewer and basin on top. There was a window, bright with sunlight glowing through its diamond-shaped panes, but the glass was clouded, and we could not see outside.

Boog looked up at the open window above us, studying the shadows. "That must be a southern exposure, with the light coming through. Is it an inn? I'm trying to place the windows."

I thought hard, too. There were over fifty inns in the city, plus numerous smaller guest houses, and Novara might be in a private residence. This was a nice place, though – definitely upper crust. That might help narrow it down, if she was even still in Frosthelm.

Boog grabbed a charcoal stick and a sheet of parchment. He sketched the window's metal framework and then started on the tapestry while the Augur held the image steady. As Novara shifted in her seat, I caught a gleam at her neck, and I motioned to the Augur to get us a closer look.

It was a pendant! Smaller than the one resting on the rune before us, but with the same moon and sun, so similar that I thought it must have been made by the same hand. As we watched, it began to glow faintly with a green light. The augur backed away, and we saw that Novara had picked up a large gemstone, a sphere, as big as a walnut. It was an odd stone – most of it was pearly white, but the central area of one side was a dark green, translucent circle. There was a sharp contact between the two colors, and the stone had been polished carefully such that both colors were smooth and bright. I'd need to check my notes, but I was pretty sure this matched the countess' description of one of her stolen gems.

Novara closed her eyes, seeming lost in thought, or meditating. I murmured, "Can we go back? To see how she arrived here?"

The Augur gritted her teeth and nodded. This required more effort and control. She raised her arms and spoke a few ancient words. We saw a series of images, called up by the web of connections between the objects. As was common, some had no apparent relevance – a stairway, a sword, a field of flowers. We saw Stennis and Novara together briefly, studying the gems, and then we saw Stennis crouching at the strongbox, forcing its lid. He had been the thief – proof, though it mattered little now.

We caught a glimpse of Novara in the Sotted Swan, with me wincing behind my warding rod. Then a flash of green, and the expensively decorated chamber again, where Novara staggered onto the bed. As she lay there, panting, she fumbled with a pouch at her belt and pulled something out, then waved her other hand over it, her mouth silently forming words. She shouted and opened her palm, and I saw the smaller moon pendant that she now wore, glowing a brilliant orange. She cast it on the table, still glowing, and fell back onto the bed. The pool went dark, the water still.

"Is that all?" asked Boog, lowering his parchment.

I turned to the Augur, then ran over to her. Her eyes were closed, and she was shaking, beads of sweat glistening all over her thin face. This was definitely not normal. "Augur? What is it?"

Suddenly, she grasped the back of my neck with her cold, bony hand. It felt as if all the heat in my body was flowing out through this point of contact. I gurgled, and my knees buckled. Boog lunged over to support me before I toppled into the pool.

Around the basin, the objects trembled on their runes. The amulet resting on the first rune flashed, coming ablaze with green light. The water boiled and seethed, then settled once again into a picture of Novara. This time, though, she seemed to peer out of the pool. She was angry, shouting, almost as if she could see us. The pendant at her neck crawled with green sparks.

The amulet on the top rune turned of its own accord, and a beam of green light shot out toward the book on the second rune. Sir Neggin's book rose off the basin's edge, floating in the air, its pages turning. As they turned, the illustrations rose as glowing specters from the pages, dancing over the pool as if alive before plunging into the water below, sending ripples over Novara's face. There was a flash and a crack, as of thunder, and the book tore into two halves. From one half emerged a small flaming sun, and from the other, a shimmering full moon – I remembered those illustrations from my studies. The two met above the pool, duplicating the amulet's pattern, and began spinning madly, faster and faster, tumbling over each other, until they reached blinding speed, and sun became indistinguishable from moon. At last, they shot down into the center of the pool, and I could see a terrible fear stream across Novara's face as the water broke into seething chaos.

That image burst as the pool erupted, spraying us all with mystical fluids. The Augur collapsed to the floor, and I would have too, had Boog not held me up. There were pages fluttering in the air, everywhere, like autumn leaves. I could feel my consciousness slipping away, but as it did, I saw another fragment of an image in the roiling puddle that still remained in the basin.

Fiery balls descending from the sky, splashing and erupting against the roofs of buildings. I saw the clock tower, the one that stood above Fountain Square, bathed in glowing fire. This was Frosthelm. Frosthelm in flames.

5

COMPLICATIONS

I awoke in my bed in my small room in the inspectors' dormitory. I stretched, languid, blinking sleepily in the stream of warm sunlight coming through my window. The dust motes danced in the golden light. Outside, a squirrel chattered happily while chewing on an acorn. One of the clouds looked like a dragon, I thought. Or maybe a butterfly. I wondered briefly why I felt somewhat damp.

Holy Bloodmother and Her Three Ugly Daughters! I sat straight up as awareness returned. I quickly hopped out of bed and ran for the door. I paused only when I realized I was a bit chilly. I looked down and saw that, while I still had my shirt, someone had taken my trousers, and I was quite indecent. The shirt I wore was moist and stained with something that I suspected derived originally from Stennis, although I tried hard not to think about that.

I stripped naked and found alternate attire, hopping around foolishly in my haste to get dressed. I burst out of my room and ran down the hall, still fastening my buttons as I ran. As I ducked through the door of our small kitchen, I saw Boog. He was hunched morosely at the table, absently chewing on some bread.

I planted both hands on the table before him, struggling to speak as I panted. "What…?" I coughed.

Boog motioned for me to sit. "We've been ordered not to go to the pool for a while." He grimaced.

"The Augur…"

"She's still breathing, although I don't think she's woken up yet. The healer says there's nothing wrong. She should recover, unless there are magical forces at work."

"Gaaah!" I yelled. "Of course there are magical forces at work."

Boog cast a baleful eye in my direction. "I talked with the Augur's chief assistant before they ushered me out. She says the pool will be out of commission for a month at least until they can enchant enough new water and get it cleaned up and re-sanctified, or whatever they need to do. That's assuming we didn't break it."

"Did you…" I began. "Did you tell Sophie what we saw?"

"She's been a bit busy, what with us destroying her favorite toy and blasting her most esteemed colleague senseless with unholy powers beyond our control. Strangely, I didn't feel like seeking her out. The clerks took my statement, and I imagine they'll be along for yours."

"How long have I been asleep?"

"Five hours, or so. Since this morning."

"Is anyone trying to track down Novara?"

"Not that I know of."

"Well, should we—"

"We should go to our chambers and try as hard as we can not to cause anything else to explode. I believe those were nearly Sophie's exact words."

I slumped down onto the table, rubbing the back of my neck with both hands.

"This isn't good, is it?"

"I have a strong feeling it's not. Not just pretty strong. Very strong." He took another bite of bread and chewed in silence.

I tried hard to figure out what to do or say, but nothing much came to mind. "I'm sorry, Boog, I…" I trailed off.

He patted me on the shoulder with his huge right hand. "It's not really your fault. Using the book was your idea, but nobody knew that would happen, and the Augur approved it, regardless. If she wakes up and isn't filled with unreasoning rage at us, she can set things right, and we'll be able to go find Novara." Boog rubbed the stubble on his chin. "Perhaps she'll resist arrest, and I'll be able to subdue her."

"That would be, uh, nice." I held out my hand. "Partners?"

He clasped it firmly with his. It hurt, but in a good way. "Partners."

I paused a moment. "So, uh, where are my pants?"

6

Anger Management

We were summoned to Sophie's office a few hours later, just after supper. The High Inquisitor was very, very angry. Red-cheeked, spittle-spewing, hair-tearing angry. I knew that I was not really guilty of causing the morning's events. Well, responsible for, but not technically culpable of. But this didn't seem like the time to split that particular hair.

"I suppose, Provisional Inspector Mingenstern, that you have some explanation for why the Augur lies in a drooling faint, perhaps never to awaken?" Her face was inches from mine. I could feel the heat of her breath. "And the sacred artifact we're sworn to protect, that has served Frosthelm for nearly a thousand years? I hear you broke it today, pursuing some crazy scheme involving a long-dead religion. Do you have anything, anything at all to say for yourself?"

I stammered, "Uh, Inquisitor, we—"

"That was rhetorical, you idiot. Don't interrupt me when I'm yelling at you." She took a deep breath. "We've got no pool, maybe for a month, maybe forever. That means no auguries, and the budget's suddenly a nightmare." She sank into her chair, suddenly deflated. "And the Augur, bless her, is a good friend."

Boog cleared his throat. "Inquisitor, we're very sorry about all this. We had no idea there was any danger."

I stepped in. "The pool has never behaved this way – there's nothing like this in any book in the library."

Sophie waved dismissively. "I know that. It doesn't help me."

I stayed quiet for a bit. "Inquisitor, as bad as this is, I think we need to address what we learned."

Sophie fixed a baleful glare on me. "And what is that, exactly?"

I'd been thinking about that since I awoke. "Well, the less important part is that we confirmed that Stennis was the thief, that he did sell the jewels to Novara, and that Novara has them, or had at least one of them, this morning, that is."

"Splendid. You've solved your robbery. How lovely."

I swallowed and continued doggedly onward. "A more important part is this. Novara is a powerful sorceress, or at least has access to powerful magic. It appeared that she transported herself out of the tavern to a secure location. That's no mean feat — how many wizards in Frosthelm have that kind of power? One? Two? I'm not even sure Bezanne could do it." Bezanne was the Prelate's court sorceress, an imposing and pompous woman with an unusually acute passion for tiny, yappy dogs.

Sophie nodded. I continued, hoping I was making sense, or at least distracting her from putting us on scullery duty. "I haven't discussed this with Boog— uh, Beauregard — but I think it looks like Novara caused the death of Stennis. She appeared to cast a spell while at the bar, and she may have finished it, causing the explosion, when she reached her residence."

Boog piped up. "That makes sense to me. It would be too much of a coincidence for it not to be Novara's doing – we know she used magic, so she may have had the ability to kill him this way. We know she had illegal dealings with Stennis, so we know she had a motive, and the blast seemed to come from the amulet, which she knew Stennis had, and which she'd cast the initial spell on." He paused. "Plus, we know Stennis was annoying."

Sophie's cheeks had dulled to pink. She thought. "So, did Novara plan to kill Stennis, or did your arrival trigger it?"

I replied, "I think we forced her hand, for a number of reasons. For one, there must be easier and more, uh, subtle ways for a wizard like Novara to kill someone. Two, I don't think she'd have given Stennis all that money if she planned to kill him. Three, and most telling for me, is that I really don't think she'd have left behind the amulet unless she had to. She really wanted it. Four would be the coincidence — our happening to show up and challenge them just seconds before she was going to kill Stennis? That seems improbable."

Sophie was nodding. She could seldom resist a puzzle, no matter what the circumstances. We were lucky we had one. "So where does that leave us?"

"Well, Chief, I have to move into the realm of speculation at this point. I suspect that Novara wasn't just looking for any set of jewels. She's powerful and probably rich. She may need these particular stones for a purpose, perhaps a magic ritual."

Boog continued, "Also, Chief, the moon and sun symbol. We've seen it on two articles Novara was interested in, both items of magical power, particularly the one we have. It must be very important to her in some way. I think Marty's guess that it was related to the cults was borne out by the events of the augury. The symbols floated out of the book, after all."

Sophie snorted. "That's great, yes. Good ol' Marty's idea was spot on. Too bad proving it left us crippled and bankrupt."

I blushed. "Chief, if I may, I fear the most important finding of this augury is that there may well be a powerful wizard loose in our town who is very well equipped and is an adherent of a doomsday cult. That may be a stretch, but we have to consider the possibility."

Sophie smirked, thinking. "And what do you think she intends to do?"

I was pretty sure this wouldn't go over well, but I had to bring it up. "Just before I, uh, lost consciousness in the Augur's chamber, I saw an image in the remaining liquid in the pool. Giant fiery balls were falling from the sky, and it looked like the whole of Frosthelm was on fire. The marketplace, the clock tower, the keep, every roof, every building... We can't let that happen."

Sophie didn't just scoff at me, as I had feared. I couldn't read Boog's expression. "You're sure of this?" asked Sophie. "It wasn't a dream that you had after fainting?"

"Losing consciousness, Inquisitor." I had some small amount of dignity left.

"Whatever. You're sure of this?" she repeated.

"I saw it, Inquisitor. I'm sure of it. And it must be related to Novara, because she was the focus of the augury."

Sophie sat back in her chair. "Well, isn't that just wonderful." She gazed at her desk for a time. "We need the Augur. But we don't have her. We need all our inspectors. But half of them are scattered about at the border serving in the damned war. We need our pool, but it's out of commission." She frowned at me. "And I can't think that the good criminals of Frosthelm will suddenly cease their felonious acts to help us out. I have much to think about, and much to plan."

She paused again, then spoke. "One thing is certain, though. This has grown bigger than what two provisional inspectors can handle. We need to find this Novara." She studied a list of names on her desk, and then she straightened in her chair. "All right, this is how it is. I'd rather put you two on another case, preferably something out in the countryside, concerning livestock, which even you couldn't mess up or explode. But you're the only inspectors still conscious who've seen Novara and wherever she is staying."

She made several marks on her list of names. "You two are no longer to work independently. You'll be part of a team, under Inspector Denault. I'll assign Gueran and Clarice as well – they've just completed a project."

Clarice. Warm thoughts filled my head. I might even have managed a goofy grin, but then I saw Boog grimace. He seemed to be focusing more on the Gueran side of things. Denault would be good – she was quiet but competent, respected and senior, and I'd worked with her as an apprentice during training on several cases.

Sophie's voice interrupted my reverie. "What are you still doing here? Get out. Go find your damned cultist wizard – I don't care how hard it is."

7

THE HUNT

Our crack team of inspectors got off to a good start early the next morning. Clarice identified the window pattern in Boog's sketch as being common in the more lavish houses of nobles and important persons found inside the keep wall. I wondered how she knew this. Neither Boog nor I were very familiar with that part of town, given our relatively impoverished childhoods. Gueran knew where all the tapestry vendors were. Of course he would. He probably had matched sets of tapestries and changed them every month. I'd never even remotely considered buying a tapestry, as I could barely afford the meager rent of the dormitory, and my decorating budget was, shall we say, strained. The proprietor of the third shop Gueran visited dimly remembered selling a green goat-covered tapestry to some noble or other a year back. He thought he remembered the delivery being on or near the end of High Street, which matched Clarice's memory of the windows.

Armed with that information, Inspector Denault split us up. We dispersed into the neighborhoods around High Street to study any southward-facing windows we came across. When we reunited after an hour of searching, Boog reported a likely candidate, and we all accompanied him there. The window did seem like a good match to his sketch and to my memory of the scene.

The building was no mansion – just an unassuming two-story house tucked into a dead end on the inside of the keep's curtain wall. The house had a low wall surrounding the property that ran back to join the much taller curtain wall behind. We spread out around the house and waited a half hour, watching the building, but there was no sign of activity. Gueran gallantly volunteered to burst in, blade at the ready, and (I think I'm getting this right) 'cut down the foul witch where she stands.' As if he could cut her down in some location where she wasn't standing. Gueran was already starting to grate on me.

Instead, Denault sent me, reasoning that I was the sneakiest. I was of two minds about this. Being sent instead of Gueran felt very good, and I hoped Clarice had noticed this. On the other hand, barging blindly into the lair of an evil sorceress wasn't sounding so lovely. I attempted a bit of a swagger as I headed out, but it set Boog to chuckling, so I quickly stopped. I hopped over the low wall and circled around to the rear door, peering through the rumpled glass panes in the small windows. I had thought to pick the lock, but it was broken, and the door swung open at my touch. I let myself in, quiet as the snow falls. There was no sound except the ticking of an expensive-looking pendulum clock over the fireplace. I drew my warding rod out of its case at my belt and activated it with my palm. I glanced into the living area and the kitchen, and then I took careful steps up the staircase, slow and soft.

It was there I found Novara. The grand battle I'd imagined in my head, where I yelled, dodged countless spells, and finally tagged her with my rod, wasn't to be. The version where I was instantly reduced to a pile of ash also wasn't to be, so I had no real complaints. Boog's dream of subduing the sorceress would probably be denied, as Novara was in no position to resist arrest, being, as she was, quite dead.

I couldn't be sure of the cause, but I figured the sun and moon pattern burned through her clothing and deep into her chest had something to do with it. I also figured it might be my fault, given that her face was frozen in the same terrified expression I'd seen in the pool moments before everything went awry. Now, it was mid-afternoon – more than a day since I'd seen her screaming image. Her corpse was just coming out of its death stiffness, and she was starting to smell a bit ripe. She was also quite cool to the touch, and her eyes had clouded over. I guessed she'd died just as our pool erupted.

I left her where she was and walked down to the front door, which I opened. It was unlocked, too. I guess Novara felt pretty secure, although given her current state that was perhaps a misjudgment. I swung the door open to invite the others in, but I had to duck as a blade whistled at my head. I fell into what passed as my fighting stance. Mistress Fennick, our combat instructor, had given my particular stance a special name: *The Cow Stands Watch*. But then I realized my opponent was Gueran.

"What are you doing coming out the front door?" he cried.

"What are you doing trying to kill me?" I responded, not without some justification, I think. Gueran stormed off. I shrugged.

"She's in here, but she's dead," I told them. Boog actually looked a bit disappointed. "Come on in and help me sort this out."

I went back inside, and they climbed the stairs behind me. Denault poked at Novara, checking her body and clothes and reading off her findings. Boog wrote them down.

"Grown woman, probably fifty, fifty-five years old. Short brown hair, graying. Black eyes. Old scar from chin to…" She pushed open Novara's collar. "…base of the neck, a serrated blade, I'd guess." She pulled on Novara's limbs and wiggled Novara's fingers, then smelled her carefully at several spots. "I'd say she's been dead more than a day." She turned to Novara's burnt chest. "Recent injury, probably the cause of death, oddly in the shape of a moon and sun…looks like some kind of magical fire. The wound is cauterized, and the intricacy of the pattern probably precludes a hot blade."

"How deep is it?" asked Clarice. She seemed unmoved by Novara's injuries, but her hand touched the small silver falcon pendant she always wore at her neck.

Denault pulled a thin metal rod from a toolkit at her belt and probed the wound. As she wiggled it in, it disappeared, nearly all six inches. She pulled it out and wiped it off on Novara's clothing. "Deep. Huh. Help me here." She and Gueran rolled Novara over. Her cloak was burnt in the back, and the moon and sun was scorched into the planks of the floor underneath, discolored by some seepage of Novara's internal fluids. Denault tore the cloak and clothing aside, and we saw the pattern in reverse, charred into Novara's back.

Gueran swore softly. "That's something you don't see every day."

Boog spoke up. "She must have died right as we were watching – from magic sent through the pool? Is that possible?"

"I wouldn't have thought so," I replied. "But the pool certainly wasn't behaving normally. It might instead have been some connection between the amulets, hers and the one from Stennis."

"Where's her amulet?" asked Clarice.

"I didn't see it, but I wasn't thorough," I replied.

Gueran and Denault rolled Novara back over, and Denault searched her, turning up a handkerchief, a money pouch, and a set of keys, but nothing else.

"She was wearing it when we saw her in the pool, right? Around her neck?" asked Boog.

I nodded. Could it have been destroyed by the magical storm that had disrupted our pool, or perhaps consumed as it burnt the symbols into her chest? Maybe, but I remembered that when Stennis exploded, his amulet was unharmed.

"All right, then," said Denault, rising from the body. She rubbed her back and stretched, then gestured to us. "Clarice, Gueran, you stay here with me and search the house, everywhere, top to bottom. You two," she pointed to me and Boog, "go talk with the neighbors, and see if they've noticed anything strange recently, or if they know anything about Novara here."

"Inspector?" I said. "There's one more odd thing I noticed. The rear door was unlocked and the lock broken, perhaps forced. And the front door was unlocked." Denault made a note of this and motioned us on our way.

As we descended the staircase, Gueran called down, "Be careful not to blow anyone up, boys. Anyone else, that is." Boog's lips tightened.

8

BAKED GOODS

We emerged from the house. The cobblestone street here was a short alleyway branching off a minor thoroughfare. Two of the three houses were pressed against the interior of the keep's wall, facing the rear of a much larger building, an inn. The third house, Novara's, was at the end of the small road. The grand curtain wall of the inner keep rose behind them, dwarfing them all.

The inn had only a few windows facing the alley, no doors. I thought the houses seemed more promising, and Boog concurred. We walked over to the neighboring house and Boog knocked on the door. We waited for some time. Boog was ready to move on, but I thought I heard voices from within. I knocked again. Finally, the door opened a bit, revealing an old woman with rheumy eyes staring suspiciously out of the dim interior.

"Madame," I began. She studied me appraisingly, then turned and noticed Boog towering over me. She gave a shriek and slammed the door. I looked up at him. "Nice going, ape man." He snorted. I knocked again and called out, "Madame! We're inspectors, with the Inquisitor's Guild."

There were more muffled voices from inside. Finally, the door opened again, and the business end of a crossbow pointed out at us. Boog's hand flew to his sword. "Don't think I won't use this! I will!" came a shout from inside, a creaky male voice this time. "Go away!"

"Sir, we can't go away. We're conducting an investigation. We mean you no harm, and we won't hurt you," I said, in my calmest, most soothing voice. I noted that the crossbow bolt's tip, though quite rusty, was sharp enough to do some real damage. Great, I thought, what a fine day to be perforated by a paranoid coot.

The man behind the crossbow was silent for a time, then spoke. "Send the big one away."

Boog chuckled and crossed the street over to the back of the inn. Sometimes, I thought, it's good to look harmless. Or be harmless. The crossbow disappeared inside, and the door opened wider, revealing a very old man with a halo of thin white hair. "Do you have credentials?"

Mother of Blood. I showed him my inspector's ring, a large garnet in carved brass. "That could be faked, you know, or stolen," he said. "With all the goings on around here, I don't trust anybody. Why, we saw you and the others casing the neighborhood not long ago."

"I assure you, sir, we are inspectors investigating the house next door, on orders directly from the High Inquisitor, Sophie Borchard."

He perked up. "Next door? That creepy old woman?"

Creepy, I'd give him, but this guy was in no position to be calling anyone else old. "Yes, sir, we have reason to believe she was involved in criminal activities."

"All right, all right, come in. We've been watching carefully, you know. We're glad to help," he said, stepping out of the doorway. "We were going to go to the City Guard, but we were afraid to leave the house after last night."

"Can I invite my colleague over as well?" I asked. He nodded, and I waved Boog back over. He had to show his ring too.

We stepped into a small sitting room. The furniture was a bit worn, but the room was immaculate. I sat on a small stool, and Boog sat gingerly on the sturdiest chair he could find, shifting his scabbard to his lap. The old lady appeared with a tray bearing tea service and a variety of pastries and baked goods. I glanced at Boog, and he smiled. This was looking up.

I accepted a cup of tea. "Thank you." It was warm and strong. "Do you recall how long the woman has lived next door?"

"Oh, about three weeks," said the woman. The old man nodded agreement. "She comes and goes at all hours. I'm a light sleeper, and I can hear her boots on the stones outside as she walks by." Well, that was one problem she'd no longer have to deal with.

"Did she buy the house, do you know?"

"Oh, I don't think so. It's belonged to the Marron family since I was a little girl. They let their household staff live there, usually. There was a darling family there up until last autumn, with the cutest little girl. Count Marron's bursar, I think the lady was."

Interesting, I thought, reaching for a macaroon. We'd need to learn more about Marron. I didn't recognize the name, but that was no surprise. My knowledge of the local nobility was limited, to be generous. I'm sure Gueran would be able to tell us Marron's heredity, approximate wealth, and favorite color of tapestry.

"Did she ever speak to you?" asked Boog. He raised a meaty pinkie as he sipped his tea.

The old man shook his head. "No, not to me. Mavis brought her a plate of her almond glazed torties when she moved in, but she refused them and shut the door in her face." More fool Novara, I thought. They were delicious. Someone needed to teach these evil wizards better manners.

"Did she ever have guests at the house?" I asked. I couldn't see Novara inviting Stennis here, but she might have had other associates.

"No," said Mavis. "Not that I saw, and I'm here most of the time." She was looking warmly at Boog, who was on his fifth cherry crumb crescent. He gave her an appreciative, crumb-filled grin.

I went on. "Did you notice anything strange over there in the last day or two?"

This got the old man excited. "Did we ever! Two nights ago, there was a flash of light from the upper floor of the house. I was coming back from Ruger's, across the street. It was quick and bright, like lightning, only green. I waited a bit, but nothing else happened. I'm guessing she's a wizard." The old man shook his head, his face full of scorn.

Mavis added, "Then, yesterday morning, I was baking in my oven, a batch of nutmeg rings. They're very good, I think, if you'll pardon my presumption. I used some lemon preserves, this time, from last spring. Won't you try one?"

I declined politely. Boog took two. I asked her to continue.

"Yes, well, I heard the most odd wailing sound, like a bunch of scared animals, only it was more unearthly than that. I was terrified, especially after my Terrence had told me what he'd seen the night before. But I went to the window and peeked through the shutters, and I could see that there was green light, again, up there – I could see it even in the daylight. The wailing got louder and louder, and there were brighter and brighter flashes of light, and I could hear her yelling—oh, it was dreadful. Then there was a huge noise, like a thunderclap. She cried out, and then everything was quiet."

Her gaze was distant. I could see her reliving the experience. "Did you investigate?"

"Oh, goodness, no. I waited for Terrence to get back, late that afternoon. We couldn't decide what to do."

Terrence spoke up. "I thought about going over there, but that seemed dangerous. I was about to go tell the city guard, but then those three came to the house."

"What three?" I asked. Boog sat up straighter.

"Oh, they looked so cruel and fierce – all three of them. One seemed to be the leader. He had on a black robe. The others wore chain mail and helmets, but they had no crest or mark. Mercenaries, maybe." He looked angry.

"Did you notice anything unusual about them? Identifying marks, scars, tattoos, jewelry?"

The old man and woman thought a bit. "The man in the robe had a beard, I think, a little one, well-trimmed," said Mavis. "No mustache. His hair was blond, the beard darker, a bit reddish. The others, I don't know, it was hard to see under the armor. Both women, though." Terrence nodded.

"Were they part of the Marron house?" asked Boog.

"I don't think so," she replied. "I'd never seen them before, and the Marrons have uniforms for their guards."

"What did they do?"

"They went up and knocked on the door. For a long time. They were pounding on it at the end, and shouting. Then one of them went around to the back, and a few minutes later the door opened and they went inside. They were in there over an hour, and then they left."

"Did you notice anything different about them then? Were they carrying anything?"

"It was getting dark by then, but no, I don't think they looked any different. Except the man in the robe – he was very, very angry, yelling at the other two."

This was something new to go on – our case hadn't died with Novara. The broken lock in the back and the missing amulet now made more sense, although not much else did. I wondered why they hadn't done anything with Novara's body, but maybe they couldn't, at least not then. Not under the watchful eyes of Mavis and Terrence.

Boog brushed a crumb from his tunic and looked longingly at what little remained of the plate of baked goods. "They didn't come back?" he asked.

"No," said Terrence. "I was still thinking of going to the guard, but I thought that maybe the men had dealt with whatever had caused the light and the noise, and I didn't want to anger them. It's been a long time since I was in a fight," he said, looking wistfully over to his crossbow.

"Then you all came this afternoon, prowling all around, and we didn't know what to think," said Mavis. "You should wear the uniforms, you know. The red is very handsome, and you wouldn't scare folks so."

I smiled, thinking how pitiful our efforts would be if we all wore our scarlet tunics and cloaks everywhere. Hello, criminals! Inspector here! Please carry about your business. "We didn't mean to frighten anyone, Madame."

"Say," said Terrence. "What's this all about? What happened to the woman, and who were the other men?"

I exchanged glances with Boog. I decided to stick with the truth. Some of it, anyway. "Your neighbor was trafficking in stolen jewelry, and I think some of that caught up to her." Yup, it sure did. "She's dead."

Mavis gasped. "Dead? Did those men…"

"No, no, we're fairly certain she was dead before they arrived." Fairly certain that they hadn't carved through Novara with the blazing insignia of a moon cult – no, that would be my doing.

"Oh, how horrible!" She held a hand to her mouth.

Terrence was more philosophical. "She was rude, and she didn't like your food. If she's a thief, too, then we're well rid of her."

Boog nodded sympathetically. "I think we need to go report back. Thank you so much for speaking with us. Your information will help us sort this out. You are wonderful observers."

Mavis beamed. I added, "If you think of anything else, or if you see anything else out of the ordinary at the house, please contact us. I'm Inspector Mingenstern, and this is Inspector Eggstrom, but you can talk to any inspector and they'll pass the word on to us." I stood. "Thank you also for your very gracious hospitality. I can honestly say I've never had better pastries."

Mavis shone even brighter. "Thank you so much, inspector! Oh, you must take some with you." She hopped up and ran back to the back of the house. Boog stood up, too, trying not to drop crumbs on the floor.

Terrence extended his hand, and I shook it. "Sorry about threatening to shoot you there, boy."

"All in a day's work, sir." Well, not usually, but it sounded good, I thought.

Mavis returned with a bulging cloth sack bigger than Boog's head. "I added some extras for you to share with the other inspectors. But keep the golden honey squares for yourself. They're a family recipe." She handed it to Boog, whose eyes widened as he thanked her. He could eat anyone under the table, especially me, but he'd be lucky to get through these in a week, or more. I wondered how Terrence stayed so thin. Mavis cleared the teacups and headed back to the kitchen.

"Thanks again," I said, and we turned to leave.

As we neared the door, I heard Mavis cry, "Wait!"

I stopped. More information? I wondered what else she could have seen. We could use some more leads.

"Don't forget yours, too." She handed another huge sack to me.

9

FROWN FOR THE COUNT

We knocked on the door of the next house down, but there was no answer. The place looked disused. I suggested we might try the inn, but Boog thought we should check back with the others. I agreed.

When we opened the front door, a smell hit me, and not a pleasant one. I thought perhaps that Novara had ripened a bit more, but as I sniffed further, it smelled more like a stuck privy. Odd. We headed toward the stairs, and the smell intensified. I noticed muddy footprints on the steps. This was not right. I gently put down my bag of treats and drew my warding rod from its sheath, and Boog followed suit, his blade gliding silently out of its scabbard.

Boog motioned me forward, and I padded up the stone steps as quietly as I could, wondering why it was that I needed to go first. I could hear rustling noises from the room above. At the top of the stairs, I pressed myself against the wall, and slowly, ever so slowly peeked around the corner.

Clarice was there, and Denault, going through a chest of drawers. She spotted me and waved. I relaxed, put away my rod, and called Boog up. "We saw footprints on the stairs," I said. "What's that smell?"

Denault mutely pointed over to the wall at my side, where Gueran sat glowering at me from the desk chair. He was covered in gray-brown grime from head to toe. He was using a rag to wipe his face but with little apparent result. I tried very, very hard to keep from laughing. "What...what happened?" I brought a hand to my mouth to cover my smile.

Boog pushed past me into the room and spotted Gueran. He snorted, then laughed, his eyes gleaming.

Clarice gestured to Gueran. "I discovered a passageway beneath the floorboards in the room below us. There was a ladder leading down, and Gueran gallantly offered to go first." Was that a hint of a smile I saw on her lips? "Unfortunately, a step on the ladder broke, and he fell. Also unfortunately, the passage connected to the privy shaft, and he was unavoidably...soiled...when he landed."

Denault could not keep a straight face, and she looked away. Boog was making little wheezing noises, and I thought I saw tears in his eyes. Clarice continued. "The passageway was dark, and although Gueran was unhurt, we decided to wait until we could return with torches." Finally, she smiled. "And a change of clothing." Gueran dropped the rag and bent over his lap, placing his head in his grimy hands.

"So," said Denault, clearing her throat. "What have you two been up to?"

Boog couldn't answer, so I had to. I tried for my most happy, enthusiastic voice. "We've been next door, having tea and tarts." Boog sat down heavily, clutching his stomach, tears running down his cheeks, whimpering occasionally in his mirth.

Once Boog could talk again, we related our findings. Denault took extensive notes. We covered Novara, the lights and sounds, and the three men and their actions. I remembered then about the house's owners. "Oh, yes, and they said that this house is owned by the Marron family and is frequently used to house their servants."

As I said this, I noticed that Gueran looked expectantly at Clarice. Curious. She said nothing, merely frowning, and finally Gueran said, without his usual abrasiveness, "They're a wealthy family of high-ranking nobility, with several generations of extended family living here in town. Their lands and full estate begin three day's ride west of here, near Belcaster."

He continued staring at Clarice as he went on. "Marron himself is not universally liked, and he has interests in many businesses and political groups, and more than a few allies. Some consider him shrewd and clever, but many would call him a ruthless bully. He's a, shall we say, complex man."

"Yes," murmured Clarice. "Complex." I waited for her to say more, but she turned to study some papers on the desk.

That ended our report. Gueran asked to go home and clean up, and Denault dismissed him. Clarice showed us a small box she'd found under the bed. "It's locked. I thought you could probably open it."

To her, I said, mildly, "Yes, I think so." Inwardly, I was dancing and singing. Clarice thought I was good at something! Even if it was normally a skill for criminals and thieves. Hmm. Maybe I should learn some more laudable talents. Saving kittens from distress, for example, or perhaps dentistry.

First, I tried Novara's keys. More than once, I've spent an hour picking a lock, only to have someone point out the owner's keys, sitting there all along. No luck this time, though. I got out my tools and set to work. It wasn't a tricky one – only a couple of pins. I opened it up and felt an unexpected bit of relief. Inside was a pile of gemstones, including black pearls and fire emeralds. This had to be the same set Stennis had stolen. At least we had completed our initial assignment. But then I remembered something. "Do you see one that's white, with a green circle?"

Clarice shook her head. "No, I don't think so, but let's have a closer look." She poured them carefully out onto the table. There was no sign of the odd stone we'd seen Novara holding. I had meant to check our records, but I forgot in the tumult of the headquarters. But I was pretty sure that the green and white jewel had been in the set of descriptions we'd received from Countess Moriff. The others appeared to be safely accounted for here, but I had a bad feeling about the missing one given Novara's interest in it. "The gems are here, but the green and white one's gone," I called to Boog.

"I wonder if it was taken by the three visitors?" asked Boog. "Must have been."

Clarice frowned. "But the box was locked."

"Maybe they opened it and took the key?" I suggested. "Or, wait, she had it out near when she died. They probably just found it on the desk."

Boog squinted. "Was it important to them, or were they just cleaning the place out, taking all the valuables? They probably took her pendant, too."

Clarice pointed to Novara's money pouch. "Ten gold pieces in here, and another thirty-odd in a bag in the chest-of-drawers. All Gortian. I don't think this was a robbery."

"It's possible the pendant and the gem were consumed in the event that killed Novara," I proposed.

Clarice looked skeptical. "Possible, I suppose, but why assume that? We have a simpler explanation."

True enough, I thought. I went downstairs to have a look at the secret passage, but on my way I saw my forgotten bag from Mavis. I selected what I thought might be a golden honey square and returned upstairs to Clarice.

"The woman, Mavis – she gave us some of her baking to take home. Would you like one?" I held out the confection.

Clarice smiled and reached for it. "Thank you, Marten. It looks delicious." Her finger brushed mine as she took it. It was warm. I stood there holding out my empty hand, grinning foolishly, for a bit longer than I should have liked, but then I recovered my wits. I skipped joyfully down the stairs.

"Hey, where's mine?" Denault called after me.

The door to the passageway was closed, but I could see from Gueran's footprints where it was. It was cleverly set into the wood of the floor, the door opening along the natural joints between floor planks. One needed to poke through a knothole in one of the planks to pull up the floor section, and there was a recessed trapdoor set into the floor underneath. I noticed little dust. Perhaps it was regularly used, but Gueran's recent adventure could also have disturbed the area.

As I opened the door, I wondered what nefarious, or perhaps glorious, purposes it might have been used toward in the long history of Frosthelm. I had heard from some of the other inspectors that many of the noble's houses were riddled with such passageways, the better to overhear a conversation, meet an illicit lover, or make an escape. Growing up as I had in a one-room cottage, it was silly to me to make such a fuss about these things. I guess when one is fabulously wealthy and doesn't need to work, one needs something to fill one's time when shopping for new tapestries becomes tiresome.

A wooden ladder led down into the murky depths below. A powerful aroma rose up from those same depths. I took off my cloak, stepped onto the ladder, and carefully made my way down, avoiding not only the broken fourth rung where Gueran had his mishap but also the moist stains marking his ascent afterward. The bottom was lit dimly from the open door above me and also from the square opening of the house's privy, over to the right of the trapdoor. The base of the ladder rested on a small landing near the dark opening of the privy chute, which I guessed must lead through the curtain wall and down into the lower section of town outside the inner keep. A breach of the city's defenses, I thought, although the city hadn't been attacked by an army in centuries. There was a sizable cesspool that lapped up to the chute opening, and there were a mass of muddy markings leading out onto the ledge. Despite the eye-watering stench, I smiled again at the memory of Gueran's discomfort.

It occurred to me that this whole arrangement might be little more than an access to clean out the jakes as needed. Perhaps that had been its original purpose, but it had taken considerable craftsmanship to hide the door in the floor. There was also the matter of the exit. Behind me, where the ledge met the stone wall of the pit, was a small passageway that led off into darkness, curving gently to the right. It was lined with rough stone. I followed it a good way, tracing my hand against one wall. Eventually, I could no longer see light from the pit behind me. I was probably forty feet down the tunnel, and it headed downward on a gentle incline. I took a few more steps, and the passageway made a sharp turn to the left. I almost lost my contact with the wall in the darkness. We'd definitely need torches or lanterns to go farther in safety.

I retraced my steps, climbed back up the ladder, and closed the trapdoor. I feared I might have become unpleasantly pungent, so I went outside to air out my clothes a bit. The clean, cold air felt wonderfully refreshing after the dank sewer. I was surprised to see a group of eight or ten city guards milling about at the main road. A man in a fine fancy cloak marched up the alleyway. He wore several long gold chains around his neck, and he had a purple cap edged with white fur on his head. He looked to be about forty years old, clean-shaven, with dark hair and blue eyes. He saw me and waved a gloved finger at me.

"What is the meaning of this? This is an outrage! What are you doing in my house, on my property?" he yelled, cloudy vapor puffing from his mouth in the cold air.

"Sir, I am an Inspector, with the Guild, and an investigation led us to a suspect staying in this house."

"What? Regardless, I gave you no permission to enter this house. I'll have you arrested!"

This came up frequently. The permission to search part, not my being arrested. "Sir, our Charter, issued by Prelate Leopold and signed by every Prelate since, including His Grace Jeroch, grants us permission to pursue suspected criminals into private homes when we have reasonable grounds to believe they are present."

He stepped closer to me, bending over so that his nose almost touched mine. "Criminals? There are no criminals here. Do you have any idea who I am?" he growled, threateningly.

An idiot, I thought. "No, sir," I replied. "I would be very interested in that information, however. Can I have your full name?" I pulled out my small notepad and pencil.

He turned and stormed back to the guards. I pulled the door open and shouted up the stairs. "Inspector Denault! We have company!"

A few of the guards followed the man back to me, one a tall woman with a sergeant's mark on her armor. I didn't recognize her, but most of my work was outside the curtain wall in the less tapestried parts of town. "Sergeant! Arrest this man!" he cried.

"On what charge, Count Marron?" asked the sergeant.

"Trespassing! Thieving! Vandalism! Who knows what they've done in there," yelled the man, presumably Count Marron if the guard knew what she was talking about.

The sergeant turned to me. "Inspector, may I see your credentials?"

"Certainly," I replied. I showed her my ring, and she examined it briefly.

"Thank you. Have you, in fact, trespassed, stolen, or vandalized this property in any way?"

"No, sergeant, of course not." I thought of Gueran's footprints. "We have inflicted no damage to the property other than in the necessary execution of our duties," I amended.

The Count seethed. "Execution. Good word. Expect yours shortly. I have friends in the Justiciary, you know."

Denault came out and stood beside me, followed by Boog. The sergeant continued. "Did you have reasonable grounds to suspect that a criminal was inside the house?"

"Yes," I replied. "Actually, she's upstairs, as is the stolen property we were pursuing her to recover."

"Do you need assistance in apprehending her?"

I smiled. "Uh, no, we have managed to subdue her."

Marron reached his limit. "Sergeant, I don't care about this drivel. I will have you removed from the guard, shackled, and hauled to the dungeon if you do not arrest these people this instant."

The guard stared at Marron, but she made no move. Denault stepped in, her voice low and smooth. "My lord, pardon my intrusion. It seems to me that there are two possibilities here. We have discovered a thief and murderer residing at a property you own, apparently with your permission. Either you did not know that your houseguest was a thief and murderer, in which case you should want us to complete our investigation as quickly as possible and clear you of any wrongdoing. Or, conversely, you did know, in which case you would likely want to hinder our investigation at every step."

Denault stepped closer to the nobleman. "So, my lord, which is it? Are you an innocent victim who wishes to assist us, or should we include you in our investigation for aiding in these crimes?"

The sergeant folded her arms across her chest. "The inspector's perspective makes sense to me, my lord. Do you persist in requesting me to arrest them?" She frowned, and her eyebrows descended to form a dark, fierce line. I imagined this look was effective deterrence for most of Frosthelm's citizenry.

Not Marron, though. His returned glare could have frozen the sun. When he spoke at last, it was in a hushed, icily polite tone. "The trauma of these accusations and of my guest's death must have unsettled me. I apologize to you all, and I wish you success in your investigation." He turned on his heel and strode away.

Boog patted Denault on the shoulder. "Nice work, inspector."

Denault shook her head. "He's far more powerful than I am. Maybe more powerful than all the Guild. I'd have preferred not to make an enemy of him."

As I turned back to the house, I saw Clarice standing in the doorway. She had eyes only for the count, staring at him until he rounded the corner at the end of the alley. Her lips made a very thin line across her face, and she clutched her falcon pendant firmly in her left hand.

"Hey," said Boog. "Did any of us ever mention to the count that Novara was dead?"

Not I, I thought. Now, how had he come by that particular bit of information?

10

CASE CLOSED

I was eating some porridge in our small kitchen when Boog wandered in. "Late night?" he asked. "You look horrible. Really bad."

"Hey, thanks," I grumped. After we'd returned from Novara's house, made our reports to the clerks, and filed all the papers and other evidence we'd recovered, I had spent four hours and run through a goodly number of candles in the library looking for further information on the cults I'd studied earlier. With Sir Neggin's book reduced to a sodden mess, there wasn't too much else to go on, and the time had been frustrating and unproductive.

I shouldn't really be complaining. Our investigation so far had been amazingly fast-paced. Starting with the report of the robbery, it had taken us less than a week to identify the thief and apprehend him. Or, well, bring him to justice. In a bag. We'd found Novara very quickly, too, in less than two days, and recovered the amulet and all but one of the stolen jewels.

Yes, except for the minor setback where we destroyed the Augur's pool, this would have been a real success story. There were obviously still some mysteries left unsolved – what Novara was trying to do, where the missing jewel was, what the pendant signified, and how Marron might be connected to the whole affair. These still nagged at me and, I thought, at the other inspectors as well.

The case was hardly my only concern. The Augur hadn't regained consciousness as of the night before, and I was quite worried about her. I supposed the healers could still give her water, and they had some sustaining magic to use, but I wasn't really sure how long she could last without regular nourishment. Or, for that matter, whether she'd recover at all. I would visit her today, I resolved.

I finished my porridge, wiped the bowl and my spoon with a damp rag, and put them in my small cubbyhole. Boog was already into his second bowl, and I saw that he had selected three of Mavis' golden honey squares as an accompaniment. I sent my bag down to the apprentices' quarters, figuring those poor wretches would appreciate it more than I.

One of those self-same wretches knocked at our door. "Inspectors?" he said, timidly. He looked to be in the newly-recruited group, a first-year, those who'd replaced our graduating class. I wondered if I'd looked as young and as wide-eyed five years ago. Probably even more so, I decided.

"Yes?" growled Boog. He liked playing with them a bit.

The boy flinched, and stammered, "Yes, sir. I mean, sir, your presence, sir, is requested by Inspector Denault in the meeting hall. Sir. Now. Sir." The boy paled as he spoke, shrinking from Boog's hulking presence.

Boog gave him a nasty glance. "Oh, really?"

The boy seemed to want to curl into a ball. "Yes, sir."

"And why should I believe you?"

The boy looked confused. "Sir?"

"There are spies and traitors about. Everywhere." Boog cast quick, paranoid glances in all directions. Then he grabbed the boy's jerkin and pulled him close. "Perhaps you are one?" The boy opened his mouth, then closed it, then opened it again. No sound came out.

"Boog, give it a rest," I said, tired of the game. I'd been the target of such jokes far more often than Boog, I'm sure, and I had a good deal of sympathy for the gangly boy.

Boog laughed and tousled the boy's hair. "Sorry, lad. We'll be along shortly." He gave the boy one of his honey squares.

"Here you go. Thanks for the summons." The boy left rather quickly.

"What do you think Denault will want to do next?" I asked, gathering my cloak from its hook.

"No idea," said Boog. We wound our way through the dormitories and then through the clerks' offices to the meeting hall, outside Sophie's office. Denault, Clarice, and Gueran were all there. Sitting across the table from them was Sophie and a woman I'd not seen before. She wore the blue and gold doublet of the Justiciary.

I glanced at the map and was surprised to see that no flag had been placed where we'd found Novara. The map was updated first thing in the morning and then as needed during the rest of the day, so it should have been marked. I was unsure of the appropriate flag color for finding a dead criminal sorceress with a magic hole burnt through her chest. Probably still miscellaneous orange. Even stranger, I saw that the case flags had been removed from the Sotted Swan and Countess Moriff's house, the site of the original robbery.

Boog and I found seats at the table. Boog sat next to Clarice before I could make my way there. The clod. I hoped his chair had a splinter.

"Marten, Beauregard. Thank you for coming so promptly," said Sophie. She didn't look happy. "This is Justice Wiggins. She's come here to follow up on a request we received late last night."

This was unusual. We had frequent contact with the Justiciary, but it was normally initiated by us, when our cases were complete and we or the city guard had arrested a criminal. I couldn't think why a justice would be interested in our case, particularly one in which both the thief and his employer were dead, and the stolen goods recovered. There seemed to be nothing and no one upon which to pass judgment.

Sophie continued. "We have been requested by the Justiciary to conclude our investigation into the jewel robbery upon which you all have been working, with great success, I might add." She looked at us, a small smile showing her pride.

The justice, a thin woman with a crooked nose, interrupted Sophie. "It is our understanding that you have solved the case and recovered the stolen property, and that both of the persons involved are deceased. There would seem to be nothing else for you to do."

Not by half, I thought. Denault agreed. "But the case has come to include more than just the robbery," she said. "There is the matter of the sorcery performed by Novara—"

"Who is dead," interjected Wiggins.

"And the matter of Novara's accomplices, seen entering the house."

"They were not accomplices. They were sent by Count Marron to investigate reports of noise at his property." That didn't ring true. For one thing, why weren't they wearing his uniform? But I was beginning to see what was going on here.

Denault was becoming frustrated. "We have not recovered all of the stolen jewels."

"Count Marron is deeply upset that such unsavory events transpired on his property, although of course he had no knowledge of Novara's intentions. He has offered to compensate Countess Moriff generously for her loss and her trouble, and the Countess has accepted this offer." Justice Wiggins sounded very regretful indeed.

Gueran spoke up. "In the course of their investigation, these two," he gestured to Boog and me, "invoked powerful magic which damaged and possibly destroyed the Augur's pool."

He paused to favor us with a look of open disdain. Thanks, Gueran, you pompous ass. He went on. "This magic was directly tied to Novara and merits further investigation for the safety of the city."

Wiggins seemed ready for this, as well. "As I pointed out earlier, Novara is dead and poses no further danger. As for the damage to Guild property, the Justiciary has ruled that the Guild may keep the gold recovered from Stennis Shortsaber to help pay for repairs. In addition, Count Marron deeply regrets his unintentional involvement, and has most generously offered a sum of four hundred gold sovereigns to help compensate the guild for necessary repairs and loss of income."

I could see from the bright pink of Boog's face that he was angry. "I suppose that's contingent on us breaking off the investigation?"

The justice didn't reply. Sophie looked very uncomfortable. "That's enough, Beauregard," she said, softly. Boog folded his huge arms across his chest and looked down at the table. Clarice sat impassive and unreadable at his side, and Denault seemed suddenly deflated. Gueran's eyes showed anger, but he said nothing.

If that was our price, at least it was a good one. I didn't know the details of the Guild's finances, but I guessed that such a sum would keep us going for three months, at least, maybe more. More than enough time to get the pool back in operation.

Sophie spoke again. "I've decided to close the case. Please file your final report with the clerks by the end of the day." Her tone was dull and heavy. She turned to the Justice. "Thank you for taking the time to help us clarify the situation. I think we're finished here." Wiggins rose and left, a smirk on her face.

We were all quiet for a while, lost in our own thoughts.

Finally, Boog broke the silence. "That's not right." His voice was cold.

Sophie sighed. "I know it. Believe me, I hate this more than you do. But what am I to do? Fire all of you, and run all the investigations myself? Stop feeding everyone? Sell the Guild Hall? Without the pool working, we can't make it. And the Prelate can't spare another copper with the fighting at the border. We have no choice."

"We're whores," said Gueran, acidly. I was surprised at his vehemence. "There is no honor in this." For once, I agreed with him.

"There is no honor in Marron," murmured Clarice. "None." She abruptly stood and left the room.

My mind wanted to tear off in a thousand directions, but I forced myself to think. "Chief. If I understand this…arrangement, we are not to investigate any further into

Novara, Stennis, or Count Marron." Sophie nodded glumly. "Does this prevent us from doing further work on the pendants and their magical properties, and the connections to the old religious groups?"

Sophie thought about this. "I suppose I have no objection to that, as long as you keep well clear of Marron. But I need you all on other cases. We've got more cases than we have inspectors, and I can't spare you for a wild chase that may never lead anywhere."

"But on my own time?" I pressed her.

"Your own time is your own business," she replied. I saw a glimmer of satisfaction play across her face. She stood. "Once you've completed your reports, please contact me for a new assignment. Inspector Denault, come with me, if you would. I want to discuss the wording of the final report." Denault looked unhappy, but she followed Sophie into her office and closed the door.

I looked at Boog. He held out his hand, and I grasped it. "I'm with you," he said. "Let's get to the bottom of this. Marron or no Marron."

Needless to say, I was quite surprised when Gueran placed his hand firmly atop both of ours. "I'm with you, too."

11

THE PURSUIT OF UNDOMESTICATED GEESE

The Augur's assistant peered out through the half-open door after I knocked. I wasn't sure if she would be glad that I was coming to visit or angry because I'd been involved with the Augur's affliction. I suspected the latter, but her neutral expression held no clue.

"Madame awakened, just an hour ago," she said. "Thanks be to the Mother. She's resting in the rear chamber. She may have fallen back to sleep, so tread softly." She gestured toward the rear of the room.

We had a small infirmary in the Guild Hall, and the Augur had understandably been granted its largest room. I padded quietly through the archway separating the two halves of the room and saw the Augur resting on a bed, her upper body propped up on a pile of cushions. Her skin looked gray, and her breath hissed in and out unevenly, so it took me a little while to realize she was conscious of me in the room. Her pink eyes showed only through slits under her eyelids, but I could still feel the power of her gaze.

She made a soft grunt, then coughed, dry and raspy. I knelt by her bed and placed my hand on hers. It felt cold, her skin like dry parchment. "Augur, I've come to apologize for what happened. I should never have used the pendant without knowing its power and history. It's my fault you're hurt."

Her lips moved, and I leaned closer to hear her whisper. "It's your fault..." she wheezed, then closed her eyes. I felt terrible.

Her injuries, the pool — I'd been hoping she wouldn't put the blame solely on me. But who else? Not the Augur herself, and certainly not Boog. I wondered if I should resign from the Guild entirely. Perhaps they'd all be better off if I did.

She opened her eyes again. "It's your fault," she repeated, "that I'm alive." Surprisingly enough, she grinned. She seemed to regain a bit of her strength, although I still strained to hear her whispering. "The pool saps strength from those who use it, as you know. When I lost control, and the pendant took over, it...drained me. I could feel my life departing my body, into the pool, and stranger still, into the amulet. It was all I could do to grab onto you, and feed it some of your strength, so that I might retain some small piece of myself."

My hand flew unbidden to the back of my neck. I recalled her cold, tight grasp at the pool, and my sudden weakness. She swallowed noisily and smiled. "I can see I should have fed it more of you, and less of myself."

"But, Augur," I replied, slowly. "It was still my choice to place the medallion among the runes. My error, that caused all this."

She laughed, a ghastly chuckle, then sank into a fit of coughing. "Silly lad. I knew better what we did than you. It was my curiosity, not yours, for which I now pay the price." She closed her eyes again and was silent for a time. After a few minutes, I thought she must have succumbed again to sleep. Though I longed to ask her a hundred questions, I thought it best to let her rest, hopefully to recover. I let go of her hand and rose, turning quietly toward the archway.

"Marten," she called at my back. "The north corner. Look there." She placed a hand over her eyes, and said no more, though I waited a long while, until her breathing became soft and regular.

I nodded to the Augur's assistant as I walked out, lost in thought. I wondered which north corner she meant. I thought instantly of the Augur's chamber with the pool, but it was circular, and had no corners at all. Perhaps I was to look in the northern corner of headquarters, but that, too, seemed unlikely. The Hall of the Inquisitor's Guild was a rectangular building running east-west, with the dormitories attached on the western end, so it didn't really have a northern corner. And it had three stories, plus below-ground storage, so it wasn't even clear which of the northern sides she could have been speaking of. No, I couldn't think that she'd refer to a northern corner in the building, although in her weakened state she might have misspoken.

Could it be Frosthelm itself? The ancient castle sat atop a steep rocky hill, its outer walls tracing the hilltop's contours, forming an impregnable barrier. Well, it might be pregnable, but it hadn't been conquered in the last four hundred years, at least, although that was more due to the strength of its armies than of its walls. The wealthy and the noble lived inside the walls of the inner keep, while the tradespeople, merchants, and commoners lived in the city below, sprawled around the hill in all directions, the houses and businesses within the large outer city walls giving way to pastures and farms the farther out one traveled, past the outer walls.

The outer city was too large and too disorganized to have anything like a northern corner, or any corner, for that matter. The inner keep wall did have something of a northern extreme, if I remembered the maps correctly. I headed to the meeting hall to check. I had already turned in my report to Denault, and I hadn't been assigned new duties, so I could spend the rest of the afternoon on my search.

Two hours later, I stood atop the wall of the inner keep, admiring the view of the city below. Would that my powers of intuition had been equally breathtaking. The wall here, definitely the northernmost point of the keep, was amazingly nondescript. It brought absolutely nothing to my mind. Nothing. There were no markings, no mysterious informants waiting with information, no messages secreted in potted plants.

I could not imagine what the Augur had meant, if she meant me to look here. Directly below me, at the foot of the wall, were a well and a pigsty, serving the kitchen of a nearby household.

I'd examined the well thoroughly, and the pigs and I had become fast friends after some initial distrust, but I was no nearer to solving the puzzle than when I'd started.

Perhaps the Augur meant for me to notice something out below me, in the city. I looked out again over the jumble of houses, roads, and businesses below, with the Serpentine River cutting a gray-brown path through them. Fifty thousand people lived in and around the city, if the Prelate's city minister could be believed. It was easy to believe this number from up here. I could see the northernmost of the city's two main markets. The southern one, hidden from my current view by the keep itself, sprawled across several blocks in the southern part of the city. The northern one, which I now observed, catered to a wealthier segment of the population. It nestled in and around Fountain Square. The fountain there appeared as a bright blue disk from this height. I scanned the panorama for several minutes, but if there was a message there, I was too dense to see it.

Dejected, I turned from the rampart's edge. At the corner of my vision, I spotted just a hint of a gray cloak flapping in the wind. A figure disappeared down the nearby stairway, but I couldn't get a good look. The sun flashed off red gems set in steel protruding from a scabbard — an ornate weapon. Probably a guard, I thought, although the walls of the inner keep were seldom patrolled in these days of relative peace in the city. But wouldn't a guard have been in uniform, wearing a dark green cloak? And the sword was fancier than most guards would carry. Hmm.

I walked down the stairs, bade farewell to the pigs, and headed back to the Guild Hall, which was across the keep grounds to the south. I tried to imagine what the Augur could have meant by a northern corner. I was obviously either missing something, or the Augur, in her illness, had been confused.

I was pretty well confused myself by the time I returned to headquarters. I opted for the meal provided for the students in training – it was never anything special, except on holidays, but it would be hot and plentiful, and I'd had a discouraging day. I entered the front door of headquarters and headed for the dining hall.

As I made my way through the building, I passed by the Augur's chamber. Curious, I ducked inside to see what progress had been made in its restoration. With the roof closed, it was dim, lit only by a torch guttering in its sconce on the back wall. It felt sterile and dead compared to the bright light, excitement, and terror of two days before.

I wandered around the room. They'd cleaned up the mess. The water was gone, the scattered book pages removed, the items I'd selected returned to storage, I supposed. There wasn't any trace of Stennis on the runes. Poor guy, I thought, struck with a sudden pang of pity. He may have been a thief, but he had been vibrant, full of life, and I was fairly certain he had no idea what he was getting into. At least he died happy and rich, I mused. As he would have liked.

Walking up the steps, I could see that the pool was empty, and it was shocking for me to see it so. It had not been drained in my lifetime, although the Guild histories told of such things in the past. The pool's waters were prepared by the Augur and her assistants from an ancient recipe, requiring rare ingredients and arduous magical rituals. Once the liquid was created, there was no place it could be stored save the pool itself. It soaked up memories and images from whatever it touched. The wood of a barrel would fill the water with images of leaves and animals. Metal cauldrons would imbue the water with images of mines, mountains, and metalworkers. Normally, the Augur and her staff would create enough liquid each week to replace what was lost to evaporation, but the pool was never emptied and refilled except in the direst circumstances. Such as I had wrought, I thought sheepishly.

Hopefully they could begin to refill the pool soon, although I thought they probably waited on the Augur's recovery. I did not doubt the estimate of a month to fill it again. I looked around the room, at the carved columns, at the benches set out for observers, and at the neat stack of cleaning cloths, in case anything messy was placed on the runes.

As I retreated back down the stairs, I wondered at the sophistication of the ancient masons who had constructed this chamber, about which the Guild Hall had been constructed much later. The room was a perfect circle, its dimensions accurate and identical beyond our ability to measure. The tiles were set perfectly, the runes carved flawlessly, the ornate decorations repeated meticulously around the chamber. And none of it had shifted or abraded in all the centuries of use. There must be some powerful magic at work at this place, and so much knowledge about it must have been lost since its creation.

It was then that I suddenly realized I was staring at the diamond pattern that made up the chamber's floor. I had seen it so many times that I barely noticed it anymore, but the tiles around the basin were a diamond of black marble, surrounded by a ring of white marble extending to the wall. In a flash, I was on my knees, examining the floor. I closed my eyes and imagined the plan of the Guild Hall and the chamber's place in that plan. I had entered from the south, so I crawled over to the northern side.

Each tile in the floor around the raised dais had, carved into it, a rune filled with gold. Many had been translated, but others remained a mystery. It wasn't anything I gave much thought to anymore — just decorations in the room. As I crawled over to the northern part of the black diamond, however, I had eyes only for the runes. And in the triangular tile that made up the northernmost corner of that diamond, I saw a symbol that turned my insides all tingly.

Carved into that tile, by hands at least eight hundred years dead, was a full moon partially obscuring a sunburst, an exact duplicate of the amulet.

12

A Rugged Fellow

Boog had our prisoner by the arm and was hauling him roughly along. "Hey!" complained the mud-spattered man, wiping a small feather from his upper lip. "That hurts!"

Boog just snarled at the man, and the prisoner promptly shut his mouth. I'd have shut mine too. Boog was in a nasty temper after having pursued this individual, a Maurice Houghton, across a field, down a stream, through a barn, and into a chicken house. Small tufts of feathers still stuck to both of them, especially their wet, muddy boots. I'd avoided being so decorated by mere good fortune, having circled around to the back of the farmhouse in case he attempted to escape.

Escape he had, but through a side window. By the time I'd seen him fleeing across the field, with Boog charging after him, I was much too far behind to catch up, and I had followed at a more sedate pace. Which fit the case, a fairly mundane one: a carpet merchant in town had discovered a dozen carpets missing from her warehouse. I wondered at the wisdom of the thieves – – there were many more portable, more valuable items to steal than carpets. Most of those the Guild apprehended were not blessed with genius.

This was our fifth case in the three weeks since finding Novara dead, with three solved and two still active. Sophie Borchard had kept us hard at work after the Novara business, and I didn't know if it was merely because the Guild was so short-handed, or whether she was trying to keep us from looking further into those earlier events. We'd split our extra time three ways. I was to work in the library, trying to figure out what the moon and sun symbol meant. Gueran was using his placement in noble circles to try to dig up more information on Marron and his connection to Novara. Boog had set out to do some legwork in the city, trying to track down anyone with connections to Novara and Stennis, and Marron too, for that matter. I know we'd been warned off Marron, but some orders seemed less mandatory than others. More guidelines, or suggestions, really. Tips. Regardless, I'd barely had time to sleep, much less make any real progress in my studies, and I was sure the same was true for Boog and Gueran.

Working with Gueran had been surprisingly less annoying than I had anticipated. I had originally doubted that it would work, but either his dunking in the privy or our shared purpose had dampened some of his more obnoxious tendencies. Not that he couldn't still be a pompous boor, to be sure. But I had to admit his competence, and he seemed to share with me and Boog a love for the Guild and a strong sense that we'd been bought off.

If only we'd had more time, but criminals don't normally wait on our convenience. This case, of the purloined carpets, had been fairly routine thus far. We'd checked out the merchant's employees, but they all seemed unlikely, and most had witnesses as to their location on the night of the robbery. The customer list the merchant provided had proved similarly unhelpful until we'd hit upon Maurice, whom the merchant described as a frequent visitor to the shop, but one who'd never purchased anything. We'd come to his farm merely to question him, but his attempt at flight made me think we might have found our man.

Boog shoved Maurice back into the farmhouse, a large, well-made building with two stories. Maurice stumbled a bit on the wood floor, and I worried that he might fall, as his hands were tied behind his back. He stayed up, though. He looked scared and sweaty, his face flushed and glowing in the light of a small oil lamp.

Boog pushed Maurice down onto a chair, causing some feathers to go fluttering about. I wandered about the house, opening doors to some of the other rooms. Oddly enough, each room I visited had a fine, new carpet laid tastefully out on the floor. One even had a small parchment tag displaying a rather exorbitant price tied to its edge. Tsk, tsk, Farmer Houghton. I untied the tag and returned to the front room, where Boog had begun questioning the farmer.

"So, Maurice, we hear you've taken an interest in carpets from the south," said Boog.

"I don't know what you're talking about," stammered Maurice. "I hate carpets. Always have."

"But you've got a carpet in almost every room," I said. "Not very common for a farmhouse. You'd think they'd get muddy."

"They're family heirlooms," said Maurice.

I held up the tag.

"I was planning to sell that one," he said. "Hate carpets."

Boog shook his head. "I saw two more in the cart in the barn. I suppose you were off to market to sell those family heirlooms as well?"

Maurice looked pretty miserable, but he said nothing. Boog pulled out his small notebook and pencil and began writing down details. Maurice squeezed closed his eyes. Finally, he spoke.

"This isn't going to go very well for me, is it?" he asked.

Boog and I looked at each other. I flicked a feather off of Boog's tunic. "No," I said. "I don't think so."

"What is the penalty for carpet theft?" he asked. "Not that I stole anything, or know of any carpet thieves," he added lamely.

"That depends on a lot of things," I said, "but it's up to the Justiciary, not us. If you confess and cooperate, that can help. If the carpets are all present here, and undamaged, that might help. If you turn in an accomplice, or someone you were going to sell them to, that might help. If you can provide us with valuable information, we can sometimes put in a good word."

Maurice looked unhappy. "But what is the range of possible penalties?"

Boog smiled. "Well, they might let you off with public flogging and a fine. Or confiscation of the property here, and all your belongings. Or, they might cut off a hand. This isn't quite serious enough for the iron maiden or the rack, wouldn't you say, Marty?"

"No, the rack would be a stretch," I replied, smiling. We'd done this routine countless times, but it never failed to crack me up.

Boog grinned back. "And there's always death."

Maurice blanched. "Death?"

"You can't rule it out," said Boog. "If the judge is a friend of the merchant, or had a bad egg at breakfast, say. They can be quite capricious."

Not strictly true, I thought. The Code of Laws described the range of penalties for most crimes in fairly specific detail. But I let Boog have his fun. He was covered with feathers, after all.

"Bad egg," mumbled Maurice, his eyes wide.

"So, what will it be, Maurice?" I asked.

He sagged a bit in his seat. "There are five in the house, four in the storage shed out back, and three in the cart in the barn."

Twelve. Excellent. That would be all of them. "Why carpets, Maurice?" I asked. I had to know. "Why not gems, or artwork? Or, chickens?" Boog shot me an annoyed look.

"I love carpets," he replied, looking miserable. "Always have."

We tied his ankles and wrists to the chair and searched the farm. All of the carpets were where he said. They looked to have been lovingly cared for. When we returned, he looked anxious.

"I've thought of something! Something that might help!" he cried as soon as we entered the house. "I was at a tavern a few days ago, and I overheard a group next to me talking about a meeting."

"Fascinating," said Boog. "A meeting. Shall we let him go now, Marty?"

"No," he cried. "It was not a normal meeting. They were bad."

"Oh, well, if they were bad, then sure," said Boog.

"Listen to me!" Maurice was getting agitated. "They spoke of stolen goods, and of kidnapping!"

Boog snorted. We'd heard this kind of tale a number of times, and Maurice certainly seemed more likely to have an active imagination than to have stumbled upon something important. I figured we should hear him out, though. There was no harm in listening. "What goods? What kidnapping? Why didn't you mention this before?"

Maurice looked at me with some calculation. "You'll get me mercy from the judges?"

"No promises," I replied. "Tell us what you know."

Maurice took a deep breath. "They said they were meeting at the empty Jezarmi warehouse on the wharf road, by the fountain there. The one with the red doors? I only noticed because it was near the carpet warehouse. That got my attention."

He paused, looking at us for approval, and I motioned for him to go on. "One seemed like the leader. She said they needed to meet there in five days – that would be two days from now. At midnight. Pick up their payment there, and drop off the goods, and their guest."

"This sounds more like a business deal than a high crime," I said, doubtful.

"But they laughed when they said 'guest' – and they were acting in a very suspicious manner."

"Suspicious how?"

"I don't know, suspicious. They were armed, and they looked mean."

"Which tavern?"

"The Burly Boar, in town—"

"I know it. How many?"

"Five or so, I think. Maybe six. They came and went."

"Any uniform, or distinguishing features?"

Maurice thought for a moment. "No, no uniform. They were all strong, tough-looking, mostly women. I was scared of them, so I moved to the other side of the tavern."

I looked at Boog. This was weak. He said, "This is the best you can do? There's nothing that says the goods were stolen, or that their guest is a prisoner."

"Look, the warehouse there is empty, and it's been closed down for years. I go by there all the time taking my goods to market. There's no legitimate business going on there."

"This Jezarmi – Boog, you heard of it? A merchant, a family, or a company?" I asked.

He shook his head, but he was thoughtful. "Sounds familiar somehow."

Maurice looked at us expectantly. "So, you'll check it out? I'll get mercy?"

Boog pulled Maurice up from his chair. "You'll get what's coming to you. But we'll see." Suddenly, he paused. "Jezarmi…Jezarmi…"

Boog looked down at Maurice, who was gazing up at him curiously. "What are you looking at?" asked Boog. He gave Maurice a shove, and we continued out the building.

13

DOWN TO THE LETTER

The next morning, before working on our report on
Maurice's ill-planned robbery, I visited the Augur first thing
after breakfast. She'd been making a steady recovery. She'd
even resumed some of her duties, which now centered solely on
refilling the pool. I pressed her for information on the rune in
the north corner.

"Ah, Marten," she said. "I wish I could tell you more. As you
may recall from your lessons, we know the meaning and
significance of only a portion of the runes in the room. The
seven around the pool, the most central, we believe simply to be
numbers, indicating the rank of the objects placed upon them.
The rest, out on the main floor, must have had great significance
to the builders, but we do not know much about them. The four
runes we think of as elements are displayed among them – earth,
air, fire, water. The others are a jumble, with no apparent
connection between even those whose meaning we know. The
four at the cardinal directions, at the corners of the diamond,
may have had some significance. We think the south one, the
flower, to be life, and the east one love, but the west appears
nowhere in our histories. The north one, though – that was the
sign of an ill-omened religious movement, back in my
grandfather's day, as I think the book you brought indicated.
Quite a scandal, with many nobles involved."

"If the south is life," I asked, "couldn't the north be death?"

"Several have proposed that interpretation," she replied, "and
I've found it plausible, but there's simply no evidence one way

or another. That doesn't necessarily fit the moon and sun symbols, but it is folly to presume to know their thinking. I was curious enough to use the amulet and the book in your augury, to my regret."

I knelt once more to study the carving as the Augur puttered about, cleaning the distillation apparatus for the creation of more water for the pool, occasionally cracking a knuckle out of habit. What the rune could mean, and why it was so important to Novara, I still had no clue. From behind me, I heard the Augur's voice. "Have you learned anything new about your mysterious rune, Marten?"

"No, Madame. Unfortunately not," I replied, rising from the floor. "I've had little time to spare, to be honest."

"And your vision of the city's fiery doom?"

"Still as much of a puzzle as ever."

She walked over to me and placed a hand on my shoulder, leaning gently on me for support. "I find that the most troubling bit of all about this whole affair, more than the amulet and the symbol, more than the strange magic of that day, and certainly more than my own incapacitation. I've never known the pool to fail in a prediction that clear, and I've not read of such a failure in any of the records."

"You're sure it was a prediction, and not an image of some distant past?" I asked.

"You said you saw the clock tower, did you not? That is less than sixty years old. I can remember seeing it built when I was a young girl. We've not had a rain of fire from the sky in my lifetime. Even as addle-brained as some think I am, I'd have likely noticed that."

"The future, then," I mused. "One of the pool's rare foretellings. But we cannot know how soon it will be. Maybe it will be centuries in the future."

"I'd rather not count on that, Marten," she said. "The pool draws its images from the objects around it, and, with the possible exception of the book, those objects were all bound together by current events, in the present time. If the connections between them inspired that terrible scene, then I fear it may not be far off."

Her voice had grown softer and more ominous as she spoke. I stood there, full of fear, pondering the imminent destruction of all that I knew and loved.

The Augur patted my shoulder. "Of course, I may be full of fever dreams and fancy," she said. "I'm just a crazy old woman who tends a giant magical bathtub, after all."

I wished the Augur good luck at refilling the pool and decided to find Boog to complete our report, although I would much rather have been working on the rune than on Maurice's petty malfeasance. The end of the world ranks a bit higher in my book than stolen floor coverings. As I was about to go, the Augur perked up. "Say, have you done anything with that amulet?"

"No, I haven't," I replied. "I guess it must have been returned to evidence storage. Frankly, I haven't wanted to mess with it since the augury."

"Well, I was thinking, I have a friend, a scholar named Monique Lenarre. She's one of the Prelate's advisors. She lives in the north tower in the castle and has a workshop there. You might want to let her examine it. She's something of an expert in ancient magic. Well, she fancies herself one, I should say." The Augur grinned, then went back to her reagents. "Moni might have some insight. I'll let her know you'll be visiting."

This sounded promising, at least more so than another late night at the library. Maurice could wait, I thought, rather recklessly, hoping Boog wouldn't be too angry. I headed over to the evidence storage chamber. Through the thick bars blocking the window, I could see the evidence clerk, Lianna Willis, there at her desk.

"Hi there, Lia," I said, trying for my friendliest, most chipper voice. "I was hoping to take another look at the amulet we were using on that case a couple weeks ago. I've got a new lead on it."

Lia looked at me dourly. "That case has been closed, and all the evidence pertaining to it is under an impound order."

Impounded. That was very rare, and usually reserved for extremely valuable items. It certainly wasn't done for an entire case, unless the case involved a top-secret investigation ordered by the Prelate.

I clenched my teeth. Only Sophie could order an impound. I was having trouble figuring Sophie out these days. I had looked up to her, almost worshiped her, during training and after. She seemed like the perfect leader, a woman to be emulated, although I could never hope to match her wisdom and judicious insight. That image had taken a tumble since she'd taken Marron up on his bribe. His offer, I corrected myself half-heartedly. I knew Sophie had been placed in an impossible situation with the loss of the pool's income, but still – there had to be a better way.

Well, maybe I could make careful enough notes that the scholar Lenarre could still tell me something. "Can I see it, at least? I won't take it from the chamber."

"That's not normally done on an impound," said Lia, reluctantly. "The case is closed."

"It's not about the case," I said, flailing a bit. "It's, uh, the Augur said I should take it to a scholar for a consultation. If I can't do that, I could at least make some sketches and take some notes."

"The Augur?" asked Lia, skeptically.

"Yes, I just came from visiting her. The amulet was part of the augury that messed up the pool and nearly killed the Augur, you know. I can go get her, if you need her authorization." The Augur ranked second only to Sophie in the Guild, so this just might work. I wasn't sure the Augur would support me over an impound order from Sophie, though. It was a gamble, but I had little to lose.

Lia considered, chewing on her upper lip. At last, she said "I suppose it wouldn't hurt to look at it here. What was the case number again?"

I told her, and she disappeared back into the crowded shelves. She was gone a long time, and when she finally returned, she looked alarmed.

"It's not there!" she said. "This isn't right." She sat back at her desk and pulled out a large ledger, flipping back through the yellowed pages and scanning through the tiny scrawled entries. It had been three weeks since the amulet was deposited, so it took her some searching. I waited anxiously.

"Signed out two weeks ago, by Sophie, then returned the next day," she said. "Unusual, but she returned it, so it should still be here…" She turned some more pages. "Aha!" she cried, tapping an entry with her finger. "It was signed out three days ago, shortly after midnight. That idiot Bernot must not have realized it's been impounded. I'll wring his neck! I'll rip out his liver! I'll fling him out of the clock tower! I'll—"

"Who signed it out?" I interrupted with some trepidation.

She looked down at the ledger again, and then looked back at me, her eyes wide. "Why, there's no name. This is even worse!"

I thanked her and left her there ranting. Bernot seemed destined to have a very bad day. I did not like where my thoughts were leading, but I could not help myself. If Bernot were even halfway competent, then there was only one person who could override an impound order. The one who issued it. I could think of only a handful of reasons why she wouldn't want her name in the ledger, and none of those were good.

I walked up the stairs and through the meeting hall to Sophie's office. As I arrived, I saw her head inside with another Inspector, Ravenna Jensen. That was just as well. I needed some time to figure out what I was going to say. It was possible Sophie had nothing to do with the amulet's disappearance. Perhaps Bernot was guilty merely of an error, and someone else had borrowed the amulet, maybe for some benign purpose. Try as I might, though, I couldn't think of a plausible scenario.

On the other hand, if I told her I'd asked after the amulet, I could get myself in a good deal of trouble. I'd been ordered directly by Sophie to leave the case alone. My invoking the

Augur might have worked on Lia, but it would be no excuse for Sophie. I knew that.

I sat there waiting, wondering, as ready to get up and leave as I was to confront Sophie. My eyes passed over the basket outside Sophie's door, where outgoing parcels and letters waited for our courier. I'm naturally a nosy person – it's really more of a career qualification, I keep telling myself – so I could not help but glance at the addresses written on the packages. Three were to various members of the Justiciary, one to a local farmer who I knew provided most of our food, one to the Captain of the City Guard, and one more, a thin envelope sealed with wax, addressed as follows:

The Right Honorable Count Marron
Marron House, Red Street

Right honorable? Not by a long stretch. But what could Sophie be corresponding about with the Count? Hadn't their business been completed?

I haven't ever figured out quite why I did what I did next. It was foolish. If I'd been caught, I'd have been dismissed and jailed, perhaps worse. It was also terribly impulsive, which I hope I tend not to be. I had no evidence, no justification, no right to do it, and I had no plan for what to do next. Be that as it may, seized with sudden foolhardiness, I scanned the hall for any observers, and, finding none, snatched the letter from the basket, tucked it under my cloak, and fled to the dormitories.

I lit a candle from the fireplace in the kitchen, scuttled back to my small room, and locked the door. Wax seals are good for show, but they provide almost no security when faced with a person of the appropriate skills. And the appropriate lack of good sense or moral character. I pulled a thin piece of wire from my toolkit, heated it in the candle and carefully scraped off the seal, lifting it with the blade of my dagger as it came up so as not to damage it. Sophie had done a careless job. The wax was thick enough in all places that I would have no trouble replacing the seal.

My heart beat fast as I opened the letter. I was sure by now that I'd risked my career for what would turn out to be an invitation to lunch, or a mere note of thanks for the Count's financial assistance. I unfolded the thick sheet of parchment that made up the envelope. Inside was a single piece of thin vellum, folded over twice. I opened it and read Sophie's neat script:

Count Marron –

I have done as you asked, under the terms upon which we agreed. I hope there will be no further requests. I am already questioning the wisdom of our arrangement. If you wish further consultation about any of the issues we discussed, please make an appointment.

Respectfully yours,
Sophie Borchard
High Inquisitor

I was filled with dismay as I read the note. My first thought was that the 'request' was for Sophie to give Marron the amulet, but I forced myself to acknowledge that the note could have been about anything, and that I wasn't even perfectly certain that Sophie was the one who'd taken it from storage. The 'issues' they discussed could be any of a wide range of topics, although I suspected they might possibly concern Novara's doings. But this was weak. For all my subterfuge, and despite my impetuous betrayal of my superior, I'd learned nearly nothing.

I carefully heated my dagger over the candle, just enough to soften the underside of the seal. Using a tiny set of forceps from my toolkit and a thick leatherworking needle, I replaced the seal on the envelope, pressing it gently into place. I inspected my handiwork through a large magnifying glass, one of the few things I'd inherited from my father. My careful touch, honed through years of toying with locks, seemed to have borne fruit again. Now, I just needed to get the letter back into place undetected. I tucked it into my shirt.

I was in luck. Sophie's basket was still full, her packages not yet picked up by the courier. I replaced the envelope in the basket and skulked away. As I walked back toward the dormitory, I saw Clarice sitting on a bench. She held her falcon pendant in one hand, rubbing it absently with her thumb, and there was a look of hurt in her eyes. I paused. "Clarice? Are you all right?"

"Marten," she replied, looking bewildered. "I've been reassigned. I'm to be sent to the border."

My heart skipped a beat. "But why? Gueran too?" I wondered if he'd pressed too hard in checking after Marron.

"No, just me. I'm to work with Inspector Aelvia."

That was odd. It was quite unusual for partners to be separated without one of them requesting it. "You didn't ask for a new partner? Or did Gueran?"

"No, I surely didn't, and he swears he didn't either."

Stranger and stranger. The barbaric clans who inhabited the mountains to our east sometimes raided border villages, but they were normally more likely to trade with them. It was hard to predict, because they were only loosely organized. But in the last year, a leader named Ganghira had arisen (actually, I think she called herself Ganghira, Lord of Steel, Fierce Lion of the Mountains, Wrath of the Clans, but maybe she was compensating for something). Ganghira had united some of the clans and conquered others, and then she had declared war on us, for no reason we could decipher. A regular civilized war we could probably handle. We had the Prelate's Brigade, after all. But the clans did not fight in the civilized way, preferring instead to strike, slay, steal, and flee back to their high hills and valleys. By the time the strength of the Brigade could be brought to bear, the clan warriors were long gone. Since the fighting began, the raids into our lands had become more frequent and more bold. Jeroch had sent most of the Brigade out to assist with border patrol and fight off the raiders, and we had a large number of inspectors posted out there assisting in the efforts, infiltrating the territory across the border and tracking the movement of the clan militias.

Those inspectors, though they shared our title and were under the High Inquisitor's command, were wholly different from us. They rode for days, they used camouflage and traps, and they moved in stealth and shadow. They were frequently called upon to fight, in small skirmishes or even in open combat, and some were proficient with poisons and assassination. They and we existed in two separate worlds, and though Sophie had dispatched a good number of the city inspectors who she felt were best suited, it was almost unthinkable that a city-trained provisional inspector in her first year of duty would be sent out there.

I didn't want to say it to Clarice, but she seemed not particularly well-suited to border duty, though I would certainly be hopeless out there myself. Our skills had been honed in the city, and we were trained for investigation and interrogation, not spying and subterfuge. Boog would possibly have been a good candidate, but Clarice's skills with research and magic would be near useless, and I doubted she'd often ridden for a full day or slept under the stars. It made no sense, except perhaps as a punishment of some sort, but there was nothing I could think of that she could have done that would earn her a rebuke such as this. The border inspectors had a hard life and a dangerous one. We'd lost ten in the past six months alone, their names entered into the book of honor in our small chapel.

Clarice seemed fully aware of her plight, and I was sure she didn't need me explaining it to her. She looked up at me with an unexpected poignancy. "Oh, Marten. I leave this afternoon, in a few hours. There's something here I'm not seeing. It makes no sense."

I didn't know what else to do, so I put a hand on her shoulder and sat down next to her. She leaned ever so gently into me, and I suddenly felt ten feet tall, Marten the Magically Magnificent.

I tried to think of what might motivate Sophie, but I couldn't come up with anything. Besides, Clarice's hair smelled really, really nice. It tore at me that she was leaving just as she might be becoming closer to me, though perhaps I flattered myself in that regard. I tried to find something to say.

"You'll do fine out there," I said, then cursed myself for the triteness of my sentiment. My tongue felt leaden, like I'd tapped it with my warding rod. "The Brigade will put down the raiders, and you'll be back by next winter."

She looked at me and smiled, a small wistful smile. "I hope you're right, Marten." She rose from the bench. My side and my arm felt terribly cold with her gone. I shrank back to normal size, Marten the Merely Mundane. She spoke again. "Keep up your work, with Gueran and Boog. I'd help you, if I could. All is not right around here."

Then she leaned over and kissed me quickly on the cheek. "Stay safe," I mumbled, my voice a traitor to me. She smiled once more and turned down the hall.

I sat on the bench for a while. My throat hurt. After a while, Boog walked by on his way to the case clerk, a stack of parchment sheets in his hand.

"Hey, Marty! Where've you been? You know I hate writing the reports. And you here sitting on a bench, lazy as the day is long. Did you just get up?" At that point he noticed my face, which I imagine looked like that of a puppy who'd been kicked. Maybe twice. His voice softened. "Oh. Well. You just go on sitting there, little guy. Er, I mean, big guy. Er, guy." He squeezed his eyes closed and rubbed his forehead with the heel of his hand. "I'll just be in the meeting hall whenever you're ready."

14

TAKE A POWDER

My back was starting to ache. I shifted silently to lean on a different crate. Boog, across the building in another loft, called out in a loud whisper. "Jezarmi! Now I remember. I saw it in the records I looked through at the City Registrar. It's a trading company owned by Marron."

Marron. I thought dark thoughts about the man and his money. And, as it turned out, here we were in another of his buildings. Sophie wasn't going to be happy about that. I brooded and pondered, almost missing Boog's signal to me as the small group entered, although the light from their torches and the creak of the door would have alerted me regardless.

Boog had a clear view of the front entrance, while I was positioned to watch the back. His fingers danced. *Four women. One man. Armed. Swords. Carrying cake.* I glanced down at the scruffy group as they filed into view below me, but saw no sign of any cake, or any dessert foods at all. At my questioning look, Boog revised and signed again. *Carrying chest.*

Ah, there it was – an ornately carved wooden chest, about four feet long and not quite as wide, maybe three feet tall. Whatever was inside must have been heavy. The two burly women carrying it were straining, using both hands and taking small steps.

Finally, there was something to watch. We'd sequestered ourselves in a loft area of the warehouse a few hours earlier, well ahead of the midnight meeting time specified by Maurice. I'd picked the lock on the small door near the wider cargo doors, and we'd locked it behind us. We'd searched the place, but it was relatively empty. Some old barrels and casks suggested that at least part of Jezarmi's business had been in wine or ale. We'd tried to leave the clutter as undisturbed as possible, so we hadn't been exhaustive in our search. It was clear that the building, though closed and empty, had been used recently, because the central part of the building was free from the dust and cobwebs covering the rest of the area. Covering me, too, now, in my hidden vantage point.

I guessed it was about a quarter hour past midnight. I'd heard the clock tower chime eighth bell for the midnight prayer, but I had no way of knowing exactly how long ago. Not long, though. At least Maurice hadn't completely made up his story. I still doubted that we'd see anything other than a business deal, but Sophie had given us permission to observe in case there was any smuggling or other untoward activity taking place.

The two large women carrying the chest moved across the room and put it down. One sat on it, while the other just sat on the floor. They looked tired. There was no sign of the guest Maurice had mentioned. Either he or she was coming later, or the guest was one of the group, but they all seemed to be similarly dressed. To me, too, they had the apparent comfort and ease of long-time companions. They were about twenty feet below me and perhaps thirty feet away towards the back of the building, almost directly under Boog. I doubted he could see them, so I signed over to him. *Chest down. They rest.*

The woman on the floor spoke. "Where is the man? He'd better come."

Another replied. I guessed this one to be the one Maurice had identified as the leader. She was tucking a large key into a pocket of her jerkin. "He'll be here."

The first shot back. "He'd better. I'm not carrying this back to the cart."

There was a soft rattle at the rear door. I saw the door handle move, and the door swung open. A man in a black cloak entered. His hood was large, and he had it pulled down over his face.

With that and the general gloom, I had trouble making out any details of his face. He walked slowly into the room, looking around at all the others.

The woman with the key greeted the new arrival. "We've brought what you asked. Both items." She gestured to the chest.

The cloaked man spoke slowly. "Excellent. And the equipment I provided?"

"In the chest as well. And here's the warehouse key." The leader pulled out the key and handed it to the cloaked man.

"How did it go?"

"It got a little hairy when we made the grab, if that's what you mean. But that was months ago and far away. And it was nothing we couldn't handle. After that, we hid the chest at our place in Jeston and went off to handle the other job, which took us a few months, to get there and set up and get back. Then we recovered the chest and came back here. In the city here, we've had no trouble. We've been hiding out at an abandoned farm the past few days at the edge of town. We drove the cart through town tonight, but we had the chest covered up."

"And the second job? You got it?"

"In here," said the leader, handing the cloaked man a small bag she pulled from her belt. "It was not as simple as you said. I can't imagine why you wanted them so badly."

She seemed to be probing for an answer, but the cloaked man remained silent. So they'd had several tasks, over the span of many months, involving significant travel? This was a major operation, whatever it was.

The cloaked man first peeked in the small bag and grunted his satisfaction. He tucked the bag into a pouch hung from his belt. Then, he opened the latch on the chest and lifted the lid. Unfortunately, they had set it down so that it opened away from me, and I couldn't see inside. The man fished around inside for a while.

"One of them is missing," he said. He didn't sound happy about this. He rose, and I could see that his hands were filled with something that shone like gold. Jewelry maybe? No, small curved knives.

One of the group, the only man, rubbed nervously at his long, braided beard. At last, he spoke. "I lost mine, in the woods. It was dark."

The cloaked man produced a small leather sack and put the knives into it. "They are important to me."

The leader replied, "He's an idiot. But we can't do anything about it now."

The cloaked man hooked the sack back over his belt and then pulled out a coin purse. He handed it to the leader. "Here's eighty, the second half, as we arranged. Divide it as you see fit." Eighty pieces of gold, I wondered? A hundred sixty in all? That would make for a really expensive box. Or maybe it was whatever was in the small bag that was expensive.

The man with the braided beard, the one who'd lost his knife, approached. "About that. We had to travel for longer than expected, and this was a gruesome business. Ellya had to learn all those patterns, too. I was hoping for a bonus, for the team."

The man with the cloak looked impassively at the man with the beard. The leader made no move. I wondered if this was planned, or if she was just waiting to see what transpired. Finally, the cloaked man spoke. "You lose my knife, and then you want a bonus? We arranged our terms at the outset, and you agreed to them. I've been more than generous." He turned back to the leader. "I would appreciate it if you'd leave town as soon as possible. I'd rather avoid any questions or loose tongues."

The bearded man stepped closer. "If it's questions you'd like to be avoiding, I have a feeling you could be more generous. That would sew my tongue up tight." He sounded a bit menacing now.

The cloaked man glanced around the room. None of the women had moved, but all were armed and within easy reach of their blades. "Our business is concluded. Please leave the building immediately. Don't try anything foolish."

The bearded man moved forward and placed a hand on the cloaked man's shoulder. "Twenty more, and I'll go quietly. You'll never see me again."

The cloaked man pushed his hand away. "Unhand me, you bastard," he hissed.

"Bastard, is it?" The bearded man raged. "Give me the knives. Those cursed things will sell for a pretty penny." He drew his sword, the steel a blur as it swung to the ready.

The cloaked man's hand flew to his belt, and he pulled out a small wand. There was a brilliant flash of light and a high-pitched sound, like the yip of a small dog.

I heard a clanging of metal, as if the sword had fallen to the floor. When my eyes recovered from the flash, I saw that the bearded man was gone. Not gone as in left the building — I mean quite literally gone. His clothing was resting in a heap on top of his boots, and all of it was covered in a coating of some orange powder, kind of like sawdust.

The other four women had their blades out almost instantly, although the leader held a hand up to restrain the others. The cloaked man held out his small wand. His hand shook, perhaps from strain or trauma. I signed frantically to Boog in the opposite loft, who couldn't see what was going on. *Magic. One dead?*

He signed back. *Go down?* He tensed for action, reaching for his staff.

I replied. *No. No. No. Wait. Danger.*

One of the swordswomen poked at the pile of clothing. "Where…is he?"

"I said to leave the building," replied the cloaked man, his voice suddenly ragged.

"You killed him?" she said, obviously upset, raising her sword. "You killed him?" she repeated, nearly screaming.

She charged at the cloaked man, and again the wand flashed and yipped, and again nothing was left of the attacker but her clothing and blade and the orange dust.

The leader shouted to her remaining two companions, "Stop! Put away your swords. Let's get out of here." She sheathed her blade, but her face was twisted with rage. To the cloaked man, she said. "We're leaving, you bast—" her eyes widened in fear. "I mean, we're leaving." She backed away from the man, and the other two followed suit, their eyes wild. As they neared the door, they turned and ran out to the street.

The cloaked man waited to ensure the others were truly gone, then stowed his rod at his belt. He was shaking, and his shoulders drooped. Finally, he pushed his hood off his face, revealing a man of perhaps thirty-five years, with short blond hair and slightly darker beard. I thought immediately of the man Terrence had described at Novara's house — this could be the one, but I had no way to know for certain.

After a moment's rest, the man checked inside the chest once more, then poked the piles of clothing and dust with his toe, probing for what, I don't know. He walked over to the front door of the warehouse and locked it, finally returning to the back door. He opened it, walked outside, and closed it, and I could hear his key turn in the lock.

Boog signed to me. *What happened?*

Two dead. Strong magic.

Go down now?

Wait until clear, I replied. At this, Boog rolled his eyes. His enthusiasm would be dampened a bit if he'd just seen two people reduced to well-dressed piles of powder.

We waited about ten minutes, in Boog's case quite impatiently. Occasionally he would yawn theatrically and examine his fingernails or twiddle his thumbs. When I was more confident the cloaked man wasn't returning, I signaled Boog. We stepped cautiously down the loft stairway and out onto to the warehouse floor.

"Where are the bodies?" whispered Boog.

I pointed at the piles. A faint tendril of smoke rose from one of them.

"What? Whoa…" said Boog, kneeling over them. "In hindsight, your caution seems warranted. I apologize for doubting you."

I wished I knew what the wizard had in the small bag. At least we had the chest, though. I walked over to it. It was made of dark wood, with no seams, maybe carved as a single piece from one tree. That would have to be a pretty big tree. It was elaborately carved in geometric patterns. There was a latch, but no lock. I opened the latch.

Boog called out softly from one of the piles, the first one, formerly the bearded guy. "Hey, I found something! A little gold knife tucked into the cuff of this guy's pants. Is this what they were talking about?" Huh. It looked as if the bearded guy hadn't lost his knife after all. Perhaps he should have settled for keeping just that one, though.

I pulled open the lid, then jumped really high, making a screechy 'eep' noise through my clenched teeth. I walked in little circles for a bit, trying not to look at the chest again. When I regained control of myself, I said, "Hey, I found something too."

15

I'm So Blue

"You found what?" asked Sophie, incredulous.

Boog looked uncomfortable. "It would be easier if you just came to see it. It's out in the evidence chamber."

It was there, but not without effort. Boog and I had barely been able to get the chest out of the warehouse. I should say, Boog had done it nearly on his own. I'm not sure what I was doing could be considered help. I did sweep up the two powdery ruffians into separate crates, although what use they would be now I wasn't sure. While Boog stood guard, I had located a city guard patrol, and they had helped to lug the chest back to headquarters. I'd barely slept in the couple of hours since, and Boog didn't look much better.

We walked out through the meeting hall. On the wall map, the warehouse was pegged with a bright crimson flag. Murder. We wound our way to the evidence chamber. Lia was there, scribbling in her ledger.

"Any sign of Bernot?" asked Sophie.

"No, Chief," said Lia, looking angry. "I had to cover for him last night. I can't do that again tonight, Chief. I'll pass out."

"Is he sick? Is he at home?"

"No," said Lia. "I sent an apprentice to check."

"Borrow a clerk from Recording if Bernot doesn't show up tonight," said Sophie. "And let me know."

"Yes, Chief. I will, Chief."

"Now, can I have a look at this chest these two brought in?"

Lia gave a low whistle. "Certainly. Now, there's something you don't see every day. Come around back."

We went through the reinforced door into the evidence chamber. We'd dragged the chest to the back of the room, the area for large objects. My back hurt just thinking about it. Boog knelt and opened the latch. "Chief," he said. "Be warned. This isn't pleasant." He lifted the lid.

Safely inside headquarters, the sight was less shocking, but only a little bit. The chest held the body of a woman, her torso facing up, her hips and legs folded back under her at an impossible angle. Her spine must have been broken clean through. I hoped it had been after she died, but even if it had, I was sure her end had been terribly painful. Her body was covered with an intricate pattern of incisions. The cuts ran in crisscrossing bands across her shoulders and neck and in curled spiral patterns on her lower chest. Her arms were folded across her chest, and the lacerations curved and scrolled around them as well. If the image were not so gruesome, and the canvas not a woman, the pattern might have seemed artistic – whoever had done this definitely had a sure hand and a careful eye. The shallow cuts were likely from something very sharp. The edges of the wounds were perfectly even. What if the woman had been alive when they were made? I shuddered at the thought.

There was one other very odd thing, as if it needed to be any stranger. The woman's skin was a uniform shade of dull blue. Boog and I had no idea why. We'd never seen anyone with such coloring. It looked far too even to be tattooing, and too pervasive to be painted on. The woman's eyes, though clouded in death, showed white, and the interior of her mouth was a dull pink.

Sophie grunted once, then surveyed the body thoroughly, occasionally touching it or probing it with her small dagger. I walked over to a bookshelf, sat down, and tried to think of puppies romping in a flowery meadow. I failed.

Finally, Sophie rose. "Well," she said. "That's definitely odd."

"Yes, Chief," replied Boog.

"Do you have any idea who the wizard was, or who the other group was?" asked Sophie.

"The other group, mostly women, had been hired by the wizard, and their service was complete," I said. "He paid them, very well, I think, and dismissed them."

"But they didn't go?"

"One challenged the wizard for further payment, and the wizard turned him into orange dust," said Boog, gesturing toward one of the small boxes we'd brought. "He's in there. Another one attacked the wizard after the death of the first. She's in that box, over there. The others fled after that."

Sophie opened one of the boxes and stirred its contents with her dagger. She looked at Boog and pointed at the box. "You seem to be making a habit of bringing back dismembered bodies in containers."

Boog looked uncomfortable but said nothing.

"Why do you suppose she doesn't smell?" asked Sophie, turning back to the ornate chest. I hadn't thought of that, given the flurry of events. "No rot, no maggots, not even any desiccation – but she was probably in here for a while."

"The woman who brought her indicated it had been many months."

"Even stranger. And, she's far from home."

"Why do you say that, Chief?" I asked.

"The tattoos on her wrist and ankle. Her hair and earring. She's clearly from one of the clans, from the mountains over the border."

I hadn't even noticed the tattoos. "Is the blue color, the cuts, something they do?"

"Not to my knowledge. Might be worth a trip to the library, I'd think."

"Look under B, for blue," offered Boog, helpfully.

"Or butchery, or barbarism," said Sophie. She stared intently at the blue body before her. "Is there anything else you have to tell me?"

I looked at Boog. I wished I could ask him what to do. In the end, I opted for the high road. "Chief? The warehouse – it's owned by Jezarmi."

"And?"

"Jezarmi is owned by Marron."

Sophie looked sharply at me. "I ordered you off that case. I ordered you to stay away from Marron!"

"It came up separately," I protested, glumly. "On a separate case. The stolen rugs."

"There isn't any other connection between the cases," said Boog.

"Unless you count sorcery, shady deals, and messy deaths…" I added.

Sophie cut me off with a glare. "When did you figure out about Jezarmi and Marron?"

"Um, last night."

"Before or after you asked if you could go to the warehouse?"

One thing in our favor, at least. "After, Chief. When we were already there. But we had no reason to suspect that Marron had anything to do with anything. You agreed, it deserved a look."

Sophie looked like she could kill us both. "If I can't trust you to be honest with me, I can't trust you at all. Do you want to keep working here?"

I felt like I was actually growing smaller as she talked. I loved being an inspector. It had come to mean more to me than anything. I'd dedicated over a quarter of my life to the Guild. I realized, though, that I wasn't sure I wanted to keep working for an institution that could be bent to the purpose of anyone willing to pay.

"What should we do about the wizard?" asked Boog, trying desperately to change the subject.

"Nothing," growled Sophie. "Absolutely nothing. Give his description to the city watch, go over your report again with the clerks, and then you're done. I'm turning this over to someone else. Someone I can trust to follow my orders."

"But, Chief!" said Boog. "We found this, tracked it down…"

"Enough!" cried Sophie. "If you're looking for something to do, track down Bernot. Can you do that? Please? Without getting anyone else killed?" She stalked back out toward her office.

We stood there for a while. Then Boog closed the chest carefully.

"Well played, inspector," he said.

"Sorry." I felt pretty miserable.

Boog stretched and yawned, looking like some gigantic ape. "She'd have made the connection eventually. It's better that she heard it from us, I suppose. Although I would have liked to see this through, at least a little farther."

"Me too." I said, relieved at his words. "Although I'm happy to have avoided getting turned into powder or turned blue and stuffed into a chest."

"They could fit two or three of you in there, Marty. For you, they'd just need a box, or maybe a small bucket." He scratched his scalp through his short hair. "I'm going back to bed. Bernot can wait."

We thanked Lia, and I followed Boog back to the dormitory. I was tempted to follow his plans, as well. Asleep, I probably couldn't mess anything else up. But I didn't think I would get much rest at the moment. There was too much on my mind. I returned to my small chamber, put on my good boots and my red tunic, and washed up a bit. There was still a lead that needed following up, whether Sophie approved or not. I suspected not.

16

THE PROFESSOR

"Yes?" came the annoyed reply to my knock. A rather polite knock, too, I'd thought.

"My name is Marten Mingenstern. I'm with the Inquisitor's Guild."

"I don't care. Go away," came the muffled voice. A woman.

"I was referred to the scholar named Monique Lenarre," I persisted.

"She's not here. Go away."

"But this is her laboratory."

"She died. This morning. Horrible accident. Terribly sad. Still dangerous in here. Burning things, evil spirits. Go away."

I cleared my throat. "I was referred by the Augur. She said Professor Lenarre might be interested in what we've found."

There was a moment of silence. "Gilla? She sent you?"

This took me aback. I actually didn't know the Augur's given name. "Madame, the Augur said you—er, Professor Lenarre, may her soul rest in peace, were interested in ancient magic, and we've found a connection to the builders of the pool."

I heard sounds of shifting metal on the other side of the door. A heavy bolt, most likely. The door creaked a bit as it opened. The woman behind the door was old and terribly gaunt. She was dressed in a simple wool gown with a belt of rope. Her hair was wispy and dark gray. "How is ol' Pinkeye doing?" she asked.

"Much better, I'm happy to say. She's been busy refilling the pool."

"Yes," the woman muttered. "Horrible business, that. Tempted to test the limits of the pool by some damn fool junior inspector, I heard."

I blushed a bit. "Er, yes."

"You, was it?" she asked, looking at me sharply.

I nodded. She twisted up her mouth, but then moved aside to let me in, and I followed her into the chamber beyond. As I suspected, nothing was on fire, and the evil spirits seemed to have departed. The chamber had archways on each side leading to smaller side chambers, and the whole suite was filled with all manner of obscure materials – flasks, glassware, hundreds of books and scrolls, bits of metal and tubing, crystals, jars of animal pieces. There was a cluttered workbench in the middle, and the woman pointed at a worn-looking wooden chair in the corner. After removing a stuffed owl, I sat. She clambered onto a stool at the bench and began fiddling with some flasks of liquid connected by tubes and various pieces of mysterious apparatus, all suspended on a metal framework mounted to the back of the bench. She didn't speak for some time.

"Madame Professor Monique Lenarre, I presume?" I asked, not sure where this was going.

"You do presume," she replied. "I'm a busy woman. What do you have for me?"

I decided to start at the beginning, with Stennis and Novara. The professor continued to work, but she shot me a glance when I mentioned Novara's magical disappearance from the Sotted Swan, and finally put down her work when I got to the unfortunate detonation of Stennis. She listened avidly as I described the ill-fated augury at the pool and our discovery of Novara's corpse.

"These amulets – do you have one of them with you?" she asked.

"No, Madame. Novara's was missing when we found her. The one we got from Stennis was in storage at the Guild Hall, but someone removed it."

"What kind of mummer's show are you running over there? Who removed it?"

"I can't say, Madame. I don't know that."

"And you say it matches one of the runes around the pool?"

"Perfectly, Madame. A sunburst behind a full moon."

She looked thoughtful for a bit. "That's interesting, now," she muttered. "Very interesting." She rubbed her front teeth with a gnarled dirty finger, her thoughts elsewhere.

"Madame?"

"That symbol has been around for centuries, obviously, since the time of the pool's construction. But as you say, it was used by a band of zealots over a century ago. The Faerans, they called themselves, if I remember correctly. They grew to great power in Frosthelm but were eventually destroyed by Prelate Karela and a group of wizards."

I was overjoyed. Progress, at last. "So, do you think they've returned?"

"It sounds as if that's possible. The Faerans originated in Gortis, and Karela only drove them out of Frosthelm – she didn't hunt down every last one everywhere. Also, the magic you saw – the amulets, the transportation, the disintegration – fits with their earlier patterns. The gems that your wizard had stolen — can you describe them?"

"Well, she stole a number of them, but only one seemed to matter to her. It had a clear green circle set into a ball of white opaque material, like a really large pearl."

Monique rose from her stool and disappeared into an archway. She was gone for some time. I heard what sounded like her searching through shelves, and then there was an enormous crash, and a cloud of dust drifted into the central room. I rose, uncertain of what to do.

"Damn it all," I heard her say. She returned carrying a book and pulling bits of wood and leather from her hair. She sat again. She flipped carefully through the pages of the book, scanning each as she went. "Ha!" she cried at last. She pointed at a page, and I came over to look. "Like this?"

The page contained several sketches. The top one matched the gemstone we'd seen Novara handling. "Yes, I think that's it," I replied.

"The Eye of Hrogar," he said.

"Huh?" I replied. "The what of who?"

"The Eye of Hrogar. The gem is ancient. You said Countess Moriff had it, and reported it stolen? I think her ancestor a century back was an advisor to Karela, maybe even a wizard. I'd have to check the histories. But the earlier Moriff probably got it from the Faerans when they were defeated."

"Is that bad? Why'd they want it back? It didn't seem that valuable. Is it magical?"

"It's not valuable or magical on its own. It's a key." Monique seemed to be enjoying lecturing me, but I didn't begrudge her fun.

"What kind of key?"

"The eye supposedly fits in a statue which stands guard over a gate to another realm, an unearthly one."

I sat down again. "And they want to open this gate? With the eye?" This was becoming more and more outlandish. "What would that get them?"

"Hard to say. Nobody knows where the gate or the statue are, although they're rumored to be near Frosthelm. All we have to go on is bits of legend and the rantings of the Faerans. But the Faerans thought it would bring them ascension to eternal life, tremendous infernal power, and a thousand years of dominion over all the planes of existence."

I swallowed. "Something everyone needs," I mumbled, but my joke wasn't even funny to me.

She noticed my discomfort. "Aw, lad, don't worry just yet. There's no telling if any of this is even true, and they probably don't even know where the statue is. Even if they do, according to their prophecy, they'd have to wait until the next time the moon covers the sun to open the gate. That could be years. Also, there are a bunch of other things they're supposed to need for the ritual, and they're hard if not impossible to find."

"Like what?" I asked.

Madame Lenarre flipped a page in the book. "Like what? Like this, for instance." She tapped the book. "The Sacred Mace of Godron. The Fingernails of The Holy Hermit. The fabled Thersian Crown." She flipped another page. "Heh – and look at this one. The ritually sacrificed body of a trueblood princess of the Golesh tribe. I doubt there's even such a princess left, much less anyone who knows how to perform the ritual."

I looked down at the page. "I have a feeling they're actually pretty far along on that front," I mumbled. The sketches showed a cut and bleeding woman with intricate scars and a small, curved knife. The book's illuminations were faded, but even so, the woman's skin showed a faint bluish tint. "We have one of those in storage."

She looked up at me, her eyes wide. "Really." I nodded. "Perhaps I'd better go check the astrological charts for that eclipse." She rose. "Why is it always eclipses with these cults? Not a shred of originality. Thousands of stars to observe, all sorts of complex lunar and solar cycles, but no!" She waggled his fingers ominously. "Oooooo! Fear the eclipse!" She sniffed. "Pathetic, really."

I followed her into an alcove full of books, where after a few minutes' search, she located a weathered leather-bound tome bearing a flaking gold emblem of concentric rings. She brought it back to the main room and set it on the workbench. She carefully opened the brittle pages, muttering as she fingered through them.

"Werole," she said, tapping the book, "was a failure in life – lost his first wife to a circus acrobat, his second to a convent, and his inherited wealth on improbable bets on lizard racing, of all things. But he was the best astronomer the city has produced." She paused at a page and ran a wizened finger down the scrawled text. "I guess when you're bitter, broke, and alone, you have a lot of time to observe the stars and think. Ah!"

She thumbed her lower lip, then grabbed a lead pencil and a scrap of parchment and began scribbling. She paused to scratch at an ear. "That's not good," she said. "Perhaps I've made a mistake." She ran her pencil over her figures, checking each calculation.

'Not good' was not what I wanted to hear. "What is it?"

"Well, I seem to have calculated the eclipse for a little over two weeks hence."

"Gaaah!" I gasped. "Two weeks?" I thought again of my vision of the city in flames. Everything I knew could be gone before the month was out.

The professor didn't reply at first, absorbed in her calculations. Then she made several corrections and slammed down the pencil. "Ah, there it is. Silly me."

A wave of relief washed over me. "We've got more time?"

"Yes, much, much more," she said. I sagged in my chair, feeling lucky and thankful. My beloved city would survive, perhaps well into the future. My children and grandchildren would play along the cobblestone streets. The Faerans were just a shadowy nightmare, easily forgotten as the new day dawned.

"We've got almost a whole six months," said Monique happily.

17

AN UNEXPECTED INVITATION

I wandered, despondent, into the meeting hall. Boog looked up from his seat at a table. "Where've you been?" he asked.

"Learning of the imminent destruction of all of us," I replied.

"Well, aren't you full of good cheer," he laughed. "Who's predicted our doom?"

"A scholar. Professor Lenarre. Friend of the Augur." I told him what I'd learned, of the cult, of the Eye of Hrogar, of the unfortunate blue woman. And of the six — no, five and a half – months until Frosthelm would burn.

"Well," said Boog, his mood a bit more serious. "So, the amulets, the magic, the orange powder– all from these Faerans?"

I nodded glumly.

Boog stood and clapped me on the back. "Well, then, you were right. All along."

True, I thought, but I took no satisfaction.

"We should tell Sophie," said Boog.

"I doubt she'll want to hear that I worked on the case further."

"But you have to tell her. You know that," he replied. "Even if she fires us."

"Or throws us in irons."

"Yes, or just cuts us down on the spot, before enjoying a bit of cheese. The problem is, though, she's out. Renne said a courier came with a message just after we, uh, were dismissed, and she hurried out."

Great, I thought. I can stay an Inspector for a few more hours, at least. "So, should we track down Bernot? It would help if we had something good to tell her, too."

"I've made some progress on that," said Boog.

I was impressed. Only a few hours ago I'd left Boog in bed. "What did you do? Check his home? Talk to his neighbors? Initiate a manhunt?"

"Heh. No. I got this." He held up a piece of parchment. I took it. It was addressed to *Inspector Eggstrom* in a careful script. "I found it tucked under my pillow."

"A secret admirer?" I asked. Boog snorted. I opened the note.

Dear Sir,

I need to speak with you. I've been in hiding. It is a matter of utmost importance. Please meet me at The Red Rabbit as soon as possible. I'll be waiting. Or, rather, I'll have someone watching. Bring Inspector Mingenstern, if you would. Tell no one else, and destroy this note at your earliest convenience. By fire, if possible. That would be best.

Sincerely,
Bernot
Clerk, Second Rank

I looked at Boog. He shrugged. "Any idea where the Red Rabbit is?"

There was a loud sniff from behind us. I turned to see Gueran. "The Red Rabbit? You've never been there? No, I suppose you wouldn't have." He smiled, or sneered – with him, it was hard to tell.

Boog looked annoyed. "What kind of place is it? An inn? A tavern?"

"Heh." It was a smirk this time. I was sure. "Yes, of sorts. It caters to an exclusive clientele. Only the finest families, and they use it only for special occasions. Very special occasions.

There are services that are only available at the Red Rabbit, if you know what I mean."

I didn't, but I wasn't going to admit that. "Where is it?"

"On Crown, just inside the inner wall. I haven't been there in many years."

"Why?" asked Boog. "You're not important enough anymore? Stuck slumming with us?"

"No," said Gueran, looking mildly irritated, but still amused. "I just don't…travel in those particular circles anymore. Enjoy your visit." He turned to go, chuckling to himself.

Boog made a face after him. A sneer, or was it a smirk? "Let's go."

18

THE RED RABBIT

"Enter, if you please," said the small man, tipping his tall, multicolored hat. Boog shot a glance at me, but he followed the man's waving hand. On the way over, we'd explored the possibilities. Would the Red Rabbit be a house of pleasure, with wanton persons available to fulfill the basest desires? That could explain the "services" to which Gueran had alluded. An exclusive private club, where the city's powerful elite cut deals and struggled for primacy? A den of thieves? A market for illicit herbs and liquors? A fighting ring, stained nightly with the blood of gladiators?

Whatever it was, it was not a secret. There was a large elaborate sign over the door announcing the Red Rabbit, including a tiled mosaic depicting a long-eared rodent. The man with the hat had seemed a bit surprised and nervous to see us at the entrance. That boded ill, I thought – if Inspectors were unwelcome, the patrons of the Rabbit might be up to no good. He'd also looked all around us, perhaps to see if we were accompanied or to make sure our entrance was unnoticed – I could not say. As I followed Boog into the dark hallway, I felt for my warding rod and dagger at my belt, and I could see the tension in Boog's broad shoulders.

The little man pushed gently past me and Boog, stopped at a trio of broad oaken doors, and turned to face us. "To which party might I direct you, gentlemen?"

A puzzle. Bernot had said that he would find us, and I doubted he'd given his name, what with the directive to burn the note and all. We had no one here to visit, at least not officially. As I pondered an appropriate response, Boog answered. "No one."

Not an appropriate response, judging from the narrowing of the man's eyes. "But… that is most irregular." He held up a delicate hand, laden with rings with large jewels. "I'm afraid I'll have to ask you to leave."

Boog scowled. I interceded. "Sir, we're just here to observe."

"Observe what? And just what would you expect to find?" He sounded irate.

I had nothing, and I managed merely to open my mouth and close it a couple times. Boog dove in. "We're investigating reports of criminal mischief in this establishment."

"Well!" shouted the man, visibly offended. He raised his eyebrows farther than I'd thought possible, narrowed his eyes to slits, and I thought I could almost see his nose bend upward into the air. "I can assure you, I run a fine, upstanding establishment. Criminals – bah! We pay our taxes, and we provide a unique service for the wealthy and noble classes of the town, one they can find nowhere else. We screen our employees very carefully — our clients demand it – and we've never had such a complaint in thirty-six years in business. This is an outrage! Just who has complained? I'm well connected, I'll have you know. This won't stand – it's slanderous."

Boog opened his mouth, but I prodded him to silence. I hoped. "Sir," I said. "None of the reports concern you or the establishment. There are merely some guests in the establishment whom we need to locate. I assure you, we'll be very discreet."

This seemed to mollify him a bit, even though it directly contradicted what Boog had said. We needed to work on our improvisational lying. "Well, then," he replied. "I still don't see how any of our clientele could be involved in such matters. They're just…incapable of any such thing."

He plainly had a higher opinion of the wealthy and noble classes than I did, I thought. He continued, "I must require that you check your weapons in the cloak room. I cannot be flexible on this point."

Boog frowned, and I shared his sentiment. We still had no idea what was going on, and I hated the thought of going unarmed into the unknown, particularly with all the trouble we'd been having recently with death cults, malevolent wizards, and exploding swordsmen. But we needed to find Bernot. I unhooked my dagger from my belt and handed it over, hoping he'd let me keep the rod. He did – I'd have some protection at least. Boog's scowl deepened, but he grudgingly gave up his own dagger and staff.

The man opened the left-most of the three doors to reveal a glimpse of a large closet with pegs on the walls. He placed our items inside and returned.

"All right, then. Which party do you need to observe?"

And there we were again. I stammered, "Our informant didn't provide a name, just the place and time." The words felt stale in my mouth. "I, uh… Can you tell me which, er, who is in attendance right now?" I tried to grin convincingly. Boog closed his eyes and shook his head.

Our diminutive host glared at me balefully. I feared he might try to evict us again, but instead he said, very slowly, as if I were an idiot nephew, "There is the Sestille party and the Harance party."

"Uh, Sestille. Yes, that sounds quite right. They will do nicely. Er, to observe." I wondered if it were possible to swallow one's own tongue. If so, I wished to at that moment.

The little man shot me a withering stare, but he pointed at the door on the right. "In there. Be very careful not to disturb them. I'd hate to see them angry." He shuddered. "That wouldn't be good."

I thought of all kinds of bad things angry patrons might do, many involving the loss of my limbs and vital organs. I was beginning to think that Bernot might not need finding. We surely had a surplus of other clerks, second rank. My reverie was interrupted by Boog shoving me toward the door with what

I considered to be unnecessary force. "So, uh, I'll go first, then." I said.

The door opened into a narrower hallway lined with red velvet. Whatever the Red Rabbit was, it had spared no expense in decorating. As we neared the end of the hall, I could hear muffled sounds of manic laughter mixed with piercing shrieks and screams. My knees felt a bit wobbly as I approached the next door. As I reached for the brass handle, I wondered what manner of depravity lay beyond. The hinges creaked ominously as I pulled.

The room beyond was very dark, the only light coming in thin streams from a lantern in the far corner. It was hooded, the shades pulled almost all the way down, so the light came out only from little slits at the bottom. There was a platform at the far end of the room. At my first glance, I could barely make out some murky shapes moving about some tables in the center. One of them bore antlers like a stag. Another, a long, sharp unicorn's horn. Still another, a pair of shadowy grotesque wings, fluttering as it moved. But they were all small, much smaller even than I. I was bewildered. A man bellowed, and suddenly, something flew toward my head. Instinctively, I yelled and ducked, and I heard a wet thud and a grunt as the object struck Boog in the chest.

I rolled to the left, behind another low table, and risked a glance at Boog. He was holding his chest, his head bent over. I thought I saw a blotch of red on his chest, but he still stood. The screams had subsided to soft anxious murmurs. I could not wait for them to hatch a plan. If Boog were injured, there was no way I could fight them off alone. I had no options.

My first combat instructor, Mistress Fennick, had been quite fond of posing hypothetical scenarios and asking for an appropriate response. Now, she'd never covered being outnumbered in a dark, unfamiliar place, surrounded by armed miniature animals, with a wounded partner, but her favorite advice was still applicable. I can still hear her rough voice: *The worse your situation seems, the more it calls for bold, daring action. If it works, you might gain the upper hand through surprise. If it fails, at least you'll die fast and more gloriously than otherwise.*

It seemed appropriate now, although bold and daring aren't exactly central to my nature. I tensed, took a deep breath, and launched myself over the table behind which I had cowered. "Cease your attacks!" I cried. "In the name of the Inquisitor's Guild! Drop your weapons, and get down on the floor, or I'll kill every bloody one of you!"

There was a moment of silence. Then a man, the one who'd bellowed earlier, said, "What, then?" A child started to cry, and another, a little girl, said "But we're already on the floor." I heard Boog snort behind me.

The man rose and raised the shades on the lantern, illuminating the room brightly. A group of children in animal costumes stared at me from the floor, blinking in the light. One, in a bear suit, was sobbing uncontrollably. The man glared at me. "Children, it's all right. Keep on romping through the forest. I'll be back in a minute." He came over to me. "What's the meaning of this?" he hissed.

"I, er, I mean, I'm…" I turned to Boog. His hand was still pressed to his chest, but I saw that instead of a bleeding mortal wound, his tunic bore only a smear of strawberry preserves, no doubt left there by the fruity tart he now held. He chuckled and popped the pastry in his mouth.

I sagged, and turned back to the irate host. "Sir, I am dreadfully sorry," I began. "We've made a terrible mistake. Obviously." I turned to the children. "Sorry, young ones! Please, enjoy your party." I smiled as broadly and kindly as I knew how. The bear boy wailed louder. A girl dressed like a fairy eyed me suspiciously, then reached for another tart from a pile on a plate.

I turned back to the man. "Sorry, sir, again, sir. We were here to investigate… er… Well, you see, we're always on the lookout for crimes. Even in the most unlikely places. But we didn't know it was unlikely. As it obviously is. This place." I felt a huge hand on my shoulder.

"We'll be going now," said Boog. "Please accept our apologies. The tart was delicious." He pulled me back out the door, and I was happy to go, and to shut up.

We retreated back down the red hall, where we met the short man again. Boog nodded to him. "Wrong party. We'll head over to Harance." The man looked ready to protest, but Boog guided me swiftly through the center door. "Nice, Inspector Mingenstern," he whispered. "Very nice."

"How was I supposed to know?" I said, my voice higher and screechier than I would have liked. "You were hit... I heard screams..."

"I'll kill every bloody one of you, you small defenseless children," mimicked Boog. I had to admit he did a good impression of me. He paused at the end of the hall and opened the door gently.

This room was nearly identical to the other, with the long tables and raised platform at one end in front of a long red curtain. A gaggle of well-dressed children sat on benches near the platform. On the stage, a group of costumed players danced and gestured – a man in fool's motley, a woman in green woodland garb, and another in a mouse costume, the player's entire head obscured with an elaborate whiskered mask. We slid softly in and sat in the back. The players launched into a song about a lazy crocodile. They were good, really good, actually. I hadn't seen many dramatic productions other than the occasional street troupe, but they were as good as I'd seen. I was a bit too busy cringing about my recent death threat to the Sestille party to enjoy it much, though.

They finished their song to raucous applause and pranced off the stage to mingle with the children. Boog leaned closer to me. "What now, brave warrior?" he murmured.

"He said he'd find us." I didn't know what to do, other than wait. If Bernot didn't show up, this was certainly going to rank among my worst days ever. Perhaps it already did - up all night watching men vaporized, then scolded and disgraced by my mentor by midmorning, and, not to be outdone, learning of the imminent destruction of my city shortly after noon, topped off with a generous helping of terrorizing innocent children before suppertime. I felt a strong desire to go to bed before I caused a flood or earthquake or maybe a plague of insects.

Over by the stage, the players were organizing the children into a line, and, as I watched, they began a parade around the room, the jester singing a happy marching tune as the others clapped and followed. That is one thing about my line of work – you never know what you'll see next.

The parade wound through the tables over to us, and I could tell the jester was surprised to see us, but he showed no hesitation as he strutted along. He and the children filed by with the green-clad maid skipping around the line. The mouse, bringing up the rear, suddenly laid a hand on Boog, miming for him to stand. I chuckled.

Boog's eyes widened, and he tried to decline politely. "No, sir, uh, mouse. I'll just watch."

The mouse waved a scolding finger at Boog and pulled harder, with both hands. Boog looked at me with growing desperation. I shrugged, trying to contain a smile. "I think the mouse wants you to join the parade."

Boog rolled his eyes. "I know what he wants, you idiot." Boog spoke loudly to the mouse. "I'm sorry, I don't march." His tone was icy.

The mouse put its gloved hands on its hips and shook its head. Then, quick as anything, it grabbed hold of Boog's ears and tried to pull him up with exaggerated yanking gestures. The children laughed and clapped. That is, until Boog yelled, grabbed the mouse's leg in an expert wrestling grip and hurled the unfortunate rodent to the floor. The children gasped. The singing stopped. The mouse writhed. Boog hauled back his meaty right fist to strike.

"Boog," I said quickly.

He looked up and saw all the open mouths of the children staring at him. There was a tense moment, and then his fist relaxed, and he patted the mouse on the chest. He smiled broadly, but there were beads of sweat forming on his brow.

"Hello, kids. Just a little fun with the mouse here. We're only playing! Ha, ha. Silly mouse. Please, carry on." He hauled the mouse to its feet, where it staggered a bit, then reached up to straighten its head.

The jester looked rather put off, if 'rather put off' can include a healthy dose of barely contained horror. Ever the showman, though, he started up his song again, and the forester maid urged the children along a path directly away from Boog. Not a coincidence, I suspected. The mouse took a few faltering steps and then limped along gamely behind the procession.

I looked at Boog.

"What?" he said. "Shut up."

I kept looking.

"That's not fair. You threatened a whole room of children with death," he grumbled.

"Yes, and you vanquished an overzealous rodent. Boog the Fearless, Slayer of Monstrous Mice."

Boog put his face in his hands. "I won't tell anyone if you won't," he mumbled.

"Fair enough," I replied.

The children circled the room a few more times, and then the jester produced small gifts for each of them from a patchwork sack. They cheered, and the three players led them to the door, where the entire entourage proceeded out to the entrance. The jester shot us an ugly look as he left.

Boog sighed. "That's it. I've had enough." He stood. "I'm going home to bed."

Before he could make good on his pledge, though, the door opened again. I feared that the little man might come in, full of wrath, and I couldn't really see how we didn't deserve it. But instead, the mouse came back in, favoring its left leg.

Boog groaned. "Look, I'm really sorry. But you can't just go around grabbing a guy's ears." He rubbed his forehead with the heel of his hand. "Let's not make a big fuss out of this."

"Murrrf fumf!" said the mouse, its voice muffled by the mask. It pulled off a glove and reached up to undo the lacing at the back of its head. The laces loosened, it pulled off the mask to reveal a stubbly face surrounded by rich brown locks matted with perspiration.

"Bernot?" I said, shocked.

"Gaah," said Boog. "I had no idea it was you. You're not......hurt?"

"No," said Bernot. "Not badly, anyway."

"What are you doing dressing up like a mouse, playing for children?" I asked.

"It's my day job," he said. "I really want to be an actor, but they don't pay enough here, so I clerk at night."

"But…nobody knows?" I asked.

"It's not something I advertise," he said. He held up the mouse head and smirked. "But that's not important now."

"Yes, why have you been away from work?" Boog asked. "And why all the secrecy?"

A look of fear flashed in Bernot's eyes. "You told no one? You weren't followed? You destroyed the note, I trust."

"Yes, I tore it to shreds and ate it personally," said Boog. "With my soup." I assumed he was joking, but when I glanced at his face, I wasn't sure. Bernot seemed convinced, at least. "What's going on, Bernot?"

Bernot took a deep breath and set the lifeless mouse head on a table. "Five days ago, I was working the night shift in the evidence room. It wasn't a busy night at first. All I checked in was a bloody dagger from a tavern brawl gone ugly." He swallowed and continued. "A little after midnight, two people, a man and a woman, came in. They said they were from the House of Marron, and they were there to collect the count's family heirloom. It was the pendant you two checked in a few weeks ago – you know, the case Sophie put on impound?"

I nodded, a vague, unpleasant feeling rising in my gullet. If Marron had the pendant now, Sophie must be involved. Bernot continued.

"I told them I had no authorization to release it, and they produced a note that said they could take it, signed by Sophie. It didn't look quite right, though."

"Not right how?" asked Boog.

"Sophie's signature looked strange, and regardless, this isn't how she does it. She signs the book for impounds – always has, the few times I've seen them. The whole thing seemed off."

"So what did you do?" I asked.

"I told them this wasn't proper procedure, and that they'd have to come back and get it in the morning, when Sophie was available to release it." He glanced nervously at the door. "They weren't, uh, impressed with that. They challenged me, and looked very threatening, but I figured they would never do anything in the headquarters. I mean, one yell and I'd have guards and inquisitors running to save me."

"Or at least to witness your murder," said Boog, with a grin.

Bernot didn't seem to find that very funny. "Finally, they insisted that I contact Sophie immediately to resolve this. I really didn't want to get her up, but there was a chance that the note was legitimate, and I didn't want to mess up."

"You woke up Sophie in the middle of the night to ask about a clerical issue?" Bernot was either braver or stupider than I was, to be sure. Maybe both.

Bernot looked unhappy and more than a touch defensive. "I've never dealt with this kind of thing, and you know Lia. She's really hard to work for. I figured that was the only way to be sure I wasn't messing up. I had the note, but it wasn't standard procedure."

"What did Sophie say?" asked Boog.

"Well, I locked up, took the note, and walked over to the residence." Sophie lived in the Inquisitor's Residence, a modest but comfortable house across from Headquarters. One of the benefits of her position. "After I knocked several times, Sophie opened the door." The corners of Bernot's mouth bent downward. "She wasn't happy." I could imagine. "But I showed her the note, and I'm nearly certain she'd never seen it before. She looked really angry, and just stood there holding it for a long time."

A forgery? But why? And why so clumsily done? Maybe they assumed Bernot would be easier to bully than he turned out to be. I had to give Bernot credit there. But, if it was forged, what had happened to the amulet? I was becoming very confused.

Bernot continued. "Finally, Sophie folded up the note and just said, 'Give it to them.' I asked her if she was sure, and she said she was. She told me not to discuss this with anyone, not even Lia."

That didn't seem like a workable plan. Lianna was very thorough, and Sophie knew it – Lia's annoying attention to detail was actually one of her major qualifications for her job. Maybe Sophie had figured on fixing the situation somehow before Lia caught on, but that didn't sound right either. This wasn't making much sense, but it was also looking depressingly as if Sophie had been bought by Marron's gold.

"I returned to the evidence room, and I should say, I can walk very quietly when I want to – all the theater training – and I have very good hearing." He looked very proud of this, so I smiled encouragingly. "Marron's people didn't hear me coming, and as I was walking down the hall, I overheard them talking. The man said that with the amulet back, they would be back on course. The woman said they had Sophie Borchard wrapped up and under control. I don't know exactly what that meant, but the man laughed, and said, yes, just a few more loose ends to tie down. I really didn't like the way he said that – it sounded like a threat."

I glanced at Boog, and he looked back at me, his face grave. "So, what then?"

Bernot continued. "I came around the corner, and they looked a little startled, and then a bit angry. Well, more than a bit. I told them that Sophie had approved, and they waited while I collected the amulet and recorded the transaction. The man, the leader I suppose, put the amulet in a pouch on his belt."

"What did he look like?" I asked.

Bernot squinted, trying to remember the details. "He had blond hair and a beard, no mustache. Probably thirty years old, maybe more. In a black robe and cloak, no obvious weapons, but a Marron heraldic sign on a patch on his shoulder." Our wizard from the warehouse? It made sense. He'd been involved with Novara as well. Obviously a close associate of Marron. "The woman was shorter, darker skinned, with mostly short black hair but a long braid coming down off the left side. No insignia at all, but she must also be with Marron. Very muscular, graceful, in chain armor with a short sword with a jeweled hilt – small garnets, or something similar, in rows along the guard."

I commended Bernot on his observations and asked for a few more details – scars, accents, and the like – but he had little else to give. I thought about the ramifications for a bit, but couldn't make much sense of things. I didn't like where my thoughts led.

Boog broke the silence. All right, so this all sounds out of the ordinary and all, but it still seems as though you resolved it. I don't understand why you've gone into hiding and are sending me secret notes."

"As I said, I had a bad feeling about the two of them and their intentions towards me," Bernot replied. "They took the amulet. I had noticed one strange thing when I collected it. In the inventory book, the item was listed as 'amulet, moon and sun, with gold chain,' but there was no chain. I looked everywhere. I was trying to decide whether to tell them this, but then the woman grabbed me by my shirt and told me that under no circumstances was I to speak of this with anyone, or I'd wish I hadn't."

"You're talking to us, though," I said.

"I was scared, I'll admit. Both Sophie and this man had told me to keep quiet, and I was quite willing to do so."

"So did you mention the chain?"

"No, I was pretty scared then, and I just wanted them to leave."

"So why are you telling us now, if they were so scary, and you were under orders not to?" Boog asked.

"I carried on as normal for a few days, but the day before yesterday, something happened. I came off my shift and headed home for some sleep. I slept for a couple hours, but I'm a light sleeper, and a noise outside my door woke me. It sounded like someone was outside my house. I went over to the door, and I could hear faint metallic sounds from the door, like someone fiddling with my latch."

Boog rubbed his chin. "So, you thought they'd come for you?"

"I couldn't think of any other reason, aside from burglary, but nobody in my part of town has anything worth stealing, myself included. I got scared, and I dropped into my root cellar, which I share with my neighbors the next house over. They never keep their trapdoor latched, so I was able to come up through their house and get out into the street. It was mid-morning, so the street was busy, and I pulled on my hood and risked crossing over to the other side of the road to get a view down the alley towards my house. It's pretty secluded there, but in front of my house I saw the woman from Headquarters – the one with the braid, who'd threatened me. I remembered them talking about loose ends, and I was fairly certain that I'd become one."

I thought about this for a while. Threatening an inquisitor was a crime, and certainly breaking into Bernot's house was as well. Given that I'd personally observed these fine upstanding citizens turn two people to powder and blow up Stennis, not to mention whatever they'd done to the poor blue lady in the box, I conceded that they might not be so concerned with the mundane details of the criminal code. "So why tell us? Why not tell Sophie?"

Bernot looked uncomfortable. "I hate to say it, but I'm not sure what side she'd be on. For all I know, she could have told them where I live. You two were the ones who turned in the amulet, and I've heard from Lia and others that you've still been following up on the case." He gestured toward Boog. "Plus, I could use somebody intimidating on my side, I think."

Boog smiled grimly at this. I considered for a moment being offended, but I'd be kidding myself if I thought that anyone found me intimidating. I asked, "So, where are you staying now? And why are you still working here?"

"Nobody from the Guild knows that I work here, other than you two now, so I thought it was still safe. I spent last night at an inn, but I don't have the coin to keep that up for long. I'm in trouble – real trouble, aren't I?"

I couldn't disagree. I looked at Boog, but his face was impassive. I thought for a bit, then replied. "It's not a good situation, to be sure. Why don't you stay in hiding for now, until we figure things out? I can give you what I've got on me." I fumbled in my coin purse for the little money I had. I heard some noises outside the door — perhaps the other players were returning. "That should keep you for a couple of days. We can meet here again the day after tomorrow. Boog and I will try to feel out Sophie and decide on our next step."

Bernot thanked me, and as he pocketed the coins, the door flew open, and three men and a woman burst into the room in quick succession, armored, blades drawn, each wearing a mask of black cloth with crude holes cut for eyes and mouth. Bernot blanched, and then made a dive for the platform behind him, surprisingly nimble in his mouse costume. I nearly followed him in flight, but I didn't want to leave Boog there alone.

"Hold!" shouted Boog. "We're inspectors on official business. Sheathe your swords immediately!"

The new arrivals didn't seem impressed with our credentials. "We know who you are," said one, his voice muffled by the mask. "Catch the clerk!" he shouted, pointing his blade at Bernot. His voice had a lilting accent I couldn't quite place. In response to his order, one of the men moved quickly over to the platform, where Bernot had just reached the curtain. As Bernot fumbled with the drapery, trying to push it aside, the man leapt onto the stage. I took the opportunity to draw my warding rod. The attacker reached for Bernot with a meaty left hand, but Bernot was quick, dancing away to the curtain's edge. The man thrust his sword at Bernot, but Bernot hurled his mouse head at the man, striking him in the face and knocking him back. The man lurched back a step and then toppled off the stage, striking his head on one of the benches as he fell. He landed awkwardly and lay still, his blade clattering to the floor at his side. Bernot ducked behind the curtain, and I heard a latch scrape and a door open.

Another masked man jumped up onto the platform and ran to the curtain. Boog began backing slowly toward the wall, and I followed. Better to have them all to our front, I reasoned. This wasn't looking good – three against two, and Boog unarmed. Boog stomped on the edge of a small bench, tipping it up to his hands, where he hoisted it easily. OK, mostly unarmed. Though I respected Boog's martial skills, I'd probably not have put money on us, furniture or no.

The man on the stage cursed and yelled "Locked!" Mentally, I joined in his cursing – Bernot had cut off an escape route for us to save his own furry hide. If I ever saw Bernot again, I'd need to discuss with him the concepts of teamwork, togetherness, and common goals, perhaps with the help of Boog's staff.

The man giving the orders spat on the floor. A bit melodramatic, I thought, though I gave him credit for launching it through the mask's mouth hole without apparent effort. Spitting indoors, though - his mother would be displeased. Unless he'd learned it from his mother. "We'll get him later," he growled. "Let's deal with these two."

Time for diplomacy. "Citizens," I said. "We can work this out. There's no need for violence."

The man on the stage jumped down, and they arranged themselves between us and the main door. The woman twirled her blade menacingly.

Time for reason. "The penalty for harming an inspector is forty lashes and imprisonment in the dungeons for a year," I continued, helpfully, I thought. "The penalty for killing an inspector is death."

They closed a few steps, moving in easy unison. "Don't give them ideas," grumbled Boog.

Time for bluster. "I'll have you know, I'm a trained sorcerer, and my partner has killed ten men in unarmed combat." Boog cast a glance my direction, his eyebrow raised.

"Have at them!" shouted the leader. They charged at us.

Time for panic. I ducked behind a chair as the woman reached me, her sword striking the chair's wooden back. The two men went for Boog. He knocked aside the leader's sword with his bench and tried to dodge the other man's strike, but he wasn't quick enough – the blade's edge bit into his shoulder. Not a major wound, but not one he could afford in this battle. He grunted with the pain and swung the bench back around, barely missing the man's head.

The woman kicked the chair at me, and it fell over. She approached warily, her sword out in an impressive guard pose. The warding rods are not very long, so she had a good foot of steel on me. I was very aware at that point that I am less than a foot thick. I struck the end of my rod with my palm, and the rod began to hum. If I were lucky enough to hit her, the rod could put her down, but that seemed an unlikely hope.

Through the mask, I could see her eyes widen at the magical effect, subtle though it was, and I had a flash of inspiration. "Kalakh! Zembul! Galooka! Wegarness!" I shouted. Other than Zembul, which is a kind of gooey cheese Sophie favors, I don't know what those words mean, or if they're even words at all, but they seemed appropriate at the time. I persevered. "Spirits of fire! Spirits of death! Attend me, and slay my foes!" I waved the rod in little menacing circles.

The woman took a step back, cringing, and the masked man who'd cut Boog looked over in surprise. He didn't see any spirits of fire or death (or even spirits of cheese, for that matter). He also didn't see Boog's bench, which connected firmly with the side of his head. I don't want ever to hear that sound again, but I must say it was welcome on this occasion. The man went down like a sack of squash.

The woman swung her sword at me, a downward, chopping blow, and I barely knocked aside her blade with my rod. Boog hurled the bench at the leader and, as the man dodged, Boog lunged for the sword dropped by the attacker he'd felled. I tried a stab at the woman with my rod, but it was feeble, even by my standards. She barely needed to dodge, and I thought from the growing look of scorn in her eyes that she perhaps wasn't thinking of me as a fearsome wizard anymore. Boog scrambled across the floor, struggling, trying to get away from the leader while getting a grip on the sword.

The woman swung at me, low, at my left side. I dodged away, but she quickly lunged, finding my abdomen, just under my ribs. I yelped at the sudden burn, and tears filled my eyes. I stumbled away, getting a table between her and me for a moment. I had been injured before hundreds of times, even cut sometimes in blade training, and I'd been in a few fights, although with Boog around they were usually short. With all that, though, I'd never been seriously hurt by anyone who really wanted to kill me. A million thoughts filled my head – had she hit a lung, or my viscera? Would I die a lingering death of coughing or disease? Or would I bleed out here? Or would none of that matter? And who was this? Why did she want me dead? I couldn't see her face, or any of these assailants. I ran over all the rivals I'd had and the enemies I'd made, but it was a short list. I was decidedly unimportant and indisputably small-time. My profound irrelevance was such that I couldn't think of anyone who'd want me to pay an extended visit to the Blood Mother.

Other than Marron. It had to be him, particularly with the connection to Bernot. Marron and his retainers had shown themselves to be ruthless, and we had disrupted their progress. If Madame Lenarre was right about the Faerans, and the unfortunate blue woman we'd recovered was integral to his plans, then we had obviously gotten in his way, not to mention the business with Stennis and Novara. But having an inspector killed? In a public place? Marron was either very bold, very angry, or very desperate. Maybe all three.

I, on the other hand, was merely very desperate. It appeared I was long on brilliant analysis but short on destiny. I imagined my entire existence ended, reduced to a little crimson flag on the map back in headquarters. I hoped my fellow inspectors would avenge me, or at least mourn my passing. I pressed my left hand over the hole in my side, and a tingle of fear ran through my jaw at the sticky dampness I felt there. I risked a glance down and to my dismay saw a large and growing blood stain. With my right hand, I held my rod up, but it seemed a meaningless gesture.

I heard the clang of steel from off to the side. Boog had recovered the dropped sword and was holding his own now, even pressing his own attack. I wished him well but could spare no more attention. The woman tried a feint to my right side, but I was either too skilled or too slow to respond, and I easily parried the following slash at my left. She kicked at my knee, but I dodged that, too, albeit clumsily. I was beginning to feel light-headed and warm, and a metallic taste grew in my mouth.

She took a step back, then attacked with new ferocity, her blade dancing around me. Strangely, I found myself momentarily entranced at her eyes through the mask – a bright hazel, and burning with emotion and effort. I snapped out of it, and through a series of dodges, blocks, and lucky breaks, I avoided serious damage. She did cut several new holes in my clothes and carved a new scratch across my chest. It burned, but it wasn't deep, or so I hoped. She broke off her attack, catching her breath, but I was fading fast. My rod was never intended or designed as a fencing weapon – its weight and balance were all wrong, and it had no hilt. Just keeping it up was taking all my concentration, and it was becoming impossible for me to hold it steady, as I was sure my opponent realized.

She circled me warily, moving around the furniture, seeking an opportunity to finish me off. I retreated, but I knew I didn't have far to go. I couldn't make it to the door without going past her, so that wasn't going to happen, even if I were willing to abandon Boog. I considered throwing the rod. If I hit her squarely, she'd go down, but that was no sure thing. If I failed, I'd be unarmed and at her mercy, and mercy didn't seem to be a defining component of her character. Better to tough it out and hope for an opportunity. Or at least, I thought morbidly, to distract her long enough to give Boog a better chance at survival.

She lunged, and I backed quickly behind another table. She took two dancing steps forward and stabbed at me again. Again, I backed up, but this time I pressed up against the wall behind me. Seeing an opportunity, she leapt up onto the table, laughing. I don't think I'd ever heard such a cold sound.

Time to do or die. Or both. Summoning the last of my strength, I pressed my right foot up against the wall and pushed off at her, knocking her blade up with my rod as I neared. As she swung back down at my head, I dove under the table, pulling off a not-half-bad tuck and roll. Sometimes small stature has some advantages, handling the low clearance of tables being one such instance. I emerged on the far side and scrambled to my feet. A glance back showed that I had thrown her off, albeit temporarily. She was bent over, her sword thrust down under the table after me. As she rose and spun around to face me, I swung my rod as hard as I could, and it smacked hard into her thigh. The magic energies discharged in a web of blue sparks. With a strained grunt, she dropped her sword, fell limply to the table, rolled off onto the floor, and ended in an awkward heap.

I'd like to say I turned and joined my friend in his fight, perhaps even saving his life through acts of noble wrath and derring-do. The truth is, I took a faltering step in that direction, wondered at how dim the room was becoming and at how strangely flexible its walls now seemed, and then I felt my cheek smack hard against the floor as the darkness swallowed me.

19

Puncturation Marks

After an indeterminate period, a dim flicker of consciousness returned. A bony hand, cold as ice, clutched at my throat. I waded through the darkness, trying to summon the strength to struggle. Was this Death himself, come to fetch me? Did I lie cold and dead in some grave, my tortured spirit trapped by my murder in some cruel undeath?

After some time, I remembered that I had eyelids, and then that they could open, and then how to open them, but such a task still seemed beyond me. The hand seemed to press ever harder, but as I felt its weight, I also felt my breath rustling grudgingly in and out. Did I still live, then? Perhaps so. A moment later, I knew that I did, because the pain in my side resolved from a dull ache to a sharp, piercing agony, and I found the strength not only to open my eyes, but to yelp. Surely the dead did not yelp – it would be far too unseemly.

My vision swam with pain, then cleared. The bony hand was not connected to some grinning skeletal specter, but instead to a pink-eyed, white-haired skeletal specter with a rather more serious expression. Instead of devouring my soul, she appeared to be daubing at the scratch on my chest with a damp cloth.

"Marten," said the Augur, gently. "You gave us quite a scare, boy."

"Guurk," I replied. "Hurkle."

"Shh, now, just rest," she said, pulling the sheet up a bit. A sheet. Hmm. I glanced around me. I appeared to be in a bed in the infirmary at Headquarters.

"Boog?" I asked.

"Inspector Eggstrom brought you here yesterday. He carried you himself, all the way from the inner keep. Covered with gore, he was, but fortunately it turned out not all to be his own, or yours. The healer cleaned and sutured him up, and after he filed his report with the clerks, he's rarely been away from your bed here. I think he's acquiring some sort of luncheon at the moment. I chased him out at last. He looked a bit wan, and I thought some food might improve his health and his mood. I'd wager he'll soon return."

Boog alive! Relief surged through me. "Why are you here? The pool... you should be filling it."

"Can't be doing that all day now, can I?" She grinned.

I was honored – I wouldn't have thought myself worthy of the Augur's attention, much less her medical ministrations. My thoughts returned quickly to the cause of my injury. "Attacked... We were attacked."

"Obviously so, unless you're given to self-mutilation. I gather from Beauregard that you acquitted yourself well."

"I barely defeated one of them, then passed out," I replied. "Not too valorous, I'm afraid."

"Mister Eggstrom credits you with two of them, and yourself unarmed."

I snorted. It hurt. I resolved to avoid further snorting. "Hardly." But Boog was surely a good partner and friend. "Did any of them live?"

"Two, I gather, but one has not regained consciousness," said the Augur.

"That's right," came a familiar voice from the door. Boog entered, swallowing noisily. "The woman you fought is the only one awake."

"Boog!" I exclaimed. "Are you hurt?"

"Not like you, Marty. I'll have a few impressive scars, though." Boog touched his shoulder gingerly. "I'm glad you're back among the living." His words had a casual bravado, but the concern I saw in his face gave it the lie.

I felt a stab of fear. "Was there... er, was I..."

"The healer said she'd not bet money on you making it to morning, with the blood you lost. But the wound seems clean, she says, and mostly through muscle. I gather that's a good thing. Shouldn't fester."

"Pff," said the Augur. "That damnable healer wouldn't let me get to work filling the pool until I 'built up my strength.' As if I could do that stuck abed here. Far too excitable, if you ask me. Scared as a mouse." Boog nodded agreement.

I was still reeling a bit from their casual dismissal of my brush with mortality. I felt gently around my wound. It was covered by a thick dressing, and there was a greasy residue all around it – probably an unguent. Or so I hoped – I'd rather not still be leaking important fluids. I lifted the sheet, but there wasn't much to see. Just a carefully folded and bound cloth, tied on with linen. All thankfully white and unsullied. I was quite naked, though, and I felt a blush coming on at the thought of the healer, a gentle, decorous older lady, casually disrobing me.

"She won't talk," said Boog, and it took me a moment to realize he was speaking of my assailant. "I think they were mercenaries from the southern lands – some of their equipment looked southern-made, and they all had thick dark hair under the masks. They didn't have much money, either, so maybe they were earning their supper chasing Bernot. Sophie's got five inspectors out trying to track down their lodgings and contacts, but without the pool, it's a challenge."

"It's Marron," I said. "Has to be."

Boog nodded his assent. "Unless Bernot's got a lot more enemies than I think he does. And they were obviously told about us as well."

The Augur seemed surprised at my accusation, and I realized then how impetuous I must sound, a provisional inspector of low birth casually indicting a respected nobleman. She leaned back in her chair. "A bold and treacherous move he's made, if you two are correct. I'd not think him capable of it, but these are unsettled times. I doubt you'll ever find evidence enough to make it stick. He's not fool enough to have hired them himself."

She paused. "If you're right, you've gained a very powerful enemy."

Boog filled the Augur in on the blue woman, on Bernot's eavesdropping, and on our suspicions. I added the professor's insights about the Faerans and their ambitions. I realized that I'd not yet told Sophie about all of that. I groaned inwardly. Maybe my current state might soften her ire when she found out? I doubted it.

The Augur listened attentively, but then her eyes grew distant as she pondered our words. At length, she spoke. "A fine mess you two have stumbled into," she mused. "But all your evidence could be portrayed as nothing more than mere circumstance. You'll need far more than inference and a few coincidences to convince Sophie, much less the Justiciary, much less the Prelate, who will surely be summoned into any matter concerning the House of Marron." She pounded the arm of her chair. "If we only had the pool – damn that wizard and her amulet."

Boog grunted agreement. "What should we do now, Augur?"

"In your case, that's for Sophie to decide. In Inspector Mingenstern's case, he should lie here, drink plenty of mead, and attempt not to bleed."

I was all too eager to comply. Suddenly, a wave of weariness washed over me. I closed my eyes, and the last thing I remember was a huge hand gently patting my leg.

20

CLOSING WOUNDS

I awoke parched. From the window, I could see the sky was dark, some lamps burning in the street below. Someone had left a pitcher of water by my bed. I drank carefully, trying not to move anything that didn't absolutely have to move, and hoping that I wouldn't see the water I drank flow out from under my bandage. My whole left side ached, and the cut across my chest still burned at the slightest touch. I tried to find a comfortable position. If there was one, I failed to find it. I let out a heavy sigh.

My struggles alerted someone in the next room. I heard a chair scrape, and then soft footsteps. The healer came through the archway and walked over to my side, her lips pursed in disapproval. "It would be preferable if you would lie still," she said. With a practiced flick, she turned down my sheet. I yelped and tried to cover my nakedness with my right hand, but it turned out she'd left me some modesty with the sheet. Barely. She clucked her tongue. "Honestly, Mr. Mingenstern. You've got nothing I haven't seen already far too many times."

While I pondered what that meant, and whether I should possibly be intrigued or offended, she inspected my dressing, lifting it gently and pressing and prodding around the area. Her fingers were really, really cold. I tried to salvage some small bit of dignity by not flinching. "Surprised you're alive," she said. I tried to detect some glint of happiness on her part that I'd exceeded her expectations but found none. She replaced the dressing. "Since you are, I suppose we can use one of these."

She opened a small drawer in the table by my bed and pulled out a ball of brown clay. "Arnaud's Poultice Mud. Very expensive, and hard to find around here. Didn't want to waste it if you were just going to die."

There was a great deal wrong with her priorities, I thought, but I decided the more prudent course would be to avoid antagonizing her. "What does it do?" I asked.

"Speeds healing, sometimes tremendously, for this kind of wound. Prevents putrefaction, usually. Enchanted, it is, or at least Arnaud claims so." She worked the clay in her fingers, spreading it out into a thin disk. "Mostly river mud from the banks of the Duyenne near Galustrina, plus elm bark, ground pearls, and organs from several kinds of squirrels." She lifted my dressing, and I saw a sizable sutured gash underneath. She pressed the disk onto my wound. The pain lessened immediately, and I felt tingly all over. The mud was hot, and it bonded instantly with my skin. "Oh, and cricket brains, and extract of goat feces," she added. I felt less tingly.

There was a tap at the archway. I looked up to see Sophie. "May I see the patient, Domina?"

"You're the High Inquisitor," she replied, not unkindly. "Do what you want." To me, she said more sternly, "Don't move, you. I'll be damned if I sew you up again." She closed the drawer and returned to the main room of the infirmary.

Sophie came to my bed and sat on a nearby chair. "So, tell me what happened," she said.

I related as best I could the events of the previous day, from visiting Monique, to Bernot's note, to our ill-fated visit to the Red Rabbit. I must admit to leaving out most of the part about terrorizing the Sestille children. When I got to Bernot's report, I wasn't sure how much to say. If Sophie had been bought by Marron, it might be better not to let her know what Bernot had overheard and what we now knew, because then Boog, Bernot, and I might all become liabilities better eliminated than tolerated. That certainly did seem to be Marron's preference. It was a horrible thought, that Sophie might intend us harm, but ugly as it was, I couldn't rule it out. Bernot's story and the note I'd impulsively stolen made the unthinkable possible.

On the other hand, perhaps knowing the scorn Marron held for Sophie and for the Inquisitors might shake her out of whatever internal negotiation she'd made to accept Marron's money. Realistically, if Marron wanted me dead, and Sophie were compliant, then it's not as if I was in any shape to resist them. Better to hope for the best. The Sophie who had trained me, who I had idolized, would never succumb to the lure of mere gold. I took a deep breath and related all of Bernot's report.

Sophie listened silently as I finished a brief summary of the fight. At last, I fell silent, and Sophie made no comment, just studying me, her eyes unreadable. What manner of discipline was she contemplating? For surely I had violated the spirit of her orders, if not also their letter, in visiting Monique Lenarre. Bernot's involvement with Marron was unknown to us when we sought him out, and the battle was not our fault, but I wasn't sure Sophie would see it that way. Worse still, could she be here to finish the task the fierce masked woman had nearly completed?

She looked down, finally, and cleared her throat. "So, in defiance of my wishes, in contradiction to my orders, you've been continuing an investigation I closed weeks ago and specifically ordered you off not a day ago? Merely because you found it interesting, and couldn't let it go?"

I believed at that point that no person before or since had ever felt so miserable as I. I thought of several excuses, of extenuating circumstances, but those words all turned to ash before I could speak them. "Yes, Chief."

She sighed and lapsed into silence again. At length, she spoke. "I'm sorry."

"What, Chief?"

"I'm sorry, Marten," she continued. "You've done exactly what I trained you to do. To sink your teeth into an investigation, and never to let go until you've run it to ground."

"But, Chief. Your orders…"

"My orders were misguided." She shook her head. "I wasn't convinced you were right. If you were wrong, you'd be wasting your time, and getting the Inquisitors into needless trouble. If you were right, then ordering you off the case would, I hoped, protect you while I figured out what to do next. Obviously, that failed, due to your willful disregard for my orders, or your tenacity, if you prefer. The situation with Marron is delicate, to be sure, and I suspected that if I let you turn over enough stones, you were bound to uncover a viper. I just didn't realize how soon it would come to pass. You've made excellent progress. I should have trusted your instincts, as I've often trusted mine."

My mind reeled. "But, you're taking his money," I blurted. None too politic, I chastised myself.

Sophie chuckled. "Yes, but where is it written that you can't take someone's money while working toward his downfall?" She grew more serious. "And we need the gold – there's no getting around that."

She rose. "Your injury is my fault. I'm very glad, but not a little surprised, that you two survived the attack. You won't be so fortunate for long, and I fear this won't be the last attempt on your lives. Despite your efforts, I don't have nearly enough to move against Marron, and unless every aspect of the case is locked down, his position and his friends will save him, and make us out to be fools. He'll receive the benefit of every doubt, so we must eliminate every doubt. It will not be easy, but if there's anything at all to this Faeran business you've dug up, we need to get to the bottom of this, and quickly."

She placed her hand on my shoulder. "You need to heal. I need to think. And to figure out our next move. If you would, please stay here. I can protect you in our headquarters, and I'd rather not tempt fate again." She turned and headed for the archway, then turned back once more. "If you're up to it, have an apprentice bring you what you need from our library or elsewhere, and see if you can learn anything else about the Faerans and this prophecy. I'll issue you a pass for the Prelate's Library also."

"Thank you, Chief," I called after her. I felt better than I had in days, and I'm sure it wasn't just the effects of Arnaud's mud.

21

INVALID

The next few days passed quickly. I seemed to be mending well. Two days after the fight, I was on my feet and walking gingerly around the infirmary. I read a great many treatises by learned authors, but information on the Faerans was hard to come by, and I didn't learn much that we didn't already know. The cult earned its name from a being called Faera or Fae-Rah, who was either male or female or neither, an ancient evil god of the underworld, or a sinister frog demon, depending on which scholar one found more convincing. The cult was ancient in Gortis, with few adherents, not considered important or threatening other than the odd murder or theft. Its rise to power in Frosthelm a century ago seemed to be a new resurgence, with local converts, not driven by or connected to the Gortian sects. As Madame Lenarre had said, despite remaining fairly secretive, they attained considerable influence in Frosthelm, with many of the noble class involved. There was the same eclipse prophecy back then as well, although what was prophesized and what form the ritual supposedly took varied from text to text. One proposed an awakening of an army of dead warriors. Another, the summoning of a fearsome ice-beast. A third, a plague of hellfrogs, and a fourth, the emergence of Faera himself (or herself, or itself) onto the land. None sounded particularly pleasant, but none seemed necessarily consistent with the pool's prediction of fire raining from the sky to burn Frosthelm.

The moon-and-sun symbol was identified in many of the sources. Some also mentioned the Eye of Hrogar gemstone, the Fingernails of the Holy Hermit, the Thersian Crown, and also the Mace of Godron, which had reportedly been recovered and taken as a prize by Prelate Karela herself. I found one other mention of a blue princess of the Golesh tribe. Apparently there had been another unfortunate dead princess found in the Faerans' possession a century ago. I supposed that if I were chief of the Golesh, I'd hope for sons. The nature of the ritual in which all these bizarre objects would be used was unclear, as all of the leaders of the Faerans had fought to the death or fled, never to return. Only rumors from the remaining minor cultists were recorded, and they were often vague or contradictory. Some seemed to involve amulets, as we'd seen the Faeran followers wear, and some referred to human sacrifice. A grim business. I soon exhausted all of the limited number of histories and official records available to me. The apprentice I pressed into my service did not seem sorry when at last I gave up the search.

Boog stopped by frequently with news. Continued investigations had turned up little about our attackers. The woman still remained stoically silent, but her companion, the one who'd fallen off the stage, had recovered, and he was more gregarious. If he was to be believed, they were mercenaries, in town only briefly, on a break from service at the border. Their leader was the one Boog had fought and slain after I'd gone down. He had found them work, but the others hadn't been party to the negotiations and knew nothing of their employer. They were to find and capture Bernot and kill us if they could do so without attracting too much attention. They'd followed us from headquarters to the Red Rabbit and overpowered and tied up the little proprietor while we spoke with Bernot. I didn't imagine we'd be very welcome at the Red Rabbit in the future.

Bernot was understandably nowhere to be found, and he'd left no more notes for Boog. I hoped he was in hiding, or better still, pursuing a rewarding non-rodent-based theatrical career somewhere rather than captured or killed by Marron. The investigation had mostly run its course. An assault on inspectors always took top priority, but all avenues of inquiry appeared to be leading to dead ends. Life in Frosthelm continued apace, as did crime and intrigue, so the inspectors had gradually returned to their other duties.

One late afternoon, I asked Boog, "Are you doing all right, considering?"

"What do you mean?" He chuckled. "Watching you lounge around all day reading books while I work? That's getting annoying."

"Well… just that you killed two people." As far as I knew, they were his first.

"Oh," he said. "Hadn't given it too much thought." He placed a huge, callused hand over his mouth, then lowered it. "We've been in fights before. I thought we did well to survive, outnumbered and unarmed."

"Yes, but we actually killed citizens."

"They were going to kill us! I believe we're covered in that case. What should we have done, said, 'Sorry, evil criminals. We'll not be able to fight back. Wouldn't want to harm you murderous rogues.' We did right. We did our jobs. We put violent, would-be murderers in jail or in the ground."

"So you're proud of it?"

"Well, aren't you?"

"All I did was paralyze one of them, and then I had to be carried home."

"Not so – without your fake wizard curse, we'd have stayed outnumbered and unarmed, and likely died. You saved us! Maybe you didn't swing the bench, but you killed that man as much as I did."

I thought about that for a while. I couldn't really dispute his reasoning. Was I, then, a killer? "I never signed up to kill people," I said. "That's not our role. I just…" I wondered what my mother would think of all this. She had been a peaceful, happy woman. Both my danger and my involvement in these deaths would have been shocking and alien to her.

Boog saw my distress. "Marten, we're officers of the law. There are evil people about. Better that they prey on us than on the citizens, and better that we kill them than they us." He patted my shoulder. "Be proud. There is no clearer case of justified killing than this, and you performed admirably against a superior enemy. Sophie's proud of us. The others are proud of us – we're becoming a bit of a legend."

He leaned in close and whispered, "Besides, the ladies love a scar and a tale to go with it."

I snorted at that – my prowess with 'the ladies' was most assuredly not a thing of legend. Boog laughed and slapped me on the shoulder. I grunted in pain.

"Uh, sorry." He patted me again, gentle this time. "But cheer up – you're alive, your enemies are dead, and you're a minor hero. Enjoy it a little."

I resolved to try.

22

NAGGING DOUBTERS

Five days after the attack, as I was re-reading a dusty history of Karela's reign, Gueran ducked his head into my room.

"So, the brave Inspector Mingenstern, in the flesh," he said haughtily. "Or what's left of the flesh. I'd have thought you too small a target to be easily struck, but you seem to have managed regardless."

I sighed. "Thanks for the sympathy, Gueran."

He snorted. "Sympathy? For being sloppy enough in your investigations to engender assassination attempts?" He laughed. "Or should I rather fear you? After all, I hear from the Sestilles that a diminutive inspector threatened an entire party of children with death. Quite the vicious warmonger."

I tried hard not to respond to his provocation, but I am not that strong. "How's the privy maintenance career going for you? You seemed to dive whole-heartedly into your new line of work."

He chuckled without any real mirth and tapped his chest. "A touch, Marten. But you do not wound me." He sat by my bed. "I am glad to see you still breathing, though. You do much to keep things amusing around here."

"I'm happy to oblige," I said. "Any reason other than amusement you've come to see me?"

"Yes, in fact," he replied, picking a speck of lint from his otherwise spotless uniform. "The woman you captured asked after you. Perhaps she'll tell you something she won't tell the rest of us, or perhaps she just wants another chance at killing you." He laughed at his joke. I didn't. He continued. "Also, I understand from Eggstrom that you've had a talk with Sophie."

"Yes," I replied, with caution.

"All is roses and spun gold once more?" he asked.

"She seems to approve of our work here, if that's what you mean. And she sees Marron as a threat."

Gueran leaned closer and spoke quietly. "Or, she convinced you that she does."

A few layers of my confidence peeled away. "What are you saying?"

"Regardless of what she said to you, she still cut off an investigation into Marron in exchange for Marron's money."

"Yes, but she's approved me researching the Faerans now."

"But not Marron, eh?"

I thought a bit. "Well, I'm in no shape to go spying on Marron."

"You think she'd authorize that?" Gueran sounded angry. "There's no doubt in my mind that Marron's behind the attack on you, but not a single inspector was assigned to pursue that line of inquiry."

I thought a bit more. "But... She said she's wary of Marron. That she was wrong before."

"And what else could she have said? You're in too deep for her to continue to stall or obfuscate. She let you dig further, because she had to, but not towards the one who has paid her off."

"Gueran!" I said, shocked. But his words found some resonance in my mind. Could it be a sham? Was Sophie that gifted an actor? That deceptive? That sinister?

Gueran leaned back. "It all may be as you say – as Sophie says. Her conversion may be sincere. But consider this – what was the root of the whole matter with Bernot? The amulet. And who now has Novara's amulet? Marron. Who is getting exactly what he wants, at the expense of our investigations, in exchange for gold?"

I closed my eyes. Gueran's words were prying open a door I'd thought closed. Did I really believe Sophie now, or did I just want to believe her? I thought back to the note I'd stolen and read. *I have done as you asked, under the terms upon which we agreed.*

Gueran continued. "Suppose Sophie's motives are pure. Even so, she's put us in an impossible place. We can't act against Marron, or even investigate him, while relying on his money. Sophie should never have placed us in this situation."

I agreed with him on that point, at least, although I didn't see where else we'd have found funding. I doubted the Prelate would be willing or even able to double our budget while we repaired the pool. I was thankful at that moment that such unpleasant decisions were not mine to make.

"Soured your milk, have I?" asked Gueran with a smirk.

"A bit," I admitted. "I have much to ponder. But we have no recourse, really, no matter what Sophie's true motivations are. What should we do?"

"Ah," said Gueran. "Finally, you are practical. I say, we must watch Marron, chart his movements and those of his lackeys, find the links between him, these crimes, and this cult of yours, if such exist. But Sophie won't let us do that, I'll wager."

"How will we have time for that, if we have our regular duties as well?"

"We'll have to find a way – cover for each other, stall on our assigned cases, whatever it takes. I'll admit to a personal motive – I've been wanting to take the House of Marron down a couple of notches for a long time."

Interesting – I knew the nobles didn't all get along, but I was oblivious as to the politics of the Prelate's court. "Why is that, exactly?" I asked. "You said before that Marron was seen by some as a bully."

"He's a powerful man, and his house has long been close to the Prelates of Frosthelm. He has the Prelate's ear, and he has often used that influence to his own benefit, at the expense of others."

That sounded like typical noble behavior to me. "Isn't that expected? Part of the game of influence you all play?"

Gueran was bemused. "I suppose it might look that way from a commoner's perspective. But Marron has, shall we say, violated the rules of the game in several ways. To those nobles willing to supplicate themselves to him, he is generous. He convinces the Prelate to add to their lands and titles, but frequently at a terrible price. And not always in gold. He often demands that those seeking his favor send their sons and daughters to his house to marry his lesser relatives, or to be little more than servants in his household, or to join his militia and go off to die fighting his battles."

"And if a noble refuses his price?" I asked.

"Those that refuse, he disparages to the Prelate, or worse. For some, he has fabricated evidence of crimes or treason, supported by his cronies in the court. He has destroyed more than one house in this way."

"But why does the Prelate not see through these ruses?"

"Marron has a tongue of silver when he needs it, and he has his people in many places – the Brigade, the Guard, the Justiciary, the Guild – who support his claims. As the Prelate has become busier with the conflict at the border, he's had less and less time to spend on matters of the court and the city. Where once he'd have launched his own investigations, he now trusts Marron to advise him and to handle more and more matters of state." He leaned back in his chair. "The Prelate is an able leader – don't misunderstand. It's just Marron dripping poisonous thoughts and foul lies in his ear."

"Has your house suffered under Count Marron?" I asked.

"No, not really. We're not of high enough stature to attract much attention, so we've stayed clear of his dealings." Gueran suddenly looked uncomfortable, and I realized he had probably not meant to admit his family's relatively lowly ranking. "But I've seen what he's done, and it's brutal, unjust, and devoid of honor."

It always came to honor or dishonor with Gueran. I suppose there are worse things to be fixated on. Something that had troubled me before resurfaced in my mind. "Clarice – you looked strangely at her before, when discussing Marron at Novara's house, as if you expected her to comment."

He frowned. "Yes."

I waited, but he didn't elaborate. "It seemed like Clarice knew of Marron."

"Yes, she does. No question about that."

"So…?"

Gueran cleared his throat, for a second time uncharacteristically uncomfortable. "If she hasn't told you, then I should respect her decision."

I was burning with curiosity. Was Clarice also of noble birth? Or even of the House of Marron herself? My mind raced. She'd never mentioned her family or her childhood. I recalled that the few times Marron had come up, she'd either remained silent or expressed discomfort and dislike. It would be bad form to press Gueran on it, though. Not honorable. "Of course," I said, reluctantly.

"Well, try not to cut yourself on the pages of these books. I hear you've lost a lot of blood already," said Gueran as he rose to depart. "If you need some fencing training, I'd be happy to oblige." I wondered how he managed to summon so much sarcasm so effortlessly. He must practice his taunts at home before bed. "The first step is avoiding the pointy end of the blade. Work on that first."

He turned, his cloak swirling like a dancer's veil, and strode toward the door. Perhaps he also practiced grand exits. I smiled at the thought of him striding and swirling back and forth in his chamber at night until he got it just right.

At the archway, he paused. "Burgeo," he said quietly, the usual sneer absent. "Her name was originally Burgeo." He vanished around the corner.

23

SPIT AND POLISH

I saw the glob of spittle fly between the bars and stick to the far wall, oozing slowly down the stonework. There was an unintelligible but definitely unfriendly comment from the cell, to which the guard responded with a scowl.

"Well, she's all yours," she said to me. "Can't see what you'll learn – she barely speaks, and then only to shower us with abuse. I've learned more than a few new insults. She's a mean one – we've not been able to go in there since she wrestled Johannsen to the ground. Took three of us to get her off him, and he'll be wearing a cap for a goodly while until his hair grows back."

I thanked her and proceeded to the cell ahead. The place smelled dank and unpleasant, a mixture of bad food, unwashed inmates, and burnt pitch from the torches. There wasn't a lot of fresh air. We were below street level under the main keep, in the Prelate's dungeon. I was a little surprised she'd been taken here, since we have a set of holding cells in our headquarters, and the Inspectors would obviously be questioning her. I suppose the guards Boog summoned after the melee decided she merited the harsher environment. After all, she was violent and assuredly guilty.

She glowered at me from behind the bars. It was strange – I barely recognized her from the fight a week before, since she'd been masked the whole time, and I'd been focused more on her blade than her appearance. There were her hazel eyes, though – I remembered them well, flashing from behind the mask. Stranger still was seeing her here, seething but powerless to hurt me, when the last time we'd met, she'd been trying as hard as she could to end my life, and nearly succeeding.

She had long black hair, unkempt and a bit stringy from a week in captivity, pale skin, with a hint of red on her cheeks, and full red lips. She was strikingly pretty, even accounting for her general filthiness, some bruises, and some rough-looking scars, one dividing her left eyebrow and one on her neck and chin. Not that her beauty had any bearing on anything. I found it strange that I could fear her so much the previous week, and now, a week later, feel not much of anything. I had thought I might feel angry, or fearful, or even pitying, but in reality, it was difficult to see her as the person who'd laughingly stuck five inches of steel into me. The whole event seemed more surreal as time passed.

I had no idea what to say. "Er, hello."

She growled at me, then said something in a language I couldn't understand. I doubted it was "Hi there, inspector! Great to see you again."

"I was told you wanted to talk to me."

She stood and came over very close to the bars, grabbing onto them firmly.

"They will kill me?" she said, her accent lilting, almost musical, the same as her leader.

An interesting question. Assault on an officer of the law was a year in prison. She was definitely guilty of that, but so would be a drunk who punched a guard trying to break up a bar fight. If I'd died from my wounds, she'd have been put to death for murder of an officer, no questions asked. What she'd done was likely attempted murder, which had a range of sentences depending on circumstances but could include death. It would actually likely be up to the justice she drew. And, I realized, what crime Boog and I, as the two arresting officers and only witnesses, elected to charge her with, and how we testified.

"They might," I replied.

"Might? What, might?" Her frown deepened.

"That depends on what crime you committed."

"I stick you with my sword! You bleed. Not complicated."

"Well, it sort of matters whether I died…"

"You not dead, yes?"

"Yes, but also whether you meant to kill me…"

"Of course I mean to kill you! Why else do I stick you with sword? Happy greeting of new friend?" She gave me a silly wave, and her voice took on a sing-song tone. "Hello, little man! Try out sword! Sharp, yes?"

I winced. "Yes, quite sharp." I took a breath. "We could either charge you with assault on an officer, or attempted murder, and there are several degrees of attempted murder."

"Degrees? What degrees?"

"It depends on intent, circumstance, premeditation, motive – lots of things."

"Who decides?"

"Well, I do, actually. And my partner."

"Big man?"

I nodded. She was silent for a bit, then spoke. "My friends – what happened to them?"

"The one who fell off the stage still lives," I replied.

She snorted. "Idiot! Beaten by a mouse man! Where is he now?"

"He's here, but in the men's cells."

"They kill him?"

"No, he'll get out in a couple of months – he didn't cause us harm, just assaulted the owner of the Red Rabbit."

"But he meant to kill you, too. Same as me. Just too stupid and clumsy to do it."

She had a point, but that wasn't how the law was written. "The law recognizes outcomes as well as intentions."

"Stupid law. I get killed, but he goes home in a couple months, because he stupid, and I good?"

I said nothing. After a bit, she said, "What about the others?"

"Both dead. One, from the blow to the head from the bench. The other, your leader, I think, killed by my partner after you and I, uh, stopped fighting."

She looked troubled at this. "Mantoo? And Goren? Both dead?" I nodded. She said something in her language that sounded like an oath, then spoke to me again. "And me, defeated by you, without even a blade. Horrible day. Goren should never have taken this job."

"What job was that, exactly?"

"Kill you, kill big inspector, capture Bernot. We were lucky, we thought, to find you all together."

"And who hired you?"

She spat at the floor. "Why should I tell you? They kill me anyway."

I considered for a moment. "If you cooperate, I can put in a good word for you. You'd get out in a year." I thought of Johannsen's recent involuntary haircut. "Maybe longer, because you fought with the guard here."

"Bah. That guard grab me, too friendly. No man can do that." She pressed close to the bars. "Why would you help me? I tried to kill you."

"I'm aware of that, believe me. But you acted just for money. I am more interested in who really wants me dead."

She chewed on her lip. "I tell you what I know, you tell them not to kill me?"

"If it's true, and useful. And if you stop fighting the guards."

She thought for a bit. "If guards not touch me, I not fight them. You swear? We have deal?"

"Yes, I'll agree to that."

"Not agree. Swear." She spat into her palm and held it out through the bars. Spitting seemed to be a vital form of conversation amongst her people.

I wasn't too excited about this, but I figured it might provide a lead for us. I worried also that she might pull my arm through or tie my limbs in a complicated knot around the iron bars. I had to give it a try, though. I worked up some spittle and spat at my hand, but I missed. She rolled her eyes as I tried to summon more saliva. I was pretty parched, and I wasn't sure if there was a specific amount required. I tried again, hitting my target, and achieved what looked like a satisfactory glob. I held out my hand, and she grabbed it, squishing the liquid together across our palms. I could see no earthly reason why this meant our agreement was more profound and more binding than if our hands were dry, but it seemed to satisfy her somehow. She finally let go. I wasn't sure of the protocol – I wanted to wipe my hand off, but I supposed that might be bad form – one wouldn't want one's word and bond smeared on someone's trousers. I decided to just let our deal air-dry.

She took a deep breath before speaking again. "We four, we're together five years, since even before leaving home. Goren was leader. Goren makes arrangements, gets jobs. Last year, he made deal, we fought at border. We were cheated — not get full pay, so we come back here, to city, to find new job. No luck for a while, but Goren find employer last week. Good pay. He have me come along to meeting in case of problems."

"Whom did you meet with? Who hired you?"

"Man named Algor, at Pampered Pig."

"I know the place. He asked you to kill us and capture Bernot?"

"Yes. 12 pieces of gold if all done right."

Well, at least our price was high. Either we'd become major annoyances, or we had a wealthy enemy. Maybe both, and both were consistent with Marron. "This Algor, what did he look like?"

"Old man, maybe fifty years. Black hair with gray spots on beard and mustache."

Didn't sound like Marron or his mage we'd seen in the Jezarmi warehouse. "His clothes?"

"Nice. High quality, no patches, silver buttons, fur in boots."

"Did the meeting go well?"

"Goren try to haggle, get better price, but Algor not interested. Goren agree."

"How were you supposed to get paid?"

"Algor come to tavern every night at sixth bell. If we do job, we meet him there."

"Any time limit to this?"

"He say as soon as possible. We must meet him for progress report every few days."

"And did you have any of these meetings?"

"No, we find you easy, first day, and we follow." I didn't feel great about that – I'd have hoped Boog and I would notice being followed by four foreigners. "We talk about splitting up to find Bernot, but you lead us to him. Little man at Rabbit place say Bernot there too, so we decide to go in. All rest, you know."

I thought for a bit. I suspected she was telling the truth. Her story sounded plausible, she had no reason to lie other than fear of this Algor person, and she had some real incentive to tell me what she knew. Under the arrangement she described, Algor probably knew things had gone sour by now. Even if he didn't know what happened at the Red Rabbit, the team he'd hired hadn't met with him. And, if he were closely connected to Marron, then he or Marron or both had probably heard of our fight. It would be a juicy rumor among the noble classes, I guessed, blood shed at the Red Rabbit.

I considered trying a ruse, where I got this woman to meet Algor and tell him she had captured Bernot. Depending on how much Algor knew, it might be tempting, and we might be able to arrest him at a meeting. Marron seemed to have pretty good sources of information, though. I supposed it was likely that Marron knew by now that the mercenary and her partner had been taken prisoner, or even that Bernot had escaped, which would ruin any attempt at deception that I could imagine.

All of that seemed complicated. In the end, the best option was probably the simplest. Do the legwork, ask around, and track down Algor. I had a name, or at least an alias, a place, and enough evidence to arrest him for questioning and possibly conspiracy to murder. I wasn't in top physical form, but I was mending well with the help of the healer and Arnaud's clay, and Boog was unharmed. If we were careful, we could probably pull it off if Algor hadn't gone into hiding.

"You not kill me now?" asked the woman, leaning close to the bars.

"If your information is useful, then I'll put in a good word for you. You'll get a year in prison, probably, maybe exile from Frosthelm afterward."

"Exile after? Hah. I want exile now. As soon as possible." She looked a bit wistful. "You good man, I think. You treat me well, with no reason to. Job to kill you was bad job."

"Er, well," I said. I felt heat at my cheeks.

"You spare my life, also, so you save my life." she went on. Her eyes widened in sudden realization. "I owe you blood debt."

That was puzzling. She didn't seem to be in a position to pay any debt, blood or otherwise. "What's that mean?" I asked.

She stood up straight. "Inspector Mingenstern, I swear blood debt to you," she said seriously, spitting on the floor. Of course, the spitting. "You need me, I come. You in danger, I fight for you. You in trouble, I help, or I take your place. Lucianna your loyal servant until debt repaid." She pounded her chest with her fist.

Great, I thought, just great. The woman who tries to kill me is now going to guard my life from her jail cell. "Lucianna? Who's that?" I asked, though I thought I knew the answer.

"Me," she said. "Lucianna Stout, daughter of Mileno Stout."

"All right, then, Lucianna," I said. "That's very kind, but I——"

"Small problem, now," she interrupted.

"What's that?" I asked. I could think of several.

"I can't protect you from prison."

It occurred to me that the only one I'd needed protection from recently was her. "I think I'll be all right, for now." She looked unhappy. "The best way you can help me is to serve out your sentence and cause no more trouble. And be more selective about what jobs you take in the future."

She sat down on the stone ledge in the back of her cell, her eyes downcast. "All right. I stay, I serve, no trouble. You tell them I sorry." She looked up at me. "I am sorry."

I thanked her, not really sure of the protocol here. Off to find Algor. As I turned to leave, she said, "When I get out, I teach you some sword fighting. So you not get hurt. Well, not so much, anyway."

24

A Man Walked Out of a Bar

Follow him? Boog signed from across the crowded tavern. Algor was straightening his cloak, having just stood. He pushed his sturdy oak chair back under his table in the back corner. A neat one, I mused.

I signed back. *I will. You come later.* I waited until Algor was closer to the door, his back turned, before getting up. I dropped a copper coin for the serving maid next to my half-full mug and barely-eaten plate of mutton on the table. Sometimes, having a mission in a tavern was a pleasant bonus, but the ale at the Pampered Pig tasted as though it was intended for actual pigs, and definitely non-pampered ones. The sheep to whom my mutton had previously belonged was wreaking revenge on humanity from beyond the grave. The meat was so gristly and tough I thought it might function better as a boot sole than as a meal.

Also, my injured side ached from sitting so long. We'd been in the Pig since before the supper crowd arrived. Why there was a supper crowd, I couldn't imagine. Perhaps they were doing penance for some sin or other. The establishment was big enough and crowded enough that we'd been able to remain somewhat inconspicuous at two positions, me at one of the long common tables in the center of the tavern, Boog against the wall at a smaller table off to the side. From then on, it was just a matter of avoiding the food and nursing our drinks. Actually, my drink needed an undertaker more than a nurse.

Algor hadn't been too hard to track down. We'd done some research, looking for records of Algor, who appeared to be an upper-class tradesman with a jewelry shop. We'd also scouted the tavern, which was close enough to his shop for convenience, although five or six others were as near or nearer. This had taken two days since my meeting with Lucianna, and now, on the third day, we were ready to execute our plan. Upon arriving at the Pampered Pig, we'd sent in an apprentice, a young dark-haired woman named Bierte, on a pretense of having a message for Algor. The tavern keeper had told her that Algor came in about the same time every night, sat at his usual table, and ordered supper. He pointed out the table and gave her a good description of Algor. Bierte had said she would try to return then, but just in case, she left her message with the tavern keeper. This was a sheet of cheap folded parchment that read: *We have Bernot. Need to stay hidden tonight. Meet here tomorrow.* This was, of course, completely false, and fairly feeble at that. Algor might well know that his team was dead or captured, depending on the quality of his information. He might even know where Bernot was, or that Bernot was dead. Even so, we hoped the note might at least trigger Algor to check with whoever was giving him orders. If anyone was. The tavern keeper had agreed to pass on the note if the apprentice didn't return.

Our apprentice had met us outside a few blocks away, passed on the information, and gone back to headquarters with our thanks. We'd taken up stations in the tavern and waited until Algor arrived, as predicted. He'd ordered his supper, and I saw that he wisely requested soup and bread rather than the mutton. The tavern keeper had sent over the note, which he opened and read with apparent interest, scratching at his beard thoughtfully. He'd gone over to talk to the tavern keeper then, and I presumed he was asking about our messenger. We'd tried to find an apprentice who looked a bit like Lucianna, but we couldn't duplicate her scars, her accent, or her attitude, so it was probably a futile attempt. Still, our only real purpose was finding Algor and learning more about him. If he bought into any of our deception, it might help, but it wasn't necessary.

Algor made his way out the door, and I followed a short time later. He'd turned left, toward the inner keep. I saw him moving up the street at a relaxed pace. We didn't seem to have scared him or pushed him to rash action with our note. I followed along, stopping occasionally in shadows. I spotted Boog leaving the tavern about forty feet behind me, and he saw me too. He followed along on the other side of the street, as inconspicuous as a big strong multiply-scarred guy with a six-foot staff can be, which is to say, about as inconspicuous as an ox wearing a dress. At least he was silent, and Algor didn't seem to be looking back. Thinking back to Lucianna, I wondered if Algor had hired another team of assassins who were following us as we followed Algor. That would be pretty funny, except for the killing us part. I couldn't help but look back to check, but I saw no one sneaking furtive glances our way.

He continued toward the keep, occasionally turning down one of the many crooked streets we passed. I followed, keeping a clear view of him as much as possible. He greeted a passing woman. A friend perhaps. I tried to record a memory of her face as I passed her. Algor was oblivious. Following people through the city was usually surprisingly easy if they didn't have reason to suspect it. We'd practiced this often in our training. On one occasion, I'd followed Gueran all the way across town to a flower shop, where he'd purchased a set of pink and yellow lilies for his ladyfriend of the moment. I'd bought a duplicate set of lilies, picked the lock on Gueran's chamber, and left them in his room with a note professing Boog's undying love and affection for Gueran. It was one of my happiest moments as an apprentice, even though I'd ended up with some extra bruises during my next weapons training session with Boog.

At last, Algor arrived at a house about a block from the keep wall. It was built of stone and wood, of modest size, two stories, with white plaster and crisscrossed wood beams on the upper level. There was a line of well-manicured hedge across the front, about three feet high, with a gap where a flagstone path led to the front door. The left side of the house pressed up against the neighboring building, but there was a small garden on the right, wrapping around to the rear. A nice house, but we were in a nice part of town. I didn't know the name of this particular street, but we'd just turned off Karela's Way, and I was confident I could find the house again.

Algor lifted the large cast-iron ring set in the door and pounded a few times. Not his house, then. I supposed he probably lived closer to the Pampered Pig. There would be no reason other than proximity to dine there. I slowed my pace and stopped behind a bush in the foreyard of a house across the street. Through the branches, I saw the door open. In the doorway stood the wizard from the Jezarmi warehouse! I shuddered a bit and tried not to think of orange dust. The two men exchanged some words I couldn't hear, and the wizard let Algor in. The door slammed shut, the iron ring bouncing a few times.

I waited for Boog to catch up, watching the house carefully. He arrived at the bush and touched my elbow. "What's happening?" he whispered.

"He's meeting the wizard from the warehouse."

Boog frowned. "That's not good."

"At least we know why he wants to kill us."

"We stole his favorite blue woman?"

"Something like that." I pulled up the hood of my cloak, making myself a mere shadow in the twilight. Or so I imagined. And hoped. "I'm going to take a closer look."

"Wait!" hissed Boog. He pointed at the side of the house. Two cloaked figures had emerged from a side door and were conferring in the garden. After some discussion, they started toward the street, and therefore toward us. Even though they weren't moving directly to our position, I worried that the bush I'd chosen wouldn't be adequate to conceal us. Winter had stripped it of leaves, and despite the dim light, we might well be spotted.

Need better hide place, I signed to Boog.

Wait. Watch. I was confused by his reply, but I followed his advice. He picked a rock from the soil at the base of the bush and hefted it in his hand. The two from the house neared our position. Boog gestured at an alleyway up the street to the left. I nodded. He then threw the rock to the right in an upward arc down the street. It soared high, then clattered down upon the cobblestones.

The two from the house looked at each other, then moved quickly to peer around the neighboring house. As they scanned the street where Boog's rock had fallen, Boog tapped my arm, and we ducked silently into the alley. I pressed myself to the ground and looked around the corner, my eyes at foot level, my cloaked head barely (I hoped) peeking past the edge of the building where we crouched.

The two spoke briefly, too quietly to be heard, then looked back down the street in our direction. One pulled his hood off his head, and I saw a head full of scraggly brown hair and an unkempt beard. He pushed aside his cloak and drew his sword from a scabbard at his belt. As his cloak parted, I saw something gleaming on his chest in the moonlight. I squinted to see better. There, hanging from a leather strap, was a metal amulet, just smaller than my palm. A full moon in beaten silver covering most of a golden sun.

I pulled back around the corner. "One's wearing an amulet!" I whispered. "Moon and sun. Faerans."

Boog looked troubled. "Should we follow them?"

A good question. They might lead us to somewhere interesting – a secret base. Or maybe the House of Marron. But we had also found the wizard, and he merited observation as well. "Split up?" I asked, uncertain. One of the first rules in apprentice training is that inspectors work in teams. Frosthelm is a dangerous place – a lesson I'd learned again all too well during our adventure in the Red Rabbit. There were situations, however, where it was unavoidable.

"Are they armed?" whispered Boog.

"Yes. A sword on one, probably the other too."

"Then I should go after them, not you." He looked uncomfortable, suddenly. "I mean, with your injury, you might not be in your best fighting form."

I grinned. "It's all right. I concede your towering superiority in battle. I am unworthy even to shine your boots." I touched my forehead in salute. "I hail you, Lion of Frosthelm, Slayer of Criminals, Defender of Justice—"

"Shut up," said Boog.

"I'll watch the house, see if I can hear anything interesting. We shouldn't try to confront them or follow them into anywhere dangerous." Boog nodded his assent. "Meet back at headquarters by second bell?"

Boog nodded again, then took a peek around the corner. "They're moving." He rose to follow. "Be careful!" he hissed, and then was gone.

I waited for a moment, pressed against the side of the building. Boog was very quiet in his pursuit. I could barely hear him moving across the cobblestones. I wished him well. After a time, I checked around the corner for any unwanted observers, and finding none, I stole quietly across the cobblestone street, between the hedges, to the front of the house. Much of the building was dark, but light spilled forth from two windows on the first floor, one on either side of the doorway. I selected the nearer one and approached, step by step, wary of any twigs to snap or dry leaves I might rustle. I needn't have been quite so cautious. The window revealed a kitchen area with a healthy fire on the hearth, but it was empty. No people in sight.

The second window might be more promising, and I crouched and dashed silently across the path. From my vantage, pressed against the wall of the house in the gloom, I couldn't see much. I stole across the small yard to the low hedge. The window was tall and wide, so from there, not eight feet away, I could see a good section of the room. It appeared to be a study or reading room of some sort, with books in shelves on the wall, large wooden chairs, and low tables around another smaller fireplace. The wizard paced around the room, occasionally speaking and making gestures. He looked angry. The man he was speaking to, or maybe lecturing to, was presumably Algor, but I couldn't make him out too well. His back was turned, and he seemed more at ease, sitting in the chair, occasionally sipping from a large pewter mug on a table nearby.

I strained to hear what they were saying, but the house was too well-made or well-insulated for the sound to travel outside. I could only catch a word now and then, and I could make no sense of them, singly or together. The wizard was angry with Algor, but Algor was remarkably unfazed by this, making unhurried statements in response to the wizard's rants and chastisements.

Something, a hand, touched my shoulder. Boog? Back so soon? I turned to look. The hand was connected not to my partner, but instead to a short woman with light brown skin, short dark hair with a long braid hanging to one side, standing behind me against the hedge. With her other hand, she held a short sword with a jeweled hilt, the unpleasant end pointed at my stomach. The gems on the sword were reddish-brown – garnets? This must be the woman Bernot mentioned, who'd come for the amulet from the evidence room. Not good.

"Good evening, inspector," she said, her voice soft and gravelly. "Perhaps you wouldn't mind coming with me."

I looked quickly around for an avenue of escape, but I was backed up against the hedge, and there was nowhere to go that her sword would not reach first. I looked wildly up and down the street. I was stuck. I wasn't going to defeat this woman, not with my daggers and warding rod hanging uselessly in their sheaths, with her blade at my chest. She touched the point of her sword to my throat and waited. I raised my hands in surrender.

25

BOUND AND DETERMINED

I tested the ropes around my wrists, but unfortunately the woman who'd captured me seemed to be quite competent with knots. A sailor, perhaps, or possibly just experienced in tying people up. Working for the Faerans, I guessed she might get a good deal of on-the-job practice. Or perhaps it was a standard part of training for all armed lackeys. Regardless, my wrists were bound expertly together behind my back, and both of them were now tied to a curved metal bar sunk into the stone wall of the house. I wasn't going anywhere.

My daggers and rod lay across the room on a table next to a stout wooden door. They might as well have been in Gortis. There was a window across from the door, but it was shuttered and inaccessible. I doubted my voice would carry more than a few feet outside, even with a full-throated yell. My shoulders were stretched uncomfortably, my side ached, and my cheek felt puffy and bruised from when she'd pressed me to the floor, her knee on my neck, while tying my hands. She'd also taken my boots. I wasn't sure why. Perhaps she thought it would hinder any escape attempts, or perhaps she just fancied them herself. If so, I hoped they pinched her toes and gave her many blisters.

I tried to hear the voices from the other side of the door. The woman had gone through it after tying me up, and from my rudimentary survey of the house before my capture, I thought it must lead to the room where Algor and the wizard were talking. I could only hear a murmur, wordless sounds of several voices.

I didn't have long to wait, though. The door opened, and my captor emerged, followed by the wizard and Algor, all looking at me with a variety of expressions ranging from disdain (the swordswoman) to amusement (Algor) to contempt (the wizard). I tried to look dignified and resolute in response, but it turns out that becomes more difficult when one is tied to a wall. The woman with the garnet-trimmed sword waved a hand at me, and the wizard approached. Algor leaned on the table, poking idly at my warding rod.

The wizard studied me for a moment. "So young, and so small," he said icily. "And yet such a nuisance."

He paused, so I figured I'd give it my best try. "I'm here to arrest you for murder," I said confidently. Well, almost confidently.

Algor burst out laughing. The wizard frowned. "Murder, eh? And whom have I slain?"

"Two of those you hired. In the Jezarmi warehouse."

His frown deepened. "The warehouse. And what evidence do you have?"

"We've got their... remains, back at headquarters."

He smiled, but it was mirthless. "That hardly implicates me, does it? People die in the city all the time, and most must leave corpses."

He was being careful not to admit anything. I suddenly suspected he didn't know Boog and I had been there. "We have a witness to the crime, as well," I continued carefully. There were three witnesses he had to know about – the remaining three women who'd left the warehouse.

"I see." He rubbed his brow. "How ... interesting." He came over close to me, his face only a few inches from mine. "Who is your witness, then? I'd love to speak with him or her."

"I can't tell you that."

"But you know who it is, do you not?"

"Yes."

"So, it is not that you cannot tell me. Rather, you do not wish to tell me."

"I suppose."

"That is important, you see."

"Why?"

I must at this point recommend never to ask such a foolish question to such a cruel person. Quick as lightning, the blond wizard stabbed two fingers into my side, upward, under my ribs, right beside my wound. I screeched and doubled over. Pain flashed through me, rushing outward from Lucianna's handiwork. The pain spread like ripples in a pond, reflecting again and again across my chest and stomach.

He chuckled. "It is important because one's wishes can change, especially when one is aware of all of the alternatives." As I raised my head back up, he slapped me across the jaw with the back of his hand. My head whipped back, and I saw stars dancing about. I tasted salty blood trickling from a new split in my lip.

I didn't lift my head again. I'm not sure I could have at that point if I had wanted to. "Who is your witness?" he asked. I didn't respond. He slapped me again. "Who?" I maintained my silence. It was the only way I could resist him.

He yanked my head up by my hair, staring straight into my eyes. The swordswoman was watching the proceedings dispassionately, but Algor looked away in discomfort. Odd, I thought blearily, since he'd not a week ago hired ruffians to kill me.

The wizard continued his questioning. "Who told you? One of those fools?" I remained mute. "My chest, that you stole – where is it?"

I didn't answer, so he slapped me again. "Now you're just being foolish. I know it's in your storeroom." Through the haze of pain, I realized he must have an informant at headquarters. Not too surprising, but something to remember. If, in fact, I ever got a chance to tell anybody.

"Did you open it?" he asked, his hand raised for another blow.

I spat out some blood. "Of course we did."

He lowered his hand. "Now, that's better. You're being more reasonable. Is the princess still inside?"

I couldn't think too clearly, but I figured that wasn't important information, and I must admit I did not want to be struck yet again. "Yes, she is."

"The amulet," he said. "Where is it?"

The amulet Novara wanted? That we'd taken from Stennis? He had to know. He was there. "You took it." I nodded my head toward the swordsman. "With her. From the evidence chamber."

The wizard slapped me again, hard. It took me by surprise, as I had answered his question. He was amazingly strong. "Do you think me a fool?" he asked.

I had caught on enough to realize I wasn't supposed to answer that one. He hauled my head back up again, and said, slowly, coldly, "Where is the amulet?"

I couldn't think. But I had no other answer. "You took it."

He punched me in the jaw, twice, with each hand. Then, with a sideways sweep of his leg, he kicked my legs out from under me. I fell to my knees, the rope scraping and wrenching my wrists and arms as I fell. I hung there, my shoulders burning with pain, my arms held back and up at an unnatural angle. Blood and saliva dripped from my mouth, but I could not then muster the strength to close my lips to stop it, much less to get back on my feet.

"Brand," said Algor quietly. "Isn't there a better way?"

The wizard glared at Algor for a moment, but then he stood and straightened his robe. Then he leaned over me. "Don't think you can resist me," he said. "We have more refined methods to break your will. You do not even know what pain is yet. But you shall."

He turned to the swordswoman. "Gag him. Bring him to the temple in the morning, Tolla. They'll be locked down now. It will be easier then. Don't let him be seen when you take him." Tolla nodded. "And post some guards – his partner may be about, or others. Wake me if there is trouble."

Tolla produced a strip of grimy cloth and wrapped it around my head twice, pulling it so tight between my teeth that it cut into my lips at my cheeks. Tolla. Tolla and Brand. I said the names over and over in my head to be sure to remember. Futile, perhaps, but if I ever regained my freedom, I'd have some small thing to show for my cuts and bruises.

The wizard, Brand, came back over to me. I struggled to raise my head, and then, with the last bit of strength and will I could muster, I looked him straight in the eye. I could not see him too clearly through my bleary eyes, but it was at least a moment of resistance. It had no discernible effect on Brand, but it gave me some small comfort. He grabbed my chin and squeezed it painfully. "Do not think you can stop us. We'll get our artifacts back. We nearly control your foolish guild. You'll rue the day you crossed us." He released my chin, and his eyes took on such a fierceness that I almost shrank back. "Faera will rise. You cannot fight our destiny." He left the room, and the others followed.

Fight our destiny, I thought. I had to get my arms to a less painful position, but I was weary and addled from the short but brutally efficient beating I'd received. Fight our destiny. As I struggled to get my legs to respond to my will, my mind filled with the pool's vision of our destiny – Frosthelm burning, yellow flames dancing across the city's rooftops.

26

THE FRYING PAN

At some point in the night, shortly after they'd left, I'd lost consciousness there, leaning against the wall. Whether it was to sleep or from my injuries I did not know. I awoke to Tolla slapping my face sharply. When I responded, she untied me from the bar set in the wall and led me toward the door. Off to the temple, I guessed. Not a trip I wished to take. My mouth was dry and very sore, and one of my eyes had swollen nearly shut. My arms and legs ached with a thousand pains, and my hands and feet flared with swarms of needles now that I was released from the wall.

"City guard! Open this door immediately!" The cry was muffled but audible. My heart leapt in my chest.

Tolla shoved me to the floor, then moved, catlike, toward the front of the room. She opened the door a crack and peered out, I presumed toward the front of the building. I breathed in as much air as I could through my nose and yelled at the top of my lungs. The gag muffled most of my cry, but Tolla looked back at me and glared. She ran across the room to the other door. She opened it, revealing to me just a narrow view of the study beyond, and let out three quick, shrill, whistles. In a moment, I heard footsteps pounding down the stairs from above.

I heard a booming thud from the front of the house. Were they assaulting the door? I hoped so. Another thud followed. Tolla slammed the door, then drew her sword. Was she going to fight them? The guard? Could Boog have summoned them when I failed to return?

There was a strange silence, then. Both sides preparing for whatever was to come. Tolla's breathing was the only sound, a controlled hiss as she crouched, listening. Finally, I heard a crunch – the door breaking in? – and then the clanking and pounding of metal-shod feet. Probably the guard. Their standard duty uniform included armored boots. I heard muffled cries and the clash of blades. Tolla moved silently to the door and opened it gently once more, a few inches. The sounds of combat came louder. I struggled to roll over to my back.

Quickly, Tolla closed the door and latched it. The latch was wrought iron, set deep in a slot in the door's frame. It seemed dishearteningly well-crafted. There was a pounding at the door. "Guard here! Open this door now, in the name of the Prelate!"

Tolla shifted her grip on her sword and turned smoothly to me. "It appears, Inspector, your time is shorter than I'd thought." She grinned. "Count this as lucky, though – I'll be far quicker and far less painful than the temple guards." She crossed over to me and raised her blade to strike.

Beaten and broken as I was, the threat of imminent perforation took precedence over my injuries. As Tolla stabbed downward, I twisted to avoid the blow. The blade pierced my tunic, and I could feel the cold steel next to my skin. Tolla hissed and raised her sword once more. As she sliced at my neck, I swept my leg across the floor, hooking her heel with my ankle. She fell back, catching herself with her left hand, as I scrabbled away toward the door.

She was back on her feet in an instant, and I was sure that whatever wellspring of luck I was drawing from had run dry. Her eyes flashed angrily. "Die!" she shouted, three quick steps bringing her within striking range once more.

I sat on the floor, holding up one foot in a feeble attempt to block her attack. Time seemed to slow, and my senses fractured into distinct flashes of perception – her face with its cruel glaring eyes, her forehead glistening with sweat, her braid tossed upward as she moved. The muffled sounds of movement and struggle from elsewhere in the house, the cool damp of the stone floor against my bound hands, the gleam of her blade's wicked tip poised above me as she considered where to strike and how to end my life. She and I stood on this precipice for one dreadful, desolate moment.

A terrible, splintering crash from the door diverted both of us. A second such crash broke open the door, sending the latch and bits of the door frame clattering to the floor. Boog stumbled through, and Tolla took a step back. She swung once at me as Boog steadied himself, but her moment had fled. I squirmed away, and Boog brought his staff up between Tolla and me. Tolla paused for just an instant, and I could see the bloodlust in her eyes, but the pendulum had swung. There were two guards in the hall behind Boog, and Tolla no longer held any advantage. She feinted at Boog, and Boog took a step back to defend. Instead of pressing her attack, though, Tolla spun away and leapt feet-first through the window, knocking the heavy shutters aside. As Boog ran to the window after her, and the other guards rushed in, I heard her quick footsteps receding outside into the night.

"Blood Mother," Boog swore. "She's gone. Our men are all on the other side." He came back over to me and sat me up, his huge hands gentle. "Your plan doesn't appear to have worked as intended," he said as he cut my bonds, pulled out the gag, and loosened the ropes from my wrists.

Fire and needles shot up and down my arms as I brought them around to a natural position. "Right where I wanted them," I gasped. My bravado rang hollow and false. After I regained some mastery over my numbed hands, I gingerly probed my swollen face. "Ow."

I struggled to get up, then thought better of it as the room danced around me. My legs were no sturdier than boiled noodles. "Brand... the wizard... Algor......" I croaked.

"We're searching the house," Boog replied. "But I think nobody's here but a few guards, and the one who just fled." He placed a meaty hand on my shoulder. "Rest now. We'll sort it out later."

The next hours swam by. Boog found a cushion for my head and a finely-knit blanket, and I lay on the cold stone floor, my injuries new and old stinging and throbbing by turn like the twisted melody of some cruel tavern minstrel. Guards came and went, along with a couple other inspectors, and Boog stopped by frequently. I think I slept at several times. I told more than one person what little I knew of my brief imprisonment, my captors, and their plans. The names I had struggled to remember, Tolla and Brand, I shared at every opportunity, along with descriptions. The face of each was etched into my memory.

Eventually, Boog tucked an arm under my shoulders and knees and carried me out to a wagon, where he set me inside on a bed of straw. Even with Boog's care, I ached all over, but despite my physical distress, I remember feeling a sense of relief and righteousness. Now Sophie and the others would have to take us seriously. My capture and torment would demonstrate what our investigation had not, that the Faerans were real, malicious, and dangerous. My pain had bought something, at least, however high the price.

I remember a couple of agonizing jolts on the ride back to headquarters, but consciousness and I had gone our separate ways well before I arrived back home.

I awoke some time later. Sunlight caressed my cheek. I was tucked into a soft bed. I felt sore, but my pain was greatly diminished. I smelled good enough that someone must have washed me, likely better than I wash myself, even. I opened the eye Brand hadn't smashed and then worked on the other. Finally, I got both open and cooperating. The infirmary glowed in the winter sun streaming through the salzglass window, and a small fire crackled in the nearby fireplace. On the small table by my bed, I saw a glass of milk with little bits of cream floating at the top and a dusky-brown loaf of fresh oat bread. I breathed deeply, ignoring the niggling aches, and let out a happy, contented sigh, glad to be both home and alive.

As I basked in my deferred mortality, I heard a voice from behind my bed. "I think he's awake, Inspector." I recognized the stern voice of the healer. She didn't sound happy at all, and while I was quite familiar with her gruff bedside demeanor, there was a note of real displeasure there.

"Thank you, Domina," came the response. I struggled to rise, but I couldn't move my right arm. As I wiggled, I realized it was stuck. Something circled my wrist. I craned my head around to see a set of leather straps binding my hand to an iron ring set in the bedpost. Fighting a surge of panic, given wings by my recent treatment at the hands of Brand, I rolled around to see a man in the scarlet uniform of the Guild approaching my bed. I didn't recognize him, and I knew all the Inspectors in Frosthelm personally, most as friends. Could he be freshly arrived from the border? My mind raced.

"Marten Mingenstern," he said gravely. "You are under arrest, under order of the High Inquisitor, charged with murder."

27

THE FIRE

I tossed my wooden spoon at the rat, nearly hitting it, but it skittered away into a narrow crack in the wall with a cheeky squeak. I bent to retrieve my spoon.

"Bad form, Marty," said Boog. "You'll never catch up with that kind of performance." He gestured to the seven dead rats propped up in a little row along the edge of his cell. I was reminded of the murals of the Seven Seers in the Temple of the Blood Mother in the center of Frosthelm, but I had to admit the parallel was somewhat tenuous.

"It's not fair," I complained. "They're attracted to your natural odor." He snorted.

To be sure, neither of us smelled very good at the moment. A week in a cell, even one as well-maintained as the Guild's, was hard both on one's hygiene and one's wardrobe, not to mention one's spirits. I had never considered how boring imprisonment was, even when one's fate and one's life are at risk every day.

We knew a good deal more now than I had in the infirmary, now a distant bittersweet memory. Denault and Gueran had been down to see us a few times and filled us in on what they knew, and we shared our recent findings with them when there were no eavesdroppers about. At other times, grueling questioning sessions gave us more details about our alleged crimes, even as we navigated their perils. My training in conducting an interrogation helped me when on the other end of the process, but I was still worn out, and I was beginning to doubt even some of the details I thought I remembered well.

Any investigation answers questions – what, where, who, how, why. In the case of our supposed crimes, some were easier to answer than others. The answer to what was murder in cold blood. The answer to how was a poisoned blade, slid between the victim's shoulders as she slept. That blade had been found, still bloody, in my quarters, and the jar of poison in Boog's, implicating both of us. The poison was a rare Gortian one, not generally thought to be available in Frosthelm, although traffickers in deadly venom didn't tend to advertise their wares.

The answer to why was complicated. That's why they had spent so much time questioning us, going over conflicting events, schedules, and motivations. In the end, though, it was irrelevant, because the High Inquisitor was convinced of our guilt. Or rather, he made a great show of being so convinced, even though he knew sure as the sun rises that we were innocent of the crime.

Yes, I do mean he. Don't for a moment think I impugn the honor of my mentor and teacher, Sophie Borchard. The answers to who and where had been the biggest shock. We were accused of murdering, in her own residence, the High Inquisitor of Frosthelm. Sophie Borchard was dead. She'd been stabbed in her bed late during the night Boog and I had followed Algor, sometime between the times of my capture and my rescue.

Boog had related the truth regarding his evening's pursuits, but he was unfortunately lacking in corroboration. The only witnesses he could draw on (other than me, but my testimony was, shall we say, discounted) were the apprentice we'd used to set up Algor at the Pampered Pig, long before Sophie's death, and the Inspectors and city guard Boog had raised for my rescue, well after the supposed time of Sophie's murder. After we parted company, he had followed the two Faerans across town, but they'd entered a tavern, gotten a meal, and gone to sleep in rented chambers. A useless venture, and even more unfortunate, there was nobody to confirm this. He'd been keeping a low profile and had spoken no more than a word or two to anyone during this time.

As for me, one might think that being captured, beaten, tied to a wall, and discovered nearly dead upon rescue by the guard might offer some exoneration for a crime committed during that period, but that alibi turned out not to be as useful as I had hoped, given the circumstances. Apparently, I'd set it up, faked my injuries, arranged my seeming rescue, or some similar unlikely scenario.

So, the answer to why remained - the question of our motivation. Those who guided the interrogation seemed to think that we had chafed under Sophie's restrictions of our inquiries. I'm not sure whether they proposed we'd decided to kill her out of anger, or in order to pursue our obsession with the Faerans unimpeded, or for some other reason. Whoever had set all of this up placed some of Sophie's valuable personal belongings in our quarters as well. That was just showing off, I think, but you can add our desperate poverty and avarice to the pile of reasons they gave for our crime.

They even, in a flourish of spurious revisionism, tried to cite the damage to the Augur's pool as intentional on our part, to prevent discovery of our crimes after the fact. The Augur herself shot this down. Of course, anybody clever enough to destroy the pool and set up an elaborate kidnap and torture ruse might also have been clever enough not to leave the murder weapon and stolen goods in his quarters. But, we weren't even given that much credit, and in the end, we were either criminal geniuses or bumbling fools as the narrative required.

If the verdict is assumed, the tale bends to fit it. This bending, and our resulting headlong sprint towards guilt, was helped along by some of the new inspectors appointed by the new High Inquisitor. It was against long-standing custom to bring in appointees as inspectors. The Inquisitor's Guild prides itself that any citizen who can survive the training can become an Inspector of full rank, regardless of background, but pride and adherence to custom were now in sorrowfully short supply.

Even with the changes in staffing, one might also think that this whole supposed crime was so convoluted and so obviously contrived that a carefully-trained group of investigators such as the Inquisitor's Guild might perhaps find the leaps in logic somewhat troubling, and begin quickly to suspect the truth and try to find not only the actual killers but also those who had falsely implicated me and Boog. And one could not be faulted for such thoughts, except for one small problem.

That problem once again manifested itself, or shall I say himself, shortly after my ill-fated attempt at rat extermination. He came swirling down the stone stairs to the holding cells, his blood-red cloak billowing behind him, the ceremonial gold key and scales emblems of office jangling at his breast. Sophie had never been one for show. I think I'd seen her in full uniform perhaps five times, but our new leader held a rather different view of the gaudy trappings of his position.

In the cell across from mine, I saw Boog's face settle itself into a cold mask, his eyes blazing with hatred. I think he could be forgiven this affront to his nominal superior.

"Gentlemen," said the High Inquisitor, a faint smile playing about his lips.

"Marron," I replied.

28

A PUZZLE

"I trust you're well?" he sneered.

Boog turned away, folding his arms across his chest in mute defiance.

"Marvelous," I replied. "The gruel was particularly well-seasoned today, and they've just changed my straw and emptied my privy bucket."

Marron sniffed, then produced a cold grin. "I don't begrudge you your impudence. It's all you have left." He placed two gloved hands around my cell bars and leaned in towards me. "We've done enough here, I think. The evidence we've connected will demonstrate you to be foul murderers. Particularly when presented in Wiggins' court. I doubt the trial will last more than a couple of hours. You'll likely see the headman before nightfall tomorrow."

I'd expected as much, but it still put a cold dagger of fear through my chest to hear him say it. I searched for something bold to say, to leave him gnashing his teeth or stomping off, but alas, I'm no poet, and nothing came to mind. I couldn't let him win, though, so I shrugged with feigned disinterest and inspected my spoon. I flicked a gray speck off it and tucked it into my belt.

Marron pushed back from the bars. "There's actually one small hope for you two," he said. This puzzled me. I couldn't see how we were of any value to him, or of any importance at all, really. We didn't know enough to hurt him or derail his plans. We had no evidence that he didn't control now as High

Inquisitor. He had his blue princess back, I thought with a pang of regret. Even if we had our freedom and enough evidence to send Marron to the dungeons twice over, we didn't have the Prelate's ear and would never get a chance to change his mind. We'd entered this whole tale as supremely unimportant fellows, and we were about to leave it in the same way, albeit also as convicted murderers. If I was going to face the headman's axe for murder, I supposed, I'd rather at least have committed one, so I could glare balefully at the bystanders and go to my end a dangerous, detestable, bloodstained rogue, feared by all.

But what was this hope Marron offered? I do have a healthy dislike for dying, but I'd not serve him in exchange for my life. Better to die with honor than live in shame. I briefly wondered if I'd feel the same way tomorrow evening and resolved to try.

"What are you offering?" I asked.

"You stole something from an associate of mine. An amulet." His eyes were cold. "Give it back, and I'll have some more evidence discovered to back you up and then send you both to the border."

Have some more evidence discovered. What a great way to run investigations. I'd have to remember that for my next case, I mused, trying not to dwell on the fact that I was likely done with cases. Brand had mentioned an amulet as well. But what amulet were they discussing? I knew of two. The first, Novara's, had been missing when we arrived, taken by Marron's guards, if Mavis and Terrence were to be believed. I felt a brief longing for baked goods. The second, the one we took from Stennis? Marron had that back already – we knew from Bernot that Tolla and Brand had convinced Sophie to release it from the evidence chamber.

I hesitated, torn for a moment, but decided to play along. The only one we'd actually ever possessed was from Stennis. "Your swordsman just couldn't keep himself together," I said, far more cockily than I felt.

Marron's eyes blazed, and I saw that with my provocation, I'd hit upon something. Stennis' amulet, then. The one Bernot had given to Tolla and Brand, after receiving Sophie's approval.

What a puzzle. Who had it if he did not? Could Tolla and Brand be working independently from Marron? No, they were first on the scene at Novara's house. I was more confused than before.

"Cease your jokes, little man," Marron seethed. "There are far more painful ways to die than beheading." He released the bars and turned sharply away from me, the trim of his cloak fluttering about. "You've got until tomorrow. Think hard about your fate." He stormed up the stairs. Boog tossed a dead rat after him, but it fell far short.

"Hey, you're down to six now," I said. Boog scowled back at me. Even if we were motivated to accept Marron's offer, that would require us to believe that he would keep his word. I'd sooner believe in Boog having magical fairy powers. Furthermore, we couldn't produce an amulet, or even another bowl of gruel for that matter. I sat down to think hard about our fate, but I feared I would find no answers. Our time grew shorter and shorter, just as we would after our appointment with the headman's axe.

29

MY BEHEADING

That was the longest night of my life. I'd been in mortal danger before, as recently as the Red Rabbit and again at the point of Tolla's blade, but in those cases, the danger was immediate, and I'd had no time to think. Come to think of it, I'd had my death threatened, even scheduled, at the house with Algor and Brand, but that already seemed surreal, and I'd been in such pain that I barely had time to consider my fate.

No, this was different. I, and my partner and best friend, were about to be run through the system I'd been part of for years, a system I knew to be efficient and effective. The fact that the evidence was false, that we were not guilty, made it seem even more hopeless. Boog and I discussed making an appeal for clemency with the Prelate, but we knew that a reprieve was nearly never granted. The Prelate was busy, and he trusted the machinery of justice, and those he appointed to run it, to accomplish their tasks. We had nothing but our word and our observations to present. No bloody knife, no alternative killer, no key witness. It was doubtful, given Marron's gaming of the system, that our appeal would even be heard.

I supposed that some of the senior inspectors could speak on our behalf, but the truth was, they knew little of our findings. We'd reported nearly all of it directly to Sophie, now silenced. Denault knew some of it, but she might not be willing to contradict her new superior, or she might have been convinced by the evidence they produced against us. Gueran might speak for us, but he was not much more important than we were, and his words would carry little weight. The Augur was perhaps our best hope, but if we were tried and convicted, even her word would likely not mean much, especially against Marron and his justices.

That hurt the most – that the system I trusted, that I worked for, could be so easily corrupted, and that criminals could operate so openly and hold positions of such power. I had no power to fight them, no way to set things right, no way even to save myself or Boog. In a few weeks, my whole life, my belief in the city and government I loved, had crumbled away.

I mourned Sophie, too. My trust in her had been shaken, but it was now restored. If she were dangerous enough to them to get herself killed, then she must have been working against them. I wanted to avenge her, to discover her killer or killers and bring them to justice. Or preferably, I should admit, to carve them open myself in a fit of battle rage, no matter how unlikely that might be. I wondered if it were Brand or Tolla who had killed her, or whether Marron had a whole army of vicious murderous followers.

Boog and I spoke of our fate occasionally, at first with anger, then regret. Then, I think each sensing the other's distress, we spoke of happier times. Our first day of apprentice training, when we stood at attention for an entire morning. After a half hour or so, an apprentice from the noble classes, Willard, had objected to the futility of the endeavor, and been silenced rudely by the instructor. He was quiet for a time, then complained again, quietly, to those around him. Finally, with increasing ire, he'd threatened to summon his father's allies, to have the instructor fired, to have the apprentice program shut down, to have the High Inquisitor thrown out of office. After several hours of this, we were ordered to take him, carry him three blocks, and toss him in the pond near the city wall, which we did with great enthusiasm. He never returned to the Guild, and none of his threats came to pass, but his name and his fame lived on long past his brief tenure.

Our first case together as provisional inspectors had been that of Brutia, a mildly notorious pickpocket. Her associate, the handler of most of her stolen goods, turned her name in to the Guild in exchange for clemency. We'd followed her to the market district in the southern section of town and observed her making several thefts from shoppers and from market stalls. My heart pounding, and with quavering voice, I'd confronted her and informed her that her days as a thief were at an end – my first arrest. In response to my laying down the law, she'd thrown back her head and laughed heartily. I'd like to say this was because of her villainous bravado in the face of certain legal peril, but I fear it was more likely because I barely came up to her shoulders and hadn't yet needed to shave.

She'd grabbed my tunic and lifted me off the ground, brown eyes bright with both annoyance and mirth. Despite what Boog says, I'm quite certain I didn't flail my arms and legs around like an overturned beetle. As I hung there, pondering my options and the next move Brutia might make, and whether it might hurt, Boog tapped Brutia on the shoulder and, as she turned, struck her with an expertly-placed fist to the jaw. A little too hard. We had to carry her back to headquarters, where we learned from the contents of her baggy pantaloons that we'd probably missed three or four of her thefts that morning despite our careful observance.

These shared memories and others helped lighten our spirits and pass the time, but not much. At length, we lapsed into silence. Unable to sleep, I watched the single torch at the end of the block of cells flicker and gutter, occasionally shooting a spark upward in the plume of smoke. Burning bright, spending its brief life. Brief, yes, but it might outlive us to shine again the next night.

After an hour or more – I had no real sense of time down there – I heard voices from the top of the stairs, where the guard stood watch. I'd had that duty occasionally myself, when we couldn't call upon the city guard to man the post for one reason or another. It was quite dull, and I'd fought to remain awake and aware. The cells were depressingly well-crafted. Even if I were as strong as Boog, I'd never have found a way out, and even if I'd had my lockpicks and tools, I couldn't have opened any of the locks without the heavy cast-iron key that hung by the guard post upstairs.

Suddenly, there was a shout and clattering from the stairs, and something red appeared, rolling down the steps. I rose from the stone bench to get a better view. It was the body of an inspector, scarlet cloak draped over scarlet tunic. I couldn't see who it was, or what injury she might have suffered, although she remained quite still. What did this mean? Were Tolla or Brand here to bypass the justiciary and hasten our doom? Or could it be rescue? My heart lifted just a shade, and I allowed myself a glimmer of hope. I saw Boog rise silently to his feet across the chamber.

Another figure appeared on the stairs, this one in a long black cloak that trailed behind it. A large hood obscured my view, but I caught a gleam of gold from the neck as the figure rounded the corner of the stairway. He or she stopped and prodded the fallen inspector with a boot, then stooped to touch the body. I couldn't make out what was going on in the dim torchlight, but it looked as if the cloaked figure pulled something, a weapon perhaps, from the side of the inspector. It turned toward us, and I saw a flicker of light reflecting from a needle or thin blade, which it held up toward us. Threatening? I took a step back from the bars.

The figure approached. I wondered if I should speak, but I couldn't think what to say, so I held my tongue. It strode to a point between our cells. Boog shot me a look, but I shrugged. Whatever it wanted, we were powerless to assist or prevent at this point. Still clutching the weapon, which I could now see was a wicked-looking dart with a long point, it reached with gloved hands up to its hood and drew it back slowly.

I gasped and retreated to the back of my cell. Boog swore softly, although the Blood Mother wasn't likely to be of much help now. The figure, now plainly visible, turned toward me. At the neck rose a dreadful serpent's head, its skin a mass of glittering green and golden scales, the eyes blood-red, cold and glassy, the mouth partly open, fangs outstretched and glistening. I scrabbled at the back wall of the cell as the serpent-man turned toward me. It pressed its terrible head up against on the bars and reached out a hand, beckoning me closer.

I swallowed, fighting down a rising tide of panic, and took a few steps to the bars. The flickering torchlight made the thing even more horrible than you might imagine a serpent-headed abomination to be. As I approached, my feet and my will faltering, it glared at me, impassive and deadly. I envisioned its fangs sunk deep into my neck, its venom spreading through my body.

I stood before it, quivering. Suddenly, it grabbed my tunic, pulled me close, and emitted a terrible sound, half hiss, half cry. I could smell its fetid breath on my cheek.

30

SNAKE EYES

I wailed and pulled away, tripping over the privy bucket and sprawling back into my cell. As I stared back at the reptilian head, cowering behind my upraised arm, I heard a muffled voice, and the head began to rock back and forth. Was it . . . laughing?

"The look on your face," the snake said in a surprisingly high-pitched voice. "If only you could see it." Its scaly lips didn't move with the speech, but who knew how such a creature would talk. It reached around to the back of its neck, and as I watched in growing confusion and diminishing horror, it pulled off its own head.

To reveal Lianna Willis, head evidence clerk, sweaty and smiling. "Great, eh?" she said. "We've had this in deep storage for fifteen years – confiscated from an attendee of a fancy ball who got into a big fight." She held up the dart. "Sleeping poison from a foiled kidnap attempt, still powerful after seven years." She glanced back at the fallen inspector. "Of course, I used a lot, just to be sure. She might not wake up for a while."

"Lia," said Boog. "What are you doing here?"

Lia smiled broadly. "Seeing justice done!"

"But…" said Boog. "You're a clerk. No offense intended, but you don't – didn't – seem like the slip-on-a-snake-disguise-and-poison-folks kind of gal."

"I know!" Lia cried. "This is so much more fun than cataloging the junk you bring back. I should have applied to be a field operative years ago. So exciting!" She produced the cell key from a pocket and inserted it in the lock on my cell.

"Why break us out?" I asked. "It didn't seem like you were involved in our case, or even cared much about us."

"I didn't. I mean, you seemed like decent folks, and you did keep things interesting, what with your blue woman, magical amulets, and all the intrigue. I didn't believe the charges, even after Marron produced the signed confessions."

"Argh," grunted Boog. This was news to me, too. Lia got the door open and I stepped out into freedom. I'd love to see what I'd confessed to, and how well they'd forged my signature.

"Also, Sophie gave me some secret instructions," said Lia proudly, turning to Boog's cell. "When you revealed to me the business with the impounded amulet being signed out, I went to Sophie right away to complain about the improper procedures." Not a surprise, I thought. Despite her recently-acquired taste for derring-do, Lia might still be better suited to her role as head evidence clerk.

She got Boog's cell unlocked and continued. "Sophie laughed, said she knew I'd be by, and gave me this," she said, fishing a small wooden box from under her cloak. "She said that if anything happened to her, I was to go straight to the two of you, no matter what, and give you this, and that I should trust you completely." She beamed.

"What is it?" asked Boog, pushing through the cell door.

Lia looked hurt. "How would I know? She never said I should look at it." She handed me the box. I tried to imagine the chances of my not opening a secret box destined for another, even if ordered not to look inside. They were probably in the neighborhood of my sprouting wings and flying over the city walls.

Boog moved down the passage to the fallen inspector. "I don't know this woman," he said.

"One of Marron's new ones," said Lia, with a sniff of disapproval. "We have to get out of here. It's late, just past first bell, but there are still some people about, and someone will probably pass by the guard post sometime."

"Do you have a plan now? Snake costumes for everybody?" said Boog. My elation at my release dimmed somewhat. What could we do now? We had to leave the city. There was no other option.

"There is a small group of us now, some of the old guard, resisting Marron and his people," said Lia. "Gueran has arranged for transport for you out of the city. The Inspectors at the border can't have been corrupted yet – you'll have to tell them what's happening here. We have to lie low for now, until we can figure out what our options are."

"Be careful," I said. "There's someone here who was reporting to Marron weeks ago, before Marron took over. Brand knew of the blue princess in our storeroom very early on. Someone, or maybe several people, were spying for him." I had a sudden realization. "You... There's so much you don't know. The Faerans . . . Brand . . . Tolla..." I didn't know where to begin.

"Gueran's filled us in," said Lia. "There's no time."

"Hey," said Boog, unhitching the fallen inspector's scabbard and sword from her waist. "What's in the box?"

I'd become distracted. So much for my pride in my great curiosity. I looked down at the box. It was roughly made, with wood hinges and a simple hook and eye holding it closed. I flipped the catch and opened it up. Inside, lying atop a tangled gold chain, was a familiar sight – an amulet, with a full moon partially covering a blazing sun. "Lia..." I said.

"Wow," she replied, looking at the amulet. "May I?" She took it from the box and looked it over. "That's the one I checked in," she said. "I remember the crafting, and the design. And look, it has my inventory mark." She pointed to a small gray 'L' marked in wax pencil on the back.

"What's that paper?" Boog pointed at the open box in my hand.

There was a scrap of parchment in the bottom of the box. I dug it out and unfolded it. It was a receipt, written in a careful script:

Received, for one Replica of Amulet provided, with
moon and sun.
The sum of Three Gold Sovereigns.
Gunther Byson, Jewelsmith.
High Street, Frosthelm.

A lot of things made more sense now. Why Brand and Marron kept asking about the amulet, even though I was sure they had it. I pondered what it all meant, and whether it was worth my torture or Sophie's murder.

Boog was more direct, and a good deal happier, but then again, he hadn't been slapped around by Brand. "Sophie gave them a fake!" he laughed.

31

PULLING THE WOOL

"You really think this was the best Gueran could do?" asked Boog.

I shoved an overly-friendly sheep away from my face. "I don't know, but I'm sure he stopped looking once he found it." Something started chewing on my tunic from behind.

We were three days' ride from Frosthelm. Well, not three days by fiery stallion, muscles rippling with strength, mane and tail fluttering wildly in the breeze. Rather, three days by sheep cart, lurching and bumping through ruts. The only thing fluttering in the breeze was the occasional bit of dislodged fluff and a nasty and nearly corporeal odor of sodden wool, an odor I now imagined soaked deep into my hair, skin and bones, never to depart my person.

After a less-than-graceful exit from headquarters through the kitchen window, and a midnight dash through Frosthelm avoiding patrols, we'd spent the next few hours after our release huddled behind a haystack on the edge of the city, just inside the walls. Our current conveyance had arrived just before dawn, complete with a dour driver, four horses, and twelve black-faced fluffy fellow passengers. We'd wedged ourselves into a small sunken space at the front of the cart, not obvious to a casual inspection, and Lia and the driver had covered us with tools, rope, supplies, and greasy sacks of millet, and then we were off into the weak gloom of morning. I don't think I'd ever been so uncomfortable, but at least my frame was not nearly so big as Boog's. This fact was hard to ignore, as my face was pressed close against his stomach, my arms pinned awkwardly over his legs.

Though the bag of grain covering my head muffled most sounds, it had been clear to me when we had reached the city gates. I couldn't make out many of the words, but I recognized the scrape and clank of metal-shod feet as the guards approached, the guttural tones of our driver's voice, and the terse reply. I imagined at that point all manner of disastrous scenarios for the next few minutes. Perhaps the guards, alerted by Marron or Brand, would search the cart thoroughly, ruining our none-too-clever disguise. Or worse, a sword, plunging, probing, thrust through the pile of agrarian junk covering our bodies. But our luck held – either the report had not yet reached the gate, or the guard was disinterested in a vigorous search of a cart full of ragged sheep, or the Blood Mother's ugliest Daughter shielded us from harm. After a few moments of agonizingly unintelligible discussion, we had rumbled through the gate and away from our home.

A wave of nervous relief had broken over me, but it receded quickly to a profound, crushing despair. Though we still had our lives and our freedom, if one can be considered free while breathing through forty pounds of coarse millet, we'd lost everything else. Our careers were over, our status reduced to escaped murderers, our home city in jeopardy ever more dire, our leader and friend treacherously slain, and our enemies firmly ensconced in positions of power and authority.

These dark thoughts occupied me for many hours, along with an ever more urgent sense of Boog's failings in matters of personal hygiene and a growing respect for the volume and variety of sounds his digestive processes could produce. We could not afford to show our faces anywhere near the city. Marron, who must now know of our escape, might well send riders along all main roads leading out of town. As time flowed by, indistinct and monotonous, I had no idea how far we had gone or what passed us by on the road. I was lost in my brooding, aware only remotely of my own growing hunger and thirst.

That day, and the first night, had been the worst. At last, the cart had jostled to a stop, and the driver uncovered us. I breathed ragged and deep, like a man held too long underwater. The sun had long since set, but even the moon, bright in the starry sky, hurt my eyes after so long in darkness. I had struggled to arise, but I was set in the hidden trough in the cart like a stone in mortar. My muscles, cramped and twitching, refused to obey, and I lay there against Boog's belly, the cold night air bathing my grimy cheek, willing my useless limbs to move. "Wuuurgh," I said, with feeling.

Apparently, Boog had weathered our confinement with somewhat more resilience, for I suddenly found myself launched up and out of the cart. I landed badly, face first, but I was too weak to protest. After a time, I rolled over to see Boog crouching unsteadily on the edge of the cart. I must admit to some small satisfaction when a sheep nudged him sharply from behind, sending him sprawling down at my side.

The drover had chuckled at us and finally helped us to sit up, to drink, and to eat. He had only stale bread, water, and some thick green soup in a leather skin, but I can truthfully say I have never appreciated a meal more. We were in a small clearing, grown tall with weeds and grasses. I knew not how far we were from the road, but it appeared the drover had found us at least some seclusion. Sleep came only fitfully, that night. Whether it was from the cramped privation of our ride, or fear of discovery, or the shambles my life had so quickly become, I knew not.

Now, on the third day, my spirits had recovered a bit, although I knew we were still in several types of danger, both immediate and ongoing. The cart did not move quickly, but we had not seen any signs of pursuit, and Boog and I had been able to ride ever more comfortably as we traveled farther from Frosthelm. There were a few nerve-wracking moments as riders and soldiers approached, but we kept ourselves concealed, and they always passed us by. Perhaps, despite Marron's growing power and his probable rage at our departure, he had been unable to mount a search. Or perhaps, I thought glumly, he was too busy bringing about the return of the undying Faera to worry about such pitifully minor annoyances as us two.

The drover seemed a decent enough fellow. I didn't know how much he was being paid, but he seemed unfazed by the situation, so I thought this might not be his first such transaction. Either that, or a lifetime of sheep tending had shown him the path to true serenity. He didn't say much other than general pleasantries and seemed more comfortable conversing with the sheep than with us, although I suspected he didn't want to know much about our situation. We took the hint and restricted ourselves mostly to topics such as ovine personalities and cart maintenance.

The plan, such a one as we had, was to make it somehow to the border, where we hoped that the Inspectors there, untainted by Marron's influence, might listen to our findings. Not that I had any idea what we could do then – Marron was the Prelate's personal choice to head the Guild, and we were nothing more than escaped murderers. We had a little money that Lia provided, but hardly enough to mount any kind of insurrection, even if we'd known where to begin. At the very least, we could warn these inspectors of Marron's treachery. We owed Sophie that.

"So…" said Boog. "Do you know anyone in Middlemarsh who could help us get farther east, out to the border?" The drover had indicated Middlemarsh was the end of his trip. I'd never been there, but I knew the basics – the largest town east of Frosthelm within the Prelate's domain, perhaps a bit more than a thousand people, with a thriving agricultural market, taverns, inns, several mills, and the like. I think there were normally a couple of inquisitors posted there, although I wasn't up to date with the recent changes in postings caused by the trouble at the border. Regardless, Boog and I didn't want to make ourselves too obvious in Middlemarsh, since it was only a few days' ride from Frosthelm, and we had no way of knowing what news or alerts (or toadies) Marron had sent out. We could hardly walk up to an Inspector and ask if he or she was supposed to kill us on sight.

For that matter, the border wasn't a sure thing, either. Some of the inspectors out there had been there for years or decades – I didn't know their names, much less their attitudes towards Sophie or towards Frosthelm politics. Everyone sent out there recently, in response to the troubles, had held Sophie's trust, though. I knew several of the Inspectors stationed there personally, and I thought (or hoped) that they had no ill impression of me or of Boog. I hoped that presenting ourselves in person, though risky, might actually demonstrate the truth of our tale. If we were truly the vile, treacherous murderers that Marron insinuated us to be, we would have no reason not to fade into the countryside and hide ourselves.

Not that this course of action held no appeal. To travel to a small backwater town, perhaps to open a store, or sell my skills with locks or with language – how simple and enchanting that seemed, compared to the uncertainty and danger that would no doubt accompany us along the much more perilous path we considered. Our training had left us with a number of skills, many of value far beyond investigating crimes and serving the Prelate's interests. Why not wash our hands of this unpleasant situation and of the Guild that had betrayed us?

Sophie, was why. And Marron, and my city bathed in flame, sacrificed to a risen god. And Gueran, damn him anyway, and Lia, and Bernot, and the Augur, and Monique Lenarre, and all those who'd gone to considerable risk to help us. They deserved whatever meager assistance we could muster in return. And Algor, and Tolla, and Brand - they deserved to taste a bit of what they'd been dishing out, although I had no earthly idea how that might come to pass.

And Clarice, who had been in my thoughts a great deal during our ride. With every mile I traveled from Frosthelm, I betrayed my home anew, but it also brought me a mile closer to Clarice. I couldn't know what she'd been through, at the border all this time, or what she might think of us, newly broken out of prison and covered with dirty bits of wool and millet – a sorry state indeed. But at least she knew the beginnings of our story personally, and I felt sure she would vouch for us to the extent she could. Whether she had any stature out there remained to be seen.

The drover cleared his throat, which took several iterations and turned into an alarmingly lengthy and gurgly process. Finally, he spoke. "Middlemarsh. It's not what you're used to, you know." He paused, picking something from under a ragged thumbnail. "Small town. People what live there know everyone and their business. You'll stick out, no question. If you let on you're Inspectors, you'll be the talk of the town. Probably will be anyway."

Boog grimaced. The drover continued. "The one saving grace ye'll have is that there are a goodly number of travelers come through, though not as many this time of year." He looked at both of us for a time. "'f I're you, I'd not be seen together. Together, you stand out like a pig in a skirt. Apart, you'd do better. Especially if word's gotten round, or if there's a reward." He poked at our small fire with a stick. "Might as like part ways there, I'd say. You'd be the safer."

Boog turned to look at me. I hadn't really considered this, although the man made some sense. The idea filled me with dread. I knew I'd rather face whatever lay ahead with someone I could trust, even if it meant some danger. But what if Boog didn't see it that way?

Boog snorted, then turned back to his porridge. "Not an option," he growled. A warm wave of relief passed through me. "But we'll lie low. Any chance to find some horses, or a ride farther east?"

"Horses? Maybe, though you'd need more coin than I think you have. A ride? Not without some trouble, and not without exposing yourselves to questions. There won't be many headed that way in these times."

"Well, we can't stay there long," I said. "We're not far enough from Frosthelm, for one thing, and the longer we wait, the longer Marron has to finish what he's doing."

Boog nodded, then licked his bowl clean. "Agreed. But I guess we'll just have to see what happens when we get there."

"So, no plan?" I asked, dismayed.

"Lighten up, Marty," said Boog, rising to his feet. "Our last plan ended with us imprisoned, convicted, and sentenced to death, only to be saved at the last minute by a giant snake-clerk. This couldn't go much worse."

32

MIDDLEMARSH

No kill! No kill! I signed furiously at Boog, who stood behind the Inspector, his staff raised with both huge arms. Boog looked at me, confused, some of his confusion no doubt related to my painful grimace and flushed face, and the fact that the near-to-being-brained Inspector was bent over, dabbing feebly at my trousers with a wrinkled handkerchief. Some of it also likely derived from my recent blood-chilling shriek, let out moments ago when the Inspector who now inspected my lap had dumped a steaming hot bowl of leek-laden broth squarely onto my privates.

"Dear me, dear me, so sorry," said Inspector Edmund in a quavery voice. "My balance isn't what it was, you know. Well, you certainly know now." He looked up at me, and noticed my raised hand, my fingers stopped in mid-sign. He squinted. "Did I get some on your arm?" Boog, still unnoticed by Edmund, lowered the staff, took a quiet step back, and frowned.

"No," I replied lamely, shaking my hand. "Just, er, hot on my fingers." Edmund stuffed his kerchief back into a pocket in his vest and turned slowly to the right. If Boog stayed where he was, he'd surely be seen. Boog's eyes widened in alarm, and he swung back around toward me, keeping behind Edmund. "Did I leave the door open?" Edmund asked, puzzled. "Thought I closed it." He had, in fact, closed it, but Boog had burst through moments before to save me. Though Boog thought he was saving me from mortal peril rather than hot leek soup.

Edmund hobbled over to the door, shoved it closed, and this time slid the latch bar into its socket. Boog glared at me, then rotated back around, staying to the rear of Edmund as the old man swung back toward me.

The meeting wasn't going well, as must be obvious by now. Nothing had gone well in Middlemarsh so far, at least for me. After bidding farewell to the sheepcart, I'd been hiding and sleeping for nearly a week in a thicket in the woods, while Boog had found warm, soft lodging at a farmstead just outside Middlemarsh. He'd embarked on a new, and I hoped quite temporary, career as a hired farm hand. Boog had been able to bring me some food and news of the town most nights, but we'd agreed that I should stay out of sight at first, and that he stood better chance of finding some kind of unobtrusive employment. The dried mutton given me by the drover was nearly gone, and what was left was so gamey that I didn't feel like risking my guts with any more. My nights in the woods had left me increasingly cold, sore, hungry, bored, and maudlin. I was a city lad through and through, and where some hardier souls than I might have been able to live off the land, I could barely even sleep upon it.

Thus, this plan, which had so far left me with well-boiled thighs and little else. It turned out there was an Inspector in town, Edmund, spoken well of by all, and apparently in the Guild since before the Blood Mother coughed up the world. There had been two Inspectors here up until a year or so before, but Sophie had reassigned the younger one to more pressing duties elsewhere. With my life as a woodland creature growing steadily worse and Boog's position tenable but leading nowhere, we'd agreed that I'd visit this Edmund. It could be that he hadn't heard of our conviction and escape and might help us unawares, or failing that, that if he were as decent a chap as reported, he wouldn't turn us in, and that we might be able to convince him of the truth behind our predicament.

Boog waited hidden outside, and I pledged to cry out at any sign of danger. Edmund had accepted my false tale of reassignment to the border without question and had asked for news from the city. As I pondered what to tell him, thinking "Well, I was convicted of murdering the High Inspector, sentenced to death, and am now fleeing from the law" was probably not my best approach, he rose and ladled a generous bowl of soup from a kettle hung over his small fire. Far too generous, I thought now, in retrospect. Initially, I'd been quite pleased by the prospect of a large hot meal, back when I'd thought I'd be eating it rather than wearing it.

Now, I had no idea what to do. Boog looked daggers at me from behind Edmund. *What now?* His thick fingers wiggled madly. *You elbow. Elbow, elbow, elbow.* Given that the sign for 'elbow' was not so very different from the sign for 'jackass,' I could infer Boog's true meaning.

I could not risk signing back, not with Edmund looking straight at me. I realized I had focused perhaps too pointedly on Boog, as Edmund looked quizzical. I cast my gaze down to my trousers, still dripping with soup, steaming slightly in the cool air. Just the day before, I'd washed them carefully in the river near my hiding place. The prison, the sheep-filled cart, and my stint as a forest hermit had left me filthy and ripe, so it was high time for a bit of laundering. I can now say confidently that there are few experiences so tiresome as huddling cold and wet in one's underthings in a forest for half a day while one's trousers aired out on a bush. And now my sacrifice was for naught. I brushed a bit of leek from my leg.

"It's all right, really, Edmund," I mumbled. "I can wash up later."

Edmund turned suddenly, and Boog flattened himself against a table. "Can I at least get you another bowl?" Boog had knocked a small pitcher in his attempt to stay hidden, and it now rolled a bit on its rounded bottom. I watched in eerie fascination for a moment as it rocked closer to the table's edge.

"No!" I yelled. Edmund looked back at me in alarm, and I wrenched my gaze back to him as Boog scuttled back away from the table. I could hear a series of tiny creaks as the pitcher still wobbled. Who would make such an unsteady vessel? Perhaps it was the work of a child, or a touchy relative, whose work couldn't be thrown away for fear of offense. It looked as though it might have been hollowed out of a gourd of some sort. I invented all manner of silent curses for the unknown rustic craftsman and his vegetable-derived dinnerware. "I mean, no, thanks, that's very kind. Look!" I said, striding gamely toward the window, though I had nothing at all in mind at which to look. As Edmund followed me over, I saw out of the corner of my eye Boog reach a finger out to steady the pitcher, and then retreat to a safer spot. He looked at me with open alarm. I pointed grandly out the window. "What a beautiful view you have," I continued gamely. "Of the back of the mill."

Edmund frowned and looked out of the window. "Well, I suppose it is," he replied. "I hadn't seen much beauty in it before, I confess, but perhaps it does have a . . . homespun charm." He raised a hand to his chin, rubbing his gray beard softly. "You know, I could have sworn I closed that door earlier." He turned back toward the door, and Boog dashed over toward me, keeping behind Edmund. As he ran, his cloak brushed the pitcher again. It teetered, swayed, rolled to the edge of the table, then rocked back toward safety. With all my consciousness, I willed it to continue to roll back, or just to stop, or failing that, to vanish in an inaudible puff of smoke. To my horror, it stopped, then slowly rocked forward, tipping farther and farther over the table's edge.

I could stand it no more. I rushed over and grabbed the thing. "And this . . . fine vessel," I said, holding it up to admire it. "I have never seen its equal. Yes, it's the best gourd pitcher I've ever seen! So clever! And utilitarian. Waste not, want not, I say. Or they say. I think they do. Yes." I set it gingerly down well back from the edge. Boog now crouched behind a chair to my left, I hoped still unnoticed. Edmund looked at me as though he was not sure whether I was merely a few steps beyond eccentric, or perhaps most of the way down the road to raving madman. I could hardly blame him.

He paused a moment, thinking, and shuffled up to me. "You know, Marten," he said, "We're not entirely cut off from the city out here." He gestured with his right hand at a pile of scrolls in the corner. "We get a missive from headquarters every few weeks. Got one just yesterday, in fact."

I tried not to let my face show my unease. "Er, I…" I looked down, and saw that in his left hand, Edmund now held a sharp knife pressed against my belly, pointy end forward. I gasped, and Boog launched himself up from behind his chair, his staff swinging downward in a fearsome arc towards Edmund's blade.

I gritted my teeth for either the crunch or the stab, but neither came. Quick as an adder's strike, Edmund dug the finger and thumb of his outstretched right hand into Boog's neck. Boog's eyes widened, his staff flew from his fingers, and he followed it down, landing with a dull thump face-first on the floor. The breath left his body in a shuddering gasp, and he lay still.

"Perhaps you should sit down now," Edmund said, quite reasonably, gesturing with his knife. I had no choice but to comply.

33

TO HAVE LOVED AND LOST

"You see, I've had some mixed messages from headquarters," said Edmund. I wondered what he meant. Had Gueran or Lia reached him? I couldn't ask, or risk betraying them, and whoever else was working with them.

"Er, mixed?" I asked. "From headquarters?" Very intelligent, I sounded. For a parrot.

"Well, I've known Sophie since she was an apprentice," said Edmund. "Terrible business."

"It wasn't us," I said, my cheeks growing hot. "She was our friend." From the floor, Boog produced a guttural wheeze. I was glad of the support, however expressed.

"Well, that leads me to the mixed messages. I heard of your crime, capture, trial, and conviction." He gestured at the pile of scrolls, then reached over to pick one up. "It all sounded quite grim. And quite hasty, I thought. And then, yesterday, a courier delivered news of your escape, and a warning to be on the lookout for a pair of desperate criminals."

"So," I said, my mouth dry. "That doesn't sound mixed."

"No," he said, "It doesn't. But then there's this." He unrolled the scroll and showed me. I was too far away to read most of the cramped handwriting, but I could see my name and Boog's in big dark letters. I'd have chuckled at the fancy 'Beauregard' under less serious circumstances. There was even a crude sketch of us, thought you couldn't get much more than our relative heights from it. I was sure I wasn't quite as scrawny as depicted, nor had I ever sported such a malevolent expression that I could remember. I could see what Edmund meant about mixed messages, though. Scrawled roughly over the neat black writing, in rust-colored ink that looked much like dried blood, was a single word. LIES.

"They've all got that, at least the ones that mention you two and Sophie." Edmund placed his knife down carefully next to his chair. Still convenient, I noticed, although if he could bring down Boog with two fingers he could probably take me out with merely a few chest hairs. "Would you care to tell me your side of this?"

I pondered. Edmund seemed open to hearing us out, at least, and he had taken no other action against us than drawing his knife, now lowered, and defending himself against Boog. I had no more cards to play. I decided to lay down my hand. But first – "I will. But, my partner, Boog…"

Edmund smiled. "He'll be all right, though he'll probably have a nasty bruise on his neck and some tingling in his extremities for a few days, and he may have bumped something on the way down. I don't get to use that trick much anymore. He should come around in an hour, maybe less – depends on how hard I squeezed. I'm a little rusty."

"Can I, uh, roll him over?" Edmund nodded his assent. I knelt next to Boog, tugged his cloak out from under him, and lifted his shoulder. To little effect, at first, but then I got a better grip and rolled him onto his back. His head hit the ground rather harder than I would like, and he exhaled sharply. His eyes were open and glassy, his mouth open, his tongue hanging out. There was a bit of wood stuck to his tongue, actually. I gingerly brushed it off and pushed his tongue back in his mouth. He gurgled, and his eyes very slowly rolled up to meet mine. I pushed his mouth closed, but it fell open again. I tried to straighten his cloak and dust off his clothing, but I didn't know what the protocol was, not having faced this particular situation before.

"That'll probably do," said Edmund.

"Right," I said, rising. I stepped back to my chair, sat, and related our whole sorry tale to Edmund. I left nearly nothing out, except the identities of my friends and the help they'd provided secretly or overtly on our behalf. And one other thing – I didn't mention the amulet Sophie had left us. If Edmund turned out not to believe us, or to be working for Marron, at least Marron wouldn't know we had the real amulet. Until he pried it from my cold, dead fingers, I thought, the odds of which were probably better than even at this point.

Edmund asked a few questions as I talked, but mostly he sat and listened. When I finished, with my none-too-glorious stay in the woods outside Middlemarsh and our haphazard plan to meet with Edmund, he sat back in his chair and rubbed the knuckles of his right hand with his left, deep in thought. Finally, he spoke.

"Well, I'm inclined to believe you," he said. I fell back in my chair with relief. "For one thing, I've seen how bad a liar you are." From the floor, Boog made an unintelligible wet noise deep in his throat. Edmund continued. "For another, I know the man of whom you speak." He paused. "I believe this of Marron, for I know he's done worse."

"Worse than killing the High Inquisitor and condemning two innocent men? Worse than resurrecting an evil god?" I could not prevent the color rising in my cheeks.

Edmund raised a hand, palm open. "I apologize. I suppose it's a matter of perspective."

I could not resist. "What else has he done? What do you know?"

Edmund looked at me squarely for a bit. "Well. I suppose there's no harm in it." He straightened himself in his chair.

"I am the oldest of twelve children. My parents were merchants in Frosthelm. They had a small shop near the noble district that sold mostly jewelry and fine clothing. Two of my sisters still run that shop now, and one brother, Roland, travels most of the year, bringing them back supplies and exotic goods. The other children, of the ten of us who lived to adulthood, anyway, have found other paths, other stations. But the favorite of the family was always the youngest, my sister Cecile.

"When she was born, I was already in my apprenticeship at the Guild. But I lived mostly at home still, and continued to, even after I became a provisional inspector. It was comfortable, and my parents had come to rely on me for help with the other children. So, I got to see Cecile grow up, into a beautiful girl, into a young woman."

He paused. This departure into his family history was unexpected, but it was far more pleasant than being stabbed, and I was interested in how Marron played into it. Edmund continued. "Often, a youngest child is spoiled, especially in a family so large and prosperous, as we were by the time she came along. And it's not as if we didn't try. She was showered with trinkets, toys, pastries... She was one of those rare people that could show true, genuine delight at receiving a gift, but all of her pleasure came from being cared for by others rather than from whatever bauble she'd been given. In fact, after a few days, we usually saw our gifts in the hands of the other children who lived nearby, usually the children of washerwomen or porters, who would never have had such a prize otherwise. She was such a wonderful girl." His gaze had grown distant, lost in his reverie.

"When she got older, she helped out in the shop, as most of us did from time to time. The shop served mostly the wealthy. Frequently the city nobility would stop by, shopping either for gifts or from vanity. Cecile was perfect. Always kind, always helpful, with a good sense of what people were really after. I don't doubt that a good part of the shop's growth and success at that time came from her working there."

"The shop became something of a status symbol." That meant nearly nothing to me. I had no idea what nobles liked, but I imagined Gueran could tell me how the lofty lived. "Our goods set trends, fashions – business was very good. Most noble families would eventually stop in, sometimes several times a month to see our new wares. That's when Marron came – not Count Marron yet. His mother, the Countess, was still alive. The younger Marron, though, then a boy of perhaps sixteen years, came to the shop, probably as a reluctant companion to his mother. And he met Cecile, and she treated him as she treated everyone, with kindness and charm and a ready laugh. One can hardly blame him for coming to love her – we all did, and she could make anyone feel their best.

"Marron visited the shop regularly, then, throwing his money about, and often bringing Cecile gifts or flowers. I don't think she had it in her to hurt him, although I'm sure she didn't respond to his wooing to any greater extent than courtesy required. And for Marron's part, he had to know it could not have led to anything – his family would never have allowed him to marry a commoner, even one of our somewhat enhanced stature. I don't know if he was after a mere tryst, or a fleeting romance, or if he even knew what he was doing.

"The thing is, Cecile had already lost her heart to another. A quiet lad, who often spent his days by a small fountain outside our shop, reading, or sketching, or writing. Though I'm sure he was shy at first, as he was with everyone, Cecile could coax words from a stone, and she would stop to chat, or share her luncheon. He was a kind and gentle boy, was Trevain. They grew to be very good friends, very close, and they fell in love.

"Though none of us knew it, the lad turned out to be a noble of a minor house. The titled noble, too – his parents had both been taken by a fever when he was ten, and Trevain was their only heir. He did not hold high station, but his mother had been a respected advisor to the Prelate, and his father well-liked. Most, if they thought of him at all, felt pity for him, but he kept well clear of court intrigues and business, and the lack of attention suited him.

"Finally, when Marron had been after Cecile for the better part of a year, Trevain asked my parents for permission to seek Cecile's hand in marriage. Something Marron had never done. They knew her heart and would have agreed even had he not been a noble. She told Marron on his next visit, and he broke several pieces in the shop and stormed out, cursing both her and Trevain. But at least it was over. The courtship was brief. They already loved each other fully and completely. They were married at his small summer estate, with all of our family in attendance, and a happier day I don't think I've ever had, nor ever will, in my life."

Edmund's eyes were moist. I could see that the story must end in tragedy, so it was no surprise. I wondered if this Cecile could really have been as perfect as he said. It didn't matter, I supposed. When people are gone, their memory is all that remains, and hers seemed a bright one. A strong echo of the old man's sorrow rose in my throat. Marron had certainly tried to destroy my life, but he had not destroyed those I loved most.

"They lived, quite happily, for a year," he continued, his voice quiet. "Then, in the middle of one summer's night, Trevain's family home in the city was burned. Both of them died in the fire."

"Was burned?" I said. "It wasn't an accident?"

"No," he replied. "It was no accident. It was made to look like one. It appeared the fire started inside, near where they were sleeping. The whole house burned down to the stonework, so there wasn't much to work with. But I got the Augur to help. We tried many sets of items – burned linens, bricks from the house, spare buttons, ash – it took many days, but I would not give up – it was my sister, and Trevain. The images in the pool finally showed the fire being set, and..." He rubbed his eyes. "...Trevain and Cecile stabbed as they slept."

The pain on Edmund's face was hard to look upon. "Could you tell... who it was? Who did it?" I asked.

"It was a thief – a common criminal. We found him a week later, his throat cut in an alley. The only thing we could get from the pool was a masked man, cutting him down, and only a glimpse of that. And that is where the case stopped."

"But you think – it was Marron, behind it?"

"There was no one else with motive. Trevain had no enemies, and Cecile surely did not. But there's more. Afterward, Marron brought evidence forward that Trevain had been spying for Gortis. Papers, notes, and testimony from some of Marron's lackeys of a meeting with Gortians. Marron had his mother's support in this, as well, though I don't know if the elder Marron really knew what was going on."

"Did you see this evidence?"

"No, I did not. It went directly to the Prelate, but I heard from some who saw it. Sophie did. It was weak. I could probably have disputed it if I'd had a chance. And Trevain had no interest in politics, no need for money – it just didn't fit. But I had no status, and it wasn't Inquisition business. And Trevain had nobody left to speak on his behalf, other than a few friends, none of whom held any weight in the court."

"So what happened?"

"The Prelate revoked Trevain's title and put his lands and estate up for auction. Marron bought them with his mother's coin, and had the homes and buildings razed. To erase the memory of the traitor, he said."

"What did you do?"

"I was full of grief and rage, but I had no evidence to go on."

"So you stayed quiet?" I asked, wondering what I would have done.

"No," he smiled, "I didn't. I kept investigating. I followed Marron around the city for a few months. Eventually, I took to the streets. I put up posters. I shouted in the town square. I got myself thrown in prison. Rather foolish, I fear."

"How is it that you're, er, out, then? And still an Inquisitor?"

"In my investigations, I found two more pieces of evidence. One showed that Trevain was innocent. He was a tireless writer, and he kept a daily journal, which, though damaged, survived the fire. On the day of his supposed meeting with Gortians in Frosthelm, he had been miles away, attending a performance of a troupe of actors and acrobats in Celeni. He had described the performance in great detail in his notes, and I verified it with some who had seen the show."

"But…" I hesitated, curious, but not wanting to offend. "Had he been a spy, could he not have gotten a description from someone else, and falsified the journal?"

"I thought of that. Not because I believed it, but because Marron might have argued it." said Edmund. "He had described his seat in the theater so well that I could actually go to Celeni and collect the chair. I put that at the Augur's pool with some of his belongings, and it showed him clearly at the theater, watching the show."

Interesting. Having been falsely imprisoned by Marron myself, I was not particularly surprised. "What was the second piece of evidence?"

"I tracked down a woman who'd been a companion of the man who set the fire. She was angry at his murder. She still had some coins she'd received from him. I bought one from her and tried it at the Augur's pool with some of his belongings."

"But money doesn't work, usually," I protested.

"It was a jumble, to be sure. But one of the images clearly showed the coin in a room in the Marron house. The Marron coat of arms was painted on the wall, and on one of the guards nearby."

"How did you get this much time with the pool? For a case that was closed?" That was certainly unusual – the pool was normally only used for at most an hour or two a day, and there were always active cases to solve, and paying clients to serve.

"The Augur took pity on me, I think. I was driven – consumed by grief and rage. And I'd been helpful to her before in several cases. I'd learned to use the pool myself, although without much control. So, she didn't have to drain herself – I took on the auguries."

I thought about it. I believed Marron capable of these deeds, to be sure. At this point, I'd believe he ate grilled kittens for lunch. "But that's not enough. Not enough to arrest or convict. Not a noble."

"No, not enough," admitted Edmund. "But it was enough for me. Until they locked me up, I spread enough rumors by shouting accusations in the town square that Marron was becoming the talk of the court, I think."

"How'd you get out?"

"If Marron had his way, I'd have been locked up for a long time, or sent to the mines, or even killed. But the High Inquisitor interceded. Dran, it was then. He pointed out my obvious distress and promised to station me far from the city. I'm not sure what the Prelate believed, or if he even cared much, but I was released and sent to the border, and then to several other posts, and for the last twelve years, here in Middlemarsh."

"And did you let it go, then?"

Edmund looked troubled. "I was in the dungeon for two months. I had time to think. None of what I was doing was going to bring Cecile or Trevain back, and it was putting me and my family at further risk. I didn't have the power to do anything, other than putting a knife in his back. And attempting that would have endangered our family, destroyed our business . . . I had others to consider, others more vulnerable and powerless than I." He looked down at his hands.

I didn't know what to say. I felt great sympathy for Edmund, and respect. I'm not sure I could have swallowed my anger and made such a decision. But I had no one to care for, or to care for me, other than Boog. I might well die unmourned, but at least I was not disappointing or endangering anyone else. I'm not sure what my parents would have made of my arrest, conviction, or condemnation, had they lived. Not the kind of thing that they'd be able to brag to their neighbors about, I thought. Well, one neighbor, Goodwife Frieden would be impressed, and would tell everybody she knew. Probably already had. I supposed every poor visitor to her fruit stall heard about how the little boy she used to know was a murderous traitor. I'd done her proud, if nobody else.

Boog made a breathy noise from the floor. He might have been trying to speak, but all I caught was "Hagooooomfffff." I looked at Edmund, and he waved a hand at Boog in assent. I knelt at the side of my friend. He tried again to speak, but his lips were stiff and rubbery. "Agghaaaaaaah."

Boog squinted hard, and his hand lifted off the ground a fraction of an inch before falling back. I took his hand and wiggled his fingers. After a time, he was able to flex them back, although feebly. I got behind him and hoisted him awkwardly up into a sitting position. He fell forward, bent double over his legs. I grabbed his shoulders and held him upward, rubbing his neck and shoulders. I panicked somewhat when he began to list leftward, but I managed to keep him up. Gradually, his strength returned, and he could hold himself up with clumsy, rubbery arms. "Thah wah noh goob," he mumbled.

Edmund chuckled. "A bit tingly?"

Boog lifted up a hand and rubbed his mouth with limp fingers. "Mah fafe hurpff."

Edmund smiled. "You'll be out of it soon, I'd wager. But it looks like you've got a fat lip."

"Ah sowwee… sorrrry… for da attackkkh…"

"It's all right. You went for the weapon, after all, not me. No hard feelings."

Boog grunted and smacked his lips a few more times. "You have…you have to teach me how to do that." He struggled up into the chair.

Edmund stabbed his fingers towards Boog's chest. "Just like this…" Boog yelped and cringed away as Edmund laughed. "No. Actually, it took me a few months of training to get it down. One of my postings was as a lookout in a tower. A tower overlooking a river ford. A ford that had last been passable over two centuries ago, leading to a country we conquered shortly before that. My partner and I had a great deal of time to pass."

He spent a few minutes showing Boog the basics, and I wandered over to the window. We'd found a friend when we most needed one. But we still had no plan, no prospects, and no apparent future. Marron still held all the cards, and, to nearly everyone we were likely to meet, we were still wanted killers on the run. I pondered this for some time and came up with no more options than I'd seen before.

A flicker of motion caught my eye. Two cloaked figures, a man and a woman, walked up the road, past the mill, toward Edmund's house. Not a problem, except that their cloaks were the crimson red of the Inquisitor's Guild. That was a big problem. I turned back to the other two. "We've got inquisitors on the way," I said, trying to keep my voice low but urgent.

Edmund acted quickly, though not in the way I would have expected. The old man leapt up and ran to the fireplace, where he gave the back wall a mighty kick, sending a shower of sparks up from the small fire. "Er," I said, wondering if his senses had abandoned him.

"Step in!" he hissed. "Quickly!"

"But…" said Boog. "We'll, uh, get burned. Sir."

"No, you idiot," replied Edmund, waving at the spot he'd kicked. A small opening appeared as the stones there swung back into a recess.

I ducked into the fireplace, stepping gingerly to avoid the hot embers. The hole opened into a small space between the rear wall of the house and the exterior wall. To the left was a pile of lumber. To the right, a passageway leading sharply downward into darkness. In the shadows, I could make out sets of rough timbers holding up walls and a ceiling of dense-packed dirt. Boog scooped up his staff and leapt over the flames, pressing me deeper into the gloom. Edmund pulled a small brass candlestick from the mantel, lit it deftly in the fire, and handed it across the flames to Boog. Then he pressed on a stone, and the wall ground back again, rotating into its former position.

We heard a rapping at the main door. As he turned to respond, Edmund hissed through the narrowing crack in the wall. "Follow the tunnel. Meet me by the western bridge at midnight."

34

STREAM OF CONSCIOUSNESS

"You look ridiculous, you know," commented Boog.

"I don't care," I replied.

"You're just going to feel worse afterward. And even then you'll be cold and sticky the rest of the day."

"Again, I don't care. Not a whit. Whatever a whit is."

Boog snorted and urged his horse past me. His undesired advice reached me from a vertical distance of perhaps ten feet, as Boog rode a tall gelding, and I was sitting chest-deep in a moderately fast-flowing part of a river. My pony drank idly nearby, his ears flipping to catch the forest sounds.

There are some who take naturally to the saddle, who develop an instinctual communion between human and steed, who can control their mounts with the faint flexing of a leg, read their thoughts through stirrup and rein, and who consider no day truly well used save those spent atop a horse. These people, I now realized, I detested. My lips and cheeks were chapped and cracking from exposure to the elements. My back and legs ached. I could scarcely walk after I dismounted, and my dismounting itself was little more than the simple application of gravity augmented by gracelessness. After five days riding, I had blisters in places I had not known could become chafed, and my posterior felt like one giant bruised slab of meat, radiating tautness and pain with every rocking nudge of my horse's bony back.

All of which may explain my choice of seating. The cool water, fed by snow, frigid in the winter air, temporarily purged the pain, along with all other sensation, from my legs and backside. Had His Grace Prelate Jeroch of Frosthelm arrived right then, I could have done him no greater favor than to offer him a seat at my side.

Not that I was not thankful for the horses, or at least for the escape they made possible. Edmund had bought them outright, for cash, from a hostler he knew who kept a stable several miles from the edge of Middlemarsh. Though I was no expert in the value or sale of horses, I thought the price nothing less than exorbitant. But Edmund had waved off my protestations, and beyond that, had given us a supply of coin that, in the city, would have lasted me for several months or more. If his family was actually as wealthy as he claimed, then I supposed he could afford it. I was grateful for his generosity.

In addition to the money, I carried a letter from Edmund vouching for us, safely stored in a wax-sealed tube in a saddlebag. If we ever reached the border, perhaps it would keep us from being arrested on sight. Or shot, or cut down, or strung up, or drawn and quartered, or otherwise eviscerated. Edmund had an eye for self-preservation. The letter did not outright say that he had encouraged us in our struggle against (or, perhaps more accurately, our haphazard flight from) Marron, but he did say that he had met us, found us to be honest and commendable, and a credit to the Inquisitor's Guild and to Sophie's memory. Probably not enough to get him arrested, should we be captured, but perhaps enough to give us a chance to tell our story to the Inquisitors at the border.

I had become increasingly aware that I had romanticized the border to an unrealistic degree. I really had little idea what the Inquisitors did there, how they were billeted, what command structure they had, how their duties were assigned and carried out, or even what duties they had. There were several, such as Clarice, with whom I'd worked in the city, and I could count a few as (I hoped) friends, several more as acquaintances. But I didn't even know if they worked together, under a centralized command, or as scouts separated by miles of little-traveled frontier. I wished I had paid more attention back in Frosthelm, but with the challenges of training and our first missions as provisional Inspectors, there had been little time (and, I admit, little interest) in a place and a job that seemed so distant and alien to what we were doing in town.

All this aside, Boog and I agreed we needed to try to act against Marron, or at least to warn others about his plans. If we were committed to this task, our only chance to avoid recapture was to meet up with Inspectors and convince them of the truth of our story. Of the other three branches of the Prelate's court – the Brigade, the City Guard, the Justiciary – none would give a second thought to returning us to Marron as escaped criminals. Even the Inquisitor's Guild was fraught with danger, since some were probably Marron's men, others likely unwilling to believe our somewhat outlandish tale of betrayal, and still others not brave enough to stand against the new High Inquisitor even if they knew the truth.

Boog broke my reverie. "Well, if we're to take a break for you to cool your fragile rear end, maybe you can help me figure something out."

My curiosity was piqued. "What's that?"

Boog stretched in the saddle. He wasn't given to long sentences or flowery diction, but I knew from our friendship that he had an active mind. He often let his thoughts gnaw at a problem, sometimes for weeks at a time, and more than once he'd found a connection or a solution that I'd never have considered.

"Well, I've been thinking about Marron and his plan, and it doesn't all make sense."

"Why not?"

"Everything he's done, that we know of, has been to further his own rise."

"Or to be horrible to people who've crossed him," I added, thinking of Edmund's tale of Trevain and Cecile.

"Right. But this Faeran business doesn't fit."

"Why not?"

"You've read some of the cult teachings, right? And other descriptions of their beliefs?"

I didn't see where he was going, but I had done some research, however rushed. "Yes."

"What's their goal?"

I thought for a moment. "To raise Faera from the underworld, or wherever he currently lives."

"Is there any promise of reward? Of power?"

"Er." I pondered. "Well, some, but it's mostly just the glory of bringing mighty Faera back, ascension to a higher form of being, and a blessed afterlife, that kind of thing."

"Right," said Boog. "The kind of thing a fanatic would go for."

"Yes," I said slowly. "I guess so. It must be convincing, or there wouldn't have been such a following now, or back the last time, a century ago."

"But Marron isn't a fanatic." Boog shifted in his saddle, sitting straighter as he neared his main point. "He's a sadist, a power-hungry criminal, a clever and ruthless player in the intrigues of the court. He's destroyed many lives, but only for a few reasons – personal gain, power, or vengeance."

"I still don't get it," I said.

Boog looked annoyed. "And you're supposed to be the smart one." He looked across the rocky ford to where the dirt track we had been following continued up the hillside, and I followed his gaze. The tall leafy trees of the lowlands were giving way to evergreens as we rose, with the gray limestone of the mountains showing through in the steeper places. Snow covered much of the ground, as we were only two weeks into the new year, but today was unseasonably warm, and some of the snow was melting. In less desperate circumstances, I would have enjoyed the scenery, very different from what I knew.

I thought a bit. "What if he's converted? Become a fanatic?"

Boog grunted. "Maybe. But he seems pretty strong-willed to have fallen so hard for a new religion. Cults like the Faerans, they appeal mostly to the powerless, who've got little to lose, or to the idle, hungry for diversion, but not to the strong. And Marron hasn't changed any of his other behavior – he's still playing the courtly game, amassing power, and hiring thugs, and murdering people, and making life miserable for those who cross him."

"Or maybe he knows something about this Faeran business that we don't – maybe he knows how to channel the power of the god, or maybe there's a specific reward for the one who works hardest or something?" This supposition sounded weak even as I spoke it.

Boog looked at me dourly. "Possible. There's a lot we don't know. But I just don't think he fits as a wild-eyed zealot, and he seems like he'd place his trust more in current, worldly power than in some long-dead prophecy."

"So why the Faerans then? Why the dead princess, the amulet, all that?"

"For that, I think we need to figure out his motivation. You know, like we learned in the second week of lessons at the Inquisitor's School."

My backside was getting a bit too cold, now. I stood, stiff and awkward, and waded toward the stony bank, water raining from my clothes.

Boog watched me waddle ashore and laughed. "Perhaps you should have worn less stretchy trousers." I looked down. The crotch of my woolen leggings now dangled to only a few inches above the top of my boots. I hoisted it up to its normal position, and it immediately sagged back down, still dripping. The leggings hadn't fit well since my attempt at laundry in the woods back in Middlemarsh, but this was definitely worse.

"Fine, laugh all you want." I squeezed my trousers to wring them out and tried with little success to restore them to their original form. "What do you think Marron's motivation is, then?"

"Well, Marty of the Extremely Short Legs, I think his motivation has always been to rise in power in Frosthelm."

"I agree, but he doesn't have much farther to rise, does he? He's already a respected noble, with lands, estate, influence.

Now he's High Inquisitor. I imagine there are a few other courtly titles he could still take over, and he could add more to his holdings. There won't be a new Prelate unless Jeroch dies, and even then he'd have to win the election. It sounded from what Gueran said that he's not universally liked. Or feared."

"Exactly. He has nowhere else to go. He's hit the limit of his birth and wealth."

I chuckled. "Not much of a limit, from where I'm standing. So he's raising a dead god because he's frustrated? Or bored?"

"No, I think he's trying to climb further, beyond his station."

I still didn't see where Boog was headed. "But Faera would end the world, right? And that would cost him everything."

"Right. But suppose he didn't really want to go all the way, but instead merely to threaten it?"

"What?"

"Aside from his family's rank and power, he's accomplished everything he's done through ingratiating himself with those more powerful and threatening those weaker."

"Or destroying them," I added.

"Right." Boog looked at me intensely. "But suppose he could cause the destruction of the world. Wouldn't that make for a really good threat?"

"That's not... But whom would he threaten?"

"The Prelate. I think he wants to be Prelate."

My mind raced. "So, he gets the Prelate to step down, to name him successor or ruler or something, in order to save the world from destruction?"

"Yes."

"That's insane! The Prelate wouldn't do it. And it's an elected position."

"He might step down. And the electors could give in too, and elect Marron."

"Only if they believed Marron would carry out the threat."

"Would you believe Marron if he said he'd do something ruthless and evil?"

I swallowed. "Well, I would, yes, but I'm not the Prelate."

"The Prelate cares about the people of Frosthelm and his lands. Always has. That's why he's committed so fully to this border struggle. It would be far easier to hold back and let the outlying villages be raided. They're not so important."

"But he's also stubborn, and I'm sure feels like he's heir to a line of bold rulers."

"But even the boldest know when to surrender. I don't think he'd be willing to preside over the destruction of everything he loves."

"The nobles – the people wouldn't accept Marron! Not under those circumstances."

"The people don't have to know. They could cover it up. Even if it got out, the people would come around eventually. The people follow the powerful. Marron didn't have much trouble taking over the Guild, did he? And we think of ourselves as independent, capable, all that."

I chewed over what Boog had said. "I don't know... I still think he might have fallen for the cult's teachings. Or maybe he thinks he'll get something important or useful out of freeing Faera, other than ending the world." I gave my distended pants one final, futile tug. "I agree that whatever he's doing, he's doing to increase his own power. I just don't think the Prelate would hand everything over without proof that the Faeran prophecy is real. And beyond that, he'd need proof that Marron could – and would – raise Faera if the Prelate refused. And that seems like a big gamble for Marron, much too big a gamble to be committing the resources he's invested."

Boog frowned. "You might be right. Maybe we're missing something."

I untied my pony from the small tree I'd found earlier. "There is a lot we don't know. The books I read on Faera were fairly contradictory on some major points. Marron probably knows a lot more. Or thinks he does." I stepped in the stirrup and swung my leg up to mount. The pony took a quick step forward, and I spun, flailed, and landed face-first on the ground, my toe still stuck in the stirrup.

Boog guffawed. "Mount and ride, brave sir knight!"

"Spluuh." I wiped trail grit from my mouth. "Very funny." The pony whickered.

35

FROM AFAR

"What are they doing?" Boog asked.

"I can't see," I replied, gingerly shifting a branch of a scrubby plant from my line of sight. "It seems like they're just sitting there."

The two riders in heavy gray cloaks hadn't moved in several minutes, sitting motionless in the saddle, facing not towards us, but west, towards the setting sun. We were perhaps three hundred yards distant atop a small mound. Our horses were tied behind us, hidden in a dry wash, nibbling the withered grass as we crouched in the brush.

"The one on the left is a woman, I think," said Boog. I strained to see. The figure he indicated was small and slender, but that was no guarantee of femininity – I would look as small. Any curves or other features were obscured by the cloak and the distance. As I squinted, the rider's hand raised, pushing back the cloak's heavy hood. The hood fell to the shoulder, revealing pale skin and short-cropped reddish hair, illuminated and tinted golden by the sun's dying colors. No visible facial hair, and a small graceful jaw and neck – Boog might be right about the gender. I felt a twinge of recognition, but nothing more – from this distance, I couldn't place the rider, not that I'd expect to know many people out here. The one on the left was bigger, more substantial – maybe a man, going only by size and physique.

"There's scarlet there, under the outer cloak," muttered Boog. "I think they might be Inspectors."

"Could be," I replied. I did see a hint of bright red, the color of the Guild. That might explain my feeling of familiarity. But they were not like the Inspectors I knew and worked with back at home. These riders were well armed, with swords, bucklers, bows, and quivers visible, strapped to the horses strategically, so as to be ready at hand. They were comfortable on this frontier, their horses disciplined, their stance easy but controlled. If they were Inspectors, what a different life they must lead than those of us mucking about Frosthelm. Riding free, living in the saddle, as armed and deadly as soldiers, facing danger and the unknown daily, while we slept in our beds in the comfort of the Guild Hall and tracked down inept carpet thieves. I felt a flush of jealousy.

"Wait—there are two more." I turned to follow Boog's gaze. There were two more riders approaching from the west, similarly clad and equipped. The woman, if she were one, raised her hand in greeting as the others drew near. The new pair slowed to a stop upon reaching those we'd been observing, and they spoke, but our hiding spot was far too distant for us to hear anything.

After a short conversation, the pair we'd seen originally, the man and woman, spurred their horses and rode west, disappearing after a few minutes behind a small ridge. The others stayed in the same spot, watching the original set depart. Was this a changing of the guard? A reconnaissance? I wasn't sure. We watched for several minutes more.

"Should we show ourselves?" I asked.

"Could be dangerous – we don't know what they think of us," Boog replied. "But we've not had a plan other than 'ride north and find the Guild' since Middlemarsh."

"True." Two weeks earlier, when we'd left Middlemarsh, I'd imagined galloping into a Guild outpost with panache and elan, decrying Marron and proclaiming our innocence. Wishful thinking, since I could barely manage a canter without bouncing about, often biting my tongue or bruising my hindquarters. Now, I wasn't sure what to do. I ran through a list of Mistress

Fennick's maneuvers for surprise engagements in my mind. *Cat Stalks Mouse. Eagle Strike. Three Talons. Break the Branch.* None was appropriate, as we wanted to demonstrate goodwill, not attack them. "We're not even sure they're Inspectors. Maybe we should wait until we're more certain of whom we're surrendering to."

"And certain they won't just fill us with arrows as we approach," grumbled Boog. "This surrender idea sounded better in the sheep cart than it does out here. Hello, what's that?"

One of the riders who remained was standing in the saddle. As we watched, he waved both arms in big circles, as if he were signaling someone or something far away. I looked in the direction he was facing, straining to see something, anything, he might be gesturing toward, but there was nothing there. Then the other rider started doing the same thing, his arms rising and falling in time with his friend.

"Are they...dancing?" I asked. They'd started waving back and forth, side to side, as if celebrating to unheard music.

"They're insane," said Boog. "Raving."

I couldn't disagree. Both of us watched the display, fascinated, as the two riders went through a series of intricate movements lasting several minutes, in what must have been some strange dance or ritual. "What do we do now?" I asked, at length.

"We ahkussst." Boog replied.

"Huh?" I asked. "Ask? Ask who?" Then I heard a dry rattle of breaking brush, and I turned to see Boog lying awkwardly on the ground, seemingly asleep. Behind him was the shorter of the two riders we'd seen before, holding a warding rod, which was already humming faintly again as it gathered power for a second strike. The bigger rider stood behind her, sword drawn, his face impassive. I'd heard nothing of their approach, and I guessed from his prone, twisted position that Boog had not either.

I'd like to be able to say at this point that I fought the two off and defended my helpless friend from these marauders, but that's not how it played out. In fact, before I joined Boog in impotent paralysis, I managed to utter only one small phrase.

Nothing even remotely glorious. Not "Die, you curs!" Not "Taste my blade, rogue." Not "You'll never take me while I still draw breath!" Not even "You shouldn't do that to my friend, you mean, mean lady!"

No, all I managed to say was, "Clarice? What…what are you doing here?" Then she struck me with the rod, and I fell into a bush.

36

A Run for The Border

"Ah, Provisional Inspectors Florin and Crozier," she said. "Newly arrived from Vigsburg."

"No, ma'am," I protested. "We're—"

"Provisional Inspectors Florin and Crozier," Inquisitor Kreune repeated, looking pointedly at me. "Newly arrived from Vigsburg." I felt a sharp elbow in my side as she continued. "Were you, for example, Provisional Inspectors Mingenstern and Eggstrom, newly arrived from Frosthelm, violent murderers, under sentence of death, I would of course have to throw you into a cell and send you back to Frosthelm to meet justice. So, it is lucky, is it not, that you are not such people."

"Er," I replied. "Yes, Inquisitor Kreune. It's just that Boog——er, Inspector Crozier—" The elbow struck again, hard enough for me to gasp.

"You be Crozier," hissed Boog, the owner of the elbow.

"Right, er, Inspector Florin and I," I went on, rubbing my side. "We were hoping to speak to you about the events surrounding the, uh, murder and flight of the provisional inspectors you mentioned. Whom we aren't."

Kreune sat up straighter in her chair and collected a sheet of parchment and a quill. She was an old woman, her hair white, her skin creased and wrinkled, but she was made of steel. If I recalled the Guild history correctly, she'd reached the rank of Inquisitor very young, and rose to lead the entire border operation nearly thirty years ago, well before I'd been born. I'd seen her in Frosthelm once, several years before, on one of her infrequent stops at headquarters, back when I was still an apprentice in training. Her every motion was strong and confident. She wrote furiously, the quill bobbing and tossing. As she wrote, she spoke further. "Those events are of no small interest to me. The murder of the High Inquisitor was a shock to all of us, and the sudden and unusual changes in leadership of the Inquisitor's Guild are still not completely understood to those of us stationed here. Not to mention the documents we've gotten recently from Headquarters, which would seem to demand your instant death, but which also have the word 'Lies' scrawled all over them. And then there's the letter from Edmund of Middlemarsh that we found among your belongings. All very interesting material."

She finished her writing, sprinkled it with grit from a silver shaker, and pushed the sheet across the desk to me. "Unfortunately, there's no time to delve deeper into this at the moment. I received word several days ago that escapees might be headed this way. Apparently they were. In the same message, it said that a team of highly ranked inspectors would be arriving from Frosthelm for a tour of our installations and an inspection of our plans, and more importantly for you, to review our staffing and question its members. These—" she tapped the parchment on which she'd just written — "are orders directing you two to report to our most distant field area immediately, and to relieve the inspectors posted there. It's seven days ride from here, in the middle of an area frequented by raiders, so I doubt the inspectors from the city will want to ride all the way out to where you'll be. There may be some, shall we say, misfiling of paperwork as well. Hopefully, you'll be safe out there while they're here, and once they've gone back home, I'll summon you back, and we can talk further about the issues you raise.

"In the meantime, the fewer people here who know your true identity, the better. I've assigned Inspector Jerreau out there with you. She's taken a particular interest in your case, and she has been riding double or triple patrols every day since we heard you might be headed up this way. She wanted to be among those who found you, if you came." I felt a warmth in my chest. "I gather from her report that you weren't difficult to apprehend." She smirked, and heat rose from my cheeks. "The others she worked with can be trusted to keep quiet."

That was a lot to take in. I didn't know what to say. "Thank you for your kindness, Inquisitor Kreune. You're taking a big risk in this."

"I know it, boy," she replied. "What's been going on in the city strains credulity. But even so, I'd be following orders had I not received a private missive from my friend, the Augur. We went through training together, and I'd trust her with my life. She speaks highly of you, and against some others we'd best not mention."

She pushed her chair back from her desk and rose, her scarlet cloak swelling around her. "Don't think of this as a holiday. You're still Inspectors. I expect you to do the work of those you're replacing. We're short-handed enough as it is." She looked hard at me and Boog in turn.

"We will not let you down, Inquisitor," promised Boog.

"Thank you," I added.

She pointed to the door. "You are dismissed, then. Jerreau is waiting for you." As we turned to leave, she called out, "Don't go killing anyone else, Crozier and Florin, or I'll have your hide."

Clarice met us outside the Inquisitor's office. I had not yet become accustomed to her changed appearance. I'd always known her to have rich red-brown hair and skin nearly the color of cream, but in the time that had passed since her departure from Frosthelm, she'd cut her hair short, and it had lightened to a red-gold from the sun. Her skin was a darker hue, and she'd grown many freckles. Her bearing, too, was changed. She had always been strong and dedicated, but not confrontational, graceful but unobtrusive. Perhaps the only feature I truly recognized was the small silver falcon pendant that still hung below her throat, but even that seemed somehow fiercer, its talons grasping ever more boldly. She stood now with confidence and pride, walked with more of a rider's saunter. She fit in well with these harder, more weathered, seasoned Inspectors. I wondered what other changes her experience out here had wrought – was she still the friend I remembered? Did she recall me as anything other than an old acquaintance? Or had our closeness only ever been a creation of my imagination, or perhaps of my heart?

We'd had little chance to talk since she'd taken us in. Boog and I had not regained mobility until we were nearly to the Guild border office. As we flopped along, limp and mostly insensate, tied to our horses like drunkards or invalids, she apologized for distressing us, but insisted that it was the safest way both for us and for our captors. The stories of our supposed crimes had reached the border, although they'd been disputed at the same time. Rumors flew, and none knew what to believe of us, although she maintained that she knew we could never harm Sophie and believed us completely innocent. I don't think that view was held universally among the Border inspectors, but at least we had an ally in Clarice, and apparently also in Inquisitor Kreune. But for those who distrusted us, or didn't know what to believe, I could see that it would make sense to bring us in incapacitated and disguised with blankets, at least until they discovered our motives and capabilities.

Upon reaching the camp office, Clarice and her partners had taken us to what must have been a holding cell. The room was sparsely furnished and locked from the outside, and we were disarmed, though not restrained. We had remained there for several hours, anxious and bored, although a man came to offer us a simple meal and then brought a basin of steaming water and some towels for our comfort. If it was a prison, at least it was more comfortable than our days spent on the run. And after a long while, they'd taken us to Inquisitor Kreune, whose company we'd just left, apparently free for the time being.

Clarice now looked at us, lips pressed close together, her green eyes inscrutable. I looked back, trying not to stare. I had a thousand questions, but none seemed worthy of being the first asked, and they all collided in a mass of conflicting emotions, weariness, and doubts. Finally, I cast my gaze at the floor, wondering what she must see. Two one-time companions, now convicted and reviled, on the run and on the wrong side of the laws she had sworn to enforce. Dirty, travel-worn vagabonds, with a checkered past and no promise of a future, dependent entirely on the tolerance and indulgence of our betters, bouncing from disaster to disaster. I felt small and worthless.

And then I was held tight in a warm embrace. I felt her skin on my cheek, and a gentle smell I couldn't have described but which I recalled perfectly then from a deep well of memory. "Marten," she said softly. "I'm so glad to see you."

The road, the flight, the fear, and the troubles all dropped away, and in that moment I was as happy as I had ever been. "Me too," I whispered in reply.

After an eternity of seconds, she slipped away and hugged Boog as well. "You too, Boog. I'm glad to see both of you."

Boog leaned down and patted her back, grinning broadly. "You had a funny way of showing it," he chided. "I'm still stiff, and I'm bruised everywhere."

"That was mostly for show, for the others," she said, eyes sparkling. "Besides, it's not my fault you were so easily distracted. You city types are so gullible and soft." She let Boog go and straightened her cloak. "I left your gear at the stable and requisitioned some new clothes. You two were ripe. And also rather hard to fit, says Conrad. But he managed. We should get to the horses. There's quite a ride ahead of us."

37

THE MONTAGE GOES HERE

The weeks that followed were a true pleasure. Though our future was uncertain, we were no longer actively fleeing, and if we were still pursued, we had friends to guard our backs. I was hopelessly bad at what we were assigned to do and discovered new inadequacies every day, but it didn't matter. We were more or less safe, far from our enemies, and able to relax and find our bearings for the first time in many weeks.

And I realized then what I'd only half-admitted to myself before — I was desperately in love with Clarice. She was the same girl I'd known from school. Clever, funny, skilled, curious. And beautiful. I could watch her ride or walk for hours, the shifting of the sun revealing new highlights of her face or eyes, and never grow tired of the sight. When she spoke or laughed it was like sweet music to my ears.

I tried to hide my adoration. I had no hope or expectation that she reciprocated my feelings, nor was I a suitable prospect for her, marked for death as I was. But on several occasions Boog had to poke me out of a reverie, in which I'd created an imagined world where things were different, where we still worked together in Frosthelm, or together at the border, where I wasn't a wanted man, a murderer in the eyes of the state and of the world, where she cared for me as I did for her. Where I knew what to say, and how to hunt and to track, and where I rode like a dashing hero rather than an ungainly child.

But I was happy, and so was Boog, and so was she, I think. We spent our days and some of our nights riding along the desolate stretch of borderland we were assigned, looking for signs of incursion. We saw some – tracks of unshod horses, ashes of campfires, a broken arrow or axe, pillars of smoke on the horizon. We crossed the border on occasion as well, to follow a set of tracks, or to reach a vantage point. The Inspectors previously posted here had left detailed notes and maps of the area, and although it wasn't a hotbed of clan activity, there was enough going on here to warrant our attention. There was a small village loyal to Frosthelm two days' ride from the border, and a few units of the Brigade were stationed there. It was our primary job to give them warning should a raiding party approach and to harry the raiders as best we could.

Without Clarice, we'd have been lost. We were still mostly lost despite her efforts, but she was a marvel. She could track both enemies and game. She could make fires from a stick and a bit of flaxen rope. She could hunt with bows and traps, and she was a superb shot with a bow, something I had known from training with her but not fully appreciated until now. She knew how to find fresh water near the ground's surface and how to dig a latrine. She knew which mushrooms were edible and which poisonous. She could always tell what direction was which, even at night, and she never, ever got lost. I marveled at how much she'd been able to learn in just a few months. Either these skills were not so difficult, or she had taken to the role naturally. I suspected the latter, and as the days passed, and I learned little and erred frequently, my suspicions were confirmed.

I expressed my admiration for her skill one night as we sat by a small fire eating rabbit stew and hard biscuits. "I knew a bit before getting here, you know. I used to ride," she replied, looking into the darkness. "With my uncle, a long time ago. That came back to me, I suppose. I did a lot of target shooting as a girl, behind our house, and I also trained with the bow with Mistress Fennick. Remember when we did *Porcupine's Quills*? I seem to remember winning." She had, indeed. Nobody else was close to her score, with a forest of arrows stuck in the center of her target. "Some of the rest of it I learned from books at the outpost. And I've had good teachers out here."

"The border suits you," I replied, trying to keep the regret from my voice. For it didn't suit me, and I didn't want to think of her out here forever. I loved the city, but if she were here, I'd have a difficult choice. Either a lifetime of bumbling out here in the wilderness, far from taverns, libraries, and the drama of Frosthelm, or a lifetime apart from Clarice. I chided myself. A choice for me? What hubris. As if she'd even be interested in a lifetime with me, anywhere. I'd be lucky even to have the opportunity to choose.

"It doesn't suit me," said Boog. "Give me the crowded streets, food on a plate, that I don't have to kill myself, a mug of ale, and a privy. The city's the place for me."

Clarice laughed. "In the city, there's a standing order to behead you."

Boog grimaced. "All right, except for that minor inconvenience."

We were silent for a time, and then Clarice slid over to her pack. "Marten, do you remember our second year in training, my birthday?"

It was an odd question. "Sure, I guess I do."

"You gave me something then."

I remembered. "The book?"

She opened her pack and pulled it out. "Yes, the book." She held it up and showed Boog. "The Personal Diary of Prelate Darima the First, a transcription by Reginald Grosse."

"What... Why do you have that out here?" I could feel my cheeks warm. I'd had the idea back then that she might like a history book, given her interest in such things. I'd scoured bookshops for something suitable, but the nicer manuscripts were well out of my price range. In my price range were books like the full inventory records of Edgaard the Barrel Maker. Twenty years of records, including the lumber sourcing for each month's barrel staves. In the end, I'd hit upon an opportunity. A noblewoman with an extensive library had died without heir, and I heard a bookseller talking about her estate sale. I'd arrived half an hour before it started, put on my most earnest expression, and asked if I could look at the books. I think the merchant tasked with selling her estate had taken pity on me. Or, she knew nothing of the value of what she had, which might also have been the case. I'd emerged penniless but with the diary in hand.

"She wrote poems about her trials and successes," Clarice said, opening it up and flipping through some pages. "The whole thing is in verse. She ruled through two wars, a serious plague, and near-constant unrest."

Boog snorted. "Great present, Marty. That's some inspiring reading."

"No, you monstrous oaf," said Clarice. She picked a bit of rabbit out of her cup and threw it at him, then licked the stew off her fingers. "It was the nicest thing anyone had ever given me. So thoughtful and personal."

I blushed and looked away. "I'm glad you liked it." I remembered that she'd seemed pleased, but I didn't remember this kind of effusiveness.

"I brought it out here to remind me of the city," she continued. "I do like it out here. It's exciting. I've been able to learn so much about riding and fighting and tactics. And the culture of the clans, which is unusual but fascinating." She looked down at the book. "But I am a city girl at heart. I miss the city, my family, the guild, the markets, the streets, the spice stores…" She tapped the pages in front of her. "And this book, and these beautiful poems, remind me that Frosthelm has survived all kinds of dire challenges, and that a woman of strength and courage helped it through some of them. Even if she failed sometimes. But mostly she didn't, even if her enemies were cruel and evil, and even if the odds were hard." She paused. "That meant a lot to me. More than you know, Marten. And it still does. Especially out here."

The next morning I woke and struggled to rise, stiff, cramped, and cold. A wind had sprung up overnight, blowing in gusts, carrying grit that stung my eyes. Boog snored in peaceful catatonia. Clarice was already up, saddling her horse and stowing our shovel and cooking tools in her pack. Our fire was long dead, and it looked as though Clarice had already buried its remains under a pile of sandy soil.

She turned and looked at me, as I massaged my neck, sore from yet another night on the ground. There was something in her gaze then that I still remember, although I'm not sure I could describe it. It was made up of fondness, gentle humor, goodwill – and I hoped, perhaps some deeper emotion, though I'm still not sure if I saw it, or merely imposed it on her features through mere force of wanting. I stopped rubbing, and we stood, wordless, looking at each other for a measureless time.

"Clarice," I said, my heart beating in my chest like a galleymaster's drum. "I want – I've been meaning, er…" I stammered. "I mean, I've been wanting…"

She smiled. "Yes? What have you been wanting to mean?"

I drew a deep breath. It felt as if I stood on a precipice, and one slip or stumble would send me plummeting into darkness. Was I ready to do this? Should I say it? Far easier to retreat, to step back from the edge, to go on with the possibility of hope rather than to risk a reality of despair. But what if she could care for me, as I did for her? Was it not worth the gamble?

I swallowed and cleared my throat. My mouth felt as dry as the arid soil that surrounded us. "Clarice," I began again.

Suddenly, she gasped. I paused, confused. I hadn't said anything shocking yet. The look on her face shifted to surprise. She opened her mouth and let out a small cough, and I saw a trace of bright red at the corner of her mouth. Her hands rose to her chest, and she scratched weakly at her jerkin. Without warning, she sank to a knee, and as I moved to her, she fell onto her side. A slender wooden shaft with three inches of colorful fletching stuck out from her back. As I knelt by her side and reached for her hand, I heard over the wind the rhythm of approaching hooves.

38

DESPAIR

"No," I said.

"Oh, come on," replied Boog, his hand reaching for my shoulder.

I leaned, as I had for most of the last five days, against the stout logs that barred the entrance to the cave where we were imprisoned. The air here at the front was fresher than in the back of the cave, and I could see a small piece of the night sky framed by the cave's mouth.

"Marten," said Boog. "We might as well do something."

I looked back at him. I imagine I looked like the very incarnation of desolation, because his face softened a bit.

"You don't know that she's dead," he said. "They took us so fast, we didn't even have a chance to check." He had an arrow wound in his left arm, bandaged now.

"She had a hole in her lung, or worse," I replied. "She couldn't even stand, or breathe."

"But she hadn't died yet," Boog persevered.

"She was dying. They took our horses. They left her to die. I left her to die. She couldn't speak. She was miles from anything, injured, bleeding, alone..."

Boog squeezed his lips into a thin line. "You could have woken me up before they got there," he said. "We might..." He trailed off as he saw the rage building in my face. "Er, never mind. Now's not the time for reviewing strategy, I can see that."

I turned back to the cave mouth. Boog continued. "She's a strong girl."

"She was shot in the back and coughing up blood."

"But they left her free."

"They left her because they knew she was going to die, and they had no need for a dead prisoner."

Boog paused, then changed tactics. "There's nothing you could have done."

"I distracted her just before they attacked. She'd have noticed them, if I hadn't been prattling on there like a damned fool."

"You don't know that. They were skilled scouts and double our number. Even if she had noticed them somehow, we'd still be in the same situation."

I snorted. "That's ridiculous." I pushed as hard as I could on the log bars, but they were as sturdy as ever, rewarding my efforts with only a faint creak. "They shot her in the back."

Boog remained silent, at last. He placed his big, meaty hand on my shoulder, and we stood there, looking at the small patch of starry sky.

After a few minutes, Boog spoke again. "I still think it would be good to train. To keep sharp, you know. So we can take any opportunity they give us to escape."

I looked up at his stubbly chin. "Do what you want." I turned back to the mouth of the cave.

"All right then," he said. Suddenly, he dug his fingers sharply into the space between my neck and collarbone. My back and knees went tingly, then limp. I gasped, and he caught me as I sank to the ground. "What do you know, it works!"

I might have cursed Boog, or Edmund, but I was already deep into other, darker thoughts.

39

CAVE INN

Our jailer was a small elderly woman who brought us food and water twice a day. She seemed a decent enough sort. She was slightly hunched over, her back the victim of age or injury, but she walked with vigor and purpose. She had gray hair, short and neatly trimmed, and a tattoo of a deer low down on her neck. Her skin was leathery and creased, which spoke of many days spent outside, but her hands were thin and uncalloused, more like those of an artisan or scholar than of a warrior or laborer. She spoke a fair bit of our language, but she told us little other than her name, Gora, and that we were being held at this camp pending arrival of the chieftain, who would decide what to do with us.

Initially, I asked her if she knew anything of Clarice. She said that she did not, but she promised to ask the others. When she returned later in the day, she said what I feared, that the warriors who'd caught us had left Clarice for dead. They hadn't been willing to kill her outright, for some reason I didn't yet understand, but leaving her to bleed to death was apparently perfectly fine with their moral code. I was still haunted by the vision of her still form, lying where it had fallen, as Boog and I, tied to our horses, were led away at a gallop from our campsite.

Gora seemed somewhat sympathetic to my discomfort. She didn't mock or taunt, and she was respectful as she shared her news. Boog spoke with her more than I, as I was occupied by staring into the black corners of my psyche, but I couldn't help overhearing them in the small space we shared. Gora asked the questions we'd expected – who we were, what our orders were, how many soldiers were stationed nearby, that kind of thing, about which we'd of course kept silent, or told falsehoods. But she also asked many questions that had no apparent strategic value – about our families, our childhoods, about Frosthelm and its customs. She knew the city well enough that she might have visited it at some time in the past, although she didn't say anything too revealing.

We'd been stripped of all our weapons and possessions. The only item I had left, my only secret remaining, was the Faeran amulet, passed on to me from Sophie. One night, while camping with Boog and Clarice, I'd sewn it up behind a thick patch in the interior of my trousers, on the inside of the left knee. On our fourth night in captivity, Gora brought my warding rod to the bars of our cage.

Gora waved the warding rod around and pointed it at me. "I found this in your things," she said. "Where did you get it?"

"Oh, that," said Boog. "It's merely for cooking. A stirring stick."

"Really," said Gora, twisting her mouth to the side. "Then why does it do this?" She smacked the end, and the rod hummed. I was surprised. It normally took a great deal of training, and not a little innate skill, to summon the magical force to get the rod to activate. I'd failed for months before getting it to work, and Boog, like most of the students at our school, had never succeeded at all.

I was filled briefly with thoughts of escape. If Gora didn't know what the rod could do, then perhaps she'd accidentally paralyze herself with it, or leave it where we could get it. I moved closer to the bars. "That's just the enhanced stirring mode," I said, trying to look angelic. "Really gets the stew blended."

"I see," said Gora. "But then, you'd still need to explain this," she said, pointing the rod in our direction. She muttered a few guttural syllables, and the rod lit up like a cold sun, casting a blue light all around the cave. A few more words from Gora, and the rod vibrated more violently, its hum rising in pitch and volume to a screech. Suddenly, it discharged a succession of seven bolts of blue energy, crackling and booming like lightning strikes, into the rocky overhang above. The screech faded, and the rod grew dim. "Your stew stick seems to have many helpful features," said Gora, her face bent into a smirk.

I could only stand silent, my mouth agape, as a cloud of acrid smoke slowly descended from the cave's ceiling. I'd never seen a rod do anything like this. Boog was likewise dumbfounded. I tried to recover my composure, but Gora had already spotted our surprise, and, I'm sure, noted our ignorance. She tucked the rod into her belt. "I'll have to try it on some of the slop our cook brews up." I thought I saw a grin cross her face, but in the dim light, I couldn't be sure.

At that point, despite my sorrow, I was, in a small part of my heart, holding out hope that Clarice would somehow receive help, be rescued, that she'd been playing dead, or something of that nature. Her death was not something I could get my mind around. My heart denied what my eyes had seen. I would probably have been content to go along like that indefinitely, but that was not to be.

The morning of the thirteenth day of our captivity, Gora visited our cave at her customary hour. She brought with her the usual breakfast – a bit of cheese, some dry biscuits, and warm goat's milk. But that was not all that she brought — she carried a large sack with her, and her face looked grim. I stood and approached the bars, and Boog came behind me, placing a large hand on my back.

"I must share this news," she began, "not because I wish to, but because honor demands it, even to an enemy. Were I in your situation, although I would not wish the truth to be as it was, I would nonetheless wish to know it." She breathed deeply. "But I delay." She paused again. "A trader came to our camp today. She brought with her this."

Gora pulled a long piece of cloth from her sack. It was scarlet red, with a brown stain in the middle. An inspector's cloak. "The trader said she'd found it on a corpse, the corpse of a western woman warrior, not far from here. She took what she could find of value and buried her in the sand." She pulled a warding rod from the sack. It looked like hers, but it looked like mine, too. They were all similar. "This, too, was there."

My mind raced, and my throat clamped shut. My chest burned, and my knees went weak. I might have fallen, but Boog slid his arm farther around my shoulder and held me up, holding me close by his side. I still could not believe – would not believe – and my mind raced through one crazy scenario after another, in which she still lived, in which it was not her buried in the sand. But then Gora pulled a final item out of the sack and held it out to me, this time without words. It was a small silver pendant on a chain, a falcon with talons outstretched. One that I'd seen many times before, always around Clarice's neck.

40

My Second Beheading

Utter despair is a strange thing. I realized at that moment that despite all we had gone through – the murder of Sophie, Marron's takeover of the Guild, our death sentences, even our attack and capture by the clans, and Clarice's grievous wound – that I'd never really lost all hope. There had always been a part of me that bore up, that went onward, that persevered, that saw every day that I still drew breath as a day where I could see my lot improved, could fight back against my enemies, could do something, however small, to better my city and the world. But the moment Gora gave us the pendant, that hope, that willingness to believe in a better future, died.

And the strange part of it was that it was liberating. I was a prisoner, but I no longer cared. My city was perhaps doomed by a cult, and it meant nothing to me. My enemies were dishonest, vicious, and evil, and they were winning, but it was of no consequence. Clarice's death left a cold pain in my heart, an injury that I knew would never heal, but the only thing I cared about was vengeance. And, I'll admit, I did not care whether I survived my attempt to gain it.

"I demand the right to face the warrior who killed my friend," I said. "In open combat. Let his blood answer for hers, or let me die for her honor." I stared boldly around the circle of warriors, meeting their gaze. I hoped my being tethered to a pole didn't diminish my ferocity. I didn't know which of them had fired the arrow, but I wanted to make him pay. "Are you all cowards?" I cried.

The chieftain looked at me for a moment, his gaze serious, brooding. Then his face broke into a broad grin, and he burst out laughing. "That's funny," he said, his accent thick, but his words precisely formed. "What do you think we are, a band of savages?"

I stood there, a bit crestfallen. "Uh…"

"You are a prisoner!" he continued. "Maybe dangerous, skilled. Why in the whole of Ganghira's broad domain would I give you arms? And risk one of my best warriors in combat?" He wiped his eyes. "You lost! You are defeated! We get to do what we want with you! Is that not how you do it in the city?"

"Well…" I started. "But—"

"Stop talking," he continued, gesturing with the large hunk of meat he'd been chewing. "Or I'll have you beheaded." He continued gnawing on his food.

I swallowed. I stopped talking. This wasn't going how I'd planned, not at all. Boog had counseled me against my current course of action, but my anger and grief had run too deep.

Stop talking, he'd said, *Or I'll have you beheaded.*

With those words, I realized something. Despair, and the madness it begets, can, like pain or disease, get better. My pointless death wouldn't bring Clarice back. Even if I somehow succeeded in killing her killer, where would I be? Nowhere. She'd urged me, before she left Frosthelm, to hunt down the source of the mystery, and of Marron's ill deeds. I'd serve her better by acting against him, in whatever way remained to me, than in any other way. Plus, I might avoid being beheaded.

So, standing there, a prisoner in a rebel camp, I came to the realization that life could, in fact, go on, something that Boog had been suggesting for days. I had been holding Clarice's pendant as I made my proud challenge, and at that moment, I clutched it tighter. Though I'd been looking for immediate vengeance, it was Marron who'd led to Clarice being sent out here, Marron who'd caused us to flee the city, where we were hidden out on the border with Clarice, Marron who'd so distressed Clarice in ways I didn't yet understand. It was Marron who needed to die. Not be brought to justice, not tried in court, not just suffer humiliation – he needed to die. I retreated a few steps back to Boog's side, but as I did so, I swore to the memory of my friend that I'd do this one thing for her. I hadn't the faintest idea how to accomplish it, but it felt good nonetheless. And I hadn't felt the least bit good in some time.

"That is better," said the chieftain, tossing the remains of his meat to a pair of long-haired dogs nearby. "So, what have we learned from them?"

"Not much, my master," said Gora. "They are inspectors, not regular soldiers. At least one of them has some skill with magic. The little one, I think. The big one is likely a warrior of moderate prowess."

"And what is their mission?" asked the chieftain.

"They will not say," said Gora. "I believe they were scouts, like others of their guild. They do not seem so seasoned as the others we've encountered."

That stung a bit, but it was true. I wondered why they were speaking in our language. It made little sense, unless the group did not share a common tongue for some reason, which seemed unlikely. Or unless they wanted us to know what they were talking about, which seemed much more probable, but I could not come up with a reason why they would. It couldn't be out of politeness.

"Green warriors? Unblooded?" asked the chieftain, picking at some gristle between his teeth.

Gora held up her hands in a placating gesture. "These two, yes. The other, the woman who was slain – she was stronger than these. We've seen her before, but closer to the Prelate's villages."

I gripped Clarice's pendant tighter at this. It was all true, but it still hurt – not that she was better, but that she was gone.

The chieftain thought for a moment, then sat up. "Well, if they won't tell us anything, they have no value. Do you think they'd tell us more under torture? Hot metal? The strop?"

That didn't sound good. I waited for Gora's reply with some trepidation.

"No, my master," she said. I let out my breath, relieved. "I don't think they have much more of value to share. Their mission can't have been too important."

"Well then," said the chieftain. "They're useless. Just another pair of mouths to feed, and unfriendly ones at that." He stood. "Behead them."

I swallowed, and I saw Boog tense, looking around for some way to escape. We were both tethered by our ankles, tied securely to a pole set deep in the hard ground of the camp, with only a few feet of freedom to move. He kicked his leg, but the tether was strong. He moved to the stout pole. It was six inches across. He pulled and strained against it, but it would not come loose. Two of the warriors picked up their axes and came towards us, grinning perhaps a bit more broadly than I would have liked. Boog turned to face them, and I stood at his side, ready to fight. Not that we stood much of a chance against armed men.

From behind us came the voice of Gora. "Wait, my master," she said. "I might have use for them." The two warriors stopped their advance, and looked to their chieftain, as did the rest of us.

"What use?" he growled.

"If they've been trained by the Guild, in the city, I might be able to learn what they know, and of the Guild's capabilities. What we might face, should the war continue. And perhaps the secrets of their magic."

Though her words were welcome, I wasn't sure what she was driving at. Boog knew nearly nothing of magic, and I didn't know much, other than the operation of the warding rods and the Augur's pool. Magic wasn't something the Prelate relied on in war. Wizards were too few, too eccentric, their spells too unpredictable to use on the battlefield. But maybe Gora didn't know this, or wasn't certain of it. But we wouldn't be the best sources for this information, even if we could be convinced to tell what little we knew. Gora already knew more about the warding rods than I. There was something here I was missing, some game Gora was playing that I did not yet understand.

The chieftain rubbed his chin. "You'll take them in? Feed them? Guard them?"

"Yes, my master."

"And share what you learn? Within, perhaps, two cycles of the moon?"

"Yes, my master."

The chieftain looked at us, the same way I had seen customers at a butcher judge cuts of meat. If I had to guess, he found us rather rank and gamey.

"All right, then," he said, at length. "They are your problem for now."

41

THE END OF THE ROAD

As we filed into the courtyard, Gora dismounted and then closed and locked the gate behind us, tucking the key back into a pouch at her belt and removing another. She unlocked the chains binding us to her horse, but only at the horse. Our wrists were still chained together, and she held the long chain like a dog's leash. I would have been angry at the image, but I was too tired. We'd been walking uphill through dry country, bearing packs full of food and other supplies, our wrists bound, for days. I pulled myself closer to the chain to give my hands some slack, and then I fumbled with the clasp of the heavy pack I carried, finally releasing the buckle. The thick leather straps flew free, and the pack slid off my back and hit the ground. I heard an echoing thud behind me as Boog dropped his burden.

I looked around me. We were in a cleft in the side of a mountain, perhaps eighty feet across. At its rear, where the trail ended, was a tall door made of a single solid slab of stone carved with patterns and runes. It must have weighed a thousand pounds. The door was set into the side of the mountain. I could not see how it opened. Above it, as the rock face rose, I could see occasional carvings or stonework, and some windows were set into the cliff face as well. Behind us was a stone wall, probably twelve feet high, with a heavy gate set into it. This wall, plus the two natural rock walls on either side of us and the back face with the door, formed an enclosed courtyard which held a few small structures and a pool of water, probably fed by a spring given its clarity.

I was happy that we seemed to have reached our journey's end, but I wasn't sure what Gora wanted now, or how she would handle the situation. It was pretty obvious that she feared that we would try to escape or overpower her. Those thoughts had been constantly on my mind, and I assume on Boog's, although we'd spoken little on the journey, not wanting to reveal anything to Gora. Not that we would be guaranteed freedom even were we not chained. The little woman was hardly an imposing physical presence, but after seeing what she had done with my warding rod, I wasn't sure that either of us was a match for her, or even both of us combined.

"Come here," she said. Her horse wandered over toward a set of stalls set against the stone wall, and Gora let it go.

"Why?" asked Boog.

"I don't want trouble," said Gora. "And I don't want to cause you further discomfort. I'd like to release you, but I need to prepare something first."

"What? Prepare what?" I asked, rubbing at the dusty edge of my mouth.

"I need to be sure you won't escape," she said. "And tear my arms off, or whatever you've been planning behind those scowls."

Boog sat down, which tugged at the chain connecting us. He glared mutely up at Gora.

"Er," I said. "See. We're not going to, uh—"

As I spoke, Gora sighed and reached under her traveling cloak. "I am sorry. This may be unpleasant." She produced the warding rod and slapped the bottom with her palm. It buzzed to life.

"Wait!" I shouted. Boog struggled to rise. I wondered if I could dodge her blow – I didn't think she'd be very good at swinging the rod at us. The rods were awkward and short, and I hoped she hadn't trained with them as I had. She might not be able to stun both of us before we tackled her, or disarmed her, or whatever we might do with hands chained together. Boog settled into a crouch, wrapping another length of the chain around his wrists. His face glowed an angry red under the pale brown dust caking his cheeks. I decided to look as fierce as I could as well. I'm not sure if I managed to seem any more threatening than a disturbed rabbit, or maybe a case of indigestion, but it's the intent that counts, right?

Gora looked at us, her face guarded, ours full of rage and would-be threat. She sighed. Then, she dropped the other end of the chain onto the warding rod. As the chain curled around the rod, sparks raced down the chain, and Boog and I dropped senseless to the ground.

42

SHOCKING, JUST SHOCKING

Gora's ageworn voice came down the hallway. "Time to get to work. I'll have your luncheon ready in four hours."

And so it was that on the morning of the third day, we roused ourselves from our tiny dormitory room and walked down the hall, bearing our brooms, brushes, and mops. Since recovering from the warding rod out in the courtyard, we'd been forced into cleaning disused chambers in Gora's home. Or whatever this place was. Excavated into the side of a barren mountain deep in barbarian territory, it seemed more like an abandoned ruin than a residence.

Boog surveyed the room as we entered. This one was cluttered with ancient furniture, mostly made of wood, much of it cracked and dried by untold years of neglect, all of it caked with yellow dust. I thought the dust must come from the dry soil outside, which had a similar color. I didn't know how there could be so much of it here, unless the stone door had stood open for many years, admitting the elements. Boog reached up to his neck and dug a finger under his iron collar.

We both wore these collars, placed upon us as we lay splayed, dirty, and insensate in the courtyard on the day of our arrival. In the subsequent days, I had examined Boog's closely, and he mine. They were uncomfortable, as wide as my hand, a half-inch thick, and tight fitting. Each had a single hinge opposite a seemingly simple clasp, but despite our struggles they would not open, yielding neither to Boog's strong hands or my futile attempts at finesse. I suspected they were held together by magic.

This was no particular leap of intuition on my part. The collars seemed to follow the design and function of the warding rods. I had no real reason to think so, but I wondered if they were produced by the same person, long forgotten. The way they functioned seemed to be simple. If we got too close to Gora, within eight feet or so, or if we got too far away, beyond a hundred yards, they discharged and paralyzed us. We'd already experienced their bite, I when I'd strayed too far from Gora while scouting the structure, Boog when he'd walked past Gora's bedchamber on the way to the privy.

"We have to get out of here," Boog said.

"Obviously." We could neither help Frosthelm nor defeat Marron from out here. The problem was the collars. We'd invented countless schemes, and all foundered or fell apart when it came to the collars. We couldn't run away. We couldn't get close enough to hurt Gora. We contemplated hurling something sharp and pointy at her, or setting a trap. If it failed, she might punish us or kill us. If we somehow incapacitated her, we couldn't approach her, and she'd just wake up angry. If we killed her, we would probably be stuck in this place, pacing the area constrained by the collars, until we slowly starved. If we killed her and were somehow able to get a rope around her body, we might be able to escape by dragging her along a safe distance behind us, but that seemed unlikely, unwieldy, and unworkable. And who knew? Maybe the collars killed us when their owner died. Or maybe they snapped open. We knew too little to act, so we waited, frustrated and tense, our anger growing daily.

Boog frowned and dropped his broom. He moved closer to me. Had I angered him?

"What is it?" I took a step back.

"There's a marking on your collar," he said, coming closer. "Faint. I didn't see it before, but there's more light in here."

"Where?"

He touched the side of my collar. "Is there one on mine?"

Sure enough, there was an engraving cut into the metal. It was simple, but carefully done. Flowing lines crossed by a jagged stroke. "Wavy lines, with another one across."

"Yours too."

I ran my finger over the sigil in Boog's collar. "It looks like one of the runes from around the pool." Like one of those set in the tiles around the pool's edge back at the Guild. The scholars who had investigated the pool over the years mostly agreed that a few of the runes represented the four classical natural elements – air, earth, fire, and water. This one resembled the air rune, but it wasn't an exact match.

"What's it mean?" asked Boog.

"How should I know?" I replied, perhaps more sarcastically than I intended.

Boog grinned. "You're the one who scored fifty out of fifty on the languages and scripts exam. I seem to remember you thinking that was a big deal at the time."

I laughed. "I only played it up because I'd done so poorly at the fencing and swordplay trial. Remember, when Gueran scored four touches in twenty seconds?"

"Mistress Fennick said she'd never seen anyone lose so quickly."

"She said my *Tiger Shreds the Reeds* was more like *Kitten Finds Some Yarn*. She suggested I eat with my hands to avoid injuring myself with the cutlery. And she told me to check my tunic for magnets." I studied Boog's collar further. Were the runes mere decoration, or some mark of trade for the maker? Or maybe they were related to how the collars worked.

Boog moved to the doorway and looked out. "It's quiet out there. You should go scouting again."

We'd been assessing the layout of the subterranean structure whenever possible. Reconnaissance fell to me, as I was quieter than Boog. I put my broom down and stepped over to the archway leading back to our room. I peered out into the hall. No sign of Gora. I set off, shifting catlike along the dusty stone tiles. I glided past the spacious kitchen and larder and then down the hall to our cramped quarters. I stole past our room, but then I paused. There were footsteps behind me. I ducked into our small chamber. Holding my breath, I peeked back around the corner. Gora was approaching down the hall, on patrol, or on some errand to the kitchen.

I was torn. Should I try to come up with some story as to why I had returned to the room? The privy was outside, the opposite direction from the room we'd been assigned to clean, so that would clearly be a lie. If I hid, our room was small enough that my collar might trigger just from her walking by.

I heard the creak of a door from down the hall. I risked a peek outside. She was standing in front of the larder, her hand on the door, perhaps pondering our upcoming meal. I seized the moment, and ducked out of the room, heading down the passage the other way. I felt a terrible tension between speed and silence. I was good at sneaking around – it was part of our training, and, unlike my fencing, I'd proved more than competent. But every soft scrape of my shoe on the floor made my lip twitch. I was committed now, though – if I were spotted, no story would excuse my furtive wanderings.

Whether it was training or good luck, I made it to the end of the hall and slid around the corner. I pressed myself against the wall, trying to control my breathing, which threatened to betray my hiding spot. I had not been down this hall before. Boog and I had looked around outside our small room the first night, but we left off exploring the first time Boog fell to the ground twitching from his collar's discharge. Now, I knew Gora was near enough, so there was no danger of going too far.

This hall was similar to the others. The floor was square stone tiles, and the walls cut from the mountainside but ground smooth. There were occasional sconces for lamps or torches, and a few banners and tapestries hung in tatters, their cloth faded, full of frayed holes from age or insects, coated in the same yellow dust we'd been cleaning for the past few days. A few archways yawned darkly along the sides, leading who knew where.

I heard the shuffle of feet from behind me. Gora was on the move again, and it sounded like she was coming my way. The only good thing about her approach was that it gave me freedom to move further away without fear of setting off my collar.

I scuttled down the hall, my hands tracing along the wall to steady myself and help me keep weight off my feet. I glanced through the archways as I went, but the rooms were all small, either dormitories similar to our bedroom, or too filled with clutter and furniture to afford an easy hiding spot far enough from the hallway. If I wanted to let Gora pass, I had to keep far enough from her to avoid falling prey to the collar.

I went through a couple more turns, wishing the hallway would fork or branch, pausing occasionally to listen for Gora. Sometimes I heard what I thought were her steps, but with the echoing of the halls and the beating of my heart, I could not be sure how close she was. I tried to imagine the layout of the passages as I moved. She wouldn't deliberately come within range of Boog, but she didn't know I was here, so she might easily come too close to me, or move too far from me, activating the collar. I didn't want to get too far ahead, or have her turn back, leaving me collapsed and dead to the world in the depths of the structure.

After a final turn, I came up short as the hallway expanded to a wide chamber with a high ceiling. An oil lamp hung above me, and in the flickering light I could see through an archway at the far end of the room. I cautiously approached the opening. This archway, twice as tall as the others I'd passed, opened into an ornate circular chamber. Inside, seven columns sprouted from the floor in a circle, meeting the chamber's ceiling twenty feet above me. Through the columns, I could see a shaft of natural light striking the back wall, admitted through some unseen window high above. The floor was white and black marble, decorated with runes. There was a raised circular dais in the center, inside the circle of columns. The walls and columns were exquisitely crafted from small stone bricks. The air was fresh and cold compared to the musty halls and rooms. Across from where I stood, a trickle of silvery water flowed from some hidden source behind the wall down a groove to a small channel cut into the floor.

But I must admit to not paying much attention to these details. I was distracted by the center of the chamber. There, set into the raised dais, was a pool of liquid, six feet wide and three feet deep, shimmering in the reflected daylight from above, surrounded by seven runes. If I weren't wearing a metal collar and hadn't walked seven days chained behind a horse to get here, I could swear I was back in our Headquarters, waiting for the Augur to finish cracking her knuckles and let me use her pool.

43

WITH A CAPITAL T

As I stood and stared, I noticed a few differences. This pool was seemingly fed by the slow flow of water through the floor channel, while ours could only be filled with great effort and ritual by water prepared by the Augur. The orientation of the small runes and decorations around the chamber seemed slightly different, but I was not sure I could trust my memory of those. The seven main runes, marking the importance of objects, were the same. The room here was slightly smaller, and the opening to the sky also smaller and much higher up. As I gazed upward, I guessed that the opening might be natural rather than shaped by the builders of this place.

My mind was full of questions. Did this pool function like ours did? Or was it merely a decoration, a motif of these forgotten people duplicated many times, something everyone had in their home, down the hall from the hearth? It seemed too carefully crafted to be merely mundane, and the near-perfect duplication of the markings and ornaments around our pool argued for some important purpose, perhaps the same one. Did this society, the ancient builders, have many Augur's Pools? Until this day, I had known of no other pools in the world. Our library made no mention of any, and the many treatises on the pool I'd read treated the pool as unique to Frosthelm. But all those scholars were working long after the pool was built, long after the secrets of its origin had been lost.

There was a noise behind me. A grunt? Sharp needles of panic raced up and down my neck as I spun around. Gora was there, standing back in the antechamber, arms folded across her coarse dark robe, looking right at me. I was caught. I opened my mouth, but I could not think of any adequate words. The shock of finding the pool here was too great. I shut my mouth again.

Gora studied me for a moment. I met her gaze, mustering up what I hoped was an expression of stiff-lipped brave resistance. To be honest, though, I'd have settled for anything that wasn't guilty or bewildered, which were closer to my true feelings.

Gora grunted again, then cleared her throat. "I can't come in if you stand there blocking the way. Unless you enjoy the bite of the collar."

Mutely, I retreated to the back of the room, circling the pool and pressing up against the back wall next to the tiny stream of water. Gora shuffled in, stopping at the edge of the pool. "So, what do you think of this?" she said, waving a hand at the pool and looking at me pointedly.

I considered my answer. I had no idea if she knew of our pool or of its purpose. She was our captor and our enemy, or at least working with our enemy. "It is beautifully made," I replied.

"It surely is." She rubbed her chin. "I'm sure it is not the first one you've seen."

I remained silent.

"Even we benighted savages have heard of the Augur's Pool, now, boy." She raised her arms. "Seeing the past, connecting memories and objects, sometimes predicting the future?" She paused. "Have you used it?"

I didn't want to give her any information, so I maintained my silence.

She sighed. "I had hoped to mend our relationship, get on better footing, before showing you this."

I couldn't help but scoff at that. "The collars aren't really the best way to foster happy companionship." A new pang of sorrow shot through me. "Nor was killing my … friend." I suddenly had trouble finding the right word for Clarice. Friend seemed inadequate, though I'm sure she'd describe me that way. Or have described.

She nodded once. "Fair enough. I regret the collars, but they are for my safety, and to keep you here, as I was ordered. And I am not the one who killed your friend."

"You serve and advise their ruler. You shackle and punish their prisoners. Forgive me if I don't see a lot of distance between you."

"I haven't punished you, ever. I saved your life, you know. You were going to be executed. And Okhot is not their ruler. He's merely a Kanur. A subordinate chieftain."

"Saved my life for what? Slave labor?"

Gora sighed, exasperated. "That was only to get you settled. And this place is dirty. It took me three days just to clean this room. Even as feebly as the two of you are working, you're faster than I am." She waved a hand in the air. "One reason I saved you is to teach me how to use this pool."

Interesting. We had something she wanted. But I decided to let that simmer for a bit. Gora seemed talkative, expansive even. During our captivity, during the long journey, during our meals here, she'd never spoken so readily. In our training, we'd been taught to press our sources when they seemed willing to speak, so I tried digging. "What is this place? This…compound."

She looked at me, calculating. "What do you think it is?"

I saw no harm in answering. "Not your home. Or else you're a terrible housekeeper."

She laughed, a dry, gravelly chuckle. "No, not my home. Sorry for the deception. Or, simplification." She leaned back against the pillar. "A trapper, one of the free riders, followed a herd of mountain goats up here several years ago and discovered this place. It had lain empty for many years, perhaps centuries. When she passed through my village, she visited me and told me of it. She mentioned the pool. I asked her to lead me back here – paid her well to do it. Once we got here, I started rummaging about. I found the pool, and the collars, and a number of old books and writings. But then my food ran short, and shortly after I returned home, Ganghira's cousin was killed, and the fighting started, and I was called to serve my clan."

That was interesting. Gora seemed, as I'd suspected before, to be quite learned, a scholar, even. I needed to reexamine my assumptions about the barbarian clans. Most in Frosthelm thought them to be uncivilized nomads, prone to violence and only occasionally literate, with little culture other than an oral tradition of tribal songs and mysticism.

The other, potentially more important part was about Ganghira. I knew from the Guild's intelligence work that Ganghira was the leader of the barbarian clans, and that she was the one who had pushed for war, uniting the tribes and starting the attacks on the border. I didn't, however, know about her cousin. "What happened to Ganghira's cousin?"

Gora looked at me again, sharply. "She was murdered, tortured, by your countrymen."

That was puzzling. I doubted it was an official act. It didn't sound like something the Prelate would order. Before the fighting, people in Frosthelm barely knew of, much less cared about, the barbarian clans. No one had heard of Ganghira until she became a threat. Even now, the people of Frosthelm saw the clans only as aggressors, the war as an unwanted burden, a reason for higher taxes and food shortages, and for sorrow in families who'd lost a son or daughter in the Brigade during the fighting.

"Are you sure it was people from Frosthelm?"

"She was stolen from her village by people who spoke your language. Her village is high in the mountains – your people never go there, so it was obvious they were foreigners. They killed three men and a woman in her household when they took her. They headed toward the border, toward the flatlands. The clan sent out all its trackers after the attack, and two of them picked up the trail. Two days out of the village, the trackers found the criminals camped by a river. They had strung up Nera, Ganghira's cousin, by her feet, and they were cutting her, over and over, with small blades. She cried out with every cut. One of the trackers was overcome with rage and charged at the attackers. He was killed. The other tracker could only hide and watch Nera die in pain."

An uneasy suspicion began to tickle at my mind. "Did the attackers escape?"

"When they finished killing Nera, they threw her over a horse and rode onward. The tracker followed them, but they moved fast and avoided the villages. She never had a chance to raise a war party to pursue them. They crossed the border and headed toward your city, and she returned to report."

"Was Nera important? I don't see how one murder, no matter how horrible, would be enough to incite war."

Gora smiled, but it was not from humor. "Then you do not know us well." She turned and traced the outline of a brick with her finger. "It was a combination of many factors. Ganghira was ambitious, and she was looking for a way to unite our clans. We lose many lives and resources to foolish squabbles and skirmishes between the clans, and together, we could be far greater than we are." Gora's voice grew stronger, and I sensed some passion building within her. "Though she serves primarily herself and her own power, Ganghira also serves our people. A common enemy, a shared passion for vengeance, can be a powerful tool to build a nation."

Gora turned back to me. "Ganghira also loved her cousin. Nera was young, charismatic, wise. A priestess by birth, one of the Kelar, and better suited to it than most. And she came from a highly-placed family." Gora smirked. "In many ways, she was a perfect martyr."

"What are the Kelar?" I asked.

"The Painted Ones, in your tongue," she said. "According to our lore, the gods choose one child in a thousand to bear their mark and carry their word to the clans. They are always trained as priests or priestesses." She fiddled with the hem of her robe. "If you ask me, though, there is nothing special about them. Just as some are born strong, or fast, or lame, or blind, others are born marked, and it has nothing to do with anything. The Kelar can be just as venal, just as stupid, as any other man or woman. But Nera was not – she was wise, even in her youth, and she felt the joys and pains of others as if they were her own. Her tongue was golden, her voice strong, her face handsome. I was honored to be in her presence."

"You knew her?"

"The Kelar often travel, journeying from village to village, spreading the word of our gods. I first met her in my village, and later, often, at the council of Ganghira. She visited with Ganghira many times. They were cousins, but also close friends. When she was killed, Ganghira was filled with rage and sorrow, but she also saw a chance to use the opportunity that fate, and you flatlanders, had provided her."

My suspicion had grown too strong to ignore. "If I'm wrong, this is going to sound strange. First, was Nera of the Golesh tribe?"

Gora's eyebrows shot up. "Yes, but… how could you know that? They're called the Gotani now, for years."

"And the Kelar, the marking. It's pretty obvious, right?"

Gora chuckled. "Yes, of course. The gods paint them blue as the sky, head to toe."

44

A NEW HOPE

The soup Gora made was excellent, although the biscuits, which had survived seven days on the trail seemingly untouched, were hard and tougher than leather. I suspected they might survive rolling down the mountain or being trampled by horses. I dropped one in my soup, hoping that at least a thin outer layer might become softer than my teeth.

Boog slurped his soup noisily next to me, then he spoke. "So, Marron started the war? Really?"

"It looks that way. But I don't think he meant to."

Boog and I ate in our small room. I had shared the day's events with him. After our discussion by the pool, Gora gave us the rest of the day off. I admitted to Gora that I'd seen Nera's body back in Frosthelm, but I said only that we'd confiscated it from criminals. That seemed to satisfy her curiosity temporarily. I told her I needed some time to think, but that we could talk more later. She seemed to accept that.

"What can we do with this?" Boog asked.

"With what?"

"With this knowledge?"

"Boog. We're enslaved prisoners, captured by an enemy force, deep in enemy territory. The man this implicates is in a position of power in our hometown, where we're murderers still scheduled for beheading."

Boog picked a hard pebble of biscuit from one of his molars. "That's all true, Marty." He pondered the bit of biscuit, then poked it back into his mouth. "But, if we get free, or can convince Gora, we could get word to the Prelate about what's going on, and maybe they could negotiate a peace. Even if Marron doesn't take the fall for it, an apology or an accord might stop the fighting. Ending the war would be good for Frosthelm, even if we're still stuck here."

"Very noble."

"And after that, we can go kill Marron. On our own time."

I poked the biscuit in my bowl with my spoon. It made a metallic clank. "What about the pool?"

"What about it?"

"Gora knows about the pool at the Guild. She said so today. She wants us to teach her to use this one."

Boog ate three more sloppy spoons of soup as he thought. "Do we even know it works?"

"It looked similar."

"Maybe ours does auguries, and this one summons fire demons from the Blood Mother's private menagerie."

"Could be."

"Helping her use it could be helping our enemy in wartime. That's treason."

"The penalty for treason is beheading, to which we are already sentenced. They can't cut it off twice."

Boog looked at me. "Very funny. You know what I mean."

"I know. I don't want to help her or hurt Frosthelm. But if we can use the pool for auguries, there's stuff we could learn, from here."

"What stuff?"

"We're trying to escape, right? Maybe we can learn how the collars work. How they come off, or how they're controlled."

"That's good. What else?"

If this pool functioned the same way, we'd need items to place on the runes. We didn't have many items. I still had the Faeran amulet sewn into my trousers, but the last time we'd used that for an augury, it had killed Novara, nearly killed the Augur, and almost destroyed the pool. "I can't think of anything else. But we might come up with something later."

Boog grunted. "A better idea might be to trade information with her for something we need."

"What? You mean teach her? I thought that was treason."

"If the pool even does auguries, it won't be a great help to them. It's far out of the way, and hard to use. I can't see what relevant military information they'd get from it, even if they could use it reliably. We've nearly never used ours for that kind of thing, have we? And we've had it for centuries."

I thought about that. Boog was right. Our pool was used to solve crimes, to uncover betrayals and intrigues, or to find lost items, but it had very little strategic importance. The glimpses it offered of the future were too rare and too obscure to be of much predictive help. I certainly wouldn't want to launch an attack or risk soldier's lives on a pool vision. If this one worked the same way, we wouldn't be giving up much of any strategic importance. "So, what can we get in return?"

"Our freedom," Boog said, scraping the last drops of the soup from his bowl. "The chance to get home."

"And what do we do when we get home?"

Boog looked at me. "Marty, I know you've been in a bad place for a while now, what with Clarice..." He trailed off. "I hate it too. And I know we're hunted criminals. On the run. And all that beheading stuff." He dropped his bowl on the table, the spoon clanging noisily. He pushed his chair back and stood up. "I'm tired of running. Tired of fleeing, tired of prisons." He tapped his collar. "Tired of being controlled. Tired of the villains winning."

I hadn't heard this tone in Boog's voice before. He had enthusiasm for his work, and for fighting, and for the occasional girl he'd pursued, but now there was real fire behind his words. He went on. "We know Marron means to take over the city, or burn it to the ground, or worse. We know he murdered Sophie, and Edmund's sister. We know he did something really bad to Clarice long ago, and it's probably his fault she was out here to begin with to get killed. He's framed us and done us wrong, and he's hurt or killed the ones we love. And now we know he started this damned war in pursuit of this Faeran stuff you dug up, by brutally murdering a blue lady who sounds pretty terrific. He's got hundreds of lives to answer for."

Boog put both hands, palms down, on the table, and I could see the tension in the muscles in his forearms. "Marron needs to die. And I want to kill him."

There were a hundred reasons to ridicule this plan, and a hundred more why it would never work, why it would be safer just to run off, hide somewhere, make a new life for ourselves. But these reasons were mere doubts, weaknesses, cowardice. Marron had stripped us of everything, and with nothing left to lose, there was nothing else to do. No other option had the least shred of honor to it. It was time to get him. And Tolla and Brand. For Frosthelm, for Sophie, for Clarice.

"Let's do it." I said, my voice strong. "Let's find a way."

45

POOL HOURS

Three objects lay on the first three runes around the pool. A belt, a dagger, and a wooden figurine of a man on a horse. I had none of the blue powder we used on the items back at headquarters, but I was mostly experimenting here anyway. I had never been sure whether the powder had much effect anyway. I pricked my finger and let seven drops fall into the pool. It roiled and bubbled just as ours did.

Gora observed from across the pool, far enough away not to set off our collars, but close enough to see the pool's surface. As the water settled, I began the Arunian chant, surprised that I could recall it as well as I did, though I'd practiced a good deal in the hours before. Almost immediately, the water glowed, and an image appeared of a table covered with tools.

"My father's workbench," Gora cried. "Where these were made!"

I was surprised. I never had this kind of success at our pool at home. As I willed the image's perspective to shift, we saw the interior of a wooden structure, a stone fireplace in one corner blazing away. A small girl entered the scene, and a bearded man placed a hand on her head.

"Papa," Gora said, her voice soft.

The bearded man picked up a small wooden object – the figurine – and handed it to the girl. The girl galloped the little wooden horseman across the edge of the table and looked up at her father in delight.

At this point, the image blurred. I tired quickly, and I was unable to maintain control of the pool. "I'm sorry," I gasped.

Gora looked back at me, her eyes wet. "It is all right. Thank you. I never thought to see him again." She gestured toward the archway leading out. "Rest now. We can try again tomorrow. And you can teach me."

When I returned to our chamber, Boog's face broke into a broad smile.

"What is it?" I said.

"Just something I found while you were in there bleeding and chanting away." His smile grew. "Some of us are trying to escape, you know."

I was too tired for this. "Just tell me, you idiot."

He slid a hand under his mattress and pulled out something dark and metallic. He held it out, still smiling.

"Now that could be useful," I said. He was holding an open metal collar, a perfect match to those around our necks.

"It hurts," I whispered, clutching my stomach, my knees pressed uncomfortably against the stone floor.

"You have to try again," said Boog.

I glared at him and stood again, my legs unsteady. The water of the pool swirled, then cleared. It was the middle of the night, and we'd stolen back here to try again with the spare collar we'd found. It was not going well. Our problem could have come from any of a number of factors – the lack of sunlight, or my fatigue from the earlier augury, or the fact we only had one item on the runes. In four attempts, I'd not produced one image, and now my head swam and my gut hurt.

"What if I stood on a rune?" Boog asked, his voice barely above a whisper.

"Ow." I considered, rubbing my stomach. It was unusual but not unheard of to use a person on the runes. Our pool could sometimes pick up connections between people and objects, but it was rare. Some scholars speculated that people had too many connections to too many things, or that their unpredictable thoughts misdirected the pool. Others thought it was just because they couldn't keep still. Still others speculated that it was the people's clothing and other belongings that drew conflicting and false connections, but experiments with naked subjects hadn't worked appreciably better. Living creatures just didn't work well.

But in this case, we had little to lose. Auguries with one object were almost always unfocused, and so far, it hadn't worked. Having Boog there might show us a connection between his collar and this one, which could be useful. Or it might produce spurious, useless connections, or none at all.

"I think I could try once more," I whispered back. "Stand on the second one. Take off all the clothing you can. And try not to move."

Boog wrinkled his nose, but he complied, stripping down to his collar and a single undergarment. His shoulders loomed large in the gloom, hunched a bit against the cold. He stood very still.

I picked up the bit of steel Boog had sharpened on the stones in our room. With it, I cut my abused finger once more. Blood welled up, sluggish, resenting yet another summons. I squeezed and rubbed, coaxing seven more drops into the pool, and began the chant once more.

The pool bubbled, then settled. In it, I saw a woman in simple dress, perhaps animal skins. She held in her hand a collar, which she placed on a shelf next to others. I was too tired to try to shift the image, but I watched, rapt. She did not look like either a citizen of Frosthelm or of the barbarian clans. She was stocky but well-muscled, her hair nearly white, decorated with colorful feathers dangling among the pale strands.

A moment later, the image shifted, and we saw the courtyard outside. But it was different –bright banners hung from the walls, animals and people bustled about, and the roadway leading up was free from the weeds and rocks we'd stumbled over. The gate and the giant stone door stood open. In the center of the courtyard, a row of ten people knelt, and behind them stood six soldiers with spears, their weapons pointed down at what must have been their captives. One by one, another spearman fit black iron collars on the kneeling figures, and the pool's perspective shifted, unbidden by me, to two of the prisoners in particular. A spearman closed the collars carefully around their necks, and then touched them with a polished black stone he carried. They sparked briefly, and the prisoners winced.

The pool blurred and cleared. Boog broke from his stillness, stretched and then relaxed. "The stone he held. It must control them."

"Mrff," I replied weakly, my face pressed against the cold floor. Strong hands helped me to my feet, and then I lost consciousness.

46

TRUST

"You don't trust me," said Gora. She pushed her bowl away from her and held out her hands, palms up, in a gesture of peace. "Let me work to gain your trust," she said. "By stating an indelicate truth. I do not support this war between our nations, at least not anymore."

"Why not?" I asked.

"The start of the struggle was useful to us, though more for the passion it inspired than the battles we won. Ganghira unified the tribes, something that has not been achieved in a century or more, and she established herself as leader. Most chieftains have sworn fealty to her, and she has set up lines of communication, standards of justice and trade, central authority, and strong military discipline. She is a good leader, and the changes she has made will serve our people well for many generations, if they hold."

She lowered her hands to the table. "Now, though, the war has outlived its usefulness. Our young men and women are dying in battle, not hunting or farming or raising children. It drains us, and you, and benefits neither. We would gain far more from a resumption of trade and a cessation of hostilities than we will by pressing onward."

"What if you win?" I asked. "Could you not plunder our towns and villages?" Boog looked at me as if I were a wart-encrusted toad, perhaps one who had just settled on his favorite pillow. I rolled my eyes at him.

Gora laughed. "We will never win, in any real sense," she said. "We cannot. You are too numerous, too well-trained, too well-supplied. When we fight in small raiding parties, with unpredictable targets and on our own schedule, we do well. We have always been riders and raiders. This suits us. Attacking hardened positions, like your outposts or your camps, would be a fool's gambit. We might succeed once or twice, through surprise or misdirection, but that is no way to win a war. And we could never in a thousand years take Frosthelm."

"Surely Ganghira knows this," said Boog. "Why doesn't she stand down, and parley for peace?"

"Our people often say that once you start a rock rolling down a hill, it is a hard thing to stop it. Our people are not yet tired of war, and our blood has not yet cooled from the murder of Nera. And Ganghira pressed hard for war, with fiery speeches and bold raids. She cannot so easily reverse what she has wrought. Nor does she want to, at least not yet."

"Why are you telling us this?" I asked. "We could inform our leaders, or we could tell Ganghira, and you could, I don't know, be beheaded as a traitor or something."

"I suspect your leaders know most or all of what I told you," said Gora. Then she waved an arm around in a circle. "And I don't see many of them around here for you to tell. As for Ganghira, I've said the same to her, several times, and she's wise enough to have known it even before I told her. I'm more valuable to her alive than dead, regardless."

"Our leaders don't know about the blue woman," grumbled Boog. "At least not the ones who matter."

Gora shot a quick glance at him. Boog pressed his lips together in a frown, realizing he might have said too much. "What do you know of Nera?" said Gora. "It was obvious when we spoke that you knew something." She looked from Boog to me and back.

I thought hard. I could see no strategic value to hiding Nera's fate, or rather, that of her corpse, from Gora. If what Gora said was true, and Nera was their rallying call, nothing I said would make much difference. I doubted I could inflame their passion more, or inspire more raiding than they were already doing. On the other hand, if they knew that she hadn't been taken as an official act of the state, but rather by a scheming criminal like Marron, there might be some basis to lessen the tension and remove heat from the conflict. I looked at Boog, and he shrugged. I pressed forward.

"While investigating a crime, we found a body matching your description of Nera – blue from head to toe, having suffered many cuts. We also found the criminals responsible for her abduction. Two of them were killed, and three escaped." I decided to let Gora believe we killed them if she were so inclined, and thus I left out the part about their being reduced to piles of orange powder while we cowered in the shadows. "The man who hired them also survived."

Gora studied my face, her eyes bright and sharp. "Criminals? Do you still have her body?"

"We brought it — her, that is, back to our headquarters, but, uh…" I trailed off, wondering how to tackle the next part. I hadn't thought this out very well at all, I realized.

"We left for the border shortly after this," said Boog, looking at me carefully. "We don't know who has the body now."

"It wouldn't still be at your headquarters?" asked Gora.

Boog looked at me, now. I swallowed again. "There were a number of irregularities surrounding those events," I began, lamely. "Our, uh, departure was abrupt."

Gora stood, and took a step toward us, then stopped, perhaps remembering the collars. She was clearly agitated. Her wrinkled chin quivered and swayed as she formed her words. "If we had her body back, that could end the fighting," she said. "That would be a powerful symbol. Ganghira could use it, tout it." She looked at us, then pointed. "Can you get her back? Talk to your leaders? I could get Okhot to release you for that."

Our leaders would most assuredly throw us into jail and execute us if we tried talking to them. Beyond that, I had no idea where the tortured blue woman was. I was certain Marron would have taken her from Headquarters immediately upon taking control of the Guild. So, even if we got back to Frosthelm without being arrested, we'd still have to find the body, which would probably mean breaking into Marron's home, or his Faeran temple, or secret lair, or whatever he had, plus killing him and defeating all of his guards. Including Tolla, who was far better with a sword than either of us, and Brand, who could turn people into powder with the flick of a wrist, all while avoiding the City Guard and the Inquisitors and trying to keep our heads attached to our necks. It was laughably impossible.

"Of course we can," answered Boog, his confidence palpable. "When can we go?"

47

OFF A GLYPH

Getting to leave was not quite so easy as that. Gora was still bent on us training her to use the pool. Boog and I were desperate to escape, so the endless auguries grated on us. But, helping Gora understand the pool also helped me. As I conducted more auguries, mostly simple trials with sets of mundane objects, my stamina increased, and my ability to control the pool grew. This pool seemed much easier to control than ours back in Frosthelm. Either that, or I had become much, much better at it, but I'd have bet good money on the pool being the difference. I wondered if it had to do with the location, or the craftsmanship, or perhaps the water trickling in from the wall. Upon further inspection, I noticed a tiny drain hole in the bottom of the basin, a feature our pool lacked, and I surmised that this was why it never overflowed. Beyond that, its construction was a mystery. It was somehow cleaner, hardier, stronger than our pool, which required such delicate care and management.

I also learned from Gora. I was not sure how or where she had studied, but she had a wealth of information unknown to our scholars and unmentioned in our libraries. She was quite willing to share her knowledge with me. Perhaps she thought it would motivate me to help her, or perhaps she was just a natural teacher, happiest when discussing obscure facts and teaching forgotten lore. Despite her vast knowledge and the skill she'd demonstrated with the warding rods, she did not take naturally to manipulating the pool. It took her several days of work just to get the pool to respond to her at all. At first, her blood didn't make the water bubble, and the pool barely stirred as she recited the chant. Even so, the experience drained her, and whether it was her age that weakened her or that the pool taxed her more than it did me, I didn't know and couldn't tell.

Gora told me that the chant, which I thought to be in the ancient Arunian tongue, was likely not Arunian in origin. The Arunians were apparently great cataloguers of knowledge, great librarians, great researchers, but most of the knowledge of magic we gained from their records actually predated their culture. The chant, Gora said, was written in Arunian characters, but the syllables were nonsense in their language. The Arunians had apparently merely transcribed something from an older tongue, being careful to preserve the words and sounds, but not their meaning. I wondered what the chant meant – was I summoning the power of some forgotten god, or promising my soul to a demon in exchange for using the pool's power? Or was it merely a disclaimer? "I agree not to hold the owners of this pool liable for any injury I may cause or incur during its use." I had no idea.

The runes around the pool, too, were of interest to Gora. The Augur taught that some represented the traditional elements – air, earth, fire, water – and that the others were just mysterious, their meaning lost. Gora decreed the whole concept of the four elements, supported and expounded upon at length by numerous Frosthelm scholars, to be, in her scholarly estimation, "goat turd."

"These four elements of yours have no meaning," she said, resting against a column across the pool from me. I could tell a lecture was coming on. "You flatlanders see them as four substances that make up all things. But they are not all substances. Air and water are simple fluids, just with different compositions. And yet when you say 'air,' you also mean to invoke wind, and weather, and thunder, all of which are completely different forces and processes that merely take place in the air. Fire is not a substance at all, but instead an energy –

heat, light, and change. Nothing can be made of fire, the way things are made of water, or stone, or air. This is foolish – you fail to understand the nature of what you discuss, and your very framing of it creates false equivalences and misunderstanding."

"And how do you know what we flatlanders think?"

"I spent six years studying in Frosthelm, didn't I?" As I'd suspected. So this was how she knew our city and its ways. I wondered where she'd lived, with whom she'd worked.

Gora waved a finger in the air, and I was reminded of Master Tolson, always one to get on a rant, although Tolson was discussing the law and philosophy, not magic and science. "The Arunians, or more correctly, those whose knowledge they stole, were wiser than you." She pointed at the runes beneath my knees, as I lounged against a column. "Those, on that side," she said. "There are far more than four, aren't there? And what do they have in common? They are all forces of destruction. Fire, there. Weather. Death. Decay." She pointed at the runes in turn, and her names for them were usually different from ours.

She continued. "Earthquakes. Violence. Anger. Freezing. Deceit. All of them, destructive forces. And these, over here?" She thrust her hands out, her fingers spread, pointing at the runes beneath her. "All forces or aspects of order, tranquility or growth. Life. Tides. Crystals. Gravity. Growth. Justice. The Moon. Seasons. Silence. Forest. Time. There are many runes, but there are only two fundamental forces. Order, and chaos. Building, and destroying. All the runes are just aspects of these two basic tenets."

I saw an opportunity. "What's this one, then," I said, pointing to a rune with flowing lines crossed by a jagged stroke. It wasn't a perfect match for the rune on our collars, but it was close. There might be some artistic license with these things, much as handwriting might differ from person to person.

"Which side is it on?" she said.

I thought. "It's close to the middle."

"Correct," she replied, seeming satisfied. "So, what does that mean?"

"It's neither chaos or order? Or is it both? We call that one air."

"Yes, but we have already established that you are idiots," she said, running her fingers through her short hair. "It is lightning, or more properly the energy behind lightning."

"Isn't lightning destructive? It causes death, and fires."

"But that is only when it is at its most powerful, most uncontrolled," she replied. "It is not always so. It arises from order," she continued, "and behaves in an ordered way. If you walk on cloth mats on a cold day, or rub a glass rod with a bit of fur, you store up energy, which then seeks discharge in an object you touch, or into the ground. A well-ordered process. The same happens to clouds. They build up energy and must discharge, either to other clouds or to the ground. The discharge can be chaotic, but the conditions and the flow are ordered and predictable. So, it shares aspects of both order and chaos."

"You were able to make my rod spark," I said. "Is that the same energy?"

"It was," she said. "That was the aspect of chaos within the lightning. Can you not do that? Or do you really just stir stew with it?" She grinned.

"I haven't shot lightning out of it. It can absorb energy directed at me," I said. "We call them warding rods, for that. And it can stun or paralyze people if I activate it properly."

"Absorbing energy is an aspect of order – free energy is dangerous, destructive. Absorbing it, such as the ground does a lightning bolt, restores order. The paralyzing effect is similar. You bring a person in motion, a person acting, to rest, exerting control, producing order. When you stun someone, the rod discharges the same kind of energy as lightning, but controlled, not deadly. This overwhelms the muscles and the mind, bringing your enemy to rest."

"Where does the rod get this energy?"

"From the person using it," said Gora. "In each of us, there is the energy of life, and of creativity, and of love — all of which reflect order. There is also the energy of anger, of passion, of violence – forces which promote chaos. The Arunians, and those who came before, fashioned many objects that harness the power within us, that amplify it."

"Can anyone use these things?"

"Some are far better suited to them than others. Like art, or carpentry, or music, or writing, or politics, some of it is innate, and some of it is learned. But the devices are rare, and their use often lost to history, so it is not very common that even someone with great potential will have an object and be trained in its use. You are lucky to have the rods. Or stew sticks."

A thought occurred to me. "The pool, here. Is it one of these objects? That focuses power?"

"Ah, you're not such a wretched flatlander ignoramus after all," she said. "Of course it is."

"Is it order, or chaos? What aspect?"

"You tell me," she said, folding her arms in a rather pompous manner.

I thought some more. "The main thing it does is draw connections, between objects." That didn't help me.

"And what does it show?"

"That depends," I replied. "Usually, it shows times when the objects were together, or events where they were connected somehow."

"So, what is it showing you?"

"Connections, I guess. In the past."

"Always in the past?"

"No, sometimes in the future," I said, thinking of the dire prediction about Frosthelm. "And sometimes the connections aren't clear at all."

"So what does this all have in common?" She looked smug.

"Uh," I said. "Connections."

Gora gave me a withering glare, as if I were a stain she'd just discovered on her favorite dress. "Connections when?"

"All different times," I said.

"And?"

"Connections at different times," I mumbled, thinking. "Is it, history? Or, time?"

"Yes!" she cried, slapping her knee. "Time. And is that a force for order, or for chaos?"

I sat silently.

"Well?" Gora demanded.

"I'm new at this, all right?" I squinted my eyes. "Time doesn't really create or destroy things. But it flows one way, at one speed, always. And it can't be reversed or altered."

"So?"

"So that sounds like a very orderly process," I guessed.

She nodded. "There are many fundamental laws that govern our world, our universe. All represent order. Time, and its flow, are one such aspect of order."

This got me thinking. "What about a wand, a device, that could kill someone. Maybe by breaking them down into dust?"

"What do you think?" Her questions were getting annoying.

"Well, that's got to be destruction, or chaos, right?"

"Of course."

"And the person who wanted to use this thing, he, or she, would have to summon chaos from inside? Or anger, or wrath, or something?"

"That's how I'd do it," she said.

"Is that how you got the rod to make the sparks?"

"Yes. I confess, I'd heard of the rods before, and studied them a bit during my time in Frosthelm, so I knew a little of how they work."

"Why can't I do that, then?"

"It's possible you haven't tried properly," she said. "Or, it could be that you are more skilled in summoning order, summoning life from inside yourself. You seem to take to those aspects more. You can use the rod by following aspects of order, and you're much better with the pool than I am. And you're a terrible liar. Maybe you just don't have enough chaos inside yourself."

I couldn't tell if she was joking. All of this was new and hard to understand. If Gora was right, it made a lot of the magical devices – the rods, the pool, Brand's wand —make more sense.

Brand likely had no trouble summoning destructive energy from within himself. I'd seen his anger on display, in magical and non-magical form.

And the collars. They were at the in-between point, along with the rods. They showed order, in that they stunned their wearers into stillness, but perhaps chaos, also, in that they caused pain, and were used with malice. But they kept people under control and in line, which was certainly orderly. I was sure I didn't understand completely.

"So what makes you so able to summon chaos?" I said.

Gora grew still. "I would rather not discuss that," she said quietly. "A flaw in my character, perhaps. Or a lifetime of experience." She stood again. "It does not seem to be helping me use the pool, though. I could use some more control, some more order. Shall we try again? Show me one more time."

I stood back while she placed some objects on the main numbered runes. Today it was kitchen items. A bowl, a spoon, a pot, a knife. The connections should be clear and obvious, the pool easy to direct. As I stood, I felt the lump at my knee, in my trousers where the amulet lay hidden. My mind shot back to the pool back in Frosthelm, and the trouble I'd had finding the northern corner suggested by the Augur. I glanced down at the tiles, and there, at the top corner of the diamond pattern of runes, was the sun and moon, the match of that one so far away in the Guild Hall. It lay along the middle of the pattern, between the sides Gora had marked as order and chaos. I remembered once thinking that the sun and moon might mean Death, because the rune opposite it was one we thought meant Life. I looked at that Life rune now, a curving line ending in radiating spokes, like a flower, or dandelion gone to seed. But that rune must mean something else entirely, because Gora had pointed out Life far over on the side for aspects of order.

"What's this one?" I asked, pointing at the flower rune.

"Destiny," Gora said. "A single path leads to many branching ones."

"And it's in the middle? Between order and chaos?"

"Your destiny could be good or bad, constructive or destructive."

"But it always ends in death, right?"

Gora turned to me. "A destiny, a life, is much more than its end, is it not? I would hope you had more ambition, or at least a less depressing view of the world. You are young. There is still time for you to build new wonders, or to destroy your foes."

I pointed to the rune with the sun and moon, the match to the amulet that I carried, that so many had already died for. "What's this one, then?"

"Ah, that one is harder to figure. In Arunian texts, they describe its name as 'fae-rah', but like your chant, that word has no known meaning in Arunian. Either the meaning has been lost, or it is once again a word of an earlier language, the sound of which is preserved in Arunian script." She placed a wooden spoon on the fourth rune around the pool. "I read a few books once on these Arunian runes. The best explanation I found for that one was Fusion, or Unity."

"Unity of what?"

"Of order and chaos, together, I believe. These two forces are opposite. They are frequently in competition, in nature, where things both grow and die, and in humans, who rage and war but also love and nurture. The sun is pure energy – a raging ball of fire — while the moon is cool and serene, settled in its orbit and regular as a clock. But the sun fosters growth, and the moon disturbs the sea with tides, which are regular in timing but can destroy. I do not think the joining is meant to be literal. They are just symbols, in this case, of order and chaos combined."

Gora waved a finger, the lecturer once again. "In terms of using magical power, or magical devices, it is the hardest thing to use these forces together. When the aspects of order act upon an aspect of chaos, it resists, often violently. Many times, there are unpredictable results, often explosive and deadly as chaos and destruction break free of their confines. The surest way to ruin, as a wizard, is to try to bind aspects of chaos with aspects of order."

As she spoke, I thought of Novara. I had sought her out with the help of the pool, and she had surely been slain by a magical explosion or discharge. I could still remember the sun and moon mark scorched into her chest. And her back, and the floor beneath her. She was certainly a powerful user of magic — she had transported herself from the tavern with ease. "What kind of magic would it take to move someone from place to place?"

"You mean, instantly? Or flying, or…"

"Instantly."

"That would have to be chaos," she said, not making me guess, for once. "It violates the principles and laws governing time, speed, and distance. You would have to weaken or ignore at least one of the three, and to do so, you would need to harness the power of disorder, of impossibility. You have seen someone do this?"

"Yes," I replied. I thought about Novara's death. All kinds of forces were in the mix then – Novara's teleportation, the pool, the amulet from Stennis – all of it must have combined to destroy Novara through the pool. This must have been what happened to Stennis, too – he had the amulet, and he blew up after Novara cast a spell on it. I remembered the sparks dancing from it, and the screaming noise. Novara must have invoked a combination of order and chaos, centered on the amulet.

"Can order win?" I asked. "If it's stronger?"

"If strong enough, and applied correctly, it could dominate, and eliminate the effects of chaos. Your warding rods do this, when they absorb magic power. But absorbing power is different from controlling it. When order and chaos aspects meet in conflict, the results are usually terrible and unpredictable."

"This Unity or Fusion symbol – what does it mean?"

"I don't know. There wasn't much written about it in what I read." By the look in her eyes, I knew she was on to me. "Why all this interest?"

"There's a group, active in my city. Long ago, and again today. They call themselves the Faerans, and they use this symbol."

"The same ones who took Nera?"

I didn't see any harm in answering. "Yes."

"Why would they kill her? She was nothing to them, unknown to them."

"They were following a prophecy, or a recipe for a prophecy, or something. My source…" I thought of Madame Lenarre and the afternoon I'd spent with her long ago. "My research indicates that they think of Faera as a being of some sort, and they're trying to raise it, or birth it, or something. Nera was supposed to be part of the ritual."

"The prophecy said, 'Go find Nera, and hang her from a tree, and cut her a lot?'"

"No, there was a ceremony, that required a ritually sacrificed princess of the Golesh tribe. And some other objects – the Eye of Hrogar – that's a gemstone – a mace, a crown. And the Fingernails of the Holy Hermit."

Gora looked at me, her brow furrowed. "Fingernails?"

"Look, I don't write the prophecies. Or prophesy them, or whatever."

"They mean to do this soon?"

"There's an eclipse coming in a little over two months. It's supposed to happen then."

"Most unusual," said Gora. A dish hung loosely in her grip. The augury was forgotten for the moment. "Most." She paced around the pool, and I had to circle opposite her to prevent the collar from activating. Finally, she looked at me, calculating. "I've never read of the symbol representing a being, but I have not read much about it."

"Where is it you're doing all this reading?" I tried again.

Gora smiled. "I have been traveling the world since before your parents were born, I wager. I've studied in Frosthelm, in Gortis, in Calenda. I even spent ten years wandering in the Serpent Kingdoms, although precious few of the people there care anything about their history, or anything else that might be useful. And the clans have a few libraries. I know we seem like rustics, like barbarians, but we have a scholarly tradition that goes back long years. There are many Arunian ruins in the mountains here, if you know where to look, and we've made good use of what we find."

The Serpent Kingdoms were far across the sea. I'd only seen two people from there in my life, and Frosthelm was a fairly cosmopolitan place. Calenda was likewise so remote, far to the south, that I knew nobody who'd ever been. "So, is this place Arunian?"

"I do not think so. But they likely used it. I think the collars are their design, and I found them here. But I think the pools would have been beyond them. The chant you taught me is not Arunian, and the runes set in the floor, though used by Arunians, were from an earlier time." She stopped pacing. "But you distract me. Surely your leaders, your Prelate, will not allow these Faerans to complete their ceremony? Especially now that they know about it, and have Nera?"

I sighed. "It's not that simple," I said. "Some of our nobles are Faerans, and they have the Prelate's ear. They've taken control of the Inquisitors, of many of our government offices. They got Nera back."

"Is the Prelate one of the Faerans?"

"I don't know. I hope not, but it may not matter." Not with Marron pulling all of the strings.

Gora resumed her pacing. "Were you sent away from Frosthelm? Because you caused trouble? By investigating this?"

'Sent away' really failed to describe the process, but I didn't want to get into it. "More or less."

Gora was silent for a bit more. "The eclipse – it is a rare one?"

"I gather they are very infrequent over Frosthelm. The scholar I spoke with said the moon would cover the sun."

"The Unity rune is a combination of aspects of order and chaos, a balance. If the eclipse changes the balance of these aspects, even by a little, the results could be unpredictable. Sunlight is a powerful aspect of growth, of life. If it is blocked…"

"The sun goes down every night, and no gods come springing up out of the ground. You're speculating here, aren't you?" I was too new to this idea of order and chaos to follow all of what she said, but I did have extensive experience watching people make things up on the fly.

Gora smiled. "Yes. Perhaps they just use the eclipse so everyone knows when to get together, kill the Painted Ones, and pull fingernails off kindly old hermits. It doesn't matter, really. The eclipse will happen whether you want it to or not. What matters is whether the prophecy is true, and if it is, whether they're able to complete the ritual."

"Our pool says they can." I remembered the image of Frosthelm in flames. "It showed me a future where the city was destroyed."

Gora's face lit up. "Fascinating! Could we see that here?"

"We don't have the objects I used, and that prophecy nearly destroyed the pool and killed the Augur. So, no, and even if we could, I'd not want to do it again."

Gora pursed her lips. "All right, then. Well, let's do the augury here, and maybe in a few days, if I ever master this, you can go off and try to get Nera back and save your city."

Once she'd placed the objects on the numbered runes, I took my place, pricked my finger, and dripped still more blood into the pool. It bubbled readily. As I repeated the chant, by now very familiar to me, I thought over what Gora had said about order and chaos. If the pool was focused on the energy of time, an aspect of order, then perhaps I could reach it better if I created more order, more calm, within myself.

That all sounded very intelligent, but I had no idea what it meant, or how to do it. When I completed the chant, I took a deep breath and closed my eyes, trying to center myself, to block out my frustrations, my anger, and my sorrow. Serenity. Or something close. I could feel my heart beat, but it slowed and quieted as I stood over the pool.

In the stillness, a few sensations became more intense. Many of them centered around coolness. I could feel the bottoms of my feet pressed against the cool floor. The collar felt cool on my neck. At first, I thought this was discomfort, but as time progressed, I realized it was just coolness, a cool presence nearby. I could feel coolness wafting up from the pool, too. A breeze? But surely that would come from the opening above.

I should really be doing the augury, I thought. But this was interesting, and I was in no hurry to discover the myriad connections between Gora's kitchen utensils. As I stood, I could almost feel the pool in front of me. My mind traced its dimensions, and those of the collar. They were both present in my mind, and they were distinctly cool. I could almost feel where they were, the way I knew where my hand or foot was even without looking. This was strange. Perhaps my attempt at meditation had brought about grandiose delusions, but I was pretty sure I could sense these two objects.

And then I became aware of a third source of coolness. A small source, perhaps the size of a walnut, somewhere across the pool. I stood with my eyes closed and visualized its location relative to me. Waist high, ten feet away. Near where Gora was standing. I directed my eyes at it, then opened them a crack. Sure enough, I was staring at Gora's midriff. I closed them again to be sure, then peeked again. There were two pockets on Gora's robe, and whatever produced the coolness was inside the left one.

Gora cleared her throat with some impatience. I opened my eyes and directed the pool. Vibrant images of shared meals flickered across the pool, some with Gora and a man, some with Boog and me, and some with people I didn't recognize. A cook prepared and served a soup. A man with feathers in his long, white hair gazed across the table at a little girl. An old man wearing an iron collar washed the dishes in a stone basin. He seemed to be whistling.

I had never felt stronger control over of the pool. I could shift angles of perspective, coming nearer or flying farther out. I could even sometimes run time forward and backward. Even as I concentrated on the images, I could still feel the cool presence of the pool beneath me, and as I stood, I could feel something emanating from me, sinking through my feet into the floor, feeding the pool. It was something akin to the coolness, although not exactly the same. An energy, or a flow. I'd felt drained when the Augur grabbed me during the disastrous augury many months before, and this was similar, but far more measured and peaceful. Or perhaps it was all in my head, a daydream given life by Gora's words, but it felt quite real.

I asked Gora if she'd seen enough. She had. She seemed impressed by the results. I think she also knew this was the best I'd done. She asked me several questions about technique and preparation, but I didn't mention my attempt at focusing myself, not sure yet if it was really effective or merely a fluke. Finally, her questions dwindled into silence. I was tired, but not nearly as drained as I had been on my earlier attempts.

"You can go," she said. "I'll go see if your friend has ruined supper again. Tomorrow, I can try the pool myself once more." She moved to the archway, and I backed away to ensure there was enough space between us.

"Hey, Gora," I called after her. "What's in your pocket?"

She turned, clearly surprised, and felt both of her pockets with a wrinkled, yellowed hand. "Nothing," she said, after a pause, but I didn't believe her. I could still almost feel the small ball of coolness there. "Why do you ask?"

"Never mind," I said. "My mistake." She didn't believe me either.

48

MIDNIGHT AUGURY

"You see coldness now?" Boog said. "Next, you'll be hearing in color. Or tasting music." He was joking, but I could tell he took me seriously. "The things you sensed..." he wiggled his fingers ominously, "were magical objects, right? The pool and the collar?"

"And whatever was in her pocket."

"And they were all part of this 'aspect of order' business you've been going on about?"

"I think so, yes."

"So, the thing in her pocket must be from order, too."

"Or life, or growth, I guess."

"Maybe it's her magical medicine pebble. Treating her creaky joints."

"I was thinking more like the collar controller."

Boog pointed at me. "That's a good thought. But it doesn't help us much. Unless you've got an eight-foot-long set of tongs we could use to get it out of her pocket."

"Maybe we could turn her upside down? And get it to fall out?"

"Hey, Madame Gora, I dare you to do a headstand? Or a somersault?" Boog laughed. "I found some rope today, and a rusty sword that should hold an edge. We'll get out of here one way or another. For now, I'm going to bed." He stripped off his shirt and trousers and, with much sighing and grunting, squeezed into his little bunk. The previous residents of this place must have been closer to my size than his.

"I'll go out scouting," I said. "Don't think I can sleep yet."
I'd had a thought over dinner, as I chatted with Gora and Boog.
More of a sad memory than a thought, actually. Of me and
Clarice learning to use the warding rods, and of how much
easier it might have been if we'd known about Gora's ideas of
aspects of chaos and order. That brought back a flood of
memories, of Clarice, of our training, of Sophie, of the happy
times I'd had at the Guild before all of this trouble began. But
mostly of Clarice. I got myself to a very sad spot in my mind,
and I truly longed to be able to see her again.

That made me think of the pool. And of Gora, seeing her
father once more in the water. As I left our small room, I
grabbed Clarice's cloak from our things. I hadn't been able to
bring myself to discard it back at the chieftain's camp, and I'd
carried it in the pack of food and supplies Gora made me wear
as Boog and I trudged along behind her horse. It was foolish,
maybe, to have taken it along, and a little disturbing, since it was
still punctured and stained with her blood, but I was in no
condition to give it up.

I also had the silver falcon pendant Clarice had always worn.
I'd taken to wearing it myself, under my shirt. It seemed like the
right thing to do. I wasn't any bigger than she was, so it fit me
well, and it was comforting, somehow, having that piece of her
with me. With the pendant and the cloak, I had two objects
bound together strongly by Clarice, so I was fairly sure I could
coax the pool into showing her to me again. I worried that I
might once again see her shot – see her killed – but even so, it
would be worth it to see her face one more time.

I hadn't told Boog of this plan. He might think it morbid, or
worse, although he'd mostly walked a careful path, avoiding
mentioning anything related to Clarice. I appreciated that. He'd
been a good friend, trying to leave me alone in my sorrow, and
to distract me from it when possible.

There was no distraction now. My throat was clenched up, a
hard ball of soreness and pain at its center. My cheeks burned
as I walked through the archway to the pool chamber. I no

longer worried about Gora finding me. She seemed to keep to her room at night, and I didn't think she'd mind me experimenting further here. It would be easy enough to explain my presence – the truth probably would serve better than any lie I could concoct.

I placed Clarice's pendant on the first numbered rune and her cloak on the second. For our investigations, we usually wanted more objects, seven if possible, to flesh out the connections between them and provide the pool more guidance. But for my purposes, I assumed the two of them would be perfectly adequate. I stepped up to the pool, pricked my finger, and let seven more drops of blood fall into the pool. My fingers were speckled with cuts and holes from all the auguries we'd done, but I didn't mind. I ran through the chant softly. It was becoming rote. I almost didn't need to think of the syllables. My mouth and tongue made them all on their own.

Once again, when the sound of my voice echoed into silence, I closed my eyes and sought to calm myself. The pain in my throat lessened a bit, shifting into a warm blanket of sorrow that draped my shoulders and chest. My eyes felt wet, and they stung. I wasn't sure if this was going to work. But again, gradually, I sensed the gentle coolness of the pool before me and of the collar around my neck. Once again, they resolved into sharply defined areas, almost like extended parts of my body, or like some outlandishly large and awkwardly engineered garment I was wearing. But I could feel them, and as I felt their coolness, I calmed further. My breathing slowed, and my heart settled into a dull throb.

I opened my eyes. The pool was already alive with colors and images. I saw Clarice and me in class, lectured by Lady Bizet on proper penmanship and grammar. This was only a bit over a year ago, but we looked much younger to me, much less weathered by time and trouble. Clarice, in particular, still had her long red hair and creamy skin, not at all the hardened, rough-and-tumble woman I'd ridden with on the border. As it was our final year of training, we'd been awarded our Inspector's cloaks, and we wore them proudly to our classes. We wore them everywhere, I remembered. She fiddled with her pendant, and I willed the pool to focus more closely on her face. Suddenly, she laughed, and even though she was silent, I laughed with her, my breath damp and catching in my throat.

I watched for some time, and then with some effort I willed the pool forward in time, watching Clarice work her way through the end of her training. Then she took to the streets of Frosthelm, with Gueran, and then the images shifted to the border, until finally Boog and I arrived on the scene again. She had certainly had some adventures – some fights, some narrow escapes, and many nights under the stars, all before we ever arrived. I was careful not to go too far, not wanting to see the end of our time together – it was vivid enough in my memory, and something I'd rather try to forget.

I do not know how long I spent there, staring into the past. My control of the pool was excellent, better even than it had been earlier in the day. Eventually, though, my knees weakened, and my stomach began to hurt, and I realized I had been at it long enough to drain my strength. But I did not want it to end, so I kept searching, watching, replaying a past I longed to live in again.

Finally, a wave of weariness swam through my head, and I lost focus. The pool jumped forward in time, and I saw me and Clarice talking, with her laughing and teasing me, on that final morning. I could not help but watch it again, as the arrow pierced her back, and she fell, and we were led away. I wept openly, shamelessly. The pool dimmed.

But then it illuminated again. I saw Clarice, on her back now, in the desert. The bloody arrow lay in two pieces by her side. She looked up at the sky, coughing. I could not bear to watch her die, but I was powerless, far too weak to direct the pool at this point. She clutched her pendant, and eventually, she sat up. As I watched, astonished, she struggled out of her jerkin and dressed her wound, binding her back and chest with long strips torn from our sleeping sacks. Her fingers frequently faltered, and she paused several times, coughing and gasping.

The image jumped again, and I saw her, hunched over, filthy, deathly pale, talking to a woman on a horse. The mounted woman looked like an explorer or trader of some sort. Her horse had bulging saddlebags, and she carried a bow and quiver at the back of her saddle and a small axe at her belt. She dismounted and helped Clarice up onto the horse.

Once again, the image shifted. Clarice was cleaner this time, and she looked much healthier. My heart leapt. She sat at a table, a quill in her hand, a long narrow strip of parchment in front of her, several long lines of neat, tiny script already in place. The falcon pendant lay to one side, its chain a pile of coils. She wore the cloak draped around her shoulders. She finished her writing, sprinkled the parchment with powder and blew on it, then rolled the strip of paper carefully into a tight little scroll, which she tied with a bit of thread. She took up the pendant, and with her thumb, she pushed on the falcon's head. It flipped back, revealing a small hole. She tucked the roll of parchment into it and then snapped the falcon's head back into place.

The scene faded and shifted once more. The rider, the one who'd helped Clarice, approached a cluster of tents bordering a rocky hillside. Horses stood tethered at the edge. As I studied the image, I realized that this was the camp where we'd been held. Our cave, with its stout wooden bars, was behind the camp, set in the hillside. The tent, in front of which I'd challenged the chieftain to let me duel to the death, was in the camp's center. The rider approached the tents, and as she dismounted, she waved at someone and beckoned, summoning.

Gora moved into the scene and spoke with the rider, who gestured out toward the direction from which she'd come. The rider stepped over to her horse and opened a saddlebag, from which she pulled first Clarice's cloak and then, after fishing around a bit, her pendant. She handed them to Gora.

I fell to my knees, even as the pool shifted to Gora handing me the items in the cave, and then to me, holding them in our dormitory room. Tears streamed down my cheeks, and I wrapped my arms around my chest.

Clarice lived.

I basked in that perfect, happy thought for a long time. The pool faded to darkness. Then I thought some more.

Gora lied to us.

The worst possible kind of lie. A flash of rage ran through me, but it was no match for my relief and joy. I let it pass.

I was an idiot.

I'd had the pendant now for weeks, and never noticed that it held a secret compartment. I rushed over to where it lay on the first rune and scooped it up. I pushed gently on the head at first, then harder. I looked for a catch or clasp, or some button to push. I saw the seam now, in the dim light of the chamber. It ran between the falcon's head and body, a line thinner than a hair. And I could see where the tiny hinge lay disguised under the falcon's neck feathers. The craftsmanship was exquisite. I really didn't want to break it, but I needed to see. I pushed harder, and it popped open.

The hole was empty.

The rage returned, and this time I let it grow.

49

STICK YOUR NECK OUT

I think I eventually slept, but I couldn't tell you when. Drained as I was from the pool, my mind still raced, as passions and hopes I'd tried my best to surrender came bursting back to life. I must have settled on fifteen different plans of escape, of interrogation, of bodily injury to Gora. In the end, all seemed lacking. In the morning, I told Boog what I'd seen. His elation nearly matched mine. He leapt about the room laughing and crowing in a manner I had not seen before or since. I think I had been too immersed in my sorrow to notice Boog's grief for Clarice. I had not been much of a comfort to him, I'm sure. He hugged me so tightly, lifting me off the ground, that I thought my spine might be permanently dented to conform to his arms.

"What's that noise?" came Gora's voice from the hall, a coarse rasping growl. "I've made porridge. Come on now, we have work to do." We looked at each other, full of emotion, and then we filed out of the room.

I will never be able to tell you how the porridge tasted, though I know I ate it. I had eyes only for the old woman, who had hurt me worse than I'd ever been hurt. And for what? No reason I could see. She sat as she always did, at the far end of the table, so that we would not be close enough to her to trigger our collars. She bent over her bowl, smacking and slurping as she studied three yellowed, curling sheets of paper, striped with neat rows of some arcane script.

I closed my eyes, seeking once again the calm focus I'd attained at the pool. It came grudgingly, but eventually I could sense the cool presence of my collar, then Boog's. I pushed outward, toward Gora, hoping to sense the object in her pocket, but it was like wading through mud. In the back of my mind, anger and frustration poked at my focus like biting insects. I couldn't shoo them away. My ire rose, and in a flash, I felt a sudden heat at the side of my left knee, a burning. I opened my eyes and looked down, thinking I had spilled my porridge somehow, but it was hotter than that, as if my trousers themselves were on fire. But only at the knee. I patted it and rubbed it, to no avail – the heat, and my agitation, increased. Gora looked over at me, and even Boog glanced up from his third bowl of porridge.

I froze. Under my fingers, at my knee, I felt the outline of the amulet in its hidden pocket, padded by the thick cloth of my trousers. "Sorry," I mumbled. "Itchy." I closed my eyes again, focusing, but feeding my anger rather than seeking calm, and again, I felt a flash of intense heat coming from the amulet. Curious.

Once again, I sought to calm myself. Distracted by my discovery of the heat of the amulet, it was easier this time, and eventually, despite being ten feet away at the end of the long table, I found the spot of coolness in the pocket of Gora's robe. I studied it, probing it, I suppose I'd say, with my thoughts, though the whole experience was alien and indescribable. You know when you taste a favorite food, or hold a loved one's hand, and you find yourself much more aware, more focused, on how it tastes or feels, just for a brief moment? I found that I could do the same, focusing this new sense.

As I studied it, I realized it was not merely a ball. When I focused more closely, it was more like a hooded lantern. The ball was an intense cool spot, but it also gave off a short emanant flare, a little lance of coolness that extended out a few inches before fading away. There was no sign of this when I looked at the pocket with my eyes open.

An idea came to me. I tried to reach out to the cool ball resting in Gora's pocket, to feed it from inside myself, as I had fed the pool during my auguries. The coolness of the ball intensified. And as I studied further, I saw the beam emanating from it grow stronger. It extended a foot or more now, well outside Gora's robe. The beam pointed toward a corner of the room, back behind my chair.

I made a soft sound, directed at Boog. "Hsst."

He looked up. *Come behind me*, I signed. *Kneel. Head even with chair seat. Face corner.*

Boog looked at me as if I were completely insane. *What?* He signed back, his thick fingers moving subtly.

Trust me, I signed, and repeated my instructions, trying to be specific about the position I wanted him in, although the Argot is hardly a precise language. Gora was thankfully still absorbed in her scrolls.

You're a duck, signed Boog. The sign for duck was pretty close to that for lunatic. He took another bite of porridge, glanced at Gora, then flipped his spoon over behind me. Gora looked up as it clattered to the floor, but then fell back into her reading. Boog rose from his seat and walked over behind the chair. He knelt to retrieve his spoon, then looked back at me.

He wasn't quite in the right place. *Left one foot,* I signed, placing my hands behind my back. *Closer to wall.*

Boog made a show of studying something on the floor, running a finger over a crack in the stone, as he crawled forward. I thought he was in the proper location now, but I wasn't sure. I glanced once more at Gora. She still read, running a gnarled finger over her text. We would have to be quick. Boog looked pretty ridiculous down there on the floor. I closed my eyes, slowed my breathing, and reached out to the ball. When I found it, I took a deep breath, calmed myself, and willed to it every ounce of energy I had.

Nothing happened. At first. But then, the ball's coolness intensified, and the beam of coolness shot out from it toward the floor behind me. Gora shifted a bit in her chair, and as the ball swayed with her robe, the spike now swung wildly around, like a beam of sunlight through leaves disturbed by a breeze, or like a drunken fencer's blade. I could feel myself tiring quickly, and my stomach twinged with pain.

Behind me, I heard a buzz of energy, and then a click. Boog's feet scraped on the floor as he stood. I gave up my focus, opened my eyes, and turned to look. I was dizzy, and it was hard to keep my eyes open.

With one hand, he rubbed his neck. With the other, he held his collar, swung open. He looked at me, nodded, then moved over to Gora.

Gora looked up at Boog's approach. "What—How did you…" she gasped. "Oh, that's not good."

Boog jammed his finger and thumb into the hollow of Gora's neck. I winced, having been the target of that maneuver all of the many times he'd practiced it since we left Edmund. Gora gurgled and wheezed and slumped in her chair.

Boog shoved Gora roughly to the ground and fished around in the pocket of her robe. He found the object. "Nice work, Marty. Very nice. No idea what you did. Here you go," he said, as he tossed me the object. It was the same smooth black stone we'd seen in the pool, or a similar one.

I'm sure Boog meant for me to use the stone to release myself, strike off my shackles, and join him in glorious newfound freedom. We've discussed it several times since then, and he's apologized profusely. As the black stone flew at me, and my arm rose to catch it, it triggered my collar, and I lost consciousness in a flurry of sparks and pain.

50

DELETED MESSAGES

I returned to consciousness in moderate comfort. I lay on a lumpy mattress, and for the first time in nearly two weeks I was free from the weight and hard, cold edges of the collar at my throat. My face felt damp, and as I breathed in, a slurping noise and the coolness on my cheek made me realize I had drooled a bit on the bedding.

I rolled onto my side, stretched, and opened my eyes. An angry face glared back at me, and I flinched. But it was only Gora, bound tightly to a chair with a soiled cloth stuffed in her mouth. As I wiped my cheek on my sleeve, I realized I must be in Gora's bedchamber – it held her clothes, folded neatly on shelves, and her travel pack, books, pens, and other materials. I must be on her bed, as well. I glanced down at the small puddle of moisture I'd made on her pillow, and as I looked back at Gora, I think I saw her face darken even more.

Behind Gora, Boog was giving the room a thorough going-over. I noted with great pleasure that my warding rod lay on a table nearby, next to the collars, the collar stone, and a small scrap of tightly-rolled parchment. There was also a stack of coins and the key Gora had used to open the outer gate.

"Oh, you're finally up," said Boog. "Sorry about that, with the stone and the collar."

"Sorry? All I get is 'sorry?'" I rubbed my neck.

"All right, I'm sincerely sorry. About causing you what was obviously such great discomfort." His tone put his sincerity into question.

I didn't think I was going to get much better than that. "How long have I been out?"

"Maybe three hours?"

I looked at Gora. She seemed even more frail tied up in the chair.

"Did you need the gag?"

"She wouldn't shut up. I warned her, twice. I got tired of listening to it." He stood, and his back cracked. "I found your stuff, over there." He pointed at the table. "Clarice's note is there too."

I thought the small scroll of parchment looked familiar. I glanced at Gora, and she looked away. I stood and took the scroll over closer to the oil lamp hanging from the center of the ceiling. The writing was very small, but very neat, and I felt a wave of warmth as I recognized Clarice's script, stretched out along the narrow strip.

2nd Nemra, 844 – M and B – I am back with our side and healing well. So sorry you were captured. My fault. I will never forgive myself if you come to harm. I have sent this message with a trader to Gora, a scholar I met on the road who has some influence with the clans, and I have asked her to find you and ensure you are treated well. She is kind – you can trust her.

[Here I snorted.]

The clans sometimes trade captives with us under flag of truce. I have informed Kreune of your situation, and I hope that you will be back with us soon. You may actually be safer as their prisoner than with our side, given your difficulties.

I have heard from Gueran. The situation worsens quickly in the city, as you might expect, and our chance to act is fading. Time is shorter than we thought. When I am fully healed, I will return there to try to set things right. Please DO NOT follow – it is far too dangerous for you there now, and you've done more than your part.

Send word when you can. I miss you both. Stay out of trouble.

C.

P.S. Please keep my falcon safe – it belonged to my mother.

I read the note through several times, savoring her words and her gentle voice, which I could not help but hear in my head as I read. The pool had shown her alive, but this note was real – she had touched it, written it, rolled it up. She lived. I gripped it tightly.

"Smitten again, I see," said Boog. "Now that she's back from the dead."

"Never stopped," I whispered, too softly for him to hear. I rolled the paper up again, tightly, and opened the falcon amulet to tuck it back in. As the falcon's head snapped back, I saw some tiny lettering set in the silver metal around the edge of the hole. I must have missed it in the gloom of the pool chamber. I squinted to read it in the soft glow of lamplight.

*TO CECILE * WITH ALL MY LOVE * TREVAIN*

Those names I remembered well. Cecile, who'd chosen Trevain over Marron, though with kindness and grace. Trevain and Cecile, stabbed and burned by Marron as they slept. Trevain, whose house, even after his death, had been wrongfully sullied and dishonored, then destroyed, a final blow struck from Marron's jealousy. This was the story related to us in sorrow and regret by Edmund, Inspector of Middlemarsh, Cecile's older brother.

But he definitely hadn't mentioned that Cecile and Trevain had a daughter. Edmund's niece. Clarice.

51

RECKONING

I looked at Gora. She gave a muffled grunt. I reached over and pulled out her gag. Boog gave a theatrical groan. Gora licked her lips and spat on the floor.

She studied me for a long time. I was content to return her gaze. Finally, she spoke. "What did you do to my collars?"

"I opened them. Well, Boog's, at least." I supposed he'd used the stone to open mine.

"How?"

"I see no need to tell you that. I have to give your future slaves a fighting chance."

"That's not why I want to know," she said. "You know that. My interest is academic."

"My interest is getting out of here, far from you."

She frowned. "There's only one reason I didn't tell you she was alive."

"I think I've got that one. You needed someone to help you understand your pool, and you knew the Guild has one in Frosthelm, so you thought we could teach you, especially after you saw I had a warding rod. You may even have talked about it with Clarice, if you're friends." I stood up. "Her note would have given us hope, and a reason to get out of here, and back to Frosthelm. Even knowing she was alive would have given us hope."

She nodded. "But I did save your life. You heard the chief order you beheaded."

"I'm pretty sure that was all staged," I said. "You and he spoke in our language. No reason to do that, unless you wanted us to follow what was going on. He even ordered us beheaded in our language. I'm guessing you have enough pull that old Okhot would have done whatever you said."

I thought I could see a hint of surprise, a hint of confirmation in her expression. "You think so? What are you basing that on?"

"You seem to know Ganghira very well. You were friends with Nera, who sounds important. You met Clarice on the road, so you're free to travel, apparently, in a war zone, and confident enough to do it alone, without warriors to protect you." I paused. "That's all assuming what you've said is true. Your credibility isn't exactly gleaming like the sun. But I think it's mostly true. No reason for you to lie about those things." I went on. "You're also one of the most learned, well-traveled people I've met. You're a powerful sorceress. And you seem very loyal to your people. They'd be fools not to hold you in high regard, and take your advice whenever offered."

Gora stared at me, her expression blank, but her eyes intense. At last, she spoke. "You must be good at your job, Inspector."

"Provisional Inspector, please. What I'm asking myself now, though, is whether you ordered us captured. All three of us, maybe? And hurting Clarice was an accident? Or maybe you only wanted me and Boog, because your sources, or your scouts, told us we were recently from the city. We'd have more useful information about the war, and we'd probably know a lot more about the pool. And maybe Clarice was meant to die, to make it look more real, and to break us."

"I wouldn't do that," she said.

"I don't know what you would or would not do," I replied. "Except that I know what you did do, which was steal us away, hold us in bondage, and try to make it look like you were helping us while you did so. And that makes most other scenarios possible."

She was quiet for a time. "I was going to let you go, you know."

"Maybe," I said. "No reason for you not to tell me that now."

"No, it's true," she protested. "There's something I didn't tell you about the Unity rune you were so fixated on. And about Fae-rah." She took a deep breath. "The cult you mentioned – the power they are trying to awaken is real. There are old texts, Arunian and some even older, that tell of a store of power infused into the air, the water, the soil of your lands. Frosthelm has been there for centuries, you know. The Arunians called it Nyria, but they captured it from its previous owners and rebuilt upon the ruins. Somewhere back in time, before the Arunians, the pool was built there, to tap into the power beneath the city."

This was confusing. I knew the pool was ancient. "What kind of power is this?"

"There is a natural confluence of aspects of order, of growth, at the site of the city. It is probably why it was settled in the first place. Crops grow well there. People build and prosper. Throughout time, they have tended to live in peace and harmony."

Marron wasn't exactly playing for the peace and harmony team, I thought. "But there's plenty of violence, greed, and hunger in Frosthelm."

"Of course. That is human nature. We each have aspects of both order and chaos of magic woven into ourselves. People make their own choices, set their own goals. But those choices are often shaped by where they live, by forces beyond themselves."

"So, all of this harmony doesn't sound like an angry god. What does Faera have to do with any of this?"

"I am not sure, but what I've read suggests that Faera is a being – a force – of pure chaos magic, which rampaged through the world, leaving a wake of death and destruction behind. Long ago, this being was defeated, captured, bound, by wizards of great power. The tales of this are legends, scraps of lore that differ as much as they agree. I cannot know how much is true. But they do say that to bind Faera, to keep it from returning, these wizards needed a prison, one that would remain strong enough to hold it long after they had died."

I was beginning to see where she was headed. "And this prison is in Frosthelm?"

"Under it. I think so. The natural strength of aspects of order, of life, at Frosthelm was enough for the wizards to fashion a cell that could contain Faera and keep it weak."

"A physical cell? Like, a room? Or a cavern or something?"

"I don't know. Maybe it is buried in rock, or merely stored energy, not physical at all. But some stories say they left a way to open the prison again."

"That sounds like a really stupid idea."

"Perhaps. The key to all of this magic is balance. With too much chaos, the world is destroyed, but with too much order, too much peace, too much stillness, creativity and ambition are killed, and life stagnates and has no meaning. Maybe they feared that there might be a need for Faera's power in the future, to restore balance."

"Or maybe they just wanted a chance to unleash Faera on their enemies. Or to be able to threaten to do so."

"That could be, too."

"So, all of these objects – the Eye of Hrogar, the Crown, Mace, Nera, the Fingernails – they are the keys to this prison?"

"I don't know, but that seems reasonable. I would imagine the builders of the prison would want to make it very difficult to open, even when – especially when — they were long departed from the world. Gathering all those objects could be quite difficult."

"And they need to do it at the eclipse, because the eclipse weakens the forces of order that contain Faera?"

"Sunlight gives life, promotes growth. When it is blocked, Faera's bonds may loosen. Or maybe the moon's power grows while overwhelming the sun, and the balance of magic is upset, allowing the release of Faera. But those are just guesses."

Boog had come over and was listening intently. He spoke. "The cult – what do they stand to gain from releasing Faera?"

Gora turned to him, looking annoyed. "You know, this conversation would be a lot more comfortable were I not tied to a chair."

Boog grinned. "You kept us in shackles for weeks. You can handle a little discomfort now. What do the cultists gain?"

"Some stories say Faera could grant eternal life to those who assist him. Others say fearsome power, and dominion over the world. Either of those may be true. But I think some people would assist in it just to be part of something bigger than themselves, or to follow a charismatic leader. Faera was very much like a god, and even false gods draw priests and followers."

"So, Faera, Unity. The rune means Faera?" I asked.

"No, the rune means the prison. Order and chaos combined, bound together. The moon and sun are a reference to his release, I think."

"And you're concerned with all of this?" I asked.

"Why would I not be? Keeping Faera from the world is good for my people as well as yours."

"Why did you wait until now to tell me all this?"

"I was trying to figure out what part of it you played, and how far I could trust you." She smiled. "Also, as you may have seen, I have some flaws in my character when it comes to telling the truth." She looked pointedly down at my knee. "Plus, as you spoke that day, I came to sense the object you carry at your knee. It is the form of the rune itself, is it not? A powerful source of chaos energy. If you bore it willingly, as you seemed to, you would more likely be a follower of Faera than its enemy."

I supposed I shouldn't be surprised that Gora could sense the amulet. Thanks to her suggestions, I too could sense such things. Surely, she had more training than I, and she'd been able to activate the warding rod and the collars easily enough, so whatever magical affinity I held, she likely shared or exceeded it. "We're definitely enemies of Faera," I said. "Or, if not of Faera, then certainly of those working to free him." I touched my knee. "What is it?"

"The stories spoke of eight master keys, one for each of the wizards who bound Faera. This might be one of those. It is powerfully enchanted."

"Why did you let me keep it, if you knew of it? Wouldn't you want an object of power?"

Gora laughed. "This whole place is steeped in order magic. I didn't want to risk mixing chaos magic with order. That can have bad results. Better you suffer them than I. And if I decided I wanted it later, I could just shock you and take it at any time." That sounded honest, if off-putting. "And, I was fairly certain you didn't know how to use it, or even what it was."

I thought for a moment. "So, it sounds like I should keep it as far from Frosthelm as possible."

Gora looked at my knee. "If that is the only key around, then yes. Without it, they probably cannot release it."

I thought of Novara, and of the amulet I knew Marron had taken from her house. "It's not the only one. They have another, back in Frosthelm."

"Then your task is harder." Gora frowned. "You could leave it with me."

Boog laughed. "Not happening."

Gora paused, thinking. "Then bring it back with you."

"Why?" I asked. "We hardly want to bring them a key, even if they might already have another one."

"Just as a key can unlock a door, it can also lock one." Gora shifted in her bonds. "If they succeed in releasing Faera, your only hope might be to figure out how to lock it up again."

This was sounding more hopeless by the minute. I rubbed my forehead.

"So, you were going to let us go?" said Boog.

"I was," protested Gora. "You seemed sincere in your desire to stop the Faerans, and I was close to figuring out the pool. At the very least, you are set on promoting discord and provocation back in Frosthelm, which could only be good for the clans. At best, you might find a way to stop the Faerans. And I meant what I said about getting Nera back. That would serve as a powerful symbol to the clans, a way to stop the fighting."

"How was that going to work? Just going to take the collars off and point us out the gate?" Boog asked.

Gora smiled. "I have a team of six warriors camped a few hours from here. If I give the signal, they'll come. They have horses, provisions. I can give you papers that will get you to the border safely."

I looked at Boog. "You'll still do this now?" I asked.

"If you untie me and let me send the signal."

"How do we know the signal doesn't mean, 'Come here and fill the flatlanders full of arrows?'" asked Boog.

Gora's smile broadened. "I guess you'll just have to trust me."

52

JIGGITY JOG

The next two weeks passed sometimes in tension, sometimes in boredom. Tension, such as when we raised a blue flag above the gate of the ancient structure and summoned Gora's warriors. Holding Gora at swordpoint, we talked them down, eventually negotiating terms of something like a surrender. True to her word, Gora gave us two horses, supplies, and papers, written in the barbarian clans' inscrutable script. Boredom, like our long ride out of the mountains.

Tension, like meeting up with clan warriors, and hoping Gora's papers didn't say "Kill these two idiots on sight and bring me their livers in a pickling jar." Whatever they said, it wasn't that, and we passed out of the clans' domain, crossed the border, and rode into the lands controlled by Frosthelm. Boredom again, as we avoided Legion outposts, Guild scouts, and all the major roads and settlements on the way back to the city, to the Guild, to Marron.

After we crossed the border, we put on our scarlet cloaks and our full uniforms, which Gora returned with our other gear. We reasoned that, from a distance, two Inspectors riding hard would draw less notice than two mysterious riders skirting major settlements. But I think we both felt good to be back in uniform, back on duty, even if it was a mission we'd set for ourselves. I thought Sophie might be proud of us, riding toward home in Guild scarlet to save the city from destruction.

Or, she might berate us as fools. We had no real plan, although talking with Gora had increased our sense of urgency.

We knew the enemy's plan, though, and we thought we knew how to disrupt it. Whether by stealing or destroying the objects they needed to free Faera, or by disrupting the ceremony long enough for the eclipse to pass, we thought we had a chance to fend off the worst of it. We could deal with Marron and his minions afterward, or fail at that, as long as the city was safe.

After two weeks of hard riding, we crested a final hill, Hearth Ridge, the locals called it. The city walls came into view below us. A lump grew in my throat as I saw my city, my home, in the valley before us. Spring had come to Frosthelm in our absence of nearly three months. I could see newly plowed fields all around the city walls, a patchwork before us, interrupted by homesteads, some alone, some in clusters in small villages. The fields gave way to roads and denser houses, and behind those, the outer curtain walls rose up, their battlements shining in the morning sun, high in the sky behind us to the east. I could see the inner keep in the center of the city, perched up on its hill, its thick, towering walls protecting the castle and the nobles' houses within. To our left, the Serpentine River rumbled out of the city walls, winding its way southward toward the distant ocean. It was gray-green in the sun, fed and dyed by the clay-rich soils all along its path through the countryside.

It was a happy sight, but it brought with it some unpleasant realities. We took off our cloaks and uniforms now, criminals again rather than Inspectors. Surely the ardor to catch us had cooled. New crimes and new criminals always took the attention of the Guild and the Guard. I was fairly certain that our descriptions would have faded from the memory of nearly all the City Guard. In the Guild, many knew us, but we hoped that only some of those wanted us apprehended and beheaded. Other than those people, it was only Marron and his cronies who would know us and seek us out, and I hoped there weren't many of them who knew us on sight.

Seeing the city also made another factor much more real – our limited time to act. Madame Lenarre had calculated the eclipse at almost six months from when we spoke. We had worked in the city for another month or so after that, been absent from the city for three months, and were now returning. If I had kept proper track, today was the 12th of Senna, and the date Madame Lenarre gave, the 20th of Mia, was little more than a month away. We had time to get our bearings and hatch a plan, but our day of reckoning was fast approaching.

We were not accosted on the way through the farms and houses, two dusty riders from the countryside being of very little note. We decided to press our luck and ride right through the open southern gate, although we went through separately, ten minutes apart. I tried as hard as I could to look nondescript and nonchalant. I was certainly more comfortable in the saddle now, after our time posted at the border and our ride back, so that was no giveaway. Our hair was far longer, more unkempt, than when we left, and we were bronzed by exposure to the elements. We had made no real effort to clean ourselves up, so our clothes were stained with the dust of the road, which I hoped added to our commonness. The horses we rode were long-haired and built for speed, not like the sturdier, carefully groomed specimens common in Frosthelm, but that was not enough to draw much notice, as trade with the clans had been common before the conflict. Still, my skin crawled as we passed under the gaze of two bored guards.

We settled at a tawdry tavern just inside the city – the Tarted Trollop, which name might have been a selling point for some. For us, though, it was small enough and quiet enough that we thought we could lie low for a while. We used the names Florin and Crozier, our false names from the border, because we were somewhat used to answering them, and because we figured our allies might know us by those names. Gora had given us more than enough coin to cover the costs of this place, along with stabling for the horses.

After an unexpectedly good meal of cheese, broth, and fresh-baked hard bread, we took stock. "We have to get word to Gueran that we're here," I said.

"Shouldn't be hard," Boog replied. "We can hire an urchin as a courier, write something careful but descriptive. Let him know where we are."

We argued a bit over the content of our note, but eventually we finished. *Dearest Gueran, your lost sheep are in town at the Tarted Trollop. Please visit soon to reminisce.* I went out, walked into town, toward the southern street market, and found a thin girl with bright eyes who looked relatively trustworthy. I gave her a coin and our note, sent her on her way to Guild Headquarters, and then bought myself a bulging sack of roasted sugar nuts. The smells, the sights, the sounds of the market were unexpectedly comforting to me. At last, I was home.

I spent a few hours wandering around the streets, mindful enough to avoid the guards and any inspectors I saw, but mostly, I felt at peace. I made it all the way north, avoiding the inner keep on its hill, to Fountain Square, where seven jets of water shot twenty feet in the air to land in a vast blue pool. I wandered the stalls of the street market there, watching the bustle, enjoying myself. At last, thinking Gueran might have received our message and sent some reply, I returned to the Tarted Trollop to check.

The tavern's interior was dark as night compared to the bright sun outside. I pushed aside the thick wood door and stood blinking in the musty air, which was rife with odors of spilled ale, baked goods, and far-too-infrequent bathing. I spotted Boog hunched over a corner table, and as my eyes adjusted, I saw Gueran himself across from Boog. I can honestly say that in the nearly six years I'd known Gueran, this was the first time I'd been genuinely happy to see him.

As I approached the table, I could see Boog's face was decidedly grim as he spoke in quiet tones. Gueran, too, seemed disturbed. I wondered what had happened. My mind flashed to all manner of ill tidings and horrible scenarios. Was the resistance discovered? Clarice captured, or dead? I pulled a chair back and sat with them.

"Nice to see you, Marten," said Gueran. "I'm always surprised by how you manage to stay alive." He was trying for humor, but he was too tense to make it work.

"What is it?" I asked, looking from Boog to Gueran. "What's wrong?"

"Not good," said Boog.

"Remember Madame Lenarre, the scholar?" Gueran asked. I nodded. "She sent the Augur a letter a few months ago. She said she'd happened to consult her astrological book, by Werole, I think it was. And that reminded her of her discussion with you."

"Touching," I said. "But that's not what's wrong, is it?"

Gueran continued. "Apparently, while reading, Madame realized she'd done her calculations incorrectly before. Something about discounting the cycle of Peristache, I believe. She'd gotten the wrong date for the eclipse."

I was beginning to see the nature of the problem. "So, when is it? What does she say now?"

"Tomorrow," Boog said. "It's tomorrow. At noon."

53

Only a Day Away

Gueran filled us in on the events of our absence. He and the other Inspectors resisting Marron's plots had been busy, and they'd redoubled their efforts after receiving the letter from Madame Lenarre. Though they had their regular duties to perform, and though Marron's appointed Inspectors kept careful watch, they had still been able to track many of the movements and activities of Marron, Algor, Brand, and Tolla, and of Marron's various guards, stewards, and employees. They had also identified a number of confirmed or probable Faerans, some of whom were lowly beggars and some wealthy aristocrats, including a number of landed nobility. One inspector, Torgen, had infiltrated the group by posing as a Faeran initiate, and his information had been among the most valuable.

They had uncovered and observed many details and events. Brand was definitely the second-in-command of the organization, taking orders only from Marron. Tolla was more of an enforcer, a strong right arm, although she seemed to believe deeply in the Faeran religion, or creed, or whatever it should be called. Algor seemed lower in the hierarchy, merely a useful adjutant. But Marron was the true leader. It was Marron's influence in the court, among the nobles, in the Guard and the Justiciary, and now in the Inquisitor's Guild, that allowed the group to grow and operate uninhibited.

The Jezarmi warehouse served as a meeting hall on several occasions, where many of the Faeran followers gathered to hear readings, read prophecies, pray to Faera, and announce plans. Torgen reported that the leaders seemed confident they had what they needed to bring about Faera's return, and they had promised all the assembled cult members that they would be rewarded for their efforts to restore Faera to life. For most of them, especially the lower-status adherents, all that was required was to come to what they called the Ceremony of Reawakening, which we now knew was tomorrow. Some others were given orders and assigned tasks. Still others were asked for donations of money or other resources. All gave of their time and money willingly. Doubters were cast out of the group, and in some cases, they vanished completely. Those that remained shared a religious fervor and strong faith in their cause.

Gueran was unsure of the Prelate's role in the organization or of how much he knew, although the cult involved enough of the court (perhaps a quarter of its members, including some of the most influential) that it was hard to imagine he hadn't heard something about it. He had not been seen at the meetings. He met with Marron frequently, but he met with many nobles, and he'd been meeting with Marron for years, even before making him High Inquisitor.

In response to all of this, Boog and I were able to fill in what Gora had told us about the nature of Faera and of the history behind the cult. I wasn't sure how useful that would be, but at least we could confirm that there was probably a reason to justify the cultists' zeal. What we said made Gueran seem more and more unhappy. "I thought there was still a good chance there was nothing to all of this," he said. "A bunch of deluded fanatics running around, killing people, stealing things, but with no truth to any of their mystical prophecy. It sounds like I was wrong. The threat is real. They might really be able to pull it off."

I couldn't wait any longer. "Is Clarice here? Is she back?"

Gueran looked at me, an odd expression on his face. "She arrived back in the city a few weeks ago, after we got her word of the shift in dates for the eclipse. She was injured but seemed to be recovering. She carried orders from Kreune, which covered her return from the border, but she wasn't about to report to Marron at the Guild. I've met with her several times, and we've exchanged information. She's been tracking Marron's movements and those of the other cultists, I believe."

A question occurred to me, a puzzle I'd earlier set aside. "Do we know why she was sent away?"

"It was Sophie's decision, at the suggestion of Clarice's uncle. Apparently, Sophie and Edmund were good friends, in close contact," said Gueran. "Sophie noted the decision in her journal, which I managed to pilfer from evidence storage with the help of Lianna. Edmund had heard of the events surrounding Marron's sorceress, and he worried that Clarice might become a target and wanted her safely out of his reach."

Except that the border was hardly safe. But there may not have been any good options. "Do you know where she's staying?"

"No idea. I haven't seen her in five or six days." He frowned. "Frankly, Mingenstern, we have more important things to deal with now."

He was right. At least she'd made it here safely.

There was one more odd detail Gueran related to us. Over the past few weeks, traffic around Novara's old house had increased. Many people came and went, nearly all of them known or suspected Faerans, and many more than seemed normal for a small home. Ten, twenty people at a time would enter the house and stay, sometimes for hours, often carrying large bags or bundles in and out. But the house stayed quiet. Whatever they were doing in there, it was not a party or a loud ceremony.

"So, what do you think is going on?" Boog asked.

"It is hard to say," replied Gueran. "The house was clearly important to Marron and to Novara."

"Could it be the temple, or the prison, or whatever it is?" asked Boog.

"Perhaps," said Gueran. "But it doesn't seem large enough, and it's… well, it's just a house. We were all in it. It looked perfectly normal."

"Not the house," I said. "Underneath it."

"What?" asked Gueran.

"Remember, the privy with the ladder? That you fell down?"

"How could I forget?" Gueran grimaced.

"There was a passageway leading away from it, one that we never got a chance to explore. I bet that leads to the temple, and that's why there are so many people going in and out. Gora said all of this was beneath Frosthelm."

"Seems like a big leap," said Gueran, considering.

"Maybe, but we should check it out," said Boog. "If we find out where the ceremony is, our job gets a lot easier."

"We have had teams scouring the city," said Gueran. "But so far, they've come up with nothing." He tapped a well-manicured fingernail on his forehead and closed his eyes for a moment. "I'll check with Torgen. He was at a Faeran meeting last night. Surely, they'll have told him where to go for the ceremony. The house is worth checking out anyway. I'll have two Inspectors meet you near Novara's house, at seventh bell. It will be dark then. Was there a tavern or park nearby?"

"Have them join us behind Number 15," I said, remembering the house next door. "Terrence and Mavis won't mind if we meet up there."

"Nutmeg rings," said Boog. His eyes grew distant.

"I'd say don't get noticed, don't get caught," said Gueran. "But if the Reawakening is tomorrow, we don't have much to lose. I'd go in hard and find anything you can."

54

An Unexpected Guest

"Are we ready?" asked Boog. He looked quite menacing, dressed all in black, his face and hands darkened with soot. The only factors detracting from his fearsomeness were the pastry crumbs and berry jam smeared on his upper lip. He carried his long staff, preserved for him by Lianna back at the Guild. Preserved as evidence, actually – it had been confiscated, tagged, and stored following our arrest for Sophie's murder. Boog seemed glad to have it back.

Terrence and Mavis had spotted me and Boog waiting for the others behind their house, and they remembered well our earlier visit. I grew briefly worried that they would know of our murder conviction and report us, but apparently Marron had not made a very good High Inquisitor. Much of the town was unhappy with the summary arrests and searches he had ordered. To Terrence and Mavis, he'd made an even worse neighbor of late. They invited us in, either not knowing or not caring about our supposed crimes.

"Hundreds of them, coming and going," she had said, holding a plate piled high with berry pastries. "Walking right through my garden, some of them! Would you believe it? And you know we've complained to Marron's steward so many times, and they do nothing at all."

"If you ask me," said Terrence, "they're up to no good over there. Serve them right if you arrest the whole lot of them."

I agreed wholeheartedly, but did not say so. I didn't think I was going to be doing much arresting that night. A short time (and for Boog, several pastries) later, Inspectors Cheliaux and Soren, dressed in similar fashion to Boog and I, arrived outside. Soren was a tall blond man. I'd met him before, but he graduated several years before us, and I didn't know him well. Likewise, I recognized Cheliaux, but didn't know her other than to exchange a casual greeting in passing. She was recently called back to Frosthelm after a stint in a small village. I'd seen her at various Guild meetings and parties. She was a sturdily built woman, a head taller than I was, and she could likely beat me in a wrestling match, probably using only one arm. After thanking Mavis and Terrance, the four of us set out into the gathering gloom. As I left the house, I saw Terrance pick up his crossbow from behind the hall table.

Novara's house, tucked back against the wall, had three guards posted at the front door. They stood together, relaxed, talking and laughing. It was relatively easy to escape their notice as we crouched behind the low wall surrounding the property. We circled around to the back, where a single guard stood watch. We waited, tense and quiet, and he eventually crossed over to face away from us, towards the far side of the property. Boog sneaked up behind him, surprisingly quick and silent for one so large, and with a sharp *Thunk* of his staff, he dropped the guard to the ground. We carried the limp guard carefully outside the low wall and hid him there under a bush. He still breathed, but I wasn't sure when, or if, he would awaken.

I stole back over to a window and peered inside. I was getting better at this kind of field work than I had been. My experience, brief as it was, riding along the border with Clarice and Boog had made me tougher, quieter, stronger. I remembered the layout of the house from our previous visit. I was looking through the small kitchen to the larger room on the main floor, where the fireplace glowed. Though the window glass here was clear, it was set in diamond-shaped panes. The glass was wavy, so it was hard to see, but I could make out three people talking. When I shifted to find a clearer pane, I could identify all three. One was Marron, dressed in a stylish, finely embroidered surcoat showing his house's coat of arms. Another, in a black robe, with short blond hair and a reddish beard, was Brand. I remembered his face well.

The third, I'd only ever seen from a distance, but even so I knew him immediately. After all, his portraits adorned all the city offices, the Guild's included, and his bearded countenance was stamped on every coin. His Grace, Jeroch, High Lord of Frosthelm, Prelate of the Northern Realm.

55

QUICK SUCCESSION

I waved the others over. Each looked, in turn, and each came away from the window with wide eyes.

"The Prelate!" hissed Cheliaux.

"We can't act against him," said Soren. "We swore an oath of fealty."

"You also swore an oath to protect Frosthelm from all enemies," said Boog. "Looks like you might have an oath problem." Soren looked away in discomfort.

"We don't know he's an enemy," I said.

"He seems chummy with some enemies," said Boog.

I looked at the window. It had a hinge on the inside, and the lower section could swing out. There was a rusted metal prop rod hanging below, connected to the window. There was a latch inside, but it was just a hook and eye. True security for the home came when the heavy shutters were closed and bolted, but they were open now, flat against the house on either side. I stuck my dagger into the crack at the base of the window and pried upward. I could see the hook inside straining against the loop of metal that held it. I put more weight behind my dagger, and the window moved upward. Finally, the small eyelet broke off the window and the hook popped free. The window came up quickly, but I caught it with a gloved hand, and it made no squeak or complaint. Those inside did not seem to notice the noise. Perhaps either the fire's crackling or their discussion was louder. I held the window open, unwilling to risk the chance of noise from using the prop rod. The voices inside were clear now.

"Your Grace," said Marron. "Our plans are about to bear fruit. You gave us your approval. You've sanctioned this every step of the way."

The Prelate frowned. "I approved you looking into this Faera as a weapon, one we might use against our enemies. You reassured me that it would be powerful and easy to use. From what my agents and advisors have told me recently, what you've got going here is much more of a religion than a weapon, and it's not clear you can control it at all if it gets loose. I've seen what you've got down there – the statue, dusty artifacts, that body – it's not a weapon you're after, or to help Frosthelm. You're nothing but a pack of damned fanatics."

"We can control it," said Brand. "The texts are clear."

"If I wanted to hear your opinion," snarled the Prelate. "I'd ask for it. No, this has gone far enough. Karela was right to crush it the last time, and I must do the same. I am withdrawing my approval. This must stop, now."

Brand glared at the Prelate. I'd seen that anger in his eyes before. "Your Grace," said Marron, still calm and cool. "I beg your pardon, but you cannot lose your nerve. The rewards are still there to be had, if we are bold enough to take them. Limitless power. Eternal life. Enough to strike fear and envy into all our enemies. Enough to keep Frosthelm safe for all time."

The Prelate drove a finger into Marron's chest. "You overstep your station when you say I lose my nerve. You are where you are, who you are, because of my support. It can be taken away as freely as it was given."

Brand spoke up. "You can't stop us, regardless. It is too late."

"Ha!" scoffed the Prelate. "It is hardly too late. Perhaps you forget who rules this city?" He pulled a sheet of paper from inside his thick wool coat. "I have here a Prelate's warrant for your arrest, signed by me. My personal agents have collected the names of all of your leaders. All are to be taken prisoner and tried for sedition. The objects you have here are to be impounded." He smacked the paper into his open palm. "This is over."

I felt a rush of elation at the Prelate's words. Whatever he had done to help Marron in the past, it sounded as though it was now finished. Completed. The threat gone.

"But, your grace," said Marron, "That simply won't do." He moved over to the Prelate, one hand outstretched in a gesture of supplication, the other at his belt.

"What do you—" said the Prelate, and then Marron shifted quickly, his outstretched hand on the Prelate's shoulder, the other pressed against the Prelate's belly. The Prelate grunted, low, in his throat. I could see him stagger, clutching his stomach. "Marron, you cur, I'll see you hang for this," Jeroch roared. Red gore flowed from his abdomen, oozing out from under his hand. He struggled to maintain his footing.

Two guards, wearing the livery of the Prelate's personal guard, rushed into view, swords drawn. They must have been waiting nearby. This was not their finest hour, to be sure, with the Prelate stabbed and bleeding before them. "Kill them!" gasped the Prelate. He fell back against a wall. Both guards attacked Marron, their swords raised, swinging, but Marron parried one and sidestepped the other. He followed his parry with a vicious stab, his bloodstained dagger flashing in the lamplight. He scored a hit. The guard cried out in pain.

The other, the one whose blow Marron had dodged, swung his sword back at Marron with a backhanded stroke. Marron was turned away, facing the guard he'd stabbed, and it seemed impossible that he would avoid the blade a second time. But then Brand held up his wand, and there was a bright flash of light, and a yipping noise, like that of a small, agitated dog. The guard's sword flew out of his grasp, past Marron, clattering on the ground. The guard's armor and clothing fell empty to the floor in a cloud of orange powder.

The other guard, her eyes wide, struggled to fight on, but Marron made quick work of her, landing three vicious blows with his narrow dagger in quick succession. The guard sank to the floor. Marron turned to the Prelate, who looked barely able to hold himself up.

"Mother of Blood!" hissed Cheliaux, "We need to save him!" She tried to push the window farther up to crawl through. I stooped to help lift her legs, but the window would not open wide enough to allow her through. She strained against it, pushing hard against the sill, but it would not yield.

"What... are you doing? You'll never get away with this," said the Prelate, his voice hoarse and weak. He slid lower down the wall.

"Ah, Your Grace," said Marron. "But I will. Thanks to the positions you have granted me, there are any number of people I can find to blame for your death." As we watched from the window, impotent, Marron stabbed the Prelate once more, in the chest. The Prelate gurgled and fell to the floor, sliding down onto his guardsman.

"That wasn't wise," said Brand, his voice unsteady. He seemed shaken, either by the Prelate's death, or more likely, from the strain of using the wand. "We can't afford the attention right now."

"It won't matter," said Marron, wiping his dagger on a kerchief he pulled from a pocket. "I doubt anyone else knows the Prelate is here. We'll hide the bodies until we need to have them discovered, later. It could even be useful. With the Prelate dead, I can make a play for the title myself."

"There won't be a need for titles, or for Prelates, if tomorrow goes as we hope," said Brand.

Marron looked back at him. "Look here, Brand, if I can engineer my way to being Prelate, we do not need to free Faera. We'll just rule Frosthelm ourselves."

Brand's eyes blazed with anger, and his voice rose to a shout. "Are you mad? Tomorrow is our only chance. There will never be another in our lifetimes. There is no turning back. With all we have done, all we have prepared, you would consider backing down? Are you weak, like the Prelate?"

"No," said Marron, looking at the wand Brand still held. "I suppose you are right." He dropped the bloodstained kerchief and turned away from Brand and from the jumbled bodies and weapons on the floor. "Have Tolla clean this up and stow the Prelate's body. We may yet need it, and she's the only one we can trust with this. We need to get to the temple."

As they spoke, the four of us outside had been frantically trying to figure out what we could do. We whispered furiously at each other. I don't think we could have acted quickly enough to protect the Prelate – it had been over in mere seconds, and we were trapped outside. But what could we do now? Boog and Cheliaux wanted to break down the back door and rush in. Soren seemed paralyzed by indecision and fear. I pointed out that Brand had killed with the wand effortlessly, so an immediate assault seemed foolhardy at best.

As we dithered, events inside carried on without us. Marron disappeared from view. Brand opened the front door and called for one of the guards, whom he sent to find Tolla. He found a pen and paper, scribbled out a note, and laid it on the Prelate's body.

Eventually, the house went quiet. The four of us were still left outside, angry and frustrated, unsure of our next move.

"Wait here," I said. I thought I might be able to fit through the window, small as I was. I handed the window to Boog, then raised a leg up and over the window sill and wriggled through the crack. I got stuck partway through, but I calmed my rising panic and kept on, the window frame scraping painfully against my neck and chest. At last, I was in. Slowly, slowly, I crept through the house toward where the Prelate lay. I heard no one else inside the house, but I couldn't be sure I was alone. We had seen neither Brand nor Marron leave.

I laid a finger on the Prelate's neck, then felt for his breath. The Prelate was dead, his eyes open and staring. A monumental event for Frosthelm, but there was no time to mourn him now. I picked up the note left by Brand.

Tolla – please clean this up. And for the Mother's sake, be discreet about it. Obviously, nobody can know of this. You can hide the body at the manor for now. We'll find a better place tomorrow if we need to.

I returned the note to where I found it. On the floor by the Prelate's hand, I found the paper he had been holding shortly before his murder, stained now with his blood. I picked it up and flipped it open. It was indeed a warrant for arrest, with a long list of names, and the Prelate's characteristically flowery signature at the base. I tucked it into my jacket.

I heard a shuffling at the door, and as quickly but silently as I could, I flew to the back door, drew back the bolt, and stepped outside. I eased the door closed behind me and circled back around the house.

"He's dead," I said. "The Prelate is dead."

"Mother of Blood," swore Cheliaux, somberly. "This is horrible. Marron must pay."

"Soren," I said. "Go report this to the Guild. No, find the City Guard. They'll be closer. I think there's a post down the street there, past the tavern, maybe three blocks." I'd have sent Boog, but he was under a death sentence, as was I. That might be difficult to explain to the Guard, if they realized who he was. "We'll hide and wait for you here. We need to get the Guard here before Tolla comes, so they can see the body."

We retreated back behind the wall, watching the side of the house carefully and studying the windows for movement. After receiving their new orders from Brand, the two remaining men seemed to take their work more seriously, walking to and fro before the house, scanning the street. But they seldom looked back to our position, and we kept low and still.

As far as I knew, Marron and Brand hadn't come out, and I hadn't seen them in the house. So, they had either gone upstairs together for some reason, or they had descended into the passageway under the house. I suspected the latter.

We waited for five minutes, then ten. This shouldn't be taking so long. The murder of the Prelate was easily the most serious crime that could be committed in the city, and it would have been taken seriously by any member of the city guard, I was sure of it.

After another five minutes passed, Boog went after Soren. He slipped silently away into the night. Cheliaux and I stayed at the wall, staring at the house, but nothing changed.

Another five, another ten minutes passed. Eight riders clattered up to the front door of the house, their horses' breath steaming in the cool night air. I was glad at first, thinking them the city guard, but I soon saw that they did not wear the green sash. They were a motley crew, men and women, all armored, all seasoned riders, all heavily armed with a variety of weapons. Some wore helmets, some hoods. Others had bare heads. They did not wear the colors of the house of Marron. In fact, there was nothing uniform in their dress at all. A band of mercenaries, perhaps? Or an elite special squad?

One of the riders walked up to the door and pushed back her hood. As she spoke to the men guarding the door, I could see in the flickering torchlight the unmistakable light brown skin, dark hair, and a long braid hanging down to one side. Tolla, who'd captured me, led me to torture, and tried to kill me. She pushed past the two men and entered the house alone.

There was a noise behind me. Boog was back, but with no City Guard in sight.

"Soren is at the guard post, but he's chained to a ring in the wall," said Boog. "I could see through the door. They were questioning him. I didn't think I should go in."

A cold feeling wormed its way into my gut. Of course Marron would have the guard posts closest to this place staffed with guards he trusted. Or paid. Or both. They weren't going to investigate one of his houses, especially not tonight. They probably had specific orders not to, no matter how serious the accusation. Even if it was the murder of the Prelate, and his body lay cooling in a pool of blood not four blocks away.

56

A MAN, GUERAN, WITH A PLAN

It was well past midnight by the time we found Gueran.
Eighth bell had rung long ago, while we'd watched Tolla
remove two bodies wrapped in blankets from Novara's house.
She'd tied them unceremoniously across the backs of two horses
and ridden off, escorted by her gang of mercenaries. Cheliaux
left, headed back to the Guild to try to report the murder. She
wasn't sure how she could report it, with Marron's influence
controlling the Guild, or how she could get Inspectors or City
Guard into Marron's house to search, but she was going to try.
We asked her to tell Gueran to meet us at a point by the Guild
hall as soon as he could.

Boog and I had watched the house for another hour, but
nothing of interest occurred. Marron's guards occasionally
came and went. Eventually they realized the guard from the rear
of the house was missing. They started a search, placing our
safety in jeopardy, and we decided to leave for the time being,
to consult and regroup. I was sure Brand and Marron had gone
beneath the house and used the tunnel we'd found. They had
never reappeared, and there was no sign of activity or movement
in the house. We needed to get down there ourselves.

But first, we needed a plan, and that meant meeting with
Gueran. He arrived outside the Guild Hall, down an alley, our
arranged meeting spot, just after we did. He said Cheliaux was
pressing for a full search. As a witness to the crime, and as an
Inspector in good standing, she was having some success. He
thought there would be a party sent to Marron's house within an

hour or two. An inspector had been dispatched to free Soren, with assistance from some trusted members of the City Guard.

All that was fine, but we needed to find Marron and Brand to have any real impact on the Faerans. Gueran suggested that if there were a big enough commotion at Marron's manor house, Boog and I might be able to fight or sneak our way into Novara's house and then be able to see where the passage led. A desperate plan, full of uncertainties, but we had nothing better.

I was dead tired from weeks of hard riding and sleeping outside, and Boog didn't look much better. We asked Gueran to let us know when the raid on Marron's home was to be scheduled, and then the two of us found a dark, sheltered doorway and sat, leaning against the wall. Boog began snoring almost immediately, and I soon after, like vagrants or beggars.

Rough hands shook me awake. "It's on," said Gueran. "It took longer than we hoped, but they're on their way. Ten inspectors, six of them on our side. With a Guard escort."

I blinked. The first hint of dawn was touching the streets and whitewashed walls nearby. We must have slept for two or three hours – too long! Boog rubbed his eyes. "All right," I said. "We'll go back to Novara's."

"I brought torches," said Gueran, "and some bread and cider. Torgen says the cultists are to meet in Fountain Square later today. Perhaps they'll be led to the temple from there. I need to get to Marron's. I can't believe he killed the Prelate."

"Thanks, Gueran," I said. "You've been …… wonderful in all this. Thank you for all you've done."

His lips curled upward in a small smile. "I did it for Frosthelm, and for Sophie. As did you." He turned to go. "Don't get yourselves killed."

We made the trip up High Street as the dim glow brightened into morning. We wiped the soot from our faces, but we were still dressed in black, well-armed, and carrying torches. Conspicuous, and clearly up to nothing good, but nearly no one was about that early, and those we did see were immersed in their tasks, preparing for another day's work. Nobody paid us any mind, and I was grateful for that. The rising light gleamed off the damp cobblestones of the street as we passed the windows of Frosthelm's finest shops. As we rounded the final corner, Novara's house came into view, and I could see the orange glow of the sunrise reflected in the diamond pattern of the windows. As during the previous night, there were three guards stationed outside the front door.

We paused, taking stock. Three was too many for us to take on. The rear door was probably guarded again as well, and it was getting light enough now that any sneaking around would be painfully obvious. They might have found the guard Boog took out. If not, we might be able to talk our way up to the door, but certainly not through it. I wished we'd brought more inspectors, but Gueran was right to take everyone he could to Marron's house. The murder of the Prelate was a much larger matter than my hunch that a subterranean passage here led anywhere important.

There was a gentle touch on my shoulder. It wasn't Boog. He was standing in front of me, studying the house. I spun, pulling at my dagger, ready to fight or kill if necessary.

"Easy, there, Marten," said Clarice. "No need to get testy." She smiled.

I know it was tactically foolish, and perhaps bad form given the recent murder of the Prelate, but I stuffed my dagger back into its scabbard and hugged Clarice as hard as I could. My throat hurt, and hot tears flowed down my cheeks. "You're alive," I murmured. "I love that you're alive."

She gave a low laugh and hugged me back. "Me too, Marten, me too."

57

In We Go

The arrow flew in a high arc, its fletching a bright red orange in the morning light. It descended gracefully, then buried itself in the chest of one of the guards. He fell backwards, his arms flailing.

"Nice shot," said Boog.

"Thanks," said Clarice. She'd already shot a second arrow and was nocking a third. The second arrow hit a second guard as he was turning to look at the first. He stumbled back, clutching at the arrow in his neck. Her third shot missed as the third guard ducked for cover. Too much to ask, I supposed. Boog and I sprinted toward the house

It was beyond wonderful to see her again. In the rational part of my mind, I had known she was all right. I'd seen her image in the pool, received her note, heard about her from Gueran. But now I knew first-hand she was healthy and alive, and I had a new memory to replace my last one, the one where she lay bleeding and dying on a dusty trail as I was carried away as a prisoner. We hadn't taken much time to catch up, obviously, but she said she'd been watching the house for most of the last few days, and there had definitely been an unusual amount of traffic heading in and out. Marron and Brand had come several times a day. Today, like us, she'd come to try to break in and see what was going on. We were out of time. Waiting and watching needed to give way to action.

We told her about the Prelate's murder. She hadn't been here last night, and she said she hadn't seen the Prelate here before.

Perhaps he had kept his distance from Marron, receiving reports at the court. Maybe he'd finally had a change of heart last night and had come to shut the operation down. Or maybe she'd just missed his earlier visits. We did not know the whole story. We likely never would.

The third guard was yelling for help. "Intruders! Attackers!" The noise would draw attention. We needed him silenced. He had his sword drawn, and he hid behind a column, one of several that held up a small portico that sheltered the house's front door. He could see us coming, but he didn't break from cover, probably for fear of being shot. A fourth guard came around from the back door, but Clarice hit him at once, and put a second arrow in him for good measure. He lay still.

Boog waved me around the right side, along the front of the house, while he took the left, running up the gravel path leading to the front door. The remaining guard, clearly scared, looked from one of us to the other. He glanced over his shoulder, checking the terrain, but escape that way would be difficult. He ducked back and pounded on the door as Boog and I closed on him.

Boog got there first, as my route had some shrubberies and bushes to navigate. He swung his staff in a ferocious arc, but the guard dashed away, his sword slicing the air near Boog's head. Boog swung again, and the soldier took the blow on his sword blade, grunting at the impact. The sword embedded itself in the wood of the staff, and the two of them struggled to get their weapons free from each other.

As I came upon them from the side, I slapped the bottom of my warding rod, and it hummed to life. I could feel a hint of coolness in it now that my senses were attuned to it, but I was much too excited and distracted for the calm meditation I had used for the pool and with the collars. I reached the guard, and as he wrenched his sword free from Boog's staff, I struck him squarely on the arm with my rod. He cried out, dropped the sword, and fell to the ground, his limbs twitching uncontrollably.

Boog and I stood breathing hard as Clarice arrived. She checked the downed guards and recovered her arrows. They lay still. "Boog," she said, "can you drag these bodies under the tree there? The longer they stay unnoticed, the better for us. I'll keep watch. Marten, can you get the door open?"

I pressed my ear to the door. I could hear nothing, but the guard had obviously thought someone inside might help. Boog dragged two of the downed guards away, grabbing their tabards, one in each hand. I tried the door handle, and it was unlocked. I pulled the door open just a bit and peered in. Nothing. Just an empty house. I waited, watching, but nothing happened. Finally, I pulled the door open a little wider and stuck my head in to look.

A strong hand grabbed my jacket and pulled me roughly through the doorway, hurling me to the floor. My rod went flying as I landed. Behind me, I heard the door slam and the bolt shoot closed. As quickly as I could, I rolled over and pushed myself up, scrabbling for my dagger.

Before me, in front of the door, stood three people, weapons drawn. Two were dressed in chain armor over padded leather jerkins. They wore helmets, visors down. The third, the one in the center, was bareheaded, with light brown skin, black hair, and a long black braid hanging down the left side of her head. Her blade, shorter than the others, had garnets set around the hilt. I recognized her at once. Tolla.

"You!" she said. "What are you doing here?"

"You three are under arrest," I said.

Tolla laughed. I continued. "And you owe me a pair of boots."

"Kill him, please," said Tolla, and lunged at me. I barely got my dagger up in time, but I knocked aside her blow. I heard pounding at the door, and the handle rattled, but it was clearly locked. Tolla's two companions were not as quick as she. The one on the right glanced at the door. I realized from the curve of the mail that it must be a woman. The one on the left circled around me, two steps behind Tolla, his sword point swinging in small, threatening circles.

Mistress Fennick had taught us several maneuvers for use when facing multiple opponents. *Wind Through the Reeds. Mantis Waits. Cornered Rat.* I could remember them, mostly, but I did not think I could pull them off against someone as skilled as Tolla, and certainly not in a small space without a proper weapon.

Tolla swung again, three times. I jumped back, parried, and ducked, but I was far outclassed. My warding rod lay on the floor behind Tolla, but it was a world away. I swung my dagger at Tolla, but she sidestepped easily, flowing across the floor as a sparrow in flight, and her sword found my forearm on the way by. I yelped and saw bright red drops of blood spill onto the floor. I backed up, and Tolla advanced.

"Why are you doing this?" I cried. "They killed the Prelate."

"Not my Prelate," replied Tolla, feinting with a quick stab at my gut. The man behind her was letting Tolla take the lead, but he was closing on my left side, pressing me, closing off my options. Not that it mattered. I think we all realized Tolla really didn't need the help. "And Faera will provide for us, better than your fool Prelate."

The woman on the right then did something I really did not expect. She crossed quickly behind Tolla, her sword out. She moved over to my left side, behind both Tolla and her male companion. Whom she then stabbed viciously in the back. He cried out, then sank to the floor.

Tolla swung at me again, and as I stumbled back, she shot a glance backward. "What—what are you doing?" she yelled. The other woman shoved the fallen man with her foot, pulling her sword free of his back, and stood ready, her sword pointed at Tolla's head.

I thought I should use the moment of surprise, so I lunged at Tolla, my dagger aimed, I hoped, at her heart. Although, really, I'd have settled for anywhere on her person, even a minor digit or appendage. Tolla struck me on the head with the pommel of her sword, a quick stroke but very hard, keeping the blade at the ready for the other woman.

My head rang with pain. I winced and tried to keep my dagger up, but my arm throbbed with pain from the cut Tolla had made, and my fingers were starting to feel numb and fumbly. Tolla saw her opportunity and swung at me. I tried to roll away, but her blade caught me in the shoulder and bit, perhaps a half-inch deep. I staggered with the force of her blow, and she took a quick step toward me to finish me off.

As she did so, the woman behind her cried out, a terrible scream of rage, and brought her blade suddenly up high above her head, then down in a flash of blood-stained steel. Tolla tried to throw herself aside, but the other woman shifted her aim as Tolla dodged, and the blade struck her at her collar. So strong was the strike that the sword passed several inches down into her neck. Blood welled up immediately, and Tolla fell to the ground, gasping, taking the sword with her. Her legs kicked out, and she clutched at her shoulder, trying to remove the blade, but I could see her movements slowing and weakening. Eventually, she let out a long rasping breath and lay still.

I stumbled, collapsing to a seat on the floor. I found I lacked the strength or the will to stand. My head ached and danced with pain where Tolla had struck me. I tried to press hard enough on my left shoulder to keep from losing more blood, but that made the cut on my right arm bleed more. I was pondering this irony and wondering fuzzily what to do about it when the woman wrenched her sword out of Tolla and advanced on me, crimson blood dripping from her blade.

I dropped my dagger and held up my hands. There was no more fight in me. She'd helped me, so maybe I had a chance throwing myself on her mercy.

She laughed. Then she lifted her visor a crack and spat on the floor between my feet. It was a good-sized blob of spit, and she expelled it with passion and artistry. It made a loud, satisfying wet splat on the floorboards. She pushed her helmet back up and off her head, revealing a tangled mass of black hair done up behind her neck.

"I told you, little man," said Lucianna Stout, daughter of Mileno Stout. "I need to teach you sword fighting. You get hurt otherwise. See?"

58

SUTURE SELF

"Augh!" I shouted. My shoulder blazed with pain, and the expensive brandy splashed all over me burned my nose and eyes. I smelled like a gutter drunk, albeit a wealthy one.

"Hold still, Marten," said Clarice. "I'm sorry to be hurting you." She jabbed the needle into my arm again and drew the thread through. My shoulder was on fire – the wound was bad enough, but the brandy rinse followed by the field sutures was tremendously painful. Boog was binding it with strips torn from an expensive-looking linen sheet he'd found upstairs, and the tighter he wrapped it, the better it felt.

"You're going to have some impressive scars," he remarked. "Girls like scars."

Clarice looked at him and snorted. "You know even less about girls than you do about Gortian courtly etiquette." She pulled the thread taut again. "It looks like the bleeding is slowing down, but you'll need to be careful." She looked at me, her eyes full of concern.

"I'm not staying behind," I said. They didn't protest.

Lucianna was standing at the door, looking through a small square window set in its center. "Why did you help me?" I asked.

"I owe you my life," she said.

"Not really," I said. "They let you out early. They saved you."

"Might not be the best time to get into this, Marty," said Boog. "How about tomorrow?"

She spat on the ground. "They let me out because they need a fighter. For greed. For them. You stop death sentence. Save me. For mercy. Not for you."

It had turned out to be for me in the end. "Thank you," I said. She laughed.

"That should do," said Clarice, "until we can get you to a healer." She wiped the needle clean on a section of Boog's sheet, then tucked it back into a kit at her belt. Boog started wrapping my arm with sheets. I pulled my torn jacket back up over my shoulder awkwardly with my left hand, and my shoulder sparked with pain in protest. I'd have to do things carefully, with both arms injured.

"Let's go," I said. "We're losing time." We had heard second bell as we approached the house, and the fight and sewing me up afterward had taken some time. We probably had not much more than five hours, maybe less. "Faerans or Marron's guards could arrive anytime."

"I'll barricade the doors," said Boog. "Might slow them down a little. Lucianna, can you hide the bodies in the closet over there?" She grunted and grabbed up Tolla's ankles. Boog left to find furniture for his barricade.

I stood up, adjusted my clothes, felt my bandages, and winced as I checked my range of motion. Not great, but I'd be all right. "Thanks, Clarice."

"I'm glad you weren't hurt worse, or..." she trailed off. "Let's get this door open."

She went over to the hidden door we'd found in the floor back during our first visit, months ago. The floorboards were already removed, presumably by Brand and Marron. She pulled at the door. It opened easily. I peered down through the hole. Someone had replaced the wooden ladder Gueran broke with a steep set of steps, and the cesspool was now walled off from the small landing by wooden panels. It smelled a good deal better. The tunnel mouth still gaped at the edge of the platform, beckoning.

After a moment, Boog returned and lit two of the torches Gueran had provided, passing them around. I asked Lucianna if she'd ever been down here, but she hadn't even known of the door. Clarice glided down the stairs, listened for a moment, and then waved the rest of us down. I went last, figuring I would take the longest. The descent was painful with my injuries. As I got to the sixth step down, I reached up and closed the door over my head. At last, we were in.

The tunnel curved off to the right, as I remembered. With the torches, we could see that it was well-traveled. There was some dust off to the edges, but it was disturbed by all sizes and shapes of footprints in the center and occasional drag marks. We worried that we might meet someone coming back towards us. Eventually, after a few hundred yards, we came to a large metal door blocking the tunnel, but I was able to get it unlocked after a few tense minutes with my picks.

Beyond the door, the tunnel floor transformed from paving stones to a series of flights of stone steps leading both upward and downward, mostly downward. The width of the tunnel varied, sometimes easily wide enough for four across, sometimes only for two, with some bigger chambers along the way. I wasn't sure why the builders of this tunnel had made it so irregular, but I had no expertise in mining or engineering. Perhaps the tunnel followed a natural cavern or seam in the rock layers. The stairs were treacherous in the guttering torchlight, and they made my injuries hurt more than they had already. Both bandages now showed red with blood, but the spots did not expand much after they made their appearance. I tried not to study them too closely, keeping my eyes on the stairs.

My sense of direction wasn't great underground, and the turns in the tunnel and the staircases had confused it further. But I knew the tunnel had started near the edge of the inner keep wall and was heading northward. That should lead us under the main keep itself, and if we went beyond the northern inner keep wall, we'd have to either come to the surface or head downward, following the steep cliff on which the keep sat into the northern quarter of the main part of the city below. For all I knew, we'd keep going, and end up in Gortis after days of aimless subterranean travel. But we didn't have days. I didn't know how long we'd been underground, but it must have been half an hour, maybe even an hour after my session with the lock picks.

Clarice raised a fist, and we all stopped. I strained to hear, although as the last one in line, I wasn't likely to hear anything in front of us. I tried to slow my ragged breathing and quiet my pounding heart. As I did so, I sensed something — not a sound, but a hint of coolness, the same feeling I got from the warding rods and augury pools when I focused on them. But this was a much larger source than those, faint only because it was distant from us – perhaps three hundred yards ahead, and significantly below our current position. I'd never detected anything so large or so far away before.

Clarice held a hand up next to the torch she carried, making it clearly visible to all of us. *Sound ahead. Two, three, four people.* Her fingers made the signs quickly but carefully. I doubted Lucianna understood, but she probably got the gist of it. Danger. We stood still as stones. Finally, Clarice signed again. *Going away. Clear now. Move quietly. Dropping light. Keep other.* She placed her torch on the ground and started moving again, much more slowly. Lucianna passed her torch back to Boog, but he didn't make me carry it. I was grateful.

Clarice signaled for us to stop several more times. Once I thought I heard voices, but it could have been some trick of the tunnels, or of my anxious imagination. When we stopped, and I concentrated, I could tell we were nearing the cool magical presence. Each time, after a pause, we moved onward. Lucianna was surprisingly quiet in her chain armor, though it jangled a loud disturbance on occasion. She'd left the helmet behind, and she let her hair down to fall over her shoulders.

At last, Clarice stopped again and signed, *Light ahead. Drop torch.* I shifted to one side to allow Boog to drop his torch on the floor behind us. We proceeded again, and I could see Clarice was right – it was getting lighter. Whatever was in front of us, it must be illuminated. We rounded a gentle turn in the passage, and ten feet ahead of us the tunnel opened out into empty space. Clarice stopped immediately, taking stock. Though I was at the rear, behind Boog and Lucianna, I could see, through the opening, a stone wall far beyond, but it was hard to estimate the distance without getting closer. I closed my eyes, and I could feel the cool presence I'd sensed before, stronger now, down below us. Whatever it was, it was in the room ahead of us, or below its floor.

Clarice signaled for us to wait, and she pressed herself against one wall of the passage and inched forward to get a better view, peering around the edges of the opening. After a few moments, she motioned for us to come forward, and then she slipped through, disappearing out of view to the right. The others followed.

As I came forward, trailing the whole party, Lucianna and Boog also ducked out of the tunnel, and my view was unobstructed. I came to the tunnel mouth. It opened into a huge circular chamber, perhaps two hundred feet across. The walls of the chamber were the same precise masonry and carefully shaped blocks I had seen at the Augur's Pool in guild headquarters and also at Gora's building in the mountains so far away.

The tunnel came out onto a ledge, ten feet wide, and I could see that the ledge continued all around the room, cut into the rock, unbroken except for a set of stairs that led down from the ledge on the far side. The upper walls, at the back of the ledge, curved in a gentle arc up into a round, flat ceiling perhaps twenty feet above us. A set of stairs were cut into the far wall, visible behind a huge circular pane of glass held up by two enormous metal arms. The stairs ran down to the right, then hit a narrow landing, then ran down to the left, presumably to the floor below. They looked like the only way down. Well, the only healthy way. All around the room, the high ledge ended in a sheer drop down to a large central circular space below. I could see various boxes, barrels, shelves and bags scattered around the ledge, and even a large metal cage or jail with iron bars and unpleasant stains nearby.

Clarice and Boog were prone, their heads barely peeking over the ledge, looking down at whatever lay below. I knelt and

pulled myself down to the floor of the ledge beside them, a very
delicate maneuver given my injuries. Very slowly, I moved my
head over the edge, just enough so I could see down into the
central area. What I saw below me was a huge circular floor. Set
into the center of the floor, made of bright gold and silver metal
inlaid into a carved floor, was the moon and sun symbol, a
hundred feet across, half the width of the floor, facing us. It was
the same pattern as the other versions we'd seen in the augury
pool chambers and on the amulet, which I still carried in the
pocket at my knee – the full moon on the right, with a golden
sun emerging behind it on the left.

Behind the symbols, standing at the top of the moon and sun,
there was a statue of a regal man in armor made of riveted metal
plates in a style I'd never seen. One of his hands clutched a thick
book. The other was outstretched in front of him, palm up. The
statue was exquisite, carved from intricately textured marbles of
different colors, black, pink, green and blue. Its only apparent
flaw was that, while one of its eyes was a pearly white stone orb
with a green center, the other eye was missing, leaving only an
empty socket. Extending to either side of the statue, matching
the circular arc of the room's wall, was a row of four rectangular
holes in the floor, two on each side of the statue. These were
perhaps three feet long by two feet wide and no more than a foot
deep, although it was difficult to estimate their size from our
vantage high above the floor. At the center of both the moon and
sun patterns in the floor below, there were small shallow
circular holes, no bigger than my hand. Behind the statue, near
the rectangular holes, was a set of boxes of various sizes. One
of them, I recognized easily – it was the box we carried from the
Jezarmi warehouse, presumably containing the blue corpse of
the unfortunate Nera, Princess of the Golesh tribe.

Farther behind the statue, near the stairs and nearly touching
the wall, was the enormous disk of pale blue glass, resting on its
edge. Connected to either side of the glass disk, holding it
upright, were huge curved arms, three feet wide and a foot thick.
The arms stretched out to the edges of the room, one to the side

with the sun, one to the side with the moon, slanting gently down to the floor. They were made of shiny black metal, and they followed the curvature of the room's wall around its edges, so they didn't obscure any of the symbols or holes set in the center. I wondered what function this might have. At the far end of each of the arms, away from the glass disk, they descended down into slots set in the floor. The whole apparatus looked terribly heavy, but the slots extended well beyond the end of the arms, suggesting that the arms could move. If the arms could be shifted or rotated upward, it might be possible to raise the glass disk up toward the ceiling of the room. I could see no point in doing that, though. The ceiling was the same featureless stone tile as the walls, and the position of the disk seemed irrelevant.

As I studied the room, I was confused about the source of light. There were six braziers burning down below, giving the air a smoky tang. These were set in a circle around the edge of the room, but they did not seem bright enough to produce the illumination we were seeing, which was steady and smooth, almost as if the bricks of the walls and floor were glowing softly of their own accord.

I've said it was difficult to estimate sizes from where we lay, peering over the edge, but we did have something to use for scale. Brand and Marron were down there, standing in the center of the sun carving, discussing something intently with a woman in robes and a soft square cap. She was a handsome woman, probably forty years old, with curly dark brown hair. She also wore one of the moon and sun pendants I'd seen the other Faerans wearing, not as big or as elaborate as the one I carried and the one that Novara had owned. A few other robed workers moved around the floor on various errands, cleaning, sweeping, carrying objects about. Spaced evenly around the edges of the room, leaning against the walls, stood ten armed warriors. Five were men, five women, with swords at their belts and small crossbows at the ready, keeping watch over the room. They wore light leather armor, covered up by loose long tabards showing the Faeran moon and sun emblem.

We observed for a minute or so and then backed silently away so that Lucianna could take a turn. No one below seemed to have a reason to look up, and nobody else seemed to be on the upper ledge level where we were. So, though we were in a precarious spot, we were probably safe from discovery for the moment.

Lucianna slid back from the edge, and Clarice waved us all back into the darkness of the tunnel.

"What do we do now?" Boog whispered, looking from one face to the other.

"This has to be the place," I said. "Nera – the blue woman – – is here, and I'm willing to bet that statue is Hrogar."

"There are too many there to fight," said Clarice. "Even with the higher ground."

"Can we get help?" said Boog.

"It took us forever to get here," I replied. "We'd have to go out and then come back again – I don't think there's time. There might be other exits, but I didn't see anything obvious, and I don't know that we can search without being seen."

"Whom would we bring, anyway? There aren't that many of us in the first place," said Clarice. "The City Guard isn't likely to follow us down here. You two are criminals, and I'm not supposed to be posted here in Frosthelm. At best, they might send a guard or two, and that's not enough."

"I don't think we can afford to leave, and have whatever they're planning go on without us," I said.

"What are we going to be able to do when it happens, if we can't do anything now?" asked Boog.

A reasonable question. I pondered for a bit. "If Madame Lenarre's books were correct, they're supposed to need all of the objects there to unlock Faera's prison. If we could steal one of them…"

Boog shook his head. "Too many eyes down there now. We'd never make it."

"A distraction of some kind?" said Clarice. "Draw the guards away?"

"That might work," replied Boog. "But it's a longshot, and with only one staircase down there, and only the tunnel to escape through, I don't really know that we could pull it off."

"We don't have to pull it off for very long," I said. "The eclipse shouldn't last for more than what, ten minutes, right? I think they're short."

"How would I know?" said Boog. "You're the man of science." He thought some more. "Even if it is minutes, they may use the objects earlier than that, to set it up, and we might lose our chance."

"Then we kill them," said Lucianna. "Easy."

She had a point. An arrow through the right person in the middle of it all could be all the disruption we needed. But it was a big gamble, that we'd have an opportunity, and that we'd succeed.

"For now, then, we wait and watch," said Clarice. "Look for an opportunity, take it if we find one, but otherwise, wait until closer to the eclipse to act. They're the ones with a tight schedule, not us."

Boog scowled. He didn't like inaction. But then he nodded his assent, then asked, "How in the six hells are they going to know when the eclipse is, buried underground like this?"

None of us had an answer. "Maybe it's obvious," I said. "Faera shows up, rings a dinner gong and sets out tea service for twenty." Nobody thought I was very funny, myself included.

Fearing that someone might come from the tunnel, we circled around on the broad ledge, finding a hiding spot behind a stack of crates and bags about halfway between the tunnel mouth and the staircase. For the next hour or so, we took turns peering over the edge of the ledge as the work continued. Boog chafed at the waiting, swinging his arms and flexing his fingers. I felt the tension too, and Clarice's mouth was fixed in a grim line as she checked over the fletching of each arrow. Lucianna alone sat still and at ease, almost as if she were meditating. In this moment of tense calm, I remembered something I needed to do. I pulled the falcon pendant out from under my jacket and pulled it up over my head. "Clarice," I said, holding it out.

"Oh," she said, smiling. "You brought it back! Thank you so much."

One detail had been bothering me. "Why did you send your cloak to Gora along with the pendant?"

"I wasn't certain you'd recognize the pendant, but I thought you'd know the cloak was mine. You found my note, right? I figured you'd find the hidden hole easily – you're so good with things like that."

"Yes, we found it," I replied, hiding my embarrassment. I could perhaps go into the details later. But me, not recognize the pendant? She clearly didn't realize just how much time I'd spent watching her every move. That was probably just as well. She slipped the chain over her neck and gripped the falcon tightly for a moment.

I wanted to say more, but I wasn't sure what. "Clarice," I began. I paused.

She looked at me, and then smiled a small, knowing smile. "We had a conversation, not so long ago, out in the hills. One that we didn't finish, but one that I very much wanted to."

My heart leapt. "I wanted to too. I wasn't sure…" She looked back at me, a hint of puzzlement on her face. Nothing for it but to dive in. "You're so strong, so confident, so clever. I admire you. So much. Have, for years." I swallowed. "I didn't think…"

Clarice smiled. "Didn't think what? That I admired you too? You were easily the top student in our class."

"Not in fencing." I grimaced.

She gave a low chuckle. "No, not in that. But in everything else." She paused. "It's funny, you know. You barely miss anything, Marten. Clues, patterns, magic – you pick it all up so easily, and see connections we all miss, can do things with the pool and the rods that none of us could figure out. You're so perceptive. Except — except you have some blind spots. Some things you don't see at all."

"Like what?" I said, confused.

"Well, there are two main areas. Two areas you need to work on, that you don't see," she said. "First, you don't see yourself.

You think you're scrawny and weak." I winced inwardly. Coming from her, that stung. But it was true. "And sure, there are others bigger and stronger. But I've never seen a man so brave. And so set on justice, and yet so kind-hearted. You've taken on Marron without a thought to the risk. That's not something I'd been able to do, even though I had far more cause. Not until you gave me hope, and showed me a way, even as it got harder and harder to find one."

My inner turmoil faded, and turned to a mix of pride and sadness as she spoke – pride, that she thought well of me, colored by sorrow at what Marron had done to her and her parents. Her eyes were bright, and I could see, I think, that she was sincere. Not trying to cajole me into happier spirits, not condescending, or just comforting an injured friend when he was down. Sincere and kind.

Something in me melted away then. Something dark and hurtful, that I'd been carrying for a while. A part of me I needed to let go. I felt stronger, more confident. Assured. If Clarice thought I was a good guy, then maybe I was. No, not maybe. I was.

"What's the other thing I don't see?" I asked.

She leaned in, quick, and kissed me. It was soft and warm, and better than any of the hundreds of times I'd imagined it.

Some time later, Boog waved us over to the ledge. His eyes were wide and dark, and his jaw clenched tight. We peered over. Brand and the robed woman with whom he'd been talking began to open the boxes behind the statue. The contents of each one they set in the four rectangular cavities. The left-most held a mace of black iron, with green gemstones set in its handle and vicious spikes at its head. In the next hole, they placed a fine crown, with many different bright jewels set in a broad circle of gold. On the other side of the statue, the woman opened a small bag of brilliant red cloth and upended it carefully over the hole. Small yellow flakes tumbled out. I supposed them to be the fabled Fingernails of the Holy Hermit I'd heard about from Madame Lenarre.

Finally, the woman summoned over some helpers, and they opened the ornate chest Boog and I had discovered in the Jezarmi warehouse, revealing the hapless Nera folded up inside. What followed was actually rather comical, in a gruesome way. They had some trouble getting her unpacked from the box. Bodies are heavy, and they found it difficult to get much of a grip on her. Also, it was a pretty tight fit in the box, and she was snugly packed inside, and had been for months. They took turns straining and pulling, trying to get her free but instead merely dragging the box around the floor, occasionally tugging on a blue arm that flopped loose. They paused occasionally for discussion and then pulled some more. At length, one of them had the bright idea of tipping the box over, and with a brave display of exertion, three of them yanked hard enough to get her to flop out on the floor, blue limbs flailing and slapping the tiles. After that, they needed to get her packed into the hole on the floor, which was not really large enough to fit. Perhaps the designers of this particular ritual had imagined a younger or smaller princess of the Golesh tribe.

It took some five attempts, with much folding and refolding of Nera's multiply-abused corpse. I was sure this part of the exercise would definitely not make it into the official Ballad of the Reawakening of Faera. Finally, they decided that it was good enough, and left her there, her head resting on top of a knee and under a folded arm. Even the best prophecies never seem to give you the practical details you need, I surmised.

All four of the ceremonial items were now in place in their holes. At this point, Marron, who'd been pacing the floor over to one side, strode over to Brand. He and Brand began to argue, with the robed woman looking on. As agitated as he was, we could hear pretty well.

"Brand," said Marron. "I must say it again: this is a bad idea. I've read the prophecies, the rituals. You don't know what is going to happen here."

"Faera is going to awaken, and reward us," said Brand, his voice rising. "It's written clearly in every book, every song, every verse. Eternal life, boundless power. What we've been working for all this time."

"There was a reason they locked him – it – away all those years ago. Those same books and songs tell of terrible destruction, of countless deaths—"

"Deaths of non-believers! Of the unworthy!" shouted Brand. "You've shown no remorse at slaying your enemies before. Why now?"

Marron's face burned with rage. "Do not question my commitment. I will always do what needs to be done. What is in question is your judgment, your sanity. Faera seems as likely to boil out of the ground and devour us as to reward us."

"Only if we stand against Faera's power," yelled Brand. "As you do now!"

"You're a madman!" shouted Marron. "You risk our lives, the whole city, for what? The dreams of long dead fanatics."

"They weren't fanatics six months ago, when you used them to spark the Prelate's curiosity and curry his favor," retorted Brand. "They were wise scholars, and their prophecy would give us power to destroy our enemies and elevate the city and all its citizens. And the Prelate himself."

"You don't understand," said Marron. "Faera was a threat and a weapon, a powerful one. But one we no longer need. We've already won. We control the city, the guild, the guard. The Prelate's dead, and I can easily win the vote of the Council of Lords. I'll be named the next Prelate. We have what we wanted – more than we wanted."

"You have what you wanted, apparently. But not what we worked for." Brand's voice was bitter, cutting.

"Worked for? We used this legend to advance our standing! And now we reign supreme. We have no more need of Faera."

Brand raised an arm and pointed at Marron, his finger stabbing the air as he spoke. "No, Count Marron," said Brand, his voice cold as ice. "Faera has no more need of you." He waved at the circle of warriors. "Take him and bind him. He will see Faera awaken, and then he will be sacrificed. Consumed with the other heretics. The flames shall burn him to purity."

Marron let out a snarl and drew his sword, but Brand was faster with his wand, and Marron stepped back, not wanting to be turned to dust. The ten soldiers all closed on Marron, threatening him with swords or crossbows. "I pay your wages," shouted Marron to the guards. "Kill *him*! A thousand sovereigns to the one who cuts him down!" he cried, gesturing at Brand with his sword.

Brand laughed. "They have no more need of coins, Marron. They are about to become gods." Three guards closed on Marron, their swords threatening. Marron dropped into a fighting stance, but then he looked around at the guards, saw his hopeless odds, and lowered his sword. "You're all mad," he spat, "Lunatics, every one." The guards grabbed him and marched him roughly over to the base of the stairs. One dug through a bag to produce some leather straps, and they bound Marron's hands and feet tightly, leaving him sitting on the steps facing the center of the chamber. He struggled against his bonds, but he seemed quite expertly immobilized.

I realized I had longed to see Marron crushed, defeated, captured, bound. But not like this. He'd been the only one down there talking sense.

59

PROPHET AND LOSS

We retreated behind a wall of crates and began a rapid-fire discussion in whispers. The events below had changed course drastically, to be sure, but we realized that our situation hadn't changed much. It was most important to disrupt the ceremony, and Marron's predicament had little to do with that. If anything, it helped us. With Marron incapacitated, we only needed to take out one of them – Brand. I wondered if Clarice was a good enough shot. She surely seemed it in our attack on Novara's house, but despite my faith in her, I hoped the fate of our city didn't come down to one arrow.

We returned to our observation of the situation below. A change came over the proceedings. The preparations seemed complete. Many of the subordinate workers crossed to the side below the moon and sun, across from the statue and the four objects in their holes, taking up positions in rows. The ten soldiers, too, moved over to that side, and all of them stood quietly together. Brand and the robed woman stood together at the top of the symbol by the statue of Hrogar, and they carried on a discussion in low tones, gesturing occasionally at various parts of the room, and more than once, at the room's ceiling. I wondered what that was all about.

Finally, Brand clapped his hands with a flourish and raised his arms. Imperious as ever, I thought. I really didn't like the guy. "My friends," said Brand, his voice clear and loud. "The day is upon us. The hour is upon us. In a few short minutes, Faera will be reawakened. He will rise again, free from his bonds. You, my brothers and sisters, you who have served him so faithfully and so well, will be the first to see his rebirth into the world. You will be the first to feel his power, to be granted his reward."

As Brand spoke, Clarice gave the signal. It was time to act. Now, or not at all. The four of us retreated to the back wall of the ledge and moved quickly but quietly around the curved ledge, heading for the staircases leading down. We could not see the floor below, so we hoped they could not see us, though perhaps a stray shadow or sound might betray us. They all seemed to be fixated on Brand, though. He continued.

"We will now begin the ritual. We must open the temple to the sky, so that the power of the eclipse can be felt down here, where Faera lies imprisoned. The legends tell us that Frosthelm itself will be pushed aside by the power of this place. There are far too many who have joined our path to fit down here, so we have told our companions to meet us up above, in the market square, where we have calculated that the city will open up to reveal Faera's prison. They, our brothers and sisters, will join us in bearing witness to Faera's release, Faera's freedom."

We reached the staircases. This was the tricky part, because we would be far more exposed running down the stairs than we were on top of the ledge. Clarice held up a hand. *Wait*, she signed. *Wait for open*. She pointed up. I could see her logic. Brand had implied that the ceiling opened up somehow, but I didn't know how that was possible. When that occurred, the attention of those below would presumably be focused solely up above, not at us on the stairs, and we would have our best chance to get down there undetected.

But that might not be good enough. I caught Clarice's eye. *We down*, I signed, *you here. If we fail, you shoot?* She furrowed her brow and slid over to take a quick look over the edge.

She returned, looked me in the eye, and nodded once. *Good luck*, she signed back. She pulled her bow off her back, checked the string, and popped the cover off her quiver.

Down below, Brand was wrapping up. "This, my brothers and sisters, is Faera's time. This is our time. For thousands of years, Faera has seethed and raged down here, below our very feet, waiting for release. Release that is now within our grasp! Today, we, my friends, will do what no others have been able to do for centuries. We will grant Faera freedom, and with that freedom will come our reward! Immortality, boundless power, and dominion over the non-believers, the weak, those who do not share our glorious truth!"

He grew quiet for a moment, then folded his hands over his chest. "My brothers and sisters, our time, Faera's time, is now." He raised a fist into the air. "Whom do we serve?" he cried.

"Faera!" shouted the throng of believers. Either they somehow were uncannily synchronized by chance, or this was a call-and-response that they had done before.

"Who is life?"

"Faera!" shouted the crowd again.

"Who is strength?" cried Brand.

"Faera!"

"Are you with me?"

"Until Faera is free!" The believers broke into applause and shouted prayers.

"Now," said Brand. "In the few minutes remaining until we open the temple to the sky, Sister Colette has asked to perform a song of praise she has composed to commemorate this great day. Please, center yourselves within Faera's benevolent presence, prepare for our great destiny, and listen."

The robed woman bowed her head and moved from the statue to the base of the stairs. We couldn't see Marron down there, nearly directly below our position at the top of the staircase, but I heard his voice, loud, mocking, and full of indignant exasperation. "Oh, PLEASE," he said. "Really?"

I worried that she would come up the stairs, but instead, she quickly came back into view carrying a lute of golden-brown wood with a wide dangling strap. She shot an angry glance back at Marron, then advanced to the center of the room, placing the embroidered strap about her neck. She bowed her head to the gathered worshippers again and gave the lute a strum. Frowning, she adjusted one of the lute's tuning pegs and strummed again. She adjusted a second peg, then played several twangy notes that bent up and down as she turned the pegs. Then again another strum. And another small adjustment of the pegs.

Brand cleared his throat loudly. She looked over, and he smiled broadly and made an exaggerated beckoning motion with his hands. The woman blushed, adjusted her square cap, plucked each string once more from high to low, then took a deep breath. And then a second deep breath. Finally, she swung her hand up high, gave the lute a mighty downward strum, and began to sing.

The song began all right, recounting a version of the imprisonment of Faera by a band of wizards which more or less matched what Gora had told us. The melody ran a little bit high for her voice at times, though, which made it sound a bit screechy. Brand kept his broad smile serene, but some of the worshippers began to look at each other. After an unfortunate rhyme of "Faera" with "terror," there was an intricate lute bridge strain, and she slowed down a little as it got harder to play. Then she sped up again and launched into the second verse, which told the tale of Faera's long slumber. Sister Colette was again not quite up to singing the higher parts, but she pressed gamely onward. This verse closed with "his power to share-a!" She got stuck in the bridge strain this time and had to restart it, her fingers twitching as she frowned, blushing. Brand's smile had faded a bit now, and some of the congregation hid smiles behind their hands. Boog tapped my shoulder and looked at me, a quizzical expression on his face. I shrugged back.

The third verse spoke first of how hard Faera's current followers had labored to bring him back. Then it shifted into an extended metaphor in which Faera played the part of a tomcat, fighting off all the other cats in the street where he lived. One of them was not-so-subtly called Blood Mother, and she met a terrible end. The feline version of Faera then granted life and leniency to the mice upon which he'd formerly preyed. It ended with a rousing rhyme, repeated twice, about the "bloodstains on his furr-ah!" This time, she nearly got the bridge strain right, and as it ended, she slowed to half-pace and chanted "Faera" in a deep monotone three times, all the while strumming a steady cadence on the lute. I thought she must be done, and so did Brand, who stepped forward to take charge again. But then Colette started up a fourth verse, this one about Faera's illustrious future as a king of the sky.

As her voice rose in shrill praise of Faera's cloudy palace, Brand shouted "Thank you!" and started clapping loudly. There were scattered echoes of applause from the assembled listeners. Colette halted, mid-syllable, and looked flustered. "Thank you, Sister Colette," said Brand. "Powerful words of praise." She played one more faltering note, then stopped. She bowed her head and walked back toward the stairs. I heard Marron murmur something and laugh, and then she reappeared, this time without her instrument.

"Sister, it is time," said Brand. "Have you the Eye of Hrogar?" We tensed up, ready to move. Colette fished a white stone out of a pouch at her belt. She approached the statue and placed the stone in the statue's empty eye socket. Nothing happened. Boog started down the stairs, slow and silent, followed by Lucianna, and I crept along after them. The worshippers flanked the statue, watching Colette work. I hoped they would not turn toward us, although we were partially hidden by the giant glass disk and its metal arms. I felt terribly exposed.

I couldn't see the statue well from the stairs, as it faced mostly away from me, but it looked like the eye she put in was pointed sideways, surely leaving poor Hrogar wall-eyed. She waited for a time, watching the statue, her lips parted. Then she crossed over to Brand and spoke to him. He muttered back, pointing at the statue.

I was struck by a sudden realization. Brand and his followers had never done this before. They couldn't do a trial run – there was only one eclipse like this in a lifetime, and the ritual had never been completed, or Faera would be free. They had never opened the temple to the sky. If it was under the city, people above would surely notice if the city was split asunder or swept apart to reveal this room. They were feeling their way through a ritual engineered centuries ago, described to them in a host of documents that had likely been translated and retranslated, lost and damaged, and subject to questionable interpretation. Unless Faera was somehow down there telling them exactly what to do, they were working through this blindly.

It was even possible, I thought, that the ritual was nothing but the ramblings of fanatics, that there was no Faera, or that whatever Faera was, it had long since escaped, starved, or died of boredom. But Marron had seemed genuinely concerned that whatever Brand was doing would work. And then I remembered my vision in the pool so long ago – balls of fire, raining from the sky. That was real enough. If that came to pass, and the Augur said the pool's predictions always had, it was likely that whatever Brand was doing would succeed.

Sister Colette went back to the statue and adjusted the eye stone she had inserted, pushing on it, then rotating it around in the socket. She looked nervously back at Brand, then pushed on it again. He came over to have a look, but as he neared the statue, there was a fearsome clanking noise, and a hail of dust and gravel fell like rain from the ceiling. The whole chamber vibrated, and a wide circular area of the ceiling, some seventy feet above the floor, began to shift. As the clanking and rain of pebbles and dust continued, the ceiling split apart into seven sections, each shaped like a slice of pie. Between the sections, black cracks widened, and more and more material fell to the floor below, bigger pieces now, including bricks and cobblestones. Brand and the others backed up, staring at the ceiling, moving to safer spots around the edges. Boog and Lucianna and I resumed moving down the stairs, but the going was difficult with the room shaking and with the noise and dust.

There was then a groaning and grinding noise as two of the sections of ceiling shuddered to a stop. The other five continued, and I could see thin blue slivers of sky showing through in places, growing as the sections separated. Tremendous cracking and popping sounds resounded through the chamber, and the two stuck wedges split apart and moved again. Where they split, a curtain of water rained down to the floor, and several of the nearby cultists were swept to the ground by the spray as it struck them. As the cracks above widened, more and more water spilled through, until the deluge finally slowed, and the curtain of water broke into dripping streams. There was a full inch or two of water soaking the floor amidst the ritual items and the debris that had fallen from above.

Through the grinding, clanking, and splashing, I could sometimes hear the frantic cries of the cultists below as they tried to dodge the falling stones and water. I could also hear shouts and yells from above us. As we reached the landing, halfway down the stairs, I could see a seven-pointed star of sky widening in the center of the ceiling as the seven sections retracted. I could not tell from what showed through what part of the city we stood under. But then a basket of apples tumbled through one of the cracks, the fruit pouring out, and the apples smashed into the floor with loud splats as the basket bounced and broke into pieces. After that came wooden boards, two melons, and a piece of gaudily painted awning advertising a fruit stand. More and more goods fell through the cracks – a rack of shirts on wooden hangers, a tray of jewelry, an entire kebab cart with skewers and fiery embers. Three wooden cages full of chickens fell through in quick succession, and they smashed apart into clouds of twigs, straw, and feathers. Though most of the birds did not appear to have survived the fall, some of them fluttered or limped about the temple floor in new-found freedom, screeching and cawing.

We reached the bottom of the stairs. Marron lay there, covered in dust and grime, feathers stuck to his face. He struggled with the straps holding him. Boog struck him hard with his staff, and Marron slumped over, moaning. I wanted to do something, anything to him, ideally something of the fatal or painful varieties, but there was no time. We had to reach the statue and try to halt the ceremony. All around us, objects crashed to the ground. They were nearly impossible to dodge, falling fast from seventy feet above. I was struck by a round loaf of hard bread, which was surprisingly painful, and I saw Lucianna stumble as a basket of rolls grazed her shoulder on the way down.

Most of the soldiers and cultists cowered along the edge of the room, their arms raised up over their heads for shelter. Some lay limp and still, limbs splayed about, unconscious or dead from the rain of articles from above. The air was hazy with dust, feathers, and debris, and the floor was slick and treacherous. I stared wildly about, looking for Brand. He and Colette were huddled next to the statue. I shouted to Boog and Lucianna and pointed.

Boog charged across the temple floor, pulling his staff back to strike, but three of the soldiers scrambled to their feet and ran to intercept him, drawing their swords. Far above us, the sections of ceiling had almost completely retracted. They were small triangles now, poking like sharp teeth out of the edges of what was otherwise a circle of blue sky. I didn't see the sun directly, but it shone in a bright band on one side of the upper wall. I knew it should be at an angle in the sky to the south of us, so the lit wall must be the north side.

Boog swung his staff at the first of the soldiers to reach him, connecting with the man's helmet with a resounding crack. The man dropped to the ground and lay still. The second one reached Boog before he had recovered, and I shouted out a warning as the soldier swung his sword down at Boog. Boog lurched back from the swing, but his foot slipped on the wet floor, and he fell onto his back. The soldier raised his sword again, this time holding it point down with both hands, poised to drive it down into Boog's chest. I did not see how Boog could escape, although he scrabbled back along the wet ground. But then the soldier's grip loosened, and he dropped the sword and fell over on his side. I was mystified at first, but then I saw the red feathers of an arrow protruding upward from his chest. Clarice.

I drew my warding rod from its holster at my belt, and I slapped the end, causing it to buzz to life, but I was too far away to help Boog. The third soldier reached Boog as he was scrambling to stand. She had her sword out, ready and deadly, but Lucianna got there at the same time. Lucianna was a flurry of black hair and steel, screaming guttural syllables in her language with each blow, and the soldier soon went down clutching her belly. Lucianna yelled and pointed behind me, and I spun around, getting the rod up just in time to knock aside a sword strike from another temple guard. As she pulled back to swing again, I thrust my rod straight into her stomach. It discharged, and she fell to the ground, her arms flung wide.

I spun around in a full circle, looking for more danger. We'd taken out four of the soldiers. Two of the others were down and not moving at the edge of the room, probably struck by something from above. The other four were up on their feet and approaching. There was a monstrous clang from above, and the clanking and grinding stopped. The ceiling was fully retracted. Debris and soil still clattered down around the edges, and water still dripped down along one side, but the flood from above was much reduced.

Over by the statue, as the dust and haze swirled about them, Colette and Brand rose. Brand held her gently by the arm, protectively, I thought. Could she be special to him in some way? One of Clarice's arrows darted down from above. It bounced off the statue only inches from Brand's arm. He flinched and ducked behind the statue, dragging Colette with him. Lucianna yelled again and spat, and then she ran headlong at the four guards, her sword arm out at her side, sword point forward. One of the soldiers suddenly lurched and fell to one knee, an arrow stuck in his shoulder, and as he reached up to paw at his injury, Lucianna struck him hard across the chest. He went down, a red gash blossoming from shoulder to hip.

Boog ran up and stood at Lucianna's side, his staff weaving and spinning as he struck out at the guards. Though there were three soldiers, my two companions were more than enough of a match. They parried, thrust, dodged, and struck, and after a few moments, the temple guards lay still at their feet. Lucianna bled from a cut over her eye, and Boog now favored his left ankle, but they turned as one back toward the statue, toward Brand and Colette. Boog stared at Brand, his eyes narrowed to angry slits, his teeth bared in a snarl, and he took a step forward.

At that moment, an enormous clanking started up again, this time from below. The entire floor lurched upward, and I fought to keep my balance. Brand looked surprised at this development, and he fell to his knees. Colette clutched onto the statue for balance. After the initial lurch, the movement upward was steady. I shot a glance skyward and saw a few heads poking over the edge of the wide hole in the ceiling. If they were Faerans, they were probably overjoyed to see us. If they were regular citizens, such as sellers of chickens, they were more than likely completely bewildered.

Once Boog was sure of his footing, he again moved toward the statue, running at an uneven jog. He swung a vicious stroke at Brand, knocking him prone. Colette drew a wand from her robe and began a singsong chant of strange words. As Boog spun to strike Colette, her wand glowed with a greenish light. Just as Boog was about to reach her, she flung her hand out, and the wand shot a bolt of green light at Boog. As it struck, Boog cried out and let go of his staff. The light swirled around him. Boog stiffened, his back arched, and then he fell where he had stood, his staff bouncing to the floor.

I shouted in anguish. Boog was down. My best friend in the world. Dead? Absorbed by the power of Faera? I had no idea. But Colette was to blame. I ran at her, howling, my warding rod in one hand, a dagger in the other. And as I raged, I could suddenly sense, below the floor, a presence, a hotness, seething, pushing upward. Was this Faera, alive beneath us?

Colette fired a green bolt at me as well, but the warding rod absorbed its power. I felt a ripple of energy as it dissipated. I reached her just as Brand struggled to his feet again. I swung my dagger at her, but it went wide as she shifted to avoid it. I turned to swing again, but Lucianna was faster. She plunged her sword deep into the priestess of Faera. The wand's glow faded, and it dropped from Colette's fingers. She gasped, and her legs crumpled. She slid to the floor.

"No!" screamed Brand. His wand was in hand. I knew what it could do. I dove aside, my warding rod at the ready. But Lucianna did not, and she did what her training told her. She yanked her sword back up, out of Colette, and swung at Brand. There was a flash of light, and a sound like the bark of a small angry dog, and Lucianna's armor and sword fell to the ground, orange powder billowing up from the pile as it landed.

A wave of acute sorrow and anger washed over me. Lucianna was gone. But I had no time to mourn. I rose to face Brand. He was breathing heavily, looking down at Colette. He was pale, barely able to remain upright. I think that using the wand took a great deal of his energy. As he stood there, an arrow flew down from above and buried itself in his leg. His knee buckled, and he cast his gaze upward as he struggled to remain standing.

It was then as if time slowed to a crawl. I shouted at Brand, not words, just raw hate, a bestial snarl. But he did not care about me, then. He had been shot. The danger was from above. He raised the wand, and I saw that he aimed it at Clarice, up on the ledge, not at me.

Not Clarice.

Not Clarice too.

As crackling energy gathered around Brand's wand, I hurled my warding rod at Brand, desperate to stop him. I had no time to think. If I had, I might have realized that throwing the rod left me defenseless against Brand's wand. But I would have thrown it even so, with no hesitation, without a second thought.

Brand was familiar with the warding rods. He had seen me use mine, and he and Marron had likely plundered all of the Guild's magical secrets. He knew that if it touched him, he would be paralyzed. So, he did that which came from instinct. He used his wand to knock aside the rod.

But his wand was an object steeped in destruction, in death, in chaos, and it was charged to strike. And my rod was an object designed to nullify magic, to cancel it, control it, and also to dissipate anger, passion, and violence with stillness, with peace. It was an object borne of control, of order. And as Stennis had discovered in the tavern, as Novara had found through the pool, and as Gora had told me, *the surest way to ruin, as a wizard, is to try to bind aspects of chaos with aspects of order.*

As my rod struck Brand's wand, the rod discharged. Order struggled for an instant to contain chaos. But only for an instant. Brand's wand exploded with a searing burst of light and heat. I saw Brand fly back from the blast, just as I was thrown back as well. My head struck something hard, and I slipped into darkness.

60

THE ECLIPSE

Claws dug into my chest, and something sharp stabbed repeatedly at my face. Over and over. Not a weapon, unless an enemy with a blade was toying with me, prodding me. I opened my eyes to see a hideous feathered face, twitching to the left and right, bulging eyes staring at mine.

The chicken pecked me again, right in the nose. I knocked it off my chest, and it squawked and fluttered off. I sat up. I couldn't have been out for long. the floor was still rising, clanking and grinding, although it was now almost level with the ledge where we had entered. The stairs we'd descended, cut into the wall, were now nearly covered up by the rising floor. Somewhere down there at the base of the stairs, now in a deep hole, was Marron. The whole chamber was much shorter now, and sunlight streamed in, replacing the darkness. I checked myself quickly for new injuries, but I seemed to be all right, other than ringing ears from the blast and a lump on the back of my head to match the one on top from Tolla's blow. My other wounds ached, but the stitches held. As I looked down at my hands, I noticed that the shadows they cast were strange. Where light passed through my fingers, instead of crisp, regular edges to the shadows, they were curved into crescents.

The eclipse! I stared up at the sky. The moon covered most of the sun. It was too bright for more than a glance, and spots danced in my vision as I looked away. The daylight around me darkened noticeably as the eclipse progressed. I stood and cast my gaze around the room. A group of the Faerans was gathered at the edge of the room, wet and filthy, some of them climbing up onto the ledge, which was now only four feet above the floor and sinking fast. I saw that they were trying to reach Clarice. She skirted them and ran around the ledge. There were too many of them to fight, but she seemed to be keeping ahead of them for now. She fired several arrows back into them as she ran, and some found their mark.

Across the room from me, I saw Brand struggling, crawling across the sun symbol. I didn't know what he meant to do, but it couldn't be good. I stumbled over to him, weak, my feet treacherous. He reached the midpoint of the sun part of the floor carving, where the small hole was cut into the floor, and then he noticed me approaching. He looked up, and I saw that his face was a burned, bloody mess. His right hand was missing. Taken, I presumed, by the explosion.

He laughed, wheezing. "You brought it," he said. "You brought it."

"What?"

"I hoped it would work without it, that one key would be enough. But you brought it! It can only be destiny. Two keys."

I couldn't figure out what he meant. I had lost my dagger as well as my rod, so I had no weapon to use. I reached down and grabbed a handful of his robe, but as I did so, he raised his remaining hand. Clutched in his grasp was Novara's amulet, the moon and sun of Faera. I pulled on Brand's robe, tugging him closer to me, and with my other hand, I grabbed at the amulet. But he was too quick.

The sky darkened. Above us, the moon slid over the sun, and the only light came from a ring of fire around the dark disk of the moon. Brand slapped his remaining hand down, pushing the amulet down into the hole in the floor at the center of the carved sun. The amulet disappeared down the hole, and its chain slid in behind it. Suddenly, at my knee, I felt a burst of fire. It was the amulet we'd recovered from Stennis, the one I'd been carrying for so long. Pain shot up my leg, and a jet of fire spewed out from the patch. My trousers burst into flame.

I let go of Brand and jumped back, pawing and slapping at my knee. I tore at the thick cloth, singeing my fingers, but the flames died out. The amulet dropped out to the ground. It glowed red. I reached for it, but it was too hot to pick up. As I pulled back my hand, I felt something incredibly hot pass through me. I realized it was not a physical object, but instead a wave of energy, rising up from below. The same hot presence I'd felt before, then trapped below the floor, pushing upward. Now, it was free.

On the ground in front of me, Brand cried out. "Faera!" he screamed. He writhed and twisted, whether in pain or ecstasy, I couldn't say. As I watched, black smoke poured out of the hole at the center of the sun carving, and it flew into his mouth and nose. His body transformed. His missing hand grew back, but not as a human hand. It was webbed, and his fingers were thin and ended in round balls, like those of a frog. He held up his other hand, and it contorted and stretched to match the other. His mouth widened, his upper lip protruded, and his eyes grew large and shifted outward, toward the sides of his head. His skin healed, then turned a dark green. His eyes turned red as blood, and his pupils expanded to vertical slits.

And he grew. His body expanded, and a rippling yellow-green mass of flesh wormed out from the bottom of his robe. As I watched, it extended, sprouting pairs of legs along the side, ending in feet with long feathery digits. His robe split and ripped as his body grew, and I saw that his whole body was yellow-green, with the backside a darker shade of green with angular spots. He was no longer recognizable as Brand. As he changed, I felt a flash of intense heat, emanating from the beast. It took me a moment to realize my skin was not blistering, and I seemed to suffer no lasting damage. I realized that the heat I sensed was not physical heat – it was the heat of chaos, of the magic I'd learned to sense from Gora's teaching. And it wasn't just Brand, or whatever he was now, producing the heat. He felt like a simmering ball, but there was a thick strand of chaos magic connecting him to something deeper, below, underground. It was so intense I didn't need to close my eyes or extend any effort to sense it. It was just there, feeding into Brand from a source below the ground.

I backed away from the beast as it reared up, supporting itself on its thick, worm-like tail. It opened its mouth, waved its frog arms around, and let out an uncanny howl. I turned to run, and though I feared it would come after me, it did not. It was still twisting and growing. Its head was twenty feet above the floor now, and its body was twice that length with the many-legged tail section stretching out behind him.

To one side, I saw the group of cultists. They had given up their pursuit of Clarice, though she still ran away from them. Some stared, open mouthed. Others cowered. A few approached Brand, their arms outstretched. The central floor of the chamber was still rising. It had reached the level of the ledge now, and if it kept going, we would emerge from the hole into the open air, into the city. The statue of Hrogar was bathed in the dim sunlight of the eclipse, as was the top of the large blue glass disk behind the statue, its metal arms stretching out to either side. Clarice stepped up off the ledge onto the rising platform.

Brand, or Faera, or whatever he was now, bent down toward the cultists who approached. He extended his long, skinny arms and wrapped his glistening fingers around their heads. As he touched them, one by one, they sank to the ground, and then they too began to twist and change. There were five of them now, Brand the largest.

I saw Clarice loose an arrow. It flew straight to Brand and struck him in the yellow flesh of his upper body, under the grinning head. But as the arrow struck, it burst into flame and turned instantly to ash, leaving no mark on Brand. She shot again, and again her arrow was destroyed. Brand paid her no heed.

The other creatures had grown to match Brand's size, though their coloring and spots were different. The platform was only a few feet below the surface now, and I could see the tops of buildings around us. Gradually the north market came into view. We had risen up in the center of the marketplace, in Fountain

Square. In fact, the opening cut through the fountain itself. That must have been the source of the water that had cascaded down on us when the ceiling opened.

All around us, there were crowds of people, staring and shouting at us as we rose up. At the sight of the monstrous creatures that Brand and the other cultists had become, most of the spectators fled through the streets or into nearby buildings, although many remained. I saw around the necks of many of those who stayed the small moon and sun pendants. These were cultists, then, secure in their belief in Faera, or wanting their promised reward.

The platform reached ground level, the clanking ceased, and the movement shuddered to a stop. Brand and his companions split up, slithering across the platform and out into the marketplace, each of them trailing a strand of hot chaos magic below them. Many of the cultists were brave enough to approach the creatures, and some of them were grasped and transformed into still more of the monstrous things. But others burst into flame and turned to ash at the creatures' touch. There was no pattern I could see in who survived and who was destroyed.

Faced with the choice of being changed into a hideous frog worm or burned to ash in an instant, the more timid of the cultists turned to flee, running through the debris and chaos of the marketplace. Once they did, the creatures pursued them, their long bodies and many legs propelling them quickly around and over all obstacles. When they caught up to someone fleeing, there were no more transformations. All those the creatures caught were burned and destroyed. I saw a city guardsman charge at one of the creatures and attack, but he screamed and dropped his sword as it hit the creature. Most of the blade was simply gone. Only the hilt and a jagged bit of blade remained. The creature's hand flashed out and touched the guard, and he was gone in a fiery instant, a cloud of black ash drifting in the breeze.

It was a terrible scene. There were now perhaps twenty of the things, and they spread out into the town, following the fleeing crowds down streets, or scaling the sides of buildings to find new prey. In the tumult, I had hidden behind a nearby market stall. When the shouts and screams receded, I came out, and I saw a few other people cowering or crawling through the destroyed marketplace.

Suddenly, ashamed, I remembered Boog. Dreading what I would find, I went over to him. He was out cold, but his chest still rose and fell. Not dead. Not yet. Relief washed over me. I rolled him over on his back and shifted one of his legs to a more comfortable position.

"Marten!" It was Clarice. "Is he…"

"Alive," I said. My voice failed me after that. She was standing nearby, on the broad platform that had been the floor of the temple. I ran to her, and she hugged me, tears streaming down her cheeks.

"It was terrible – Lucianna, and all the others… What are those things?"

"We've failed," I said, miserable. "I think…… the city is lost. Maybe the world." I realized I hurt all over, bruised, burned, carved up. I sat down heavily, and Clarice knelt beside me. Above us, the moon crawled across the face of the sun, dimming the daylight and twisting shadows into bizarre arcs and curls.

"Is there anything we can do?" she said. "There must be something."

"We can't fight them," I said. "I don't think they can die."

"We can't run," she said, ferocity in her voice. "I won't let them kill all of us. There must be something we can do."

I tried to calm myself, to think. Something nagged at me, and I realized what it was. The pool's foretelling had shown the city destroyed by fire, not by immortal overgrown amphibians. Had the pool failed? Or did the fire come later, once Faera really got going? Perhaps the monsters were merely the first of countless plagues to come.

As I thought, my breathing slowed, and my mind became clearer. I closed my eyes, and I sensed once again the cool presence I'd detected earlier, at the end of the tunnel when we neared the temple. It was directly below me now, under the temple floor, still vast, bigger and stronger than anything I'd felt before. This must be Faera's prison, I supposed, that had kept us protected for centuries. But it was cracked, torn, shuddering. I also felt something nearby, a small but intense spot of coolness. I opened my eyes to look, and saw the amulet, the one that had burned itself out of my trousers.

Just as a key can unlock a door, it can also lock one, Gora had said.

I went over to it. Why was it cool now? I had only sensed it before when angry, and then it was a hot presence, chaos magic. But now it was cool, the same as the pools, as the warding rods. How could it change?

Then I remembered – fae-rah, which Gora said meant fusion, or unity. Perhaps it was both. The prison had been both, in a way. A huge, strong presence of control, of order, locking down its destructive prisoner, itself an immense power of chaos and death. If the amulets were the keys, as Brand had said, then perhaps they too had both types of magic combined. But chaos and order were supposed to be opposed. When my rod touched Brand's wand, it had exploded. Had the ancient builders of this place found a way to combine them? Perhaps that was the only way they found to contain Faera, to nullify it. Maybe Faera was more properly the name of the prison and its prisoner together rather than just the being.

I stretched my mind downward, to where I presumed the prison lay. I felt the broad cool presence I'd felt earlier. Order. Control. The wall of Faera's cell, I thought. Above it, I felt another focused mass of coolness, now distinct in my mind from the larger field below and the amulet at my feet. What was this? It was about six feet below ground, centered in the carved floor, and it was icy cool. It almost felt as if it were connected to the cold field below it. Generating it?

I took a jagged breath and breathed out slowly, pushing my senses deeper. I could feel the frigid ball slip by as I reached out, then the layer of cold below it, connected to it, deeper. It was thick. As I moved my mind across, I felt it shudder, and bright flashes of heat broke the coolness. The layer I had sensed before the ceremony was no longer uniform – it had cracks, fractures, running through it. Or rather, moving through it - the strands connected to the creatures roaming the square. It seemed Faera's prison was crumbling, torn apart by his servants above. Reluctant, but curious, I pushed deeper.

Suddenly, searing heat. I cried out. Not just static heat, but waves of movement, angry blows, striking at the coolness above. Down there, something raged. I felt the coolness shudder with every onslaught. Faera was trying to break free. The intensity of the energy blazed at my senses. I had to withdraw – it was too much, like trying to hold onto white-hot steel in a forge. I opened my eyes.

Two keys. Brand had used one at the center of the sun carving to awaken Faera. But there was a second hole, and I had a second key. One that radiated coldness now. I picked up the amulet and walked over to the center of the moon part of the carving, to the second small hole.

"Marten, what are you doing?" said Clarice. She knelt, checking Boog for injuries.

"I have no idea," I said. "Just a hunch." I bent down, holding the amulet over the hole.

"You do remember that when Brand put his amulet down one of those, it started the end of the world," said Clarice, coming over to me.

"Things can't get much worse, can they?" I replied. I opened my fingers, and the amulet fell down the hole.

Nothing happened at first. But then there was a clanking noise, much softer and gentler than before. It came from the center of the floor, where the moon met the sun. As I turned to look, a small section of the floor slipped aside, and a metal shaft emerged. Set into the top of the shaft was an orb of clear blue glass, as big as my head. This was the source of coolness I had sensed. It rose up until it was waist high, then stopped. I closed my eyes, and I could feel its icy cold presence. An aspect of order, stronger than the rods, stronger than the pools, stronger than anything I'd felt, other than Faera raging below. It began to sparkle in the dim sunlight of the eclipse, and as I watched, wisps of flame rose from its surface.

I moved over to it. Clarice followed. "What is it, Marten?" she asked.

"I'm not exactly an expert in this, you know," I said.

"Well, you're the one who brought it here."

As I approached, I circled around it to get a look from all sides. At one point, my shadow crossed it, distorted and curved by the eclipse above. The wisps of flame died out under my shadow. I stepped aside, and when the light returned, the thin flames rose again. I shaded the orb with my hand, and where my hand blocked the sun, the orb was dark and lifeless. Everywhere else, it rippled with the wispy, translucent flames.

I reached my hand around behind the orb, so that I could touch it without casting a shadow upon it. I realized the flames weren't fire – they weren't hot, just bright and warm, like a sunbeam. In Gora's view of magic, I supposed, this made sense. Sunlight promoted growth and life, while fire destroyed or killed. This magic emanated from the sustaining part of the sun. Augmenting it, because of the eclipse, was the moon's regular cycle, the rhythm of the months and tides, which represented order of a different kind. Maybe the orb used sunlight, or special eclipse light, to function, and the wisps were a kind of concentrated solar energy.

Looking at the blue glass of the orb made me think of another object of blue glass – the disk behind the statue, with the long metal arms set into the floor. The purpose of the disk had been a mystery before, but now, exposed to the dim sunlight, a possibility occurred to me. A lens. In our investigations, we sometimes used magnifying lenses to study details of the evidence we uncovered. At the border, I'd seen inspectors carrying distance glasses with special lenses, which they used to study objects far away. And as a child, in my father's shop, he'd used magnifying lenses to work on small, intricate lock mechanisms. One day, he'd shown me how the biggest one could be used to scorch a leaf using only the sunlight, focused down into a small point of light.

"Can you help me?" I asked Clarice. I went over to the large glass disk and bent down, placing my hands under its curved lower edge.

"That looks heavy," said Clarice, but she took the other side. I counted to three, and we lifted together. There was a scraping sound, and the disk slowly rose. My wounded shoulder burned in protest. It took considerable force to get the disk moving, but it must have been counterbalanced or geared in some way below the floor, because it was easy enough to control once it started moving.

The glass disk rose up into the sunlight, suspended on its metal arms. At the opposite side of the chamber floor, I saw the shadows of the disk and the arms move into view. There was a splash of light at the center of the disk's shadow. As the glass rose further, the shadow and the splash of light moved toward the center of the floor, toward the orb. The light condensed and grew more focused, into a ring of light surrounding a dark spot – an echo of the moon against the sun above us. I ran to where one arm met the floor and pushed back on it hard, slowing the ascent of the glass disk. Clarice followed my lead, rushing to the other side.

When the shadow of the lens first crossed the orb, it dimmed, and the wisps of light vanished. But when the intense, focused ring of light hit the orb, it blazed with energy. We had not slowed the movement of the arms enough, though, so the circle of light overshot the orb, and it went dark again. We stopped the arms, and together, we slowly nudged the mechanism back. At last, the bright spot of concentrated sunlight was focused directly on the orb. It blazed back into life, the wispy, writhing bits of flame growing larger and brighter.

"Marten," said Clarice, her voice low and intense. "They're back."

I looked around. I had been intent on the orb and our careful manipulations. Approaching us on all sides, worming their way through the ruins of the market, were the colossal beasts, the former worshippers of Faera transformed. They flapped their mouths open and closed and screeched at us, waving their long slender arms.

A purplish-gray one reached the temple floor first. Clarice ran from it, ducking through its arms as it followed.

"Run!" I shouted. "It'll kill you!"

She dodged again, rolling behind a crumbling wall as the beast surged after her. "Save the city, Marten," she yelled. "I don't matter." She vanished from my view.

Not true, I thought, not at all. I looked at the glass orb. I didn't know what it was doing. But I did know she had no chance against that creature. Nor did I, or anyone. I couldn't see Clarice, but I could see the creatures swarming over the walls. The one following Clarice stopped, twisting its grotesque head around. It seemed to have lost her for the moment. But with the others coming, one was sure to find her. And me, eventually, but it was focused on her.

I wanted to be elsewhere. I wanted to be back in training, two years ago, with my friends unhurt and a career in the Guild ahead of me. Those days were the happiest of my life, before all this. Before Marron, before Faera.

Clarice climbed up onto the wall. She looked at me, flashed a smile, and shouted at the creature. "Hey! Over here!"

It saw her. It gave a grinding squeal and flowed toward her on its many legs. It was fast. Too fast. She ran, hopping from the wall to a crate, then running along a stall railing, but it would catch her. I couldn't watch that. I had to act, to do something. Across the market square, another creature, and then another, closed on our position.

I was too scared, too distraught, too angry to center myself and work with the magic of order. So, I gave in to chaos, to anger, fear, and rage. As the beast closed on Clarice, I bellowed, as much to summon its attention as anything. It hesitated, craning its distorted face around to look at me. Clarice gained a few steps. I shouted again. Not words, just a long angry scream. At Brand, at Marron, and at Faera. For Lucianna, and Sophie.

As I howled, I suddenly felt the orb's coolness. My sensing of magic had always before been triggered by calm contemplation, but now it seemed just as strong at the other end of my emotional range. I could feel the icy presence of the orb, tinged with a heat from the sun and ripples of coolness from the moon, mixed together by the lens. Below us, I felt the cold of the prison wall, now penetrated, cracked, by Faera's efforts to emerge. And below that, the raging heat that was Faera.

Gora had told me, what seemed a lifetime ago in the ancient fortress in hills of the barbarian lands, *The surest way to ruin, as a wizard, is to try to bind aspects of chaos with aspects of order*. But wasn't this what the ancient ones had done? They had bound Faera, without ending the world. And ruin was surely here, now, already, flowing across the wrecked temple floor on dozens of legs. The creature left off pursuing Clarice and turned to me.

The orb was steeped in order and calm strength. But it was faltering, weakening. Faera was chaos ascendant. Two opposing powers, one waxing, one waning. And the stronger one was sure to bring death in its wake. There was no choice. I could not make the situation worse, but I could try to change its course.

I cried out again, my throat raw, and reached my mind out below me. Where Faera's heat broke through the prison barrier, I pulled at it. Attracted it to the heat from my own anger. It flowed to me, sought me out, whether as a kindred spirit or merely as new prey, I did not know. I felt it swirl around me and through me, intensifying. The beast neared, but slowed, perhaps seeing a hint of its master in me now. It opened its jaw, wider than any creature should have been able to, and let out a howl of its own. Then it struck at me, its glistening head darting downward toward me, a breaking wave of death.

As it opened its mouth to consume me, I hurled the energy from Faera at the orb. From the prison cell below, to me, to the orb, a gushing channel of white-hot energy, like molten steel. As it struck the orb, there was a terrible blast, and a wave of energy knocked me away from the orb, flat on my back. The creature fell back as well, dazed for a moment, sparing my life.

The glass orb sparkled, heat competing with cold, then dimmed, cool for a moment. Then it flared. A ball of bright light shot from it, striking the creature directly in the side. Where the ball of light hit, the gray flesh broke apart into steaming, sizzling bits, and the damage spread from the impact along its whole length. The creature squealed as it fell, twisting and twitching. Eventually it melted away entirely, leaving a dark stain on the ground. As it died, a black haze flowed from its melting body, coalescing into a dark cloud, like smoke, but swirling and flowing almost like a living creature, with intellect and intent. It still radiated the heat, the chaos, I'd sensed, but tinged with a chill not present before. The smoke surged upward, away from the temple, reaching skyward, but then it was sucked quickly back down, disappearing into the hole in the center of the moon carving, where I'd placed my amulet.

The other creatures slowed their approach, but the orb's intensity was growing. More balls of light shot forth from the orb, at the creatures and in all other directions. Some blazing balls of sunlight soared high into the sky, descending like shooting stars. Some smashed into the surrounding buildings, exploding with light but causing no apparent harm. But many found their mark, and one by one, the terrible creatures were struck and melted away, even as they fled. Each released a cloud of dark smoke as it died, and each cloud was sucked down into the temple floor, even as it struggled like a living creature to escape the pull.

Clarice came over to me and took my hand as I watched the display. "What did you... do?"

"I don't know." I embraced her, holding her close. The orb, fed by Faera's own power, continued to spew forth balls of light even when the creatures had all been consumed. The balls of light seemed harmless to all but the monsters. They flashed and exploded when hitting the buildings and the ground, but they did no more damage than the light of the sun. It was actually rather beautiful. I suddenly laughed.

"What's so funny?" said Clarice.

"Look!" I said, pointing at the clock tower rising above the marketplace. Balls of glowing sunlight rained down upon it, blazing with energy, protecting the city from Faera, who now seemed locked back in the prison below us. "The pool's foretelling. Frosthelm in flames."

61

AFTERMATH

Eventually, the sun moved along in its path through the sky. The moon left the sun behind, the light returned to normal. Faera's power, or whatever was triggering the orb, faded. The bright spot from the giant lens shifted away from the orb, and it went calm once more. The balls of light ceased to fly. Curious people looked out at us from windows, and a brave few crept cautiously out of doorways and along the streets.

I heard a crunch, a footstep, from behind us. Clarice turned, and said only one word, but it was cold as ice, and dripped with venom. "You!"

I spun around. There before us, covered with dust and grime, but free from his bonds, was Count Marron. He must have freed himself and made it up the staircase earlier, before the temple floor reached the surface and blocked the way. It would have been easy for me to miss. The whole series of events had been chaos, and I'd blacked out for part of it after Brand's wand exploded.

Marron held a sword. I was still unarmed. I shot a look at Clarice. She'd set down her bow to help me with the lens, and I could see her quiver was empty regardless. She took a cautious step to the side, trying to reach Marron's flank, but I didn't like our odds taking on an expert with a blade.

"A good show, boy," said Marron. "You've saved the city."

"One you tried to destroy," I said.

"I never wanted it destroyed."

I was curious. "What did you want, then?"

Marron laughed. "What does anyone want? Power over one's destiny. Power over others. That's what you wanted here, what you've been struggling for this whole time. Power to protect your interests."

"A nice speech. But you've killed hundreds."

He grinned. "I didn't. Brand did. I tried to stop him. I've only killed tens."

"You helped him! The whole time."

"Brand was useful, and smart, but he didn't understand. The Prelate did, at least until he lost his nerve." Marron swung his sword a few times through the air. "Real power doesn't come from actual violence. It comes from the threat of violence. A credible threat."

"So that's all you wanted? Power? To rule? How shallow."

Marron glared at me. "Have you read anything, boy? Throughout its history, Frosthelm has lurched from crisis to crisis, hampered by its nobles and its weak elected Prelates. With a strong leader, assured of power, and without the ridiculous machinations of the court, Frosthelm could be so much stronger."

I couldn't fault his assessment of the court. But that was the game he'd played his whole life. "Sounds like a lot of justification to me. For nothing more than a lust for higher station. One that you'll not have once people understand what you've done."

"No one left alive knows my role," he said.

"I know it!" I protested.

"No one of consequence," he amended.

"You killed the Prelate! There are witnesses."

He looked surprised at that, but quickly composed himself. "Witnesses can be managed. Testimony changed. You, of all people, should know that. It's especially easy when one is the High Inquisitor. Or the Prelate himself."

"You'll never be Prelate," I said. "Jeroch's warrant lists your crimes, and your accomplices. You are finished."

"And how do you know about that?" asked Marron. He paused, thinking. "You came through the tunnel. Through the house. You have the warrant, don't you, boy? Well, that's rather convenient." He took a step forward and brought up his sword.

I was tired and hurt, but I was far too angry to run. "Count Marron, you are under arrest," I shouted. "For high treason against Frosthelm, and for the murder of Prelate Jeroch."

"Silence, boy," said Marron. He took a swing at me, but I ducked away, dancing back. I was back at the edge of the temple floor now, near where it met the market.

I looked him in the eye. "You're finished," I said. "It doesn't matter what you do to me." He moved his sword back and forth, then lunged at me. I turned aside, and he missed. As he pulled back, I anticipated his next swing, and took another step to dodge it, but my foot hit a loose cobblestone and slid. I fell awkwardly to the ground, and Marron stood over me.

"I'm not the one who's finished," he said. "Good bye, at last."

He raised his sword to strike, but I felt no fear. I was at peace. I might be about to die, and at the hand of a hated enemy, but I had saved the city, and perhaps the world. I could make a case for saving the world, anyway. That's not a bad legacy, not at all. If the Blood Mother were real, perhaps she would let me hang out with Sophie and Lucianna in the afterlife. Or if she got all stuffy about it, maybe I could convince one of her Ugly Daughters to look the other way.

As Marron brought the sword down, Clarice jumped at him. She lowered her shoulder and hit him, hard, in the chest. He tried to change his swing to hit her instead, but she came too fast, and they both went down in a sprawl. She got a couple of punches in as they fell, but Marron maintained his grip on the sword's hilt, and he was quicker to his feet than she was. He aimed a quick stroke at her, and she tried to stumble out of its way. But I heard her grunt as it connected. She took a few more unsteady steps, holding her side. She'd gone pale.

I struggled back to my feet. Clarice had saved me, but at too great a cost. This was bad. Both of us were hobbled by injuries, though I couldn't tell how severe hers was. Marron looked at us both, glancing back and forth, his sword making small circles in the air as we faced him. I wondered at his hesitation. He could likely have finished both of us off, but perhaps Clarice's unexpected assault had made him cautious. He gave a low laugh and took a step towards me.

I risked a glance at Clarice. She wore a grim expression, still holding her side. She shot me a look. I tried to see how much blood she'd lost, but her cloak was dark, and its folds hid her injury. I noticed her fingers twitching as she held her side. Was she in pain? Had her wound caused spasms or palsy?

No, I was a fool. The Argot. *Behind him*, she signed. *Distract.*

I looked back at Marron, trying not to alert him, but also looking frantically for what she had seen. And I saw it. It took all I had not to focus there, but instead I stared at Marron's eyes. They were cold and gray.

"What you don't know, Marron, is that I've spent the last few months learning sorcery," I said. "You thought Brand's spells were strong? The clans' mystics are far stronger. I have learned their ways."

"What?" said Marron, his voice full of scorn. "That's weak, even for you. You expect me to believe such a pathetic lie? I'm insulted."

I couldn't disagree. But this was the only road I could think of. In for a penny, in for a sovereign, I thought. "You saw what I did with the machine here." I held my arms up in what I hoped was a threatening, magical pose. He took a step forward and raised the sword again. I started the Arunian chant, the one that activates the pool, the one I knew by heart now, from my earlier training and from my time with Gora. But I didn't use the singsong rhythm of the pool ceremony. Instead, I spat out each syllable, twisting my fingers into aggressive gestures.

And Marron hesitated. Not much. Just for a second. It could have been the host of terrible things we'd seen that day, or some fear borne of seeing Brand's wand snuff out people in an instant. Or my convincing acting. Or maybe a change of heart, Marron deciding, no, surely, I've killed enough Inquisitors already, time to turn over a new leaf? Definitely not that. Whatever it was, it was what we needed. Just as Marron took another step toward us, his face frozen in a grim snarl, a huge arm slid around his neck from behind.

In a continuous motion, Boog ran his other arm around the back of Marron's head, hugging Marron tight against his chest, squeezing his neck from both sides between bicep and forearm. Anatomically, I knew, he was pinching off the two vessels that brought blood to Marron's head. I'd seen him do it to a few belligerent drunkards before, and I'd had it done to me back in the training yard under Mistress Fennick's careful gaze. If Boog had a good grip, Marron only had few moments of consciousness left.

Marron flailed for a second or two, then reversed his grip on his sword. He wrenched his hips to one side, then swung the sword down and plunged it backward, stabbing at Boog. Boog grunted and fell back. I could see him struggling to maintain his grip on Marron, but Marron stabbed again, and Boog had to release him to avoid it. I could see a wet hole in Boog's leather jerkin on his lower left side. Marron's sword had found its mark.

For a moment, the four of us stood, Marron gasping for breath, his sword at the ready, his head spinning from side to side as he tried to watch all of us at once. Boog prodded the wound at his side, his eyes fixed on Marron. Then he ran his tongue around the inside of his lips and turned to face the count. Clarice pulled hard at her cloak, and the pin popped, and it fell away, floating to the ground. She raised both fists in a perfect rendition of Mistress Fennick's ready stance.

Clarice clicked her tongue. Marron spun to her, and as Boog and I watched, she signed in the Argot. *Topple the Wolf.* This was one of Mistress Fennick's drills in unarmed combat, a complex one from the fourth year intended to take down an armed opponent safely. Or mostly safely. *Me bird,* she continued, her fingers obvious to Marron. This could be dangerous, if Marron had learned the Argot. But even if he had, he hadn't sweated in the yard getting pummeled by Fennick for five years running. With any luck, he wouldn't know what we were up to.

I slid sideways so that I formed a triangle with my friends. Marron stood at the center, spinning to keep us all in view, blade out. *Me turtle.* I signed.

Me noodles, signed Boog. Of course, he meant *Me ram,* but the signs were easily confused. The important part was that he was on board.

Clarice darted in toward Marron, her fists swinging, but favoring her injured side. He swung at her, more to fend off her fists than to attack. She ducked, took a step back, then lunged again. Marron stabbed at her, and if she'd really intended to land her punch, she'd probably have been run through. But the role of the bird was to draw attention, and as Marron thrust at her, she spun back. He took a step forward at her, trained as some fencers are to pursue weakness with strength.

The role of the turtle in this scenario was not glamorous, but it was dangerous. As Marron stepped forward and his weight shifted to his front leg, I dove in to crouch next to his legs. My injured shoulder flared in protest. This put me well in range of his sword, but at an awkward angle, or so I hoped. He looked down at me, puzzled, but raised his sword to strike. And as he did, the ram, or perhaps the wrathful noodles, struck him from behind. Boog hit him at a run with shoulder lowered, and Marron flew over me and sprawled on the ground. He let out a grunt as he landed on loose rocks, all that remained of the broken pavement of the market square. His sword clattered away across the temple floor.

I hopped to my feet, and Boog took a step back to steady himself. Clarice ducked down to grab Marron's sword, and she spun towards him, blade raised. The three of us stood over him, panting, but he didn't move. A pool of red spread from his head as he lay face down on the stones. Boog touched his shoulder, then rolled him over. Marron's eyes stared up at the brightening sky. His pupils were large and uneven, and a trickle of blood spilled out from a dent in his temple. No breath issued from his mouth, and his tongue hung to one side. Marron had met his end.

Epilogue

I stood in the small chapel in Headquarters, turning pages in our Book of Honor. There were two new entries since I'd last looked a couple of weeks earlier. Both of them posted at the border. A real shame, since the conflict was essentially over now. The body of Nera had been returned to the clans, along with a personal message of explanation and apology from the new Prelate. Ganghira, or maybe Gora, had convinced the clans that this was enough. The hostilities were mostly ceased other than small skirmishes. Prisoners were being exchanged, and new border and trade treaties were in the works, to be pursued as soon as the peace agreement was final. It was much easier to negotiate with Ganghira's central government than it had been with each clan independently, before the war. It would take time, but the situation was improving.

The city was putting itself back together. The rampaging Faeran monsters had killed around two hundred people, many of them Faerans. The total was not exactly known, as the dead left no bodies behind, but the Guild was keeping a list of those missing. Removing the Eye of Hrogar from the statue had caused the strange temple to sink down once more and the roof to close up. Nobody had been willing so far to build anything on top of it, but hopefully it would stay closed for centuries, or forever, and it would pass from memory as it had before. I had strained to reach my consciousness down to the prison below the temple, but I could not penetrate the wall of coolness, now whole and strong and thick. I could not find Faera, but I am sure it was still below, slumbering, or perhaps still raging, but contained.

Along with the unfortunate Nera, the four other artifacts were removed from their holes in the temple floor. They'd been sent far away. The new Prelate, Corienne, voted in by what remained of the Council of Nobles to succeed Jeroch, had ordered them placed in remote, inaccessible places, hoping never to see them used again. The crown was buried deep in a mine in the eastern part of the lands controlled by Frosthelm, and the mine was then collapsed, and the entrance covered up and buried with no markings or signs. The mace she'd ordered transported by heavily-guarded barge along the Serpentine, through Kantis to the south, to the ocean, where it was to be placed on a seafaring ship and dropped overboard in deep water. I wasn't privy to the fate of the Fingernails or the two moon-and-sun amulets, which had been fished out of their holes in the floor, but I assumed it was something similar. I hoped that would be good enough. The events that transpired and the presence and nature of the prison were recorded, but all mention of the details of the ritual had been destroyed, even from libraries, in the hope that it could never be repeated.

Boog and I were back at work. Our names and crimes were cleared right away, and we had been awarded the Order of the Prelate along with Gueran, Clarice, and many others who'd helped. The purge of the remaining Faerans and of Marron's lackeys and minions had mostly run its course. We'd even been promoted, early, to the rank of Inspector. Along with the rest of the Guild, we were still tracking down the last few remaining names from Jeroch's warrant. None of Marron's appointed inspectors remained in the Guild. Kreune, back from the border and newly named High Inquisitor, had seen to that. Most of them were awaiting trial. Some of the Faerans, especially those who were nobles, had killed themselves or fled the city rather than face justice. I was sure that Marron had more friends and allies than those listed on the warrant, but as the murderer of the Prelate and the chief sponsor of the Faerans, Marron's name was poison now, and all in the court were busy placing as much distance between him and them as possible.

Gueran passed by the open door of the chapel, noticed me, and stopped. "Mingenstern," he said, his voice cool, and with its ever-present mocking edge. "The Augur was looking for you. Perhaps she needs someone to destroy the city again." Once, his needling would have bothered me. Today, I thanked him and smiled. He went on his way. The Augur was fascinated by my report of the other pool, and she'd had me go over all the details again and again. I was now nearly her equal using our pool, and I knew she wanted me to take over as Augur when she stepped down, which she hinted would be soon. But I was certain that my place was in the field, with Boog. And Clarice.

I looked down at the book again and ran my finger up the page to the earlier entries. *Sophie Borchard, High Inquisitor, murdered by unknown agents of Count Marron during the Faeran Incident. Her actions and leadership helped save the city.* They certainly had – without her protecting the amulet, we'd all likely be dead at the webbed hands of the Faeran monsters, or ruled by Marron. My guess was that the 'unknown agent' was Tolla, even though I'd seen her at Brand's house before and after Sophie died. But it didn't matter much now.

Below Sophie was the entry I had come here to see again, the one that I had a harder time letting go. I'd argued with Kreune to let it be included in our book, even though such a thing had never been done before. It was a touchy matter among some of the inspectors. But there it was. *Lucianna Stout, ally and friend to the Inquisitor's Guild, murdered by the wizard Brand during the Faeran Incident. Without her heroic efforts and skill at arms, the city would have been lost.* My throat closed up, and my eyes grew moist. I had barely known her, and she had tried to kill me when we first met, but she protected my life and died for me and my friends out of nothing but loyalty and duty. I glanced around to make sure nobody was looking, and then I touched her name in the book and spat on the floor. I was sure she'd understand and be pleased.

I closed my eyes, thinking over all that had gone by. My physical wounds were healing, but it would be a long time before the memories faded. If they ever did. I didn't really want them to.

An arm slipped around my waist. "Mother of Blood, but you're quiet," I swore.

Clarice laughed. "Boog wants to know when you're coming for dinner," she said, her left hand playing with her falcon pendant. "It's meat pie tonight, your favorite." She kissed me on the cheek, and I felt warm all over. I looked at her, smiling at me, her cheeks full of freckles under her green eyes. She'd let her hair grow out since her return from the border, but it was still short. I thought it was the prettiest thing I'd ever seen. Other than her smile, of course.

The new Prelate had offered to restore her house name, and this was working its way through the arcane procedural maze of laws, titles, lands, heraldry, and pervasive snobbery. She said she didn't care whether she was a Jerreau or a Burgeo, commoner or noble, as long as she was with the Guild.

I took her hand in mine. "Let's go now," I said.

NOTES AND ACKNOWLEDGMENTS

Thanks for reading this book. I hope you have enjoyed it. It's been a long time coming. I started the book in 2005, and I have worked on it for the past fourteen years, although I took multiple long breaks. My wife, Christina, has always been the book's biggest fan, so I finished the first draft in 2012, in time to give it to her for our 20th anniversary. In the next seven years, I got the book professionally edited, I sent queries to lots and lots of agents, and I wrote and rewrote. Then, there was a pretty long hiatus while I served in a faculty leadership role at the college where I work, but once that was done, and as I neared my 50th birthday, I committed to finishing. And here we are.

I have lots of people to thank. Many of my family and friends served as readers for various versions over the years, and they offered advice, encouragement, ideas, and a lot of the fire that kept me going. There's not much in this world that's more rewarding than somebody you know and respect taking the time to read a story you've written and then sharing their excitement about your characters, your story, and your world that you've made, and laughing at your jokes. So many of my friends and family have given me that gift over the years. I'll name some of them here, but there are others I'm likely forgetting to mention. My apologies for this. Know that you are appreciated even if I suck at acknowledging you.

My wife was my first and best reader, and she's always loved Marty and Boog. In the early days, I used to send her a few paragraphs at a time, or a page, or whatever I'd written each day, and she always loved it and wanted more.

Once the first draft of the book was finished, I prevailed upon many more people to read it and to help me with it. My father-in-law, Brent Farmer, shared it with an editor at his company, Karen Boss, and reading her early comments, full of help and enthusiasm, was one of my happiest experiences of this whole process. My mother-in-law, Jackie Farmer, also provided really helpful early feedback, as did my kids, Bri and Nick. Nick created the image of the Faeran amulet that graces the book cover and the website.

My father, John Dobson, read the book and worked over a lot of the plot and details with me during a family car trip. This echoed back to my childhood, when he would make up and tell me and my brother stories in the car over long drives on our family vacations. These stories, and his creativity, are very important inspiration for this work. I wish I had recordings or transcriptions of those tales, told serially across the American Southwest from the 1970's to the 1980's, but I remember them fondly.

My good friend Derek Hagen read the book early on, and his pure joy in talking about it was another of my favorite memories of this project. I can remember him saying, "I love that it's the hellfrogs! I so wanted it to be the hellfrogs, and it was!" Nobody mourned Lucianna harder than Derek, too.

My friends Jeff Vanke, Dan Hurwitz, and Adam Hauerwas all provided support and valuable comments. Alex Reutter, with whom I've played many a game of Little Green Guys with Guns, but whom I've never met in real life, posed some great questions. I got helpful feedback from another editor, Monica Perez, at Charlesbridge Publishing, in exploring if the book could fit into the Young Adult genre, and in providing a professional critique and some things to work on. Early on, I was helped by some writing groups online who read the first chapter and other parts and offered feedback. Some of those folks were part of Critters.org.

My friend Rankin Willard gave me a ton of help in considering covers. You should check out his art at RankinWillard.com. I was originally considering using a painting I commissioned (not one of Rankin's) as the cover, and he helped with many, many variations of that. Although in the end I didn't go with that painting, seeking instead something that better fit the book and the market, his advice stuck with me as I moved onward in cover design.

One of the most helpful readers and editors of my work was Rose Fox at Copymancer.com. They provided a thorough developmental edit for the first draft of the book and showed me the value of getting professional help. I was too stubborn to take all their advice, but I did take a lot of it, and anything you enjoyed in the book probably should share credit with them. In particular, they urged me to balance the gender of all of the characters in the book, something I should have done as a feminist and supporter of women's rights, but didn't do initially, because I suck. Rose also gave me loads of other great advice, some of which I followed, including changes to the plot, and about Marten's character and the relationship between him and Clarice.

Two of my colleagues at Guilford College read the book, Mylène Dressler and Heather Hayton. Both of them are better writers than I. Each of them gave of their considerable talents to their geologist colleague who was writing a silly fantasy novel, and I'm beyond grateful to both. Mylène has a number of published novels, and I've loved each one I've read. See more of her work at MDressler.com. You'll be glad you did. Heather is one of the most creative and dedicated teachers I know, and I am lucky to be team-teaching with her for the first time this coming academic year.

My deepest thanks go to my wife and family for all their support of this project, both direct (reading and talking about Frosthelm) and indirect (not minding when I disappear into the basement for hours, or take my laptop with me in the car, in the hotel room, or at band camp). Especially to Christina, whose love of me and support for my silly ideas have always been unconditional.

My parents, also, fostered in me a love of books and of reading at every opportunity. My mother, Cynthia Dobson, is a professional college librarian, and she ensured during my childhood that we would get to the Ames Public Library every week or two to get a fresh batch of books to read, providing endless new adventures to explore. My father's stories, and his own novels and history books, are likewise an inspiration.

In short, I have a wonderful wife whom I dearly love, and a terrific family, and some of the best friends in the world. I hope you do too.

May the Bloodmother's Ugliest Daughter cut you some slack when you need it. Thanks again for reading.

Dave Dobson
June 11, 2019

THINGS TO TRY

If you liked this book and want more, you have two options. There's a sequel to this book that follows the further adventures of Boog and Marten (mostly Boog) called *The Outcast Crown*. It's another full-length novel of the Inquisitors' Guild. There's also a novella, *Traitors Unseen*, which is a completely different adventure set about ten years before this book. That story follows provisional Inspector Emerra Denault, a character from this book, in her earlier career in the Guild.

If you want to keep current on all the news from Frosthelm, including the sequel to this book that's currently in the works, please visit my site at http://davedobsonbooks.com. I'll update my blog there with news, reports, ideas, and tidbits about my writing and other projects.

There's also a mailing list you can join at the site above. I promise e-mails will be infrequent and juicy with news.

If you like puzzle games or escape rooms, I've created a card game that includes a bunch of escape room style puzzles. It's called Doctor Esker's Notebook. It's fun solo or with a group, as a game night, to put out on a coffee table, or to enjoy during a lazy afternoon. It has hints to help if you get stuck. For more information see http://planktongames.com/esker. You can also find it on Amazon.

ABOUT THE AUTHOR

A native of Ames, Iowa, Dave loves writing, reading, boardgames, computer games, improv comedy, pinball, pizza, barbarian movies, and the cheaper end of the Taco Bell menu. Also, his wife and kids.

Dave is the author of Snood, Snoodoku, Snood Towers, and other computer games. He first published Snood in 1996, and it became one of the most popular shareware games of the early Internet. His most recent games are Scryptix and Polaric (coming soon). He also designs and publishes boardgames though his company, Plankton Games. You can see his games at the PlanktonGames.com website.

Dave teaches geology, environmental studies, and computer programming at Guilford College, and he does improv comedy every week at the Idiot Box in Greensboro, North Carolina. He's also played the world's largest tuba in concert. Not that that is relevant, but it's still kinda cool.

Flames over Frosthelm was Dave's first novel.

Made in the USA
Monee, IL
02 December 2021